TORTOISE STEW

P.C. ZICK

Copyright ©2006 Patricia Camburn Behnke
Second edition copyright ©2012 Patricia Camburn Zick
Cover Design: Travis Miles
Formatting: The Manuscript Doctor

ISBN: 0-9888-782-1-6
ISBN-13: 978-0-9888782-1-1

DEDICATION

For all the underdogs who fight for justice.

ACKNOWLEDGEMENTS

I originally published this book in 2006 under my former name, Patricia Camburn Behnke. In 2012, I revised and republished *Tortoise Stew* under my new name of P.C. Zick.

I thank everyone who encouraged me to write this book. I also thank everyone who supported its original publication in 2006. It still holds a message about listening to others even if we're opposed to their position. If we're all shouting, who's listening? So many people contributed to the creation of this novel, from politicians to newspaper colleagues to the regular citizens who just wanted their voices to be heard about the fray.

I thank my daughter Anna for encouraging from the very beginning to go out and pursue a career as a writer. She's a trusted reader of my work and an artist whose opinion I value in all I undertake.

To my husband, Robert: Your support and understanding as I continue to pursue this gig as a writer keeps me going every day. You're my inspiration and confidant in all matters of the heart and mind. Thank you.

And thank you to all the readers who continue to buy my books and give me the courage and the energy to continue creating novels with a message, whether about politics, love, or the environment. You are the reason I can call myself an author, and I am appreciative every single day for your support

WORKS BY P.C. ZICK

Florida Fiction Series

Native Lands – A novel rich in intrigue and history as a tribe of Native Americans, thought to be extinct, fight to save their beloved heritage.

Tortoise Stew – Politics, murder, and chaos in rural Florida reign supreme in a story where love triumphs over it all.

Trails in the Sand – Family secrets, an oil spill, and redemption create a roller coaster ride for journalist Caroline Carlisle.

Other Works of Fiction

The Grateful Fates - Four women. Four decades of friendship. Four secrets that seal their fates.

Live from the Road (A Magical Route 66 Novel) – The reader heads out on an often humorous, yet harrowing, journey as Meg Newton and Sally Sutton seek a change in the mundane routine of their lives. Joined by their daughters, they set off on a journey of salvation enhanced by the glories of the Mother Road.

Nonfiction

Civil War Journal from the 2nd Michigan – An expanded version of Civil War Journal of a Union Soldier, this book contains the complete journal of Harmon Camburn (1842-1906).

Civil War Journal of a Union Soldier (Memoir nonfiction) – My great grandfather's journal from his days as a soldier. It's a personal account of war and all its causes and effects from the eyes of a man who fought it.

Eclectic Leanings - Musings from a Writer's Soul: Essays, Creative Nonfiction, and Short Stories - Award-winning author P.C. Zick offers up a collection of her writings, which span the course of more than two decades.

From Seed to Table - Gardening techniques, organic gardening, canning vegetables, and recipes.

Ichetucknee Springs – A History and Culture of a Florida Spring – Oral and written history of the springs before it became a state park.

Garden to Table – More tips and recipes galore using fresh vegetables.

Odyssey to Myself (Essays nonfiction) – The people of Morocco, Italy, Panama, and Chile come to life through the experiences of the author as she absorbs the cultures so different from her own.

The Author's Journey: A Road Map for Writers – From Draft to Published Book - a reference book to take the mystery out of writing and publishing a book, whether through traditional channels or as an Indie Author. And if your questions aren't answered, Zick provides a lengthy bibliography for all aspects of writing, editing, publishing, and promoting your book.

CHAPTER ONE

THE BOMB SAT IN a bag on Kelly Sands' desk for an hour before she noticed it.

She didn't see the white shopping bag because she had a deadline to meet, and tunnel vision ruled when the clock ticked toward the newspaper's witching hour.

The rest of the debris on her desk also prevented her from noticing anything new. Two stained cups still holding cold coffee from the morning sat next to a pile of files on long-term stories she kept meaning to investigate. A box that once contained donuts lay on top of the papers.

Even if she had noticed the shopping bag, it wouldn't have registered as anything unusual. Her colleagues were always depositing things on each other's desks, either from absentmindedness or from the numbing blindness of a daily paper's deadline focus.

The Braidwood Tribune went to press at eleven most nights. Kelly glanced at the clock on the wall ticking away the minutes as she put the finishing touches on the story she had begun on her laptop at the meeting.

She sped from the Commission meeting before it was even over. More than one hundred residents from around Zion County came to Calloway, a town ten miles from Braidwood. Braidwood was the largest city in north central Florida, standing in the middle of some of Florida's last remaining natural landscapes.

Five commissioners representing 6,000 residents had decided to annex 2,000 acres of land into Calloway. The land represented one of only few tracts of farmland left in the county. The annexation bothered some of the residents who believed the increased acreage into Calloway would stress already limited city services such as sewer and water.

1

Buddy Tills owned most of the 2,000 acres for several decades, but he'd been selling off small parcels over the past several months. The names on the annexation requests were not local. The rumor mill kept mentioning Industrial Pines as the developer of the property.

Just the name Industrial Pines evoked fear in some residents because they were a company that developed in Florida with little regard to anything but its own profits. B.J. Winters, president of the giant company, attended all the public hearings, but Kelly's calls to him remained unreturned. She planned to corner him after the annexation meeting, but when it ran over her deadline, she was forced to leave without accosting him in the parking lot.

Now Kelly had to write a fair, impartial article on a controversial annexation in Calloway in less than an hour. She knew if she didn't get it down to bare bones reporting, the night editor would hack away at the piece until it fit into a twelve-inch space on the first page of the local section.

Kelly would be thirty-five in a few months, but she still looked like she was in her twenties. Her long black hair contrasted with her light blue eyes, unusual in their intensity and translucence. She was a tall 5'4" only because she held her head high and kept her shoulders back.

Thirty-five seemed like a milestone birthday to her. She had worked hard and earned a decent position with *The Tribune* yet she hadn't accomplished much else in her life, except a divorce from Jerry, a college sweetheart. The marriage lasted only two years. Her parents, who lived in Palm Beach, could not understand why she hadn't finished law school. It disappointed them she settled for the job of a reporter.

"I don't understand why you would work so hard for so little return," her father, a pediatrician, often said.

But her father did not understand what happened to her when she first caught the newspaper bug. She'd never gotten it out of her system after she worked on the University of Braidwood's student newspaper throughout her undergraduate years.

After she received her bachelors' degree, she struggled through one year of law school, hating every minute of it, even more so because she no longer had time to write for the paper.

When she finished the article, five minutes before deadline, she rubbed her eyes and then rested them on the bag for the first time.

Carl Handler, a fellow reporter and friend, came by her desk and looked over her shoulder.

"What are you doing here so late?" Kelly asked.

"I had that forum for the school board election tonight," Carl said. "What did you buy? A new set of knives to slice the fat off the developer's plans out in Calloway?"

"Must be a secret admirer," Kelly said as she pulled out the tissue paper tucked in the top of the bag.

"What is it?" Carl asked as Kelly stared at the contents of the package.

Kelly motioned for him to take a look. "It can't be what I think it is."

Carl and Kelly stood with the shopping bag between them. Kelly held the handles wide enough apart for them to get a good look at the contents. Neither of them had ever seen a real bomb, but both knew enough to recognize that the plastic pipe with the small digital timer and battery attached with duct tape could not be anything else.

CHAPTER TWO

RICK BELLOWS, *THE TRIBUNE'S* city editor, did not like to be disturbed at home unless absolutely necessary. When the phone rang, he and his wife had just gone to bed, and he thought about not answering. Kelly Sands began yelling as soon as he said, "Hello." He wished he'd followed his instincts.

"Rick, you better get down here; I just found a bomb on my desk," she said.

"A bomb? What kind of bomb?"

"Boom, you're dead kind of bomb," Kelly said. "Everyone has been evacuated while security takes a look. Carl and I are out in the parking lot staring at the stars."

"I'll be right there. Don't call anyone else, especially Bart. No sense in getting people upset if we don't have to," Rick said.

Bellows left his bed and sleeping wife and thought about showering before heading to the paper. Even though he hated to do it, he pulled on the clothes he had worn that day.

Richard Bellows had been born and raised in Dansville, a small town in an adjoining county, to a family rich in land, but not much else. He spoke with the soft drawl of the Deep South, giving away his status as a Good Old Boy.

He attended the University of Braidwood where he made life-long friends with the business leaders of the area. Braidwood was the ruling city of Zion County with the university as its centerpiece. Several small towns northwest of Braidwood made up the rest of the county. *The Braidwood Tribune*, the only daily in a hundred mile radius, had a circulation of 50,000, and Rick began working at the paper soon after graduation.

One of Rick's friends was the president of Zion County's Chamber of Commerce. As Rick drove to the office, all he could think about was how tourism would be hurt if word got out that one of his reporters received a bomb threat. He was certain someone wanted to warn Kelly about those articles she had been writing lately.

He would have to talk to her. She was going into too much detail about annexations on the western edge of the county near Calloway, the second largest city in Zion County. The public didn't need to know every detail from the commission meetings. Rick thought people should attend the meetings themselves if they wanted that much information. The pressure from his colleagues in the Chamber had increased steadily over the past few weeks, and he knew he had to rein her in. However, that was not an easy task, since his boss, Bart Stanley, let Kelly do whatever she pleased. Rumors floated around the office for years about those two, and Rick suspected some of them might be true.

The newspaper's security officers took one look inside the bag and called the Zion County bomb squad, and then evacuated the building. Rick found Kelly and Carl behind the hastily draped police tape on the sidewalk leading to the front door of the building.

"Any news?" Rick asked his two reporters.

"Nothing yet, but we haven't heard any explosions either," Carl said.

"And we probably won't, just somebody trying to make a point," Rick said. "I decided to call Bart on my way over, and he ordered that the pages be emailed to Ocala for printing as soon as they let us have access to one of the computers in production."

"Then we can write something on my laptop and email it to them," Kelly said. "There's still time to change the front page."

"I don't think that's necessary," Rick told her. "We don't need to give these creeps any attention. If we do anything, it will go on page seven."

"And *The Calloway Chronicle* and *The Millstone Monitor* don't follow the police scanners?" Carl asked. "Come on, Rick, you know we've got to run the story on the front page before the weeklies come out in a few days."

Just then, an officer from the bomb squad came outside and told them it looked like the real thing. They were going to detonate it in the back parking lot on the edge of the swamp that surrounded the building.

"Now is it news, Rick?" Carl asked.

"I don't think the public handles this kind of thing very well. It could start a whole chain reaction."

"This is news, Rick," Carl said.

"It doesn't have to be. I think for everyone's sake, we should keep quiet about this for now. Did it come with a note?"

Kelly searched the top of her desk before the evacuation and could account for every piece of paper there before security had insisted on kicking them out. Even though she wasn't known for her neatness, she knew where everything was on what Carl called "Kelly Mound."

"I didn't see one on my desk or on the bomb, but I didn't spend a whole lot of time looking either."

"Before I make a decision, let's see what happens when they detonate it," Rick said.

"This will make the public understand how desperate the developers are," Kelly said.

"I don't want to hear any more of your talk about the developers or you're done covering these meetings, Sands," Rick told her.

"Who else would do such a crazy thing?" she asked.

"Lots of crazies out there. What about that group protesting the annexation? They spout venom at the commission meetings all around the county," Rick said.

"Protesting the actions of the commissions at meetings and handing me a bomb are a little different. Besides they all like me. I don't see the connection, do you, Carl?"

"No, sure don't. Rick, be reasonable. We've got to go with this story. It's not quite midnight, and we haven't emailed the paper to Ocala yet. We can put in a little front-page piece about one of our reporters getting a present of a bomb. We can't bury the story. You know the weeklies will be all over this. They've been following this annexation process closely, too. It's been more exciting than the upcoming presidential election."

"Right now we're not doing anything. Not until we find out more. And that's final."

Kelly stood back from the men and watched them argue about the news. To her, it was simple and not all things in life came this simply. Someone had threatened her in order to force her silence. She knew it just as she knew that the phone calls in the middle of the night attempted the same thing. So far none of their tactics had worked.

CHAPTER THREE

INSTEAD OF BEGINNING HER second year of law school, Kelly enrolled in the journalism graduate program at UB. When she received her master's degree, her love for the news became even more ingrained. It had gotten into her blood, and she had no choice but to follow her heart.

She decided to stay in Braidwood even though her father assured her if she really wanted to be a journalist, he could get her a job on the *Palm Beach Post*. But Braidwood had also gotten into her blood and when *The Tribune* offered her a beginning level job working on the city desk, she took it and bided her time. She had moved up the ranks as much as one could as a reporter. First, she did police reports and obituaries, an important part of the paper, but pieces that didn't require much in the way of writing or reporting. Then they sent her out to the smaller towns surrounding Braidwood for little stories.

She wrote about a runaway pig in Hope Springs, a sinkhole in Calloway, and a leaky roof at the Millstone school. When she proved she could handle those two or three paragraph stories, she began attending commission meetings in the outlying areas.

Some of the smaller towns had more exciting news than the larger city of Braidwood. Developments sprang up overnight and during the decade she had been at the paper, Calloway had become the fastest growing city in the county, encroaching on the city limits of its mother city, Braidwood.

Now it was clear someone wanted Kelly to stop reporting what went on in those commission meetings. As she continued to wait in the dark parking lot with the moon providing slight light and the stars twinkling, Kelly let her mind wander, which she rarely allowed because when she did, she inevitably thought of Joely. And that she didn't want to do.

At the annexation meeting, when the people had a chance to voice an opinion, the Mayor of Calloway, Tim Murray, shot down anyone who tried to speak about any zoning changes.

"Today we are only concerned with the annexation of these parcels into Calloway," the Mayor said. "I know many of you want to talk about what will happen on this property once it is brought into the city, but that will come at a later meeting, if and when the owners request any zoning changes."

Kelly continuously heard rumors about what might happen on this property, and if the rumors circulating were correct, then zoning would most likely be changed from its current agricultural designation to commercial or — in a worst-case scenario to many residents — changed to industrial usage.

"You will be asked to sit down if you address anything other than the annexation when you come to the microphone," Mayor Murray concluded.

Although Kelly was grateful the Mayor limited citizen comments to the annexation and not any possible zoning issues, she was sympathetic to the residents' concerns. Those in attendance came to speak their mind, and they opposed any efforts to censor them.

Kelly heard developers hoped to turn the 2,000 rolling acres into a movie studio with a landing strip. She asked around the county and most of the planners she consulted agreed that 2,000 acres was much larger than either of these entities would require. And Industrial Pines' name kept popping up as that potential developer and that is why Kelly most especially wanted to speak to B.J. Winters, the man behind it all as president of I.P. In a situation typical of the Good Old Boy system, Winters' daughter, Betty Duncan, served as the city manager for Calloway.

Members of a newly formed activist group, Smart Growth for Calloway, sat in the audience. They took notes as the presentations and discussions continued. One SGC member, Karen Thorne, spoke, but the Mayor pointedly asked her if she was a resident of Calloway.

"I do not live in the city limits of Calloway, but my property is next to what is being annexed tonight," Karen replied. "I have a right to voice my opinion."

The Mayor smiled. "I know you have the right to speak, Miss Thorne, but I want the citizens to know that you don't pay taxes in the city of Calloway."

"I just want to ask one question of the Commission," Karen continued. "Do you really want an airport within the city limits of Calloway? What about the residents who bought their homes here expecting a nice quiet town? Now they'll have piper cubs and John Travolta jets bombarding the quiet. And even though I don't live in the city limits, I live closer than you, and you can't tell me I won't be bothered by the noise of planes landing and taking off."

"Miss Thorne, I have to ask you to sit down and allow others to address the issue regarding annexation," the Mayor said.

The president of SGC rose to speak. He was not popular with the Mayor or with Commissioner Jackson Stewart. But his presence at the podium could always assure the audience of an excellent show.

"Cowan Garcia, citizen of Calloway. Mr. Mayor, you can stop this nonsense now or expect a lawsuit in the future for violating county noise ordinances."

"I'm warning you, Garcia, you are to speak to the annexation, not what might happen on this annexed land," the Mayor said. "We don't know what's planned for that property. That will come back to us, and we'll have to approve or disapprove whatever is requested as far as land usage goes. Besides I do believe there is a difference between a landing strip for jets and one for the smaller planes, but that's not what we're discussing here tonight."

"What's wrong with putting a landing strip on the outskirts of town?" asked Jackson Stewart, a 30-year veteran of the Commission. "You'd think no one wanted to see our town develop. Millstone got that cement plant just down the road, and an asphalt plant even closer, instead of us, all because we have commissioners here who refuse to let Calloway grow. And now we've got a way to bring in the businessmen to make our town even better. I'd be mighty proud to have John Travolta walking the streets of Calloway, eating in our fine restaurants, spending his money here. I don't understand why anyone would doubt the good business sense in that."

Commissioner Stewart's comments brought silence from the crowd. Kelly turned around from her seat at the press table and saw heads bent together possibly concocting a response to Stewart's view of smart growth.

"I am here representing those who voted me into office, not the developer," said Commissioner Chelsea Godfrey. "And there is plenty wrong with having a landing strip in our town, even though John

Travolta would always be welcome to come and live here and spend his money. Obviously, Commissioner Stewart has been meeting with the developers because we as a Commission haven't been told anything about this development."

Zion County had enough problems handling their own money woes and keeping its largest city under control. Kelly heard from her county sources that they were happy to let Calloway have the headaches of any future projects on the property in question. The county often forgot about the other towns lying to the northwest. While sometimes the rural communities complained, these cities — especially Millstone, Hope Springs, and Calloway — did pretty much what they pleased. At least they had until recently.

South Floridians, disillusioned with rapid growth and harmful environmental practices in the south, flocked to what they thought were idyllic small towns in northern Florida. They became vocal and hostile to growth in their newly adopted homes.

So when the landowners petitioned for the voluntary annexation of the 2,000 acres into Calloway, the county gave it their blessing. Some of Calloway's officials decided that the annexation and the rezoning would be lucrative for their town and for their pocketbooks. Betty Winters Duncan first brought the matter to the attention of Commissioner Stewart, who had long been at the forefront of pushing through developments and projects that would line his pockets, so the rumors went. So far, no one had been able to prove anything against the aging politician. Stewart managed to get whatever he wanted at the state and federal level, as long as he pushed through the programs necessary for the development of this portion of the Sunshine State.

Mayor Tim Murray also walked with full pockets, although his were filled with promises of power at the state level, not gold. As Mayor, he helped direct the focus of Calloway at least in the eyes of the public.

Betty Duncan came by her power naturally. Her father, B.J. Winters, helped make Calloway more than just a small town by selling the land where the very private and exclusive Calloway Golf and Country Club was built. Close to Braidwood, the club drew its membership from all over the county.

"And I'd like to know about the gopher tortoise population on that property," Cowan continued at the podium. "Those gopher tortoises have got to be protected from your good business sense, Commissioner Stewart."

"That's it, Garcia," shouted the Mayor. "Chief, throw this man out. We will be civil in these chambers above all else. Now get out of here before I come down there and throw you out personally."

Muscles straining in his tight uniform, the Chief of Police, Thomas Jefferson, came forward to escort Cowan Garcia from the podium, but Cowan held up his arms and willingly walked out of the building without Chief Jefferson doing much of anything but walk toward him.

Even though most of the residents spoke against the annexation, the five Calloway commissioners still voted 3-2 to bring the land into the city limits. Under the city's charter, the Mayor didn't vote, serving more as a sergeant at arms during meetings. Lately he had been kept busy.

"It seems you just received a threat," said the lieutenant from the Sheriff's office who arrived first on the scene, bringing Kelly back to the present moment and danger. "Just an empty tube made to look real enough to scare you."

"And a message taped to the bottom," the other officer continued. "It said, 'Shut up.'"

"What happens next?" Rick asked.

"Next we do an investigation. I'd like to talk to all three of you tonight before you go home. Get a statement."

"Fine," Rick said.

"You can go back inside now, and maybe you could find me an office where I can talk to each one of you privately," the officer said.

Kelly stood staring at the lieutenant. She knew him, but he had not really turned and taken a good look at her. She wondered if he would remember her.

CHAPTER FOUR

"RICK, ARE YOU GOING to ask Bart about the story?" Carl asked as they walked back into the building. "Since he already knows about the bomb, won't he expect a story?"

"You've made your point, Carl."

"Yes, and he'll tell you the same thing I've been telling you. We have to put something in the paper. It's still not too late to get it in."

Rick ignored him and went into his office and shut the door. He knew Carl was right, but he worried that his friends would rather keep this story contained. It was the middle of the University's football season, and the revenues from home games floated some businesses for the entire year.

Bart Stanley, the executive editor of the paper, arrived at his office to find Carl and the investigators shut behind Bart's always open door. A window looked out over the newsroom, but Bart also liked to keep the door open so he could hear the banter. Occasionally he would enter into it with one of his one-liners, usually stolen from a favorite movie.

"I picked a bad day to give up drinking beer," he now said as he waited next to Kelly's desk. "I guess I'll wait to give up sniffing glue."

Kelly looked at Bart and smiled. He stood there with a boyish grin and crinkled eyes waiting for a response from her. When there was none, his grin disappeared.

"You okay, kiddo?"

"I'm okay, Boss, just thinking about who might have left me the gift from Macy's."

"You know how relieved I was to hear it was a fake and that you were all right?" Bart's voice dropped so no one else could hear.

When Kelly first starting writing real news stories at *The Tribune*, Bart taught her about working on a daily newspaper. He saw her enthusiasm for the news and writing, something he had never lost, and he gave her attention not given to the other reporters.

He took her around to all the city halls, the county administration building, and police departments. He introduced her to his sources, giving her an edge over the other reporters. Bart was a trusted journalist in Zion County, and his recommendation meant easy access for Kelly.

Even though he was fifteen years older than her, he maintained a vitality and strength that had not disappeared since his days as a linebacker for the University of Braidwood. He married his college sweetheart, Joyce, and they had the obligatory two children. And even though he had followed a fairly logical and normal career path up the ladder at the paper, he remained interested and excited about journalism. Sometimes Kelly thought he desperately missed being a reporter.

His excitement attracted Kelly because she felt the same thing. She found herself dreaming about him and fantasized about touching the dimple in the middle of his chin and running her hand over his buzz cut hair.

A couple of years after she joined the staff of *The Tribune,* they went to Tallahassee together to cover a controversial legislative session on the revamping of education in the state. Kelly filed stories late every day, while Bart did background work. They were gone a week, and although they worked hard and conducted interviews and sat in on debates and votes, they fell in love during long dinners and longer nights.

On their second night in the capital city, they ate at a small French restaurant around the corner from the capitol. Over wine and candlelight a flirtation began that followed them up to Kelly's room.

Kelly knew she was lost at that dinner when Bart began telling her about his troubled marriage and his wife's severe depression.

"It kills me, you know," he said. "And I don't see any way out. If I left, I don't know what she'd do, and I couldn't live with that. But it's been awful for the past ten years for a man like me."

Kelly did not want to interrupt to ask if he meant what she thought he meant. She just knew that she wanted to wrap this big man in her arms and take away his pain.

"Do you want to come in for a minute?" she asked him when he had escorted her to the door of her hotel room.

"I can guarantee if I come into this room with you, it won't be for a minute," he said.

He towered over her but bent his head so it was even with hers. She reached up and ran her fingers through his short, graying hair. His brown eyes sparkled almost as if covered with a film of tears. They overshadowed all else on his rounded face. Even the dark circles under his eyes seemed to disappear as he looked at her in the bright hallway lights.

She opened the door, and he followed her into the room. She wanted to turn to him, but she knew once she did, there would be no turning back. She went to the small sliding glass door and walked out onto the balcony. Bart followed and stood very close behind her.

"Sweet, sweet lady," he said softly into her thick black hair. He pulled it aside so he could touch her bare neck with his lips. "You're beautiful."

And then she turned to him and buried her face in his chest. "Bart, I'm scared," she whispered.

"So am I."

Later, lying in bed side by side, he asked what scared her most.

"That I'll fall in love with you," she told him. "And my life will never be the same again."

"And that's a bad thing?"

"It is as long as one of us is married."

"Kelly, I need to tell you something. I think I've been in love with you from the moment you walked in my office asking me how to read a police report." He held her face between his hands.

"Please, Bart, don't say things like that."

And he hadn't the remainder of the week. But they shared one room each night for the rest of their stay.

Now Bart stood looking at Kelly in the middle of the newsroom, telling her how worried he was when he heard about the bomb.

"Bart, please don't," Kelly pleaded as she looked into his glassy eyes once again.

"Have you been questioned yet?" he asked.

"I'm next. The Sheriff's office and the FBI are working this one together, I guess."

Kelly had never stopped loving him, even though they made every attempt to stop seeing one another outside of the office. Bart had never been able to leave his wife, despite attempts to bring her depression under control. Somehow they managed to continue working together and remained friends.

"Miss Sands, we're ready for you," said the lieutenant who Kelly recognized earlier in the parking lot.

"It's not so bad, Kelly," said Carl as he walked out of Bart's office. "Just don't tell them about the hidden stash of donuts."

"I'm Lt. John Carson," the officer said as he held the door open for Kelly. He still showed no sign of recognizing her. "We'll try to be as quick as possible."

Afterwards, as Kelly prepared to go home, she was grateful that Bart and Rick were in Rick's office discussing safety and security measures in the newsroom. She gave a wave as she walked by, but neither man seemed to notice.

In the parking lot, Mike Green pulled up next to her.

"I was finishing up my piece on the annexation when the police scanner at *The Chronicle* said you had a bomb left in the building. What happened?" he asked.

"It was a fake bomb left on my desk," she told him.

"You're not kidding, are you?"

Mike and Kelly had been dating for a short time. He worked for *The Calloway Chronicle*, a 5,000-circulation paper covering the northwestern section of Zion County. She knew either Mike or her friend Molly Hale would write the story for *The Chronicle*.

"You got the scoop here, Mike. A note on the bottom said, 'Shut Up.'"

"What kind of bag?"

"How did you know it was left in a bag?"

"Just a good guess. Now let's go have breakfast and talk," he said. "Then I'll go back and write a story about the bomb threat. We should be able to get something in this week even though the paper is almost laid out. You'll need to give me some juicy quotes."

"Good, be glad to," she said. "Bellows might try to bury it."

"That would be a stupid thing to do," Mike said. "By the way, are there any suspects yet?"

"Not a one."

CHAPTER FIVE

LUCY BURCH PULLED HER BMW convertible into the parking lot of Burch Realty in downtown Braidwood and hurried into the building. As usual, she arrived at the office at seven o'clock before anyone else.

She picked up *The Braidwood Tribune* from the sidewalk and unlocked the door. Before she entered her office, she saw the paper's headline.

"*Tribune* news reporter threatened with bomb."

Lucy read anxiously about the fake bomb left on the desk of Kelly Sands, not one of her favorite writers. She'd been chiding Rick for weeks about how unnecessary it was for Kelly to report every detail of the commission meetings. Kelly even wrote in one article about how Lucy and one of the developers sat and snickered through the first public hearing on annexation any time someone stood and spoke against it.

Maybe the little bitch would get the message now, Lucy thought. But just as quickly, she had another thought. The businesswoman in her took over, and she knew she needed to start a major public relations campaign to overshadow the news that someone in Zion County threatened people with violence when they disagreed with them. Lucy wondered who was responsible and secretly wanted to wring their necks. There were other ways that drew less attention.

When her phone began to ring soon after she saw the headline, she knew who would be on the other end of the line even before she picked it up.

"Good morning, Jerry," Lucy answered.

Jerry Mueller, president of the Zion County Chamber of Commerce, didn't waste any time in the mornings either. He couldn't afford to. His paid position at the Chamber was only as strong as his relationship with the business community. The bomb scare would definitely put a damper on public relations in the entire area.

"Have you seen the paper?" he asked.

"Yes, just now. Can't say I disagree with the sentiment, but the method leaves a bit to be desired."

"Exactly my thoughts. We've got to do something and quick. The Tennessee game is this weekend."

"Believe me, I know, Jerry. I've got two different couples flying in from Miami to look at property on the river, and then I'm taking them all to the game. They'll be my first calls this morning."

"Any ideas about containment? Maybe get Rick to let us run one of our public relations pieces? We could get someone to spice it up, you know, extol the virtues of this wonderful college town and surrounding area."

"Good idea. I'm sure Rick will agree. Should we take him to lunch today?"

"I'll call him and set it up. The Legacy Club at one?"

"Good, good. Maybe I'll see if Jackson can join us."

"Fine. We'll keep it low key, real sympathetic like, and then mention how we need to make Braidwood look friendly. Don't want to push Rick too hard. He hates to be told how to do his job," Jerry said.

"If he'd control his reporters, he wouldn't have to get instructions."

Cowan Garcia lived in one of the Victorian homes that graced the tree-lined Main Street of downtown Calloway. The morning after the meeting, he went out on his porch to retrieve *The Tribune*. He shook his head when he read the headline, and felt sympathy for Kelly Sands. Two weeks ago, his tires were slashed while he was inside city hall picking up a public records request.

He took a deep breath and glanced up and down the street. He wondered how such a beautiful area as Calloway could contain such greed and hostility. He found himself caught up in the negativity and sometimes he responded in worse ways than those with whom he had disagreements.

"Good morning," yelled Chelsea Godfrey as she rode her bike into Cowan's front yard. "Thanks for trying last night."

"Lot of good it did with those scum-sucking morons up there. We've got to find the right person to run for the March election against Simmons."

"Cowan, what is that?" Chelsea pointed to an object lying just a few feet from the front porch steps.

Cowan came down to the yard to inspect. "Damn it all!" He picked up a dead gopher tortoise from the ground and held it out for inspection.

"They were busy last night," Chelsea said. She indicated the paper Cowan had tucked under his arm. "You saw the bomb story?"

"This is going too far."

"What are you going to do with it?" Chelsea asked as Cowan headed into the house with his paper. He placed the carcass on the porch. Chelsea followed.

"I'm going to bury it in the front yard and put a tombstone up that reads 'RIP Gopher Tortoise, Killed by Developers,' and then I'll call my favorite reporters and hold a memorial."

CHAPTER SIX

ON WEDNESDAY, TWO DAYS after the bomb threat, the Living section of *The Tribune* had a front-page color spread entitled "Zion County, Living the Easy Life since 1888."

Kelly read the report with little excitement. So this was Bellows' and his friends' answer to the bomb threat. She noticed her story on Cowan Garcia's gopher tortoise grave received third page placement in the local section. Even though she sent Lonny, her favorite photographer, out for a picture, Rick must have decided not to run it. Kelly hoped Molly had better luck with her editor Greg Panzer at *The Chronicle*.

She drove the short distance to Big Meadows Park and took a long walk to begin her day. The beautiful late October weather threatened to keep Kelly outside instead of working on an article she hoped to submit to *Atlantic Monthly*. *The Tribune* was only a stepping-stone in Kelly's plan for herself as a writer. She admired journalists who used passion and literary license in their investigative reports. Her favorite journalist carried this talent over into autobiographical books, going so far as to win the Pulitzer Prize. She read his work with awe and envy, but Kelly also knew she could do the same thing.

She wanted more for her career than writing about underhanded developers and crooked politicians and criminals. She had her own stories to tell. Someday she would be ready to share them with the world.

But for now Kelly approached her job with single-minded determination. One thing had been bothering Kelly for a few months now, and she hadn't been successful in her research. She came up with nothing each time she tried. She wanted to know who actually owned the annexed property in Calloway. The deeds listed different landowners, but they seemed to be working as a team, and she hadn't been able to make a connection yet. She would next try to match names from the deeds with names listed as board members of Industrial

Pines. But she knew a company as powerful as I.P. hid their tracks very well.

The residents also wanted to know who owned the property. Many of them approached Kelly at the meetings and asked her questions. Those questions moved her to continue her research. She wouldn't be surprised if I.P. planned a purchase or transfer of the 2,000 acres now that the annexation was complete. It was a tactic to quiet the rumor mill until the legal process was complete.

I.P. supported the annexation in all the public hearings. Kelly had concerns about B.J. Winters, the president of I.P. He also served on the county's zoning board. It was just one of the many tasks she had on her list to investigate when she had spare time.

When Kelly returned from her walk, a message from Lt. John Carson awaited her. He wanted to ask a few more questions. She called him back and invited him to come over to her house.

"Who do you think might have left the warning?" he began after he settled in Kelly's comfortable, yet small, living room.

"Besides the obvious?"

"Why don't you let me decide the obvious? Tell me everything you know or suspect, then we'll decide what to investigate."

"I've been covering the Calloway City Commission for about five years now. People make comments to me all the time about my articles. Some positive, some not. I also cover the other surrounding towns like Millstone and Hope Springs. Again, I usually make the pro-developer commissioners mad as well as some residents. I get a lot of hang up calls at night."

"Why do your articles make people mad?"

"Lt. Carson, are you telling me that you don't read my articles?"

"Not regularly, but now I will, that's for sure. They must be something for you to get such lovely fan mail."

"I write what everyone says. If a commissioner comes out and says, 'What's wrong with an asphalt plant in the middle of downtown? Everyone needs roads and an asphalt plant would bring jobs and revenues,' I put it in my article. Now some folks think I should just record the votes on motions and not add the extra. I feel strongly that my job as a reporter requires me to report who voted which way and why. How else will the voters know who to support?"

"Pretty noble ideals for a journalist. Your bosses at the paper ever try to get you to tone it down?"

"Rick Bellows, the city editor, tries. But luckily the executive editor, Bart Stanley, thinks like I do. And our publisher, Mr. Collings, also likes my stuff, so Bellows is usually outvoted. It's probably the reason I'm not rotated to different beats like the other reporters. I'm the only one who really enjoys covering the outlying areas."

"Is there any person you would suspect of doing this? Someone who might have access to the newsroom?"

"No one who has access, unless ..." She let her sentence drift off because she didn't know if she should continue.

"It's okay, I'll probably hear about it somewhere else, so it might as well be from you," Carson said.

"The Millstone weekly, *The Monitor*, some of those writers come around *The Tribune* quite often. Particularly Gary Dregs who's sometimes listed as editor, sometimes as staff writer. He's pushy."

"You think this Dregs fellow might have something to do with the bomb?"

"The general opinion among news people in the area is that *The Millstone Monitor* is really a front for the developers. I've been trying to investigate that. I've got anonymous sources that tell me there's a group of developers from throughout the county who meet regularly, and they pool resources and work very hard to harass opposing forces through mailings and phone calls. Threaten to close down businesses, that kind of thing. And they pick candidates to run for different seats within the county. Some people believe the connections go even higher up and further than that."

"What does that have to do with the Millstone paper?"

"They started up two years ago, and we all suspected something immediately. The paper ran the first few months with hardly any ads."

"And? I'm not sure I understand."

"It takes big money to support a paper without ad revenue. Sales of the paper don't pay to run four sections filled with color pictures. The people at *The Calloway Chronicle* could give you more information. *The Millstone Monitor* became their direct competitor, especially when they began selling ads and undercutting whatever *The Chronicle* charged. *The Chronicle* also protested that some of the legal ads run in *The Monitor* were done against state statute."

"okay, so some rich person starts a paper and another local paper feels threatened by the competition. Doesn't seem strange so far."

"Then you have to read the paper and compare what they write about the commission meetings and what we write and what *The Chronicle* writes. They are definitely pro-developer. If you want, I've saved some of the articles. Like I said, I've been researching this stuff quietly for a while now. I think there's a stinking pile of mess under all the development in this area."

"I'd like to see those articles so I could understand a little bit more. The world of the journalist is news to me." He grinned showing dimples and lots of white teeth. Kelly looked away because she found herself mesmerized by his good looks and friendly manner. But he still did not seem to recognize her.

"Interview Mike Green and Molly Hale at *The Chronicle*," she told him. "They both write about the local politics in Millstone and Calloway and Hope Springs. I think they've both had some experience with Gary Dregs. They call him Dregs of Humanity, but I don't advise that you use that name."

"Thanks for the advice."

After he finished writing in his notebook, he looked closely at Kelly.

"You seem familiar to me," he said.

"I've got one of those faces I guess; people are always saying that to me."

"No, I don't forget a face, but the one I remember was sadder."

Kelly sighed. She never liked subterfuge and what did it matter now if he remembered.

"About fifteen years ago, you saved my life."

John looked puzzled at first but slowly the vague memory of a girl in a car passed out against the window came back to him.

"You were that girl out at Mullet Swamp?"

"Yes."

When Officer John Carson received a call over his radio at 6:37 p.m. in the fall of 1985, he dreaded responding. He was working alone, and the report didn't sound promising.

"We have a report of a woman who seems to be passed out, sitting in a car in the parking lot of Mullet Lake," the dispatcher said. Mullet Lake was a part of the prairie on its western edge.

He always hated this type of call, especially if the call had come in too late.

When he pulled into the parking lot, he saw a lone vehicle parked haphazardly, ignoring the painted lines on the pavement. The vehicle reminded him of hundreds owned by the college students who poured into Braidwood each fall.

As he approached, he could see the slumped figure with dark hair resting against the driver's side window.

He rapped on the glass several times before the head moved. And then he saw the saddest thing in his short career. An obviously drugged head turned toward him. Her hair, black and shiny, framed her small face. When she managed to open her eyes, he could see the intense blue peering at him as the flashlight poured light on the girl.

"Open the door," he shouted. He remembered the dispatcher had called back with a name. Sometimes it helped to use the familiar term in order to gain trust.

"Kelly, please open the door. There are many people concerned about you right now."

She shook her head.

"Please, Kelly. We can go into my car and just talk," he said.

She looked into his eyes and saw kindness. She unlocked the door.

"Things have changed for you, haven't they?" John now asked Kelly.

"Yes, thank you."

"I'll go now. I may have to call again, if I have more questions."

After he left, she called both Molly and Mike to tell them the lieutenant would probably be asking questions about *The Millstone Monitor.* Molly chortled over the good stories she could tell about Gary, but Mike seemed annoyed that she had given the police his name.

CHAPTER SEVEN

MOLLY AND DAVID HALE HAD lived between Hope Springs and Calloway for the past twenty years. For most of that time Molly had been busy raising their two children, while Gary developed a computer web design business. Now both of their children were in college, one in Tallahassee, the other in Tampa, and Gary and she enjoyed the freedom afforded by an empty nest.

Molly had helped David with the business for the past several years, but found herself becoming increasingly interested in local politics, especially when property next to hers outside the city limits of Hope Springs was annexed into the city. She found it difficult to get access to public records and documents. Her frustration became paramount, and she began writing letters to the editor of *The Calloway Chronicle*.

One day three years ago, she dropped off a letter, and Greg Panzer stood at the counter reading a paper. When he discovered Molly was his prolific letter writer, he told her he admired her guts and writing ability.

"How about coming to work here?" he asked her. "I can't pay a whole lot, but I could use someone to cover the commission meetings. Interested?"

Molly, usually not left speechless, stared at the young hotshot editor, who was beginning to cause a stir in the community with his in-depth reports and investigations into the activities around the area, not only in Calloway, but in Hope Springs and Millstone as well.

After Greg starting publishing consistent and thorough reports on the meetings, coupled with Kelly's attention in the larger daily newspaper, things started to change in local politics in the rural areas. As long as elected officials and developers with an eye on the big prize can get away with running the show, they will. The media's scrutiny brought awareness to the public about environmental and economic concerns. Molly could tell things changed just by looking at the increased number of residents attending the commission meetings in recent years as compared to when she first started going herself. So Greg's offer intrigued her.

"Mr. Panzer, I do believe you are one of the first people to make me speechless," Molly said. "I've never considered working for a newspaper."

"Why not consider it now? You've got the background because you've been attending the meetings for quite awhile now, right?"

"Right, but do you really think I could write an article on the meetings?"

"Sure. Why don't you come to Calloway's meeting with me on Monday night, take notes, and I'll quiz you on what would make a good lead for the story. Then you can submit the piece, and we'll talk."

"okay, but the lead? I don't get it."

"You don't write about everything that happens in a meeting — most of the time there wouldn't be enough space. And you don't write the piece chronologically. You begin with the most newsworthy item from the meeting, and that's your lead."

Molly still seemed puzzled so Greg gave her his favorite example of how not to write about a Commission meeting.

"Let's say the last thing to happen at the meeting is the shooting of one of the commissioners by the city manager," he said rubbing his hands together and licking his lips. "If you wrote it chronologically that would be the last item to appear in the piece on the meeting. Does that make any sense? You've got to lead with that story and probably wouldn't even write about the rest of the meeting, which becomes a moot point as soon as the body hits the floor."

Molly caught on immediately, as Greg knew she would. One of his talents as editor was the ability to attract and sense someone's nose for the news. He could tell from the first letter to the editor that Molly had that nose. She had not disappointed him during her three years at the paper. She covered Hope Springs exclusively and sometimes Calloway and Millstone, depending on whomever else he had on staff at the time.

These days Greg wondered if he was losing his touch. Mike Green hadn't turned into the type of reporter Greg suspected he might become. But maybe Mike was a slow starter.

Mike Green wet his bed until he turned thirteen at which point he grew into his body and bladder. His condition, while not uncommon, never went unpunished in his home.

The only child had great expectations heaped upon him by his father from the moment of Mike's birth. His father owned the largest cardboard box company in the south. The business, located in Dansville — an hour's drive from Braidwood — had begun with a slight investment but provided packaging for most of the manufacturers in the southeastern states. Mr. Green demanded perfection and most of the time he got it.

He also demanded that same perfection from his son, but his son had been uncooperative. One morning when he was five, Mike woke up to soaked pajamas and sheets and the odor of old urine. He tried to call his mother to his room, but his father came instead.

"What did you do, you stupid kid," his father told him before yanking him out of the mess and slapping him twice across the face. "Do you need to go back to diapers?"

"No, Sir, it was asident," Mike told him the best a five-year-old could do.

"We'll see about that. If you act like the dogs then tonight you'll sleep like one." Mike's father turned away to summon his wife for the task of cleaning up the mess.

All day Mike wondered what his father meant, but by the time five o'clock rolled around, and Mr. Green drove in the driveway and opened the trunk of his car, all doubt left Mikes' mind about sleeping with the dogs.

The trunk contained a folded cardboard box that Mr. Green opened on the lawn into a 3-foot by 4-foot box. This container, and others like it, would become Mike's home whenever he wet his bed for the next eight years.

And if he wet the box, he had to sleep inside of it, damp as it was, until he had a night when he didn't wet it. Mike could go long periods without wetting the bed, but that meant that he stayed awake most of the night in fear that he would. On those nights when he became so exhausted from the lack of sleep, he would drift off and wake to the stench of his body's urine.

During this time, Mike had no friends because friends in elementary school stayed over at one another's houses on the weekends and camped in the woods during the summer. Mike could not trust himself to go away on any of these excursions. Neither could he trust having one of those boys stay at his house. So whenever he was asked to do something overnight, he refused, and soon they stopped asking.

Mike played alone and developed his mind, but he also thought the rest of the world looked upon him with disdain. And so he learned early on to give off the same attitude.

When the bed-wetting naturally stopped, things changed only slightly in the Green household. Mike hated his father and refused to have anything to do with the cardboard box business. When his father tried to get him to work summers, he refused and instead got a job at a local bookstore stocking shelves. His father thought it was a job for a weakling and never let Mike forget it.

Mike graduated from high school and decided to leave Dansville to attend Banks Community College for two years and then the University of Braidwood. His father assumed he would major in business. Mike chose journalism instead. But none of that mattered because by the time Mike graduated from high school, his father was dead, and Mike didn't have anyone calling over his shoulder and reminding him what a failure he was.

He never graduated from college even after spending six years trying, while working at odd jobs to support himself. He finally gave up. No one in the school of journalism encouraged him to continue. He had no prospects for a job until he came across an ad in the paper. A small newspaper in Calloway needed a stringer. He knew he could write. It was one thing he had always done with confidence. His days with the Dansville paper while still in high school had shown him he knew how to take an event and turn it into a story. All that junk they had tried to teach him at the University seemed worthless.

After he had been working there a few months, Molly Hale, his colleague and friend at the paper, wondered why he always had a pained expression on his face when he wrote. One day she broached the subject.

"It's an agony for me to write," he explained. "I suffer over every word I put down on the page. Don't you?"

"Heavens, no. Writing is absolute joy for me. Why do you write if it gives you so much pain?"

"It's the only thing I can do well."

Molly had read a few of his pieces, because that's all he'd been able to muster in his few short months at *The Chronicle*. Unlike Molly, who wrote six or seven articles for each week's paper, Mike could only produce about one a week. And Molly knew they weren't very good. He wrote above the reading ability of the average reader. Greg always reminded them the average newspaper reader read at about an eighth grade level or lower and writing at that level and below should be the goal of the journalist. Mike wrote using words that even he had to look up in the dictionary first – another mistake according to the world of Panzer. Greg said if a reporter had to look a word up in the dictionary first then the word should not be used. Mike hated Greg for editing his words.

CHAPTER EIGHT

LUCY BURCH, OWNER OF Burch Realty, grew up in Braidwood and married often and divorced quickly. Most of her six marriages ended when she grew tired of the companionship of her latest conquest or if her current husband lost interest in her zealous efforts to make money at any price. Most of the husbands decided the abundant sex was not worth the sale of the soul.

But Lucy learned to cope very nicely. Ever since she turned forty more than a decade ago, she celebrated each divorce with a little nip and tuck handled out of state. Whenever she left, she told everyone she had gone off to a spa to recover from the trauma of the break up. She would come back a little trimmer and tighter and her short blonde hair even brighter.

She earned her realtor's license nearly twenty years ago when she realized that as a secretary she had been sealing deals for her boss at another Braidwood realty company for years and not getting a commission. Whenever she became bored with real estate, she would switch gears and concentrate on another aspect of the business. Two years ago, she began dealing in river properties on the Hope Springs River, twenty-five miles north of Braidwood. Lucy found it lucrative to lure investors from south Florida with the promise of some of her rental properties for a family weekend. She bought property almost as fast as she sold it.

She would do renovations, use the houses as guest cottages for out of town visitors, and sometimes end up selling the house to her guests. She made a handsome slice of cash on the resell.

These secluded river parcels, with boat access and rural acreage, were a popular attraction for urban dweller. However, a drought in the last year had slowed down that business as some of the property turned to mud flat frontage instead of river. Lucy still invited investors to the area, and with her contacts, continued to speculate and process large tracts of land all around Zion County and even across the river into adjoining Banks County.

She also worked with the Zion County Chamber of Commerce in promoting some of the new subdivisions growing at a speedy rate on the northwest section of Braidwood and rural, undeveloped parts of the county.

As far as Lucy was concerned, the movie studio and landing strip would be the ultimate attracter of new residents to the million dollar homes built around the landing strip. She also knew that the development in Calloway was only the beginning.

She had at least a dozen interested parties across the country. Zion County's rolling hills and rivers with fresh-water springs, coupled with a mild winter, made it an ideal location for northerners hoping to cash in on Florida's sunshine. Mild, yet noticeable changes in the seasons made the area an easy sell. Leaves fell off the trees and sweet gums glowed red, marking the start of autumn; a slight chill in winter made it ideal for wearing sweatshirts and brought forth flowering camellias; a mild spring filled with first the blooms of the red bud tree and then the azaleas and wisteria, followed by the blossoms of the magnolia in May filled the hearts and souls with promise and hope. While the summers could be unbearably humid and hot, Floridians living in the middle of the state away from the ocean breezes kept indoors in the ice-cold air conditioning.

In contrast, south Florida's weather remained constant twelve months of the year and many grew tired of the sameness broken only by the winds and floods of an occasional hurricane.

One property that Lucy kept strictly for her own use was located just over the county line in neighboring Banks County on the Hope Springs River. At this secluded river location, developers, politicians, and power brokers came from around the state to talk about furthering the development of north Florida.

Kelly walked out of the Zion County Courthouse the day after she had spoken to Lt. Carson at her house and almost bumped into him as he ran up the front steps of the building.

"How's the case going?" Kelly asked.

"The FBI decided to leave it to us since it was a fake, but I haven't really proceeded very far. Still have lots of interviews to conduct, that sort of thing," John said. "You having any problems or any more threats?"

"No, everything has been smooth, no problems. But then there haven't been any meetings since the scare."

"So I've noticed. I've been watching for your byline so I could see what you do to get everyone so riled up. When's the next one?"

"County Commission tonight at seven."

"Anything exciting on the agenda?"

"Discussion of a lawsuit the county has brought against Millstone and a land owner there. That's why I'm here today, and that's why I'll be at the county commission meeting tonight. I usually only cover the municipalities. They had a hearing on the case today. Annexing property that forms an enclave isn't taken lightly around here. They're also going to discuss the annexation of the 2,000 acres into Calloway. Seems a couple of county commissioners think they can stop that from happening."

"Is that true?"

"It might be if they can prove that it's a threat to the welfare of the entire county. But the two environmental commissioners have strong opposition from at least one other commissioner so the talks could be stormy. No decision will come up tonight, just discussion. I'm surprised it made its way into a regular meeting, instead of a workshop."

"Why?"

"A workshop gives them more time to consider all options before voting on it at a regular meeting. But perhaps that's the point."

CHAPTER NINE

THE BOAT PULLED UP to the dock at the secluded cottage on the Hope Springs River in Banks County. The landing had space for four boats to dock easily. The other three spaces were filled as the 22-foot StarCraft pulled into its spot and let out the six commissioners from Hope Springs and Calloway. Already at the location were elected officials and interested parties from around the county. Sometimes they came from around the state. This group of the powerful and rich met several times a month in secrecy, not just because of the matters discussed, but because of the Sunshine Laws, which forbade elected officials from the same board to meet and discuss in private matters which might later come up for a public vote. But that had been the way of politics in Florida since its beginning, and no laws could change this southern tradition of meeting behind closed doors in the back woods of the state.

The Sunshine Laws became a part of the Florida Statutes in the late sixties to ensure the public's right of access to meetings between members of governing bodies. The public generally supported the Sunshine Laws because supposedly, if followed, governments become responsive to the public's needs and responsible for protecting their constituents' safety and welfare.

Lucy Burch greeted the men as they disembarked from the boat onto her dock. She had driven out earlier with Rick Bellows so she could let the caterers into the house to prepare the barbecue lunch that would follow. The meeting was simply a formality. Everyone knew that the important deals took place with a barbecued rib in one hand and a cold draft beer in the other. Lucy had iced down a keg the night before. A bar down the road brought them over whenever she called for one.

"We're pleased to have you with us, Senator Jones," Jackson Stewart said to begin the meeting.

Murmured greetings to the state senator, Sam Jones, came from around the group. Most just lifted a beer mug to their old fishing buddy who had just been elected to serve in Tallahassee.

"Now the annexation is just the beginning," announced Jackson to the assembled group. "I want to hear what's happening with the development on Boat Ramp Road outside Hope Springs."

Jackson looked directly at Billy Winterrowd when he made his request. Billy owned the largest contiguous property and some of the last available land in Zion County on the Hope Springs River. He also served as a commissioner in Hope Springs. But Jackson worried about Billy, who had a penchant for trying to be funny in public. He usually ended up alienating everyone around him with his jokes unless his audience consisted only of his Good Old Boy buddies.

Jackson heard that at Tuesday's Hope Springs Chamber meeting, Billy said, "Wish they'd filled that pipe with something real at *The Tribune*. Then I'd know who to ask to do the same thing over at *The Chronicle*."

Some Chamber members laughed, but a few became uncomfortable. Jackson heard the story from several different sources. He looked at Billy for a straight answer on the prime property just waiting for condos and townhouses.

"Don't you worry, Jackson," Billy said. "I've got it under control. We'll get those deeds turned over quickly and quietly with Lucy's help. Then we've got to annex the land. It could come before us in the next two months."

"What's the chance of Hope Springs rejecting it?" Rick asked.

"Hard to tell," Billy answered. "That nigger and the faggot always make a mess when it comes time to vote."

"Billy, you've got to stop talking like that," Jackson said. "That almost cost you the election two years ago, and we can't afford to lose you in Hope Springs. Think, boy, before you open your mouth. Not everyone is amused by your nicknames."

"okay, Mammy and Boy George, then. But when I'm here drinking beer, I ain't gonna call them by name," Billy announced. "They want to change our way of life, Jackson. We can't let them take a majority on the Commission; we've got to stop that. Sometimes I wonder about J.D. He seems to lean toward them 'til he sees me staring at him. So far he's always voted the right way."

The governments within Zion County had long been ruled by a society common in the south since reconstruction. The Good Old Boy system or GOB, as the opposition disparagingly called it, had held power for so long in the county that for years no one dared cross it. The GOBs kept getting richer and richer by selling off large tracts of their granddaddies' farms to the developers who took the perfect opportunity to buy thousands of acres real cheap.

And when the Commissions consisted solely of GOBs, as they had traditionally in the rural parts of Zion County, these developers could get all sorts of perks, from tax breaks to roads built, subsidized by the taxpaying public.

The requirements to belong to the society, besides land and money, were a strong belief that the white male remained at the center of decision-making and power brokering. It also helped if members could chew tobacco and spit without anyone noticing, enjoy a large appetite for whiskey and beer at the same time, and show a love for big expensive cars and boats and women. Sometimes others would be let into the group, but only if they had learned to play the game.

Jackson Stewart, the king GOB in the county, drove a new Cadillac every year. His mistress Mazie Kane was an open secret. He took her everywhere while the wife stayed home and handled the ranch. Jackson could talk a pig out of his mud if he took a mind to do so. But instead he concentrated his energies on swindling the little folks around him by buying their property deeply discounted prices.

"You know there's going to be a sinkhole on that property real soon," he'd tell them. And because he was Jackson Stewart, they usually believed him and practically gave the land to him. And he had folks so convinced that he knew every thing, they never questioned why he would want land with a sinkhole on it.

When Jackson was elected to the Calloway Commission over three decades ago, his power base became complete. Most politicians lose money while in office, but Jackson became the richest man in the county almost over night.

The last time someone had opposed him, the challenger lost big time. During the last election when his nemesis on the Calloway Commission, Chelsea Godfrey — or Godawful as Jackson called her — ran for the first time, he had gone to the Calloway Chief of Police and asked for officers to tail her and fine her with any violation. He also wanted a complete investigation into her background. She had not grown up in Calloway, and worse, came from Ohio.

The Chief at the time refused. And that was the last time he refused Jackson anything. He never got the chance. Rumors started in the community about ticket quotas. An investigation headed up by Commissioner Stewart ended in a few short weeks with the dismissal of the Chief. Then Jackson made sure Thomas Jefferson replaced him. A black man in a high profile position gave Jackson a certain leverage that only those raised with a plantation mentality could understand. Chief Jefferson could never refuse Jackson Stewart a thing; he was one of those "different" ones allowed into the inner circle, as long as he played by the rules set by Jackson.

"I've been thinking about something, and I'd like to pass it by this group," Rick said. "What are the biggest stumbling blocks to our plans in Zion County right now?"

"Environmentalists, liberals, radicals, vegetarians, tree huggers, gopher lovers. Anyone against growth," Lucy said.

"Right. And where do they get fuel for their arguments?" Rick continued.

"The newspapers," Jackson said. "But we've done about as much as we can there. *The Monitor* is making a difference in Millstone, for sure."

"Let's start another one," Rick said. "This time focus more on the overall County."

"*The Zion County News?*" Jackson Stewart stared out the window toward the river as he contemplated starting another paper.

"Everyone suspects *The Millstone Monitor* is pretty slanted, but with this one we could make it strictly a rural community paper at first," Rick continued. "You know, school carnivals, stuff *The Calloway Chronicle* does now, but we'd have more writers and better resources, and we might even put them out of business."

"If we do it, I suggest this time we blindside them," Lucy said. "I've heard rumors that *The Monitor* became suspect immediately when it started with so few ads. Let's do a national search for a legitimate editor and get real writers and then slowly we begin getting our agenda across, a little more subtly."

"Rick, how much will it cost us?" Johnny Waine, another commissioner from Calloway asked.

"It wouldn't be cheap because I propose if we do this thing then we do it right, like Lucy said. And then we may find that we start to save money."

"Can you give an estimate?" Lucy asked.

"Probably a half million to start. That's getting an office in a central location in downtown Calloway, real visibility. We may want to consider just buying *The Chronicle* outright. I keep hearing rumors about the publisher looking around for a buyer. That would make our job a whole lot easier. Now we're talking a million."

"Who would run the daily operations?" asked Lester Simmons.

"With the right kinds of enticements, I could be persuaded to leave *The Tribune*. I've been unhappy ever since Collings came in as publisher. I'd also suggest that we find someone as a figurehead to represent the publisher. We keep ownership of the paper buried just like with the other paper."

"Let's bring this idea to the full group at our next regular meeting," Jackson said. "I frankly think it's brilliant, but of course, we need financial contributions. In the meantime, why don't you all think of people who we might hire to aggressively write and pursue stories with one goal in mind: To become the only newspaper in the area."

"I like it," said Tim Murray, mayor of Calloway. "We do this right, we can just shut down *The Monitor,* get *The Chronicle* out of the way and then we become the voice of Zion County."

Lucy looked around the large deck in front of her river house. She was the only woman present; she actually preferred it that way. Other women could complicate things. Sometimes Mazie would show up with Jackson, but she usually sat at his feet throwing adoring glances his way. She was his pigeon at commission meetings besides serving as his mistress for twenty years. These men treated Lucy as one of them because she had shown she had the balls to give as well as take.

Several sitting on the deck drinking beer had been her lovers over the years. Occasionally, she still slept with two of them when it was convenient. She almost married one of them, but thankfully they both had come to their senses before anything formal could take place. Lucy's gaze came to rest on two of the most powerful men in attendance, yet neither had spoken a word.

B.J. Winters and Anthony Marcetti had met when they were both in their twenties. They grew up in Miami, smart and ambitious. In their early teens they began dealing drugs — mostly heroin — to clubs. In those days, cocaine had not made the big splash that it did in the seventies, and those who hung out in the beat clubs dug the down side of life and chose their drug accordingly.

Winters and Marcetti only gave the customers what they wanted.

CHAPTER TEN

SOON B.J. AND ANTHONY had boys of their own to do the actual street dealing, while they sat back driving muscle cars and got all the girls. School never loomed high on the list of priorities and before long neither B.J. nor Anthony bothered to go. Why go to school when they were making three times the money as the teachers who thought they could control them.

Both teenagers found they were financial wizards and neither consumed the drugs themselves, which made them an anomaly among the drug dealers of Miami. Instead, they bought a few things for their pleasure such as cars and girls, but soon they began investing their money in tangible things, like real estate. They ventured out of Miami and became known for making magnificent real estate deals while still in their twenties.

During spring break 1962, while hanging out at Fort Lauderdale Beach, B.J. met his future wife and that was the end of his Miami stint. Lois lived in north Florida. In fact, her father owned 1,500 acres of farmland near Braidwood, and there was plenty of cheap property all around it that attracted B.J. He could see growth would eventually seep north, and if the rumors of a Disney explosion in Orlando proved correct, the movement toward the north would most likely follow.

The day before his wedding on the ranch of his future in-laws, B.J. bought 2,000 acres adjoining his father-in-law. The young couple would live on the ranch until their own ranch house was built. Throughout the 1960s, he continued to buy property around both ranches. By the early seventies, he helped create the Calloway Country Club, and Lois and he lived in the grandest house of all overlooking the fairway on the ninth hole.

This area, north of the University of Braidwood, remained part of the Deep South, maintaining a balance between southern charm and the Wild West. Crackers, who migrated from the ranches in central Florida nearly a half century before, held a supreme attraction for B.J. Winters.

These cracker immigrants were real cowboys who herded their cattle throughout pastureland, now nonexistent. Their small horses were agile and quick and steered the cows in the right direction. When needed, the cowboys cracked their whips and the sound alone would bring the cattle into compliance. Soon the moniker of *cracker* stuck. And the horses became known as cracker horses. The cracker cowboys scattered across the state, mostly in the northern regions, buying up small ranches.

B.J.'s father-in-law was one of those men. He first came to north Florida with a pocketful of change and found that he could buy any piece of property for just $100. He began by setting up turpentine camps on the outer edges of the newly acquired property where the longleaf pines grew in abundance. These trees produced the best sap for turpentine, a highly demanded product in the shipping industry. Offering itinerant black men a place to live and earn a pittance, he made a killing in the business of drawing sap from the trees. He didn't worry he was making his fortune on the broken backs and lives of men who found themselves in a form of peonage uncomfortably close to that of their parents and grandparents who had been slaves. When the state finally intervened and shut down the camps, B.J.'s father-in-law was a fat cat with connections everywhere.

But even his connections in Tallahassee could not prevent the closure of the camp. When the conditions of the men and their living quarters were revealed in the local press, it was all over.

B.J. knew the story and knew to be successful in business pursuits he needed to control the press. He never had much success at it until Anthony Marcetti showed an interest in the area, moving his operations further and further north. The two men formed their first legal partnership in Industrial Pines by the early 1990s.

"I think it might be worth looking into starting up another paper, don't you, Anthony?" B.J. spoke for the first time at the meeting.

"Do your research, Bellows. I'm interested," Anthony finally decreed.

"Where's Tony?" Lucy asked after looking around the room.

"He's in court," Tim Murray said. "Remember that annexation deal last year with that property I own in Millstone? Some county officials are crying enclave."

"I told those boys on the county commission to let the arbiter decide, but no, those newly elected hot shot commissioners think they know it all," Jackson said.

"Tony always says it ain't illegal till they take him to court," Billy said. "Will he win it?"

"Hard to tell," said Tim. "Hard to tell because the judge is new to the bench."

"He'll be fine," Anthony said. "Tony knows what he's doing."

Tony Mayberry was the city attorney in Millstone and Calloway. He kept a low profile most of the time, and when questioned about anything with a hint of impropriety he liked to say he was just a country lawyer, and he'd have to look into it.

"That reminds me. We need to start talking about elections in March," Jerry Mueller told them. "We've got to put up some good people, friendly to our business concerns. Calloway will be especially crucial."

Zion County held all local and county elections on the first Tuesday in March. That way the election in November was devoted solely to state and federal candidates and issues. The November election of 2000 was just a week away, but this group of power brokers and elected officials knew it was the local elections that really made a difference in their world. They paid little attention to the race for the presidency, although most of them at this meeting liked the idea of having a Bush in Washington as well as in Tallahassee.

"Who's up this time? Anyone here?" Lucy asked.

"Johnny and me," said Lester Simmons.

"J.D. and Billy in Hope Springs," Jackson said. "Also crucial seats if we're going to get the river development through."

"Plus those two environmentalists on the county commission, don't forget," added Rick.

"Maybe we can have *The Zion County News* up and running right before the election and give very fair and unbiased reporting of the candidates and then endorse our boys," suggested Jackson. "It could be our debut issue."

"That's moving pretty fast, but it could be done if we get to work on it now," Rick said. "Maybe some of us should meet in a few days, and I'll have some preliminary plans by then."

They decided to meet with the whole group again in two weeks, when Rick would present a full report on starting the new paper. Getting the paper up and running in time for the elections could mean defeating anyone who dared challenge the incumbents.

The rest of the lunch and meeting was taken up with the suggestion of names to run in the elections. One more anti-growth candidate in Calloway and Hopes Springs would mean a majority, and the opposition knew it as well as this group of well-heeled politicians sitting in the shade of the live oaks on this pleasant autumn afternoon.

As soon as they left, Rick and Lucy began cleaning up the kitchen.

"Your suggestion for the new paper was brilliant today," Lucy said as she came around the counter in the center of the kitchen. She pressed herself against Rick's back. "I think you're pretty sexy when you get all fired up like that."

"Oh, yeah? That turns you on, huh?" He turned around and began fumbling with the buttons on her blouse. "Seeing these two babies out in the open turns me on." His voice had deepened and his eyes glazed over when he saw her manufactured breasts with their perfect nipples standing at attention.

"Modern science does a pretty good job, don't you think?" Lucy asked him as she proudly displayed her $5,000 breasts.

"I'll say. Let's go back there and look over the rest of its experiments. Modern science impresses me every time. You look sixteen."

"You flatter me. It's a twenty year old body I pay for."

She led him into the bedroom to finish their lunch, which was over in a matter of minutes. Rick couldn't control himself. After all, the meeting itself had been a great aphrodisiac with his ideas taken seriously and then Lucy wanting him was almost too much for one day. He promised Lucy he'd be ready to go again in a little while, if she would just be patient.

"It's not my strong suit," she said. "But you just might be worth it."

CHAPTER ELEVEN

TIM MURRAY, MAYOR OF Calloway, along with three of that city's commissioners, Jackson Stewart, Johnny Waine, and Lester Simmons, plus Billy Winterrowd and Oren Krantz, commissioners from Hope Springs, talked over some of the issues mentioned during the lunch meeting on their way back to town while cruising down the Hope Springs River. Canoers and kayakers passed them regularly, but with their baseball caps pulled low over their foreheads and dark shades hiding their eyes, they felt confident no one would recognize them.

"Billy, have you figured out how to dump your property before voting on the annexation?" Tim asked.

The annexation of the river property would most likely not happen if Billy had to recuse himself from the vote.

The planned development included a 200-room hotel, with fountains and narrow canals leading into the river, along with dozens of million dollar homes close by, and would be a gem in the crowning glory of all those who met regularly. Billy owned an old piece of family property downriver. This development would only be a twenty-minute drive from the movie studio complex and landing strip.

"Got it covered," Billy answered. "Lucy transfers the deeds to her name. She's handling everything."

"Make sure," Jackson warned as they rounded the bend toward the boat ramp just outside Hope Springs.

"Keep it down, boys. There's Molly Hale and her husband," Oren announced.

"You mean that bitch writer for *The Chronicle*?" Lester asked.

"That's the one. Hey, watch out, Lester," Johnny yelled. "You're going to run into that tree ahead."

Lester craned his neck to see the reporter and failed to turn the boat soon enough. He'd been traveling along the north bank, but when

Oren mentioned the other boat with the reporter, he looked away long enough for them to run into a low hanging branch from a live oak tree.

With a loud bang, the boat's windshield took the brunt of the hit, but Lester and Johnny, standing in the bow of the boat were hit on the head with the branch, momentarily blinding them to anything else. The jolt to the boat knocked Billy and Oren, who had been standing, into the water. Jackson and Tim remained calmly in their seats and felt the splash of their two friends as they fell into the river.

Lester and Johnny reached for the branch to steady them when the boat stuck on the sandbar jutting up from the water. Fire ants, the nasty biters who care only about eating raw flesh, fled the banks of the river, scurrying up the tree limb. It took just a second before Lester and Johnny realized the pesky creatures had crawled up their arms before the ants' leader gave the signal to bite. Both men began screaming when the pinchers bit into their flesh depositing poison.

Molly and her husband David looked up from their poles in time to see Billy and Oren splash into the water. Lester and Johnny began stripping off their clothes trying get the ants off of them. The ants invaded their pants so off came all the clothing. But the ants embedded themselves in the skin of the commissioners so not even being naked in the boat helped.

Molly had difficulty helping her husband paddle over to the men. The sight of Winterrowd and Krantz in the water and the naked bodies of Simmons and Waine just before they willingly jumped into the water to rid themselves of the fiery bites, filled her with mirth. When Molly was amused, no one could top her laughter, which began as an abrupt hoot, and then merrily escalated into a loud giggle.

Nevertheless, she managed to control herself long enough to help David paddle over to the disabled ship hidden in the shade of a live oak tree. They threw their cushions to Billy and Oren who were being swept downriver toward the white water of the shoals ahead. Even though parts of the river were shallow, in the middle of the current, the water remained fairly deep and fast, making it impossible to stand at certain points. Molly only had two cushions in her canoe. Lester and Johnny would be dependent on the smart thinking of the two men left on the boat that wouldn't start.

"What's up, Commissioners? Out for a swim?" Molly looked down at them struggling in the water. "Grab the cushions and relax. Hey,

Commissioner Stewart, throw your other two buddies something to float with."

David looked up at the boat stuck on the sandbar. He recognized the two commissioners from Calloway.

"What do you know, Molly, we got a meeting of the small towns of Zion County right here on the Hope Springs River," David remarked. "Sure was nice of them to invite you so they'd be sure not to be breaking any Florida statutes or anything."

"Someone call for help on the cell phone," Johnny yelled.

"No service out here," Jackson yelled back after checking the phone in his shirt pocket.

"Very cozy, gentlemen, very cozy," Molly said. "David and I will go back to our car; we're just past the bridge at the boat ramp. My cell phone is in the car, and if I have service, I'll get you out of here in no time at all."

They mumbled something that Molly decided must be "thank you's." She pulled her waterproof camera out of the bag. She hoped for a few shots of a gator or a great blue heron on today's river excursion, but a picture of these commissioners out for a cruise would do just as nicely for the front page of this week's paper. She was sure her editor would agree to move the Garden Club picture to page two, even though this week's issue was just a few hours from going to press.

"Smile, boys," she said just before snapping. "No need to look so grumpy now. The sun is brightly shining, and you'll be on your way soon enough."

She waved; then David turned the canoe around and headed for the boat ramp and her phone. However, the first call she made was not to the towing company.

"Greg, you'll never believe who David and I ran into fishing today," Molly began.

She hoped her editor, Greg Howzer, had not finished the paper yet. Their deadline was late afternoon Thursday, and Molly saw that it was just 3 p.m. "I hope the paper hasn't gone in yet."

"Who? The Governor?" Greg asked.

"No, not the governor," Molly said. "This is better. And by the way you better find space on page one for a lovely photo of Zion County's own version of Noah's Ark. Two by two they came from the commissions in Hope Springs and Calloway to take a cruise on the river."

"They were all on a boat together?" her editor asked.

"Two of them still are with their large boat stuck firmly on a sandbar. Winterrowd and Krantz got so freaked, they fell into the water. I had to throw them my cushions to save them. I think they're clinging to the boat's back ladder now. The best part was seeing Waine and Simmons stark naked before they jumped in the water, too. Sorry I didn't get a picture of the nude commissioners, but I'm pretty sure I got some great shots. Want me to take it for one hour processing?"

"Hell, yes, but what about writing a story? Did you ask any of them what they were doing? We can quote the statute about meeting in the sunshine even though we can't prove anything at this point, but we need a quote or something from at least one of them," Greg said.

"They're still stuck out there. They're waiting for me to call a tow truck," Molly told him. "I'll do that next, and then go back out and keep the boys company until they get unstuck, although that might take more than a tow truck at this point."

"Molly, thanks," Greg said.

"For what? You need to thank our wet politicians. I was just leisurely cruising with my husband."

"Thanks for giving me the biggest thrill of my career so far. Listen." She heard Greg yell to the rest of the office, "Stop the presses. Molly just reeled us in the big one."

Molly made one more call before letting someone know at the towing place in Hope Springs that they had a little business on the river. When she called Kelly's office she only got her voice mail. She left a message and then waited for the main office at *The Tribune* to transfer her call to Carl Handler.

"Carl, it's Molly Hale with *The Calloway Chronicle*," Molly said.

"How are things out in Calloway?"

"Pretty exciting today, I'd say. I just left a message for Kelly. Know where she is?"

"Down at the courthouse – on that case in Millstone with Tim Murray's property and Tony Mayberry's enclave annexation."

"That's right. You might want to page her for this one. It would make more of a story. The mayor of Calloway certainly wasn't in court this afternoon with his buddy Mayberry."

"No? Where was he?" Carl asked.

"He was cruising down the river with his fellow commissioners and two from Hope Springs. Even granddaddy GOB Jackson Stewart was there. The two Hope Springs commissioners are floating in the river right now with my boat cushions trying to keep their heads above water. Two of the Calloway commissioners are skinny dipping."

"Sounds like they'd better worry more about what will happen when their flotation devices are removed," Carl said.

"You got it. They're depending on me to call the tow truck, but I had a few calls to make first. You know in this business we've got to take care of ourselves."

"I'll try to reach Kelly. She just might be interested in interviewing a few wet politicians this afternoon."

CHAPTER TWELVE

AFTER KELLY FINISHED TALKING to Lt. Carson on the steps of the courthouse, she walked to her car. Her beeper, which she always left in the car during meetings, was summoning her. Two calls from the office – one from Carl, and one from Bart. She called Bart first.

"Kelly, we're getting a pretty interesting report on the police scanner. You might want to check it out," Bart Stanley said when she reached him from her cell phone.

"What is it, Boss?" she asked.

"A rescue truck has been called to the boat ramp off 441 in Hope Springs," he told her. "Seems they've found some pretty strange things floating in the water today."

"Like what?"

"Billy Winterrowd and Oren Krantz, for one. Seems they took a little dip together in the Hope Springs River."

"Winterrowd and Krantz, the real estate commissioners from Hope Springs?"

"That's right. Carl just came in and told me that Molly Hale called here for you about it. Why does that name sound familiar?"

"Molly writes for *The Calloway Chronicle*. That's probably why Carl called me."

"Want to cover it?"

"I'm on my way," Kelly said as she backed out of her parking place. "Bart, thanks for giving me this. You know it's right up my alley."

"Hey, somebody's got to do it. It might as well be you. Our really good writers are busy today," he said.

Kelly could picture her editor smiling in his lazy, slow way as he leaned back in his swivel chair. Bart still made her heart do flip flops, but she concentrated on keeping a tight lid on those feelings. She was an expert at burying those feelings because when she didn't, she ended up in places where she had no intention of going.

Kelly hung up before she could say something that might betray the sinking feeling in her stomach whenever he teased her that way.

Bart slipped into Kelly's thoughts again as she drove down US 441 toward the Hope Springs boat ramp, but she tried to push him from her mind and concentrate on what might lie ahead.

The rolling hills and richness of the landscape dotted with red sweet gums of autumn and green live oak trees reminded Kelly of what the developers would like to do with that landscape. She wondered if Mike Green had any leads on a couple of rumors that had been floating around about Industrial Pines. The rural area on the northern edge of the county contained some of the largest tracts of undeveloped land. Buddy Tills, was just one of a handful selling off his property at an alarming rate.

Not for the first time Kelly wondered about the propriety of B.J. Winters sitting on the County's planning and zoning board. To her, it seemed a conflict of interest, and she watched carefully for developments in that area.

Mike and Molly shared information with her as did Kelly with them on IP and deeds and sales of parcels of land, but so far none of them had found anything amiss, just that gut feeling all reporters shared when after a big story. They decided to work together on these things without worrying about scooping one another. Kelly knew for sure that Molly and she felt the same way about watching the developers and politicians, without thought as to who scooped whom. But she was not as sure about Mike. She wondered if he resented her potential to scoop his stories given her position on a daily paper.

Last week Mike asked her about Bart. "What is it between the two of you?"

"What do you mean?"

"I've seen you two at meetings, sitting close, heads bent together, and the way you look at each other sometimes, and he always seems to give you some of the best stories, yet he's got reporters who've been doing this a lot longer than you."

"You don't think I do a good job?"

"That's not it. You know what I mean. Besides people talk, and they talk about you two."

"Let's just say that once, a while back, Bart and I were very close," she told him. "Leave it at that."

He hadn't asked her anything more, even though he asked more and more questions about what she did when they weren't together. Kelly thought it was a shame because she might eventually love Mike, but not if he made her feel like a prisoner. Now she was sorry she had admitted anything at all about her relationship with Bart.

When she pulled down Boat Ramp Road, she saw one rescue truck and lots of people standing around. She had been so absorbed in her thoughts about Bart and Mike, she hadn't thought to grab a photographer to come along with her. Maybe Molly had a camera, and they could work out a deal.

She pulled off the road and walked several feet to the crowd of people. In the center of the group sat Winterrowd, Krantz, Simmons, and Waine. They all had towels over their shoulders. Simmons and Waine seemed to have little else on their bodies. The paramedics were kneeling down next to them taking their blood pressure.

"Commissioners, is everything all right?" Kelly asked when she got close enough to be heard and seen.

"No comment," Winterrowd said.

"You mean you're not going to tell me why you and Commissioner Krantz were out on the river together?"

"They're not talking, Kelly," Molly said from the crowd. "But it wasn't just them. Don't forget these others from Calloway, a quorum of them. Isn't that right, gentlemen?"

"What happened?" Kelly asked.

"When they saw David and I coming toward them, they plowed into a sandbar and got hung up on a tree. Two of them, Jackson Stewart and Tim Murray, are still on the boat waiting for something to pull them out. Seems no one knows quite how to get them out of this mess."

Kelly and Molly walked away from the crowd and spoke quietly.

"Did you get any pictures?" Kelly asked.

"Sure did. David just took them to the one hour place."

"Think we might work out a deal? We could just buy them outright from you or if your editor agrees we could give *The Chronicle* photo credit."

"Sure, I took a whole lot, so there'll be different ones for each of us to use. Kelly, you should have seen them."

"Any idea what they were doing?"

"A leisurely cruise down the Hope Springs River? I think they were coming or going to one of their meetings we keep hearing about."

"Hey, ladies, quite an afternoon to be out on the river, isn't it," Mike said as he approached.

"Why aren't you in Millstone at the budget workshop?" Molly asked him. "Or did they cancel it because their commissioners are out boating, too?"

"No, they're still meeting, I guess. I didn't think it was as important as this," he told her. "Any news here?"

"Just a little bit. Six commissioners from two municipalities might be in violation of the Sunshine Law," Kelly said.

"But what can you really prove?" Mike asked. "Where's the real news story?"

"There's the real strong perception that they may have violated the Sunshine Law," Molly told him.

"And do you think people around here really care?" he asked. "Did you hear them talking about anything that would indicate a violation of the law?"

"What's with you? You're just as adamant as us about keeping these guys honest, at least in public," Kelly reminded him. "What's the matter? Someone paying you off to keep this quiet?"

"That's the stupidest thing I've ever heard and disgusting, too," Mike said.

"Come on, Mike, where's your sense of humor?" Molly asked. "We're just teasing you because you usually want to get these guys without as much proof as we have now."

"I just think we need more. Where were they coming from, for instance? What brought them together today in this boat?"

"Then I guess we all better get back to our offices and make some phone calls," Kelly said just before turning around and walking away.

Mike followed but had to hustle to catch up with her.

"Kelly, I didn't mean that back there."

"It doesn't really matter. I've been thinking we might need a little break from one another," Kelly told him when she finally broke her stride.

"You get back with Bart?"

"That's unfair, and that's what I mean. You go too far sometimes. Let's just give it a break."

"okay, okay, but just remember I won't be sitting around waiting for your phone call." Mike turned around and walked back to his car.

Kelly felt relief more than anything. Although the sex with Mike had been sweet, it wasn't enough to make up for his shallowness when she really began to dig beneath the surface of his carefully polished exterior. He was beautiful to look at, but she wondered why he always wore those tailored suits and fine leather shoes while driving a beat up Toyota to investigate stories for *The Chronicle*. It was a good paper for its size, but this community probably felt uncomfortable around Mike Green. And his interview pieces showed it. They were stilted and without life. She never felt like she knew the person any better after reading those pieces. Come to think of it, the other stuff he wrote about the commission meetings never seemed clear either. She never thought much about it, but Mike wasn't much of a writer. Perhaps that caused jealousy on his part. Most writers have a fairly good grasp on who writes better than them or at least the really honest ones do.

Mike may not be that honest, she thought as she drove back to Braidwood. But at least she had the break from him she needed. She turned her attention to how she would approach the boat ramp incident once she returned to *The Tribune*. She only had three hours before the county commission meeting.

Kelly went directly to Bart's office when she returned.

"What did you find out?" he asked.

"It was just like you said – four from Calloway and two from Hope Springs," Kelly told him. "In my excitement, I forgot to take a photographer. But Molly Hale took some pictures and said she would share for acknowledgement."

"Sounds good. What do you think?"

"I've been wondering how to approach it," she began. "I saw the four who went in the water, but they refused to talk. I was hoping you'd help here. And Jackson Stewart and Tim Murray were supposedly on the boat, too, but I never saw them because they hadn't towed in the boat yet."

"Quite an afternoon cruise. While you were gone, I pulled the statutes on public officials and meetings. So we go with that and then with what happened out on the river. Do you think Molly would allow you to interview her for our story?"

"I could probably persuade her. Her colleague, Mike Green, doesn't think they should run anything."

"Eddie Lewis will insist," Bart said, referring to the crusty old publisher of *The Chronicle*. "So will Panzer. They've been waiting for something like this for a while. Let me call Ed and see what he says about the interview and pictures. We might be able to give them some info, too."

"Anything else?"

"Yes, in the meantime, contact the state attorney's office for their take on this situation. Find out if any charges might be filed and what the penalties are for violating the statute.

"How about we go out in my boat and see where these boys have come from or where they were headed as soon as you get something written?" Bart asked Kelly as he picked up the phone. "If we leave in the next thirty minutes, we could have an hour on the river before dark."

"I have a hunch they were returning, coming back to the boat ramp. I saw Stewart's car on the side of the road – you can't miss a Caddy that color of gold."

"Then we'll go downriver for a little ways. I bet they left Zion County. Who knows? Maybe we'll see something."

"I've got to attend the county commission meeting tonight on the Millwood stuff, remember."

"Carl will be there anyway, so just ask him to cover if they begin before you get back. It will be dark by seven with that blasted time change last week," Bart told her before he picked up the phone to call Eddie Lewis.

Kelly smiled and nodded before leaving Bart to what he did best: talk to other seasoned news people about breaking stories. It ran in his blood, and she could see the flush in his face and the sparkle in his eye. She recognized that excitement when he was in hot pursuit of a story, and she recognized it as the look he got whenever they had gone to bed together. He wore his passions right out front for the world to see.

CHAPTER THIRTEEN

SOMETIMES MIKE GREEN WROTE insulting pieces about the residents of the rural towns he covered. A few cool, intelligent heads prevailed among the readership of *The Calloway Chronicle* and complained loudly to Greg about Mike's condescending attitude. Some of them wrote letters to the editor calling him on the carpet. In one particular column, he wrote about those who attempted suicide, calling them fools and stupid for not being able to do it correctly. It was entitled "Ten ways to mess up a suicide." Greg pulled it, and Mike never forgave him. Mike never wrote another column.

After the incident at the river, Mike went back to the office to see what else might be happening this week. Greg hadn't assigned him anything yet for next week's paper, except the Millstone annexation follow up.

"Greg, you wouldn't have believed it," he heard Molly say as he came down the hallway to Greg's office. "They all looked like drowned rats, yet indignant we were there and accusing them of improprieties. It was a sight."

"How about the pictures?"

"Monster Mart promised to call when they're ready, probably any minute now."

"Mike, come on in. Did you find out anything more than Molly?" Greg said when he saw Mike lingering outside his door.

"No, and frankly, Greg, I can't see where we have a story. So what if these six guys were out in a boat together? What does that prove? They would have to have been discussing something that would come up for a vote for a violation to occur anyway. Who will prove that?"

"It still could be a violation of the Sunshine Laws. How do we know that they didn't discuss some future issues before the commission? It's perception of impropriety more than anything, even if we can't prove

53

it. We go with the story, even if it's brief with the picture," Greg told him. "We state the statute they may have violated, and Molly gives her account of what she saw. Then we contact each city's attorney and our own attorney for comments, and we state that the commissioners in question refused comment, if they still do by the time we go to press, which is almost immediately. It will then be up to the state attorney's office whether to file ethics charges against these yo-yos."

"He's right, Mike," Molly told him. "Besides you know Kelly will have something in tomorrow's *Tribune*, and we have to follow up as the advocate for rural Zion County."

"Anything else you want me to work on?" Mike asked.

"I think a sidebar piece of sunshine violations in the past would go nicely with next week's follow up story. You should be able to get information from the library, maybe the state attorney's office. Try to concentrate on violations in this area, not necessarily Zion County, but at least in the northern part of the state. Jackson Stewart has had a few warnings himself so be sure to do a search on him. Now, Molly, you've got half an hour to get your piece together and get the pictures back here. You need any help?"

"Mike could call the city attorney for Hope Springs. No sense in bothering with Tony Mayberry, do you think?"

"Probably not. I'll call our attorney right now. What about the pictures?"

"David said he would pick them up and bring them over. *The Tribune* wants to use one, too."

Mike went off to do his job, but not happily. It still ticked him off that Kelly had brushed him off. *Who the hell did she think she was anyway?* He got tired of all this cloak and dagger reporting that Molly and Kelly seemed to thrive on anyway. It had been that type of reporting that had caused the most trouble in his short life so far.

Bart kept a boat at a friend's house near the boat ramp in Hope Springs even though he had a house downriver. This way Bart could get out on the river more often when he just wanted to do a little fishing. The small boat was perfect for putting in the Hope Springs River. He kept a bigger boat at the house in Banks County, which took about a half an hour longer to reach than the boat ramp.

Kelly and Bart drove to Hope Springs speculating about politics, threats, and developers. Anything to keep the discussion from turning personal, Kelly thought. It wasn't an uncomfortable talk because it attracted them to one another in the first place. Kelly had missed these talks the most when they stopped seeing one another.

After they had returned from Tallahassee five years ago, they tried very hard not to see one another outside of the office, as Bart attempted to get help for his wife. After a month of avoiding anything personal, Bart came by her desk one day and dropped a small note. "Meet me at the Alamo," it said.

The Alamo, a small motel on the edge of Dansville and a forty-minute drive from the paper, was noted for its home-cooked food in the attached restaurant rather than its accommodations.

Kelly smiled at his words. Despite the promises she made to not continue the affair, she drove to meet him.

"It's been driving me crazy," he said as he held the door open for her.

"We shouldn't be doing this," she told him as she entered the room, "not until you get things settled."

"I can't wait that long," he said.

They stood staring at one another in the gloom of the shaded room; turning on the lights would have revealed the shabbiness of the furniture and accessories.

"We especially shouldn't be here, Bart."

"Maybe this will cure us, cheap motel room and all. Bring us to our senses?"

He reached for her then, and she went to his arms. Cheap accommodations or not, they fell back on the bed and became reacquainted with one another.

"We can't do this again," Kelly told him even as she touched the dimple in his chin.

"I know, just this once."

Except it happened more than once during that late afternoon on the highway leading west toward the Gulf of Mexico. Afterwards as they dressed, they repeated their vows to never let it happen again.

Three years ago, Bart and Joyce separated; however, within a few months, Joyce stopped taking the anti-depressants and slipped back into a serious depression, which left Bart helpless to do anything but take her back and try to get her help once again.

Those few months during the separation brought Bart and Kelly closer together, but the pain of pulling apart afterwards tore Kelly apart. Only the promise of seeing him at work and the sparkle in his eyes when he looked at her allowed her to survive without him in her bed.

"Do you know where Lucy Burch has that house on the river?" Kelly now asked Bart as they began slowly moving downriver toward the springs that gave the river its name.

"I've heard Rick speak of it, but I'm not sure if it's after Rainbow Springs or not," Bart said.

Rainbow Springs were the small, but popular diving springs right before the tributary that led off to Hope Springs, the largest of the many springs on this river.

"Rick used to come out here quite a bit with Lucy. Seems like that relationship might have cooled a while back," Bart said.

"Lucy and Rick? Now that's a match made in heaven."

They both laughed to think of the real estate mogul with Rick who seemed to always be led by those with more power and money.

"You know what they say, 'Life is like a box of chocolates' and those two together are just one of its many surprises," Bart said.

CHAPTER FOURTEEN

LUCY AND RICK DECIDED to stay at the river house after their session in the bedroom. There was plenty of food left over from lunch, and they took the leftovers down to the dock. Boat traffic was light since it was a Wednesday afternoon, but the weather was mild and the sky clear.

"You know you were brilliant today, Rick," Lucy said. "The idea for another paper – a paper with only the community's best interest at heart – that was a stroke of genius." She rubbed his arm.

"Thanks. I always thought they were too aggressive at *The Monitor* in Millstone. Everyone knew from the very beginning that the paper had an agenda, and it lost legitimacy immediately. Instead of getting converts, that paper simply preaches to the choir."

"That's true. Now with this one, we can be more subtle. Maybe we should concentrate on winning a few awards first before moving too fast."

"I'd like to see a school-oriented section. Maybe let some students write and draw for it. That'll bring the parents and grandparents on board. Sell lots of subscriptions that way."

"Fantastic, along with a great sports section concentrating on the local kids. We need good photographers and a top notch sports writer."

"Why don't you work with me on it, Lucy? We'd make a great team."

"I'll keep behind the scenes. I can sit on the board. How's that?"

"Great, great. Now how about another barbequed rib?"

"Bart, look up there," Kelly said when they rounded the curve just past Cypress Island, a popular swimming hole for the locals. "Isn't that Lucy and Rick on that deck?"

"I'll be damned. Let's pull up a little closer and say hello."

"Isn't that your boss and the nosy reporter down there?" Lucy asked Rick as they sat finishing the last of their dinner.

"Damn, what are they doing out here?"

The boat pulled closer to shore, and Bart killed the motor before hollering up to them. "Hello, you two. Lucy, this must be your new river place I keep hearing so much about."

"Hello, Bart. What brings you two out here?" Lucy asked.

"Kelly needed to investigate a story so I brought her out. I grab any excuse I can to get out on the river."

"What story, Kelly?" Rick asked.

"Seems commissioners from several different towns decided to take a boat cruise today and ended up swimming back to shore instead," she told him.

"Really? And you think there's a story there?" Rick asked.

"When the six commissioners come from two different cities, I do. There's a possibility they violated the Sunshine Laws, don't you think? Or at the very least it reeks of impropriety."

"What is it with you, Kelly?" Lucy spoke to the reporter for the first time. "Why do you want to bother those poor schmucks? They work hard for their communities and deserve a little leisure time."

"Besides they're really not violating anything unless you can prove it, right, Bart?" asked Rick.

"That's true, but you know as well as I that perception is everything in this case. And the public will perceive that something shady occurred today."

"Anyway that's why we're investigating," Kelly told them. "How long have you two been out here today?"

"We came out for lunch," Rick said.

"Did you see Johnny Waine or Billy Winterrowd or any other commissioners out here today?"

"I don't recall seeing anyone like that," Lucy responded. "But I'm not sure I'd recognize this Waine fellow if I saw him."

"How about Oren Krantz? Didn't you almost marry him?" Kelly asked.

"Kelly, knock it off," Rick told her. "Lucy isn't under scrutiny here. If she told you she didn't see anything, she didn't see anything. I was out here, too, and I'm telling you I didn't see Waine or Winterrowd or Krantz."

"Thanks a lot, Rick, Lucy," Bart said. "Sorry to have disturbed you two. Kelly, we'd better head back, or we'll get caught in the dark out here."

"She's got balls, I'll give her that," Lucy said as she watched the boat pull away from her dock and head upstream. "She reminds me of myself when I was that age."

"Kelly's too serious. She takes everything to heart. Somehow I don't see you in that ballpark," Rick said.

"You didn't know me before I started getting married."

"Besides Kelly has some dark secret I've never been able to figure out. Around the office hints get dropped by the other reporters, but she doesn't reveal much of anything about her personal life."

"Probably a man broke her heart in a big way somewhere down the line. She'll get over that soon enough," Lucy said. "Do you think Bart will say anything to Bonnie?"

Bonnie was Rick's wife, and Bart and she had gone to school together in Boca. Bart's wife, Joyce, was one of Bonnie's best friends.

"He won't say anything," Rick assured her. "Then one of us would have to admit the reason Bart saw us was because he was giving the beautiful Kelly Sands a boat ride on the Hope Springs River as the shadows deepened and the swallows came home to the cypress trees."

"How come I never knew you were a poet?" Lucy leaned over and gave Rick a big kiss. "How about we give it one more try for old time's sake?"

"What do you think?" Kelly asked Bart when they were out of range of Lucy's deck.

"Pretty quick on the defensive."

"Lucy or Rick?"

"I'd say Rick. I wonder what the two of them were doing out there all cozy on the river having dinner?"

"You know as well as I do what they were probably doing," Kelly told him. "And we're fine ones to talk."

He looked at her sharply. Kelly never mentioned their previous relationship. In fact, sometimes Bart thought she had forgotten all about the intimate moments they once shared.

"Do you ever think about it?" Bart asked

"It? You mean us? Together?"

"No, about my dog and me together. Of course, I mean you and me."

Kelly took a deep breath. She didn't really want to discuss this, especially while they were so isolated and alone on the river with dusk making them nearly invisible to anyone on shore or passing by in neighboring boats. He was too close and accessible for her to think of those times without wanting to be held in his arms.

"You tell me. Do you think of it?"

"I can't help it. It slips into my head before I can ward it off. Like now."

Kelly remained seated to Bart's left as he maneuvered the boat. He was staring at her now and not watching the river.

"I think about it," she said. "Let's leave it at that."

"That's all I needed to know." He smiled as he turned back to the river ahead of him.

Mike did his search of Sunshine violations and fumed about Kelly. Finally, he decided to call *The Tribune* and apologize. He knew her well enough to know that she could go forever without seeing him again. That was something he didn't want to risk. He suspected he was falling in love for the first time.

"Hi, Mike." Carl Handler answered the phone on Kelly's desk. "No, she's not here. She and Bart went out to the Hope Springs River to investigate the boat dumping. Then she's headed to the county commission meeting for all that Millstone stuff. I doubt she'll be back in the office before then. Want me to transfer you to her voice mail?"

"Sure, Carl." He left a message and then went back to his work.

Now he knew the real reason Kelly had called it quits earlier.

CHAPTER FIFTEEN

WHEN KELLY FINALLY MADE it home shortly after eleven o'clock, she had three hang ups on the answering machine. One caller left a message, saying "Leave the river story alone." A muffled voice, barely audible, issued the warning. She called Lt. Carson immediately and left her number on his pager.

"Something happen, Kelly?" John asked when he returned her call minutes later.

"I've got some hang ups on my answering machine and one warning," she said.

"What's the warning?"

"To leave a new story alone."

"I better come over and listen to it."

John played the message repeatedly before asking her if he could send someone over to record the message.

"I'd like the lab to do some tests on the voice," he told her. "They can sometimes determine if it's a male or female, or if it was made from a pay phone or cell. That kind of thing."

"I'll give you my code to access the messages. I'd appreciate anything the lab could do."

"So some big boys got dumped in the river today. I bet that was fun to see."

"How did you know?"

"We got called to the scene. When the rescue call came, we weren't sure if there was criminal activity or not, so two officers were dispatched. Were you there?"

"Not when it happened." She laughed. "But my friend Molly Hale from *The Calloway Chronicle* saw it all. I wish I had been there. Those boys were caught with their pants down, that's for sure. Two of them literally had their pants off."

"What happens next?"

"If someone files a complaint with the Commission on Ethics, they might conduct an investigation. The commissioners could get fined and warned, but at least the public will be aware that something might be amiss."

"Those folks must really hate you."

"Which ones?"

"All of them. The politicians, the developers. It seems you don't let them get away with anything."

"There's probably some truth to that. It used to be the reporters in this area were a part of their group, too. They got paid off and sat high on the hog and just reported about drunken brawls in Millstone and wife beatings in Calloway."

"What changed?"

"The journalism school at UB started producing some top notch journalists who wanted to stay in the area. Journalists with integrity and ethics like Bart Stanley, my editor. Just because you see me reporting the news, doesn't mean that all my fellow reporters report what they know. There's still a few writers and editors in the back pockets of the money-makers and shakers here."

"Why Zion County?"

"The same thing happened in south Florida when there was still land to develop. Zion County has large tracts – at least for a little while yet – of undeveloped land, and compared to Dade and Broward and Hillsborough counties, it's still cheap. Plus the municipalities are eager to make deals and offer incentives."

"Like what?"

"The city of Calloway gave away property to have that Monster Mart distribution center built out on Spencer Road."

"Great piece of property, I hear, covered with sinkholes and all."

"That's a problem all over the county. But the developers and real estate people don't care that this area is like Swiss cheese underground. They'll get their money out of the deals before the buildings fall into a sinkhole. It's an environmental nightmare. And the thing is those sinkholes would never have happened if they had made smaller and shallower retention ponds around the compound instead of digging one deep hole in the middle or provided for better drainage around the asphalt parking lots."

"With you on top of the situation, hopefully things will get better. You're our own Lois Lane."

"Thanks. Now I just need Superman or at the very least Clark Kent."

"How did the meeting go tonight?"

"Nothing much happened. I just got back from the paper. I had to write up a piece on the meeting and on the river dumping. The river story is a masterpiece; the other article just says people are upset on both sides of the issue. Nothing was decided. I don't think legally the county can do anything about the annexation."

John's pager beeped. He asked if he could use her phone to call in because he had left his mobile in the car. She took him to the portable in the kitchen, and then she came back to her living room and began sorting through the past two days' mail. Some weeks she waited until the weekend to look at her bills and letters.

"Kelly, I need to go up to Hope Springs. Seems another reporter received some kind of warning or threat. What's your friend's name up there?"

"Molly Hale. Why? Did something happen to Molly?"

"I think she's okay, maybe just shaken. When she came out of the office tonight, the tires on her car were slashed and a dead armadillo was left on her windshield. They left a note, too."

As Kelly prepared to leave for Hope Springs after saying good-bye to John, the phone rang.

"Kelly, did you hear about Molly?" Mike asked her.

"Yes, how is she?"

"Fine, you know Molly; she's joking about making armadillo soup."

"I was just on my way there. Is Molly still at the paper?"

"Yes, lots of cops around asking questions taking pictures. Kelly, I'm really sorry about earlier. I don't know what got into me, but I should have kept my mouth shut."

"That's all right, Mike. It's been a tense week. About to get tenser, I sense."

"How about Saturday night?"

"okay, Saturday night, and I'll probably see you in a few minutes."

Kelly decided not to call Bart. She was certain he would tell her to go for it. She definitely wouldn't call Rick. He'd probably say it was just some redneck pranksters having some fun. However, this time she remembered to call her favorite photographer, and she swung by Lonny's house before hopping on I-75 and heading north.

"You just couldn't stand it could you, Molly," Kelly said as she embraced her friend. "You were jealous when I got all the attention over the bomb, so you decided to do something a little more exciting, a little more Calloway."

"That's right. I'm thinking about doing a weekly column on ways to use an armadillo. First hollow him out, tie his legs together, turn him over, and there you go, your very own armadillo handbag."

"That would go over big in Texas."

"Or you could line your driveway – drill a hole in the back, put in a candle and instant luminaries for the holidays."

"I can see this is just going to get worse and worse."

"I've got to do something. David's really freaked out, saying he doesn't want me to work here anymore, and I can't do that."

"What were you doing here so late? Didn't you go to press hours earlier?"

"Yes, but we were all so excited about the wet commissioners that several of us went out after the paper was done. I left my car here and rode with Greg and his wife."

"Good evening, ladies," John Carson said as he walked up to the two women standing in the parking lot.

"Hi, John. Molly, this is Lt. John Carson with the Sheriff's Office. He's working on my case, too."

"Hi, lieutenant. Do we get a group discount?"

"Let's just say we won't charge you extra for the armadillo."

"If you're going to take it into evidence, I should charge you," Molly said. "I've got lots of uses for that little hard-backed critter."

"Want to tell me about your day? I heard it was a little unusual?" John began questioning.

"I'll leave you two to the gory details. Molly, talk to you later." Kelly walked over to where the photographer was leaning over the hood of the car taking shots of the poor dead animal.

CHAPTER SIXTEEN

"LUCY, TELL THEM TO stop," Rick yelled into the phone after he heard about the armadillo and slashed tires when Kelly finally called him from *The Calloway Chronicle* parking lot.

The night editor also called Rick when he heard it come over the police scanner, but Rick told him to not do anything about it; he hadn't counted on Kelly hearing about it so soon.

"What are you talking about? Lower your voice, and tell me what's going on."

"Didn't Johnny or Jackson call you?"

"No, I haven't heard a word from any of them since their dip in the river. Why?"

"Someone left a dead armadillo on Molly Hale's car parked at *The Calloway Chronicle*. They also slashed her tires."

"Why would I know anything about it?"

"I don't know," Rick said. "I thought they might have consulted you."

"And I would have told them not to do anything so obvious."

"This looks too suspicious. The bomb thing can be written off to some nut who just didn't like Kelly. But this thing right after the incident on the river makes us look bad."

"Then make sure your paper plays it up," Lucy directed. "Do an editorial on violence. We get the commissioners to make statements abhorring the incident."

"Good, get the old publicity machine working. Maybe offer a small reward."

"Now you're thinking. That's one thing I like about you; you think on your feet and do other things on your back." Lucy lowered her voice. "I really enjoyed this afternoon and the dinner later. Why have we waited so long between meals?"

"Not sure, but let's not do it again. I mean, wait so long."

Jackson Stewart began working the phones as soon as he heard about Molly Hale's tires and windshield. As many people as he called, he still couldn't unearth the perpetrator. He was not sorry it happened. But he was sorry he and his friends would receive the biggest share of blame. He knew he couldn't keep this out of the paper. No way to control Greg Panzer at *The Chronicle*. That damn paper, he thought as his phone rang.

"Jackson, it's Rick. Have you heard?"

"About what? It's been a pretty hectic day."

"The latest with Molly Hale and the armadillo."

"Yes, and I've been trying to figure out what's going on," he said.

"You don't know?"

"No idea, and I've tried everyone to find something out."

"That's bad. Either way it would be bad because it reflects poorly on the commissioners," Rick said. "Lucy and I were just talking and think maybe we should counteract by going pubic with outrage over such a thing happening."

"Explain."

"You know *The Chronicle* will be all over it with indignant righteousness, just like they did with that creep Garcia's gopher grave," Rick said. "And Kelly will sweep down on this like a turkey vulture after that dead armadillo. I did the best I could with Garcia's story by burying it, but Kelly will be sure to go to Bart if I try to do the same thing again."

"What do you suggest then?" Jackson asked.

"I can write an editorial deploring that kind of vandalism. You and Billy should also publicly denounce it. I bet I can get Bart to offer a small reward for information leading to the arrest of the perp. He can say an attack against any member of the press is an attack against us all, that sort of thing, and mention the bomb."

"It might just work. I'll leave it all to you," Jackson said. "Rick, you'll be rewarded greatly for your diligence and quick thinking."

"Thanks, Jackson, I'm just here to serve."

He conveniently forgot to mention the idea had been Lucy's. *What did that matter,* Rick thought. Lucy had plenty of money. Rick needed to seal his future. Working as a city editor did not pay him enough to settle into the type of retirement he envisioned. He still wanted a 24-footer docked in Fort Lauderdale in front of his beach home. It didn't have to be an elaborate place, just enough for he and his wife and his Jaguar and other toys.

When he started the Zion County paper, he knew his salary would increase, as would the perks. Plus, the pressure of fighting Bart daily about what went in the paper and keeping the lid on Kelly was taking its toll. He was tired of being constantly vigilant and mostly losing. With his own paper, everyone would defer to him, or he be the one doing the winning. He couldn't lose.

After hanging up the phone, Jackson Stewart looked over at Mazie and slapped her bare bottom. It wasn't as firm as when they had first begun their affair nearly twenty years ago, but Jackson owned that ass, and he could do with it whatever he wished.

"Stop, Jackie, that hurts," Mazie whined.

"It never bothered you before. Besides it's time you got up and fixed me a drink."

He could never boss his wife around the way he could Mazie. It was part of the attraction. Mazie liked what he provided for her. The house, the clothes, even the sex, most of the time. His wife took it all for granted because he married her money. They gave up on sex as soon as the children were born. His wife only tolerated him and tolerated it in one position only, with her head turned away from him and her eyes closed.

His father-in-law had run one of the state's largest turpentine camps, alongside that of B.J. Winters' father-in-law, and both made a fortune off the labor of blacks during the twenties and thirties. Zion County was one of the last holdouts after the state starting shutting them down.

The camps consisted of shacks for sleeping, a small store where checks were cashed after paying off the week's groceries. The men were not allowed to leave the camp during turpentining season. They spent their days forcing spigots into the hardy long leaf pines and carrying bucketfuls of the pinesap, which provided the basis for turpentine. Florida provided Germany with the majority of their turpentine and so strained relations with the European country during the first half of the twentieth century would have eventually shut down the camps through economics, not law anyway. These camps remain one of the dirty secrets of northern Florida, but many of the richest people in Zion County could trace their wealth back to some part of the industry. Now all that remained were scars on the stunted pines that survived.

Jackson's legacy could nearly equal that of turpentine farmers. He believed just like his daddy and granddaddy before him that a man could do whatever he wanted with the property he owned. The Stewarts had rented their properties out to sharecroppers until the land became so nutrient-poor from over-farming they couldn't get a crop to grow. Many of the sharecroppers owned adjacent lands and just wanted a bit more to farm. The Stewart General Store in downtown Calloway provided all the supplies, and Jackson's grandfather extended credit whenever the farmers hit hard times. As the land began to deteriorate, those hard times increased until the farmers couldn't even make the monthly credit payments at the store.

However, the Stewarts had a foolproof plan. They helped those poor farmers by settling for the adjacent lands in exchange for wiping out the debt at the store. The farmers were grateful until they realized years later that the Stewart holdings had quadrupled in value. By then it was too late. The Stewart land acquisition continued to grow.

In the sixties when Jackson took over running the family's holdings, he went to school and became a licensed realtor. That way he could buy and sell without paying a middleman. His daddy's buddies came to him for real estate help and advice. Jackson did many things with the thousands of acres owned by his family. He rented out portions of it, and when lucrative enough, sold to developers. He made sure zoning was changed on certain areas to industrial so he had a variety of choices when it came to selling and renting.

These things were easy to do in the 1960s and '70s and most of the '80s. Changes came as the power structure and citizenry within rural Zion County changed.

Yankees and south Florida refugees arrived daily, wanting to live in Zion County. That wouldn't have been so bad in Jackson's mind because he had always welcomed the developers showing up from Jacksonville, Miami, and Atlanta. But this new breed stood for all that Jackson was against.

They called themselves environmentalists, but Jackson thought they were just a disguise for property-rights thieves. They wanted to control zoning and land usage.

Jackson would proclaim loudly and often, "Damn it, they even want to tell me what to do with the gopher tortoises on my property."

His daddy shot at a man once for trying to remove a tortoise from Stewart land. The man just wanted to make soup, but Jackson, Sr. said no man had a right to walk on another man's property and steal what wasn't rightfully his.

Good thing his father hadn't lived to hear these environmentalists talking about forcing property owners to relocate the tortoises when fields were plowed under or developments began. He would have shot one of them for sure. It is not that the Stewarts cared for the gopher tortoise – but they cared passionately about who told them what they could do regarding the property they owned and the property they stole.

Jackson wondered if some of the old-fashioned techniques of his forefathers shouldn't be applied now. Not only did he have to deal with these folks as a landowner, but also as a commissioner he had it up to his bushy eyebrows with these vegetarian, tree-hugging, tortoise-loving meddlers.

They even wanted to tell him he couldn't use his property for cellular phone towers. Allowing cell phone companies to place towers had become one of the most lucrative business deals in years for no outlay. The property used by the towers was minimal but the rent paid by these companies paid enough to keep Mazie.

"Here's your drink, honey," Mazie said as she came back from the den. She wore no clothes, but Jackson didn't notice.

"Mazie, I want you to start attending commission meetings again," Jackson told her.

"Why would I want to do that?" she asked. "You know I can't stand it when Commissioner Godawful starts talking about sidewalks and bike paths."

"Because I told you to. I need someone out in the audience watching and listening. Most folks don't know who you are, and even if they do, it doesn't matter because you have a way with people. I need to know what's going on with the public because there's too much noise from the left these days. I need to know what they're thinking."

"What do I get for it?"

"Me and maybe those new diamond earrings you've been crying about."

CHAPTER SEVENTEEN

ON THE FIRST FRIDAY in November, Kelly walked outside to retrieve her paper from the box. Fog enveloped the old tree-lined street. Kelly's small house sat in one of the oldest neighborhoods in Braidwood right across from the University. Even though her street was off State Avenue, the main drag in town, it ended in a cul de sac just five houses down from her.

She loved her house, purchased soon after her divorce and right after landing the job at *The Tribune*. Not much room, but it was cozy, and that was fine with her.

When she came back inside, she went into her living room with her cup of coffee. The room, filled to capacity with comfortable lounging furniture, contained windows on two sides with a sliding glass door that opened onto a small stone patio in a heavily shaded area. Right now, the camellias were budding and by December the bushes would come alive with pink and white flowers, just in time for Christmas.

Her story made the front page and so did Molly's picture of Winterrowd and Krantz attempting to swim ashore with the boat in the background. She laughed when she saw the headline, "Commissioners go for a swim in the shade." They had fun with that one at the paper last night, but she didn't think Bart would let it fly. It was a little too cute for his style, but she had been so late in filing the final story that Bart probably hadn't seen it.

She looked at the rest of the front page and saw beneath the fold line her article on Molly. Too bad, it took her friend's problem to bring her two front-page bylines in one day.

The editorial surprised her. Rick had probably written it. She figured he probably fought to keep both stories off the front page so when the editorial decried the vandalism done to Molly's car, she wondered briefly if Bart wrote it, but it was definitely Rick's style. He used cheap tricks and big words to sensationalize the situation. Bart would never stoop to that. When he wrote the editorial, it was clear, Hemingway-style writing – clipped sentences, no adjectives, no inflammatory images.

The Tribune offered a reward of one hundred dollars for information leading to the capture of the guilty party. *What was up with that*, she wondered? The newspaper was notoriously cheap. They hadn't even done that with the bomb.

When Kelly finished reading the paper, she thought about the weekend ahead. Even though she tried to cool things with Mike, she remembered she agreed to a Saturday night date. It would be her only social event of the weekend, and she now wondered if she made the right decision by relenting. They usually had a good time, but the other night he had been so strange, it had unnerved her some. Maybe she would try to get him to talk about himself. He usually shied away from any mention of his family or his roots. Anything to do with his past was kept quiet. As a reporter who wanted to know everything, that bothered her. She talked about her life before Braidwood, although she would never willingly go back to Palm Beach and live the life of her childhood. She lived a sheltered life there, and in many ways that eventually hurt her deeply and led to the biggest scars of her life.

Until she turned seventeen, she assumed everyone operated on the same honest level she did. What they said and how they looked determined what could be expected of them at all times.

She learned quickly one summer night at a beach party that words can hold lies and looks can change as quickly as the direction of the breeze during a Florida thunderstorm.

Since she had the day off, she decided to clean house instead of sitting around remembering, which led her to a place she didn't want to explore. She didn't want to think about her daughter Joely today or any day. The pain came quickly and made her short of breath. If she kept busy, those dark moments passed. Otherwise, they'd overtake her and leave her lying on the couch all day with her mother's crocheted afghan pulled up around her and the Kleenex box close by.

Now the dark days only came once or twice a year, and she usually fought them just like she was doing today. Only on February 10, Joely's birthday, did she allow the grief to wash over her. She always took the day off work and stayed in the house with the shades pulled and the telephone off. That day she gave over to mourning her daughter who probably still lived somewhere in south Florida.

On this next birthday Joely would be seventeen, the same age Kelly had been when she conceived her. That scared Kelly most of all. Had Joely been raised to read behind the words? Or did Joely trust everyone she met and allow them to talk her into things that shouldn't be?

"Mike, come in," Kelly said as she held the front door open for her date on Saturday night. "How about a drink before we leave?"

"Sounds good. I made reservations at the Carriage Gate, but we've got half an hour or so."

"The Carriage Gate? I haven't been there in awhile. *The Tribune* used to do their Christmas luncheon there until Sal's opened."

"I've got a confession. I've never been, but I read a review in that paper you work for and thought it might be nice. Maybe even romantic."

Kelly handed him his drink and smiled. This evening would turn out all right. She had been worried for no reason.

"Great job in yesterday's paper. Two front page stories," Mike said. "You deserve to be on the front page more than you are."

"Problem is I'm usually doing the rural thing, which I love, but front page has to be really big, and it usually has something to do with the Rattlers."

"We call it *The Rattler Tribune*. Anyway, I just wanted to tell you that I was proud to be your friend."

"Thanks, Mike. That's sweet. What about you? What are you working on?"

"I'm still researching violations of the sunshine law for next week's paper. I'm not coming up with much."

"How far back have you gone?"

"1968 when it was instituted."

"How about this angle. I seem to remember that charges weren't filed against him, but I heard that Jackson Stewart received a reprimand and strongly worded warning in the early eighties."

"Maybe I've been looking for the wrong thing?"

"Right. It's very hard to prove some of this stuff so actual charges that would result in getting records on violations probably are rare."

"But warning letters, reprimands would be listed as something else," Mike said. "Thanks, Kelly, that's a great tip."

"Enough of work. I've got several meetings and workshops beginning first thing Monday, and I need to be totally entertained tonight with something other than the politics of this crazy county we live in."

"I agree. So I see the county is up to their old tricks of holding those meetings during the day."

"They go back and forth. Trade off. It's crazy and not citizen friendly, I can assure you. But that's the way three of the commissioners like it, and until there's a majority on the commission who feel that elected officials work for the public and not the other way around, it will stay that way."

"I know you want to stop talking about it, but let me ask one more question. What do you think about the elections in March?"

"I haven't heard yet on the county level. I think there might be a shake-up in Calloway. Two seats are up, and I'm hearing rumbles about two radicals, one of them black, running. Could change things."

"People in Calloway are getting tired of business as usual. At least that's my sense when I attend the meetings and talk to folks."

"I agree. Things might change out there. Maybe the other towns will start waking up. People have felt powerless for so long that it might take some time. But if things like the gopher tortoise incident and now the armadillo warning keep up, folks are going to start asking questions."

CHAPTER EIGHTEEN

"HOW COME BART TOOK you out on the river the other day?" Mike asked Kelly as they lay on her bed after making love.

"He's got a boat; I needed to investigate."

"It seems you would try to avoid being alone with him."

"Bart and I are very good friends." Kelly said, "Please don't bring it up again because it's not worth discussing."

"I'm just insanely jealous of any other man who has been with you," Mike said as he kissed her shoulder, "especially knowing how closely the two of you work."

Kelly turned toward him and kissed his forehead. "None of that matters. I'm here right now with you. Why don't you tell me about growing up in Dansville."

"Dansville? Now why would you want to hear about that?"

"Because I've been covering these towns around here for some time, and I'm curious. Dansville may be in Banks County, but it's very similar to towns like Hope Springs. Second, I want to know all about you because we've been just about as intimate as two people can be. You know about me; I want to know about you."

Mike looked at her for a long time before he launched into a very choppy and sometimes inconsistent story. His father was a drunk, and his mother ran off with a neighbor when Mike was seven. His father drank more, but he took Mike out fishing on the Gulf every Sunday where some of the best days of Mike's childhood occurred. He loved his daddy for what he had done. He had kept Mike with him even after his mother left and even though two aunts begged his father to let them take Mike in with them. He hated his father's drinking.

Even though Mike had told her more this night than in all the months they had been dating, Kelly still sensed there were things that he was keeping from her.

"How did you decide on journalism?" Kelly asked him.

"I got a job with the *Banks County News* in my senior year of high school. They had me taking pictures at football games, you know, inexperienced stringer stuff. But it was enough."

"Enough?"

"You know, enough, to get me hooked," he told her. "The first time I saw my name in the paper under an article on a football game, I was so proud. Even my father said he was proud of me. And at school the kids paid attention to me for the first time. Everyone wants to get in the paper, as you already know, so for an unpopular geek like me it was quite heady stuff."

"You went to UB?"

"I had to start at Banks Community College, but most of the kids around here do that – even the smartest – because of scholarships and things. Then I transferred to UB, but I never graduated. My father died, and there was no money. I had to pay for his pitiful funeral."

"And?" Kelly asked.

"And then one day I walked into the office of *The Calloway Chronicle*. I met Greg Panzer, and he was pleased to have anyone show up with any type of training. Small papers miles from the largest city don't attract a whole lot of writers."

"And you still feel it? That feeling when you see your name, when you're on a really good story?"

"Not as much, but yes, I feel it. What about you?"

"Every day. That's why I love doing what I'm doing now. Covering politics gives me a great rush. This week was a good example; it shows you anything can happen. Most journalists want to move away from covering the small towns, thinking it's not as good as covering the large city. But I love writing about Hope Springs, Calloway, and Millstone. Forget Braidwood. These towns are the next hot spots over managed growth. And as the commissions become better balanced between the GOBs and the environmentalists, smart growth people and the no-growth folks will come out of the woodwork to make the conflicts even more intense."

"I've never thought about it that way, but you're probably right. I've been a little bored covering the Calloway and Millstone stuff, but I can see what you mean. Things did change in town with the last election. Things don't just pass through like zoning changes without an argument from Chelsea Godfrey or Richard Nichols on the Calloway

Commission at least. Plus, it empowered people who have started coming to the meetings just to inform themselves."

"Hang tight, Mike. I predict all hell is going to break loose very soon. Look what's happened in the last month with me and now Molly. And don't forget Cowan's dead gopher tortoise. Some people are real scared for some reason."

"Their way of life is being challenged. More than one hundred years of maintaining a tight control over the process of government and the electorate; they're not going to give up easily."

"That's true. If you take it all the way back to Reconstruction, it's easy to see the connection. Back then they suddenly discovered that if they didn't do something to preserve a way of life already being challenged by the federal government, then the carpetbaggers and even worse, former slaves, would start running the show. In a way, this new challenge to the status quo is actually taking a swipe at their great grandpas."

"Do you want me to stay tonight?" Mike asked her.

"I'd like that."

"Then let's go to sleep. I'm beat."

Sleep eluded Kelly, although Mike fell asleep as soon as he got under the comforter. She thought back to the questions Mike asked her about Bart, but then her thoughts drifted to Bart himself.

She remembered their second time in Tallahassee. She was sent to cover a story on proposed changes to the University's affirmative action policy; she didn't know until he knocked on her hotel door that Bart had come to Tallahassee, too.

"The big guy sent me," he told her. "He thought someone should supervise."

"Oh, really," Kelly said. "Then I guess you'd better come inside the room before you get arrested for loitering."

They made love almost immediately. No talking, just the silent and mutual realization they were totally alone in a strange city – the city where they fell in love.

The hearings lasted a week. During that week, Kelly tried to fulfill every sexual fantasy that Bart dreamed up. He brought out a side of her that she didn't know existed. She lusted after him every waking moment and said things to him that shocked her. The freedom afforded them in the hotel room left little time for discussion or questions about right or wrong.

"Thank you," Bart said to her one night just before they turned out the lights after a rather strenuous session.

"I should be thanking you, Boss. That was something; I never knew I could get in that position."

Bart pulled her into his arms and looked down into her laughing face. "Thank you for not talking about my marriage this week. It has been so bad lately that I don't know how much longer I can take it."

For the first time since he arrived, Kelly could see the dark shadows deepen under his eyes. He seemed to shrink as his shoulders drooped, and his head bent over her. In those moments, Kelly forgot all the other baggage and only wanted to prevent this man from suffocating under his burdens.

"I can't leave her because she's in bad shape right now," Bart said. "But I also can't live without passion in my life. So I thank you."

She put a hand on either side of his face and pulled him toward her. She kissed him deeply and then cradled him in her arms until he fell asleep.

The next morning, Bart came up behind her as she put the finishing touches on her make up before heading to the last legislative session on whether to change admission standards at the state universities.

"What are you doing this afternoon?" he asked on what looked to be the final day of hearings, ending with a press conference with the governor.

She stood at the bathroom mirror applying mascara. She was fully dressed for the day.

"I've got this big mean old editor who will probably make me hang around the governor's mansion until Jeb comes out to make a statement."

"Your editor sounds like a beast," he said. He approached her from behind, but she could see him clearly in the mirror. She put down the mascara wand.

"What else does he make you do?"

"You wouldn't believe the things he makes me do," she said as she reached behind her and began fondling him. "But what he does to me may be even more shocking."

"Like what?"

She directed his hands up her thighs and under her dress. She maneuvered his hands until they found the perfect spot.

"Is this what that old letch does to you?" he whispered as he moved his hands very slowly.

They didn't make it out of the room for another hour or so as they played bad editor versus hard working reporter.

Kelly turned and looked at Mike sleeping in her bed. He was sweet, but he wasn't Bart, and at this time of the night, she wondered if anyone could ever satisfy her as Bart had. She learned to live with the pain of not being with him; all that remained was an overwhelming sadness that the one man she loved could not be with her, as long as he felt committed to taking care of his wife. Ironically, the very attributes that Kelly admired most in him were the ones that kept them apart.

She eventually slept and when she woke the smell of fresh coffee hit her. Mike was no longer next to her on the bed, but she could hear him in the kitchen opening and shutting cupboards. She smiled to think about him attempting to find something to eat in her kitchen. Cooking was not one of her strong points.

She went out front to get the paper and then joined Mike in the kitchen.

"Find anything to fix for breakfast?" she asked as she came up and kissed him on the neck. Unlike Bart, he stood only a few inches taller than her, and she could reach him without standing on her tiptoes.

"Not much. But I've managed coffee and toast with some marmalade that hopefully isn't too old," he said. "I take it you don't eat here much."

"No time. Meals are usually on the run. Then on the weekends I enjoy going out."

"I'll have you over to my place one of these weekends. Don't forget I'm a great cook."

"I'd like that."

"What's in the paper today?"

"I don't believe it!" Kelly yelled when she saw the front page of the local section. "Why didn't they call me when these guys made this statement? Carl got the story."

"What is it?" Mike came from behind and read over her shoulder.

Billy Winterrowd and Jackson Stewart made a joint statement deploring the actions taken against Molly Hale. They were joining the fight to find the vandals because they didn't want either of their communities overrun with hoodlums.

"Kelly, you can't get every story. Even you have to have time off," Mike told her after reading the small piece.

"I know, but this is mine. This particular piece is mine because I've been covering it. Someone should have called me. Who assigned it?"

CHAPTER NINETEEN

"THIS SHOULD BE INTERESTING," Molly whispered to Kelly as Tim Murray banged the gavel and brought the Calloway Commission meeting to order on Monday night.

Luddy Gregors, a community activist and the first black city commissioner elected ten years ago, stood up from the audience when it came time for citizen input. Kelly kept hearing persistent rumors that she might run again for the commission.

"State your name for the record, please," the mayor said.

"Now Junior, you know as well as I do who I am, but here goes. Luddy Gregors, citizen and former commissioner of Calloway."

Luddy called the mayor by his nickname. Even though his daddy, Tim Murray, Sr. had long ago passed away, Tim could not get rid of his childhood moniker of Junior.

"Good evening, Luddy," Junior said. "What can we do for you tonight?"

"What you can do is tell my why three of our commissioners, and you, Mr. Mayor, were out on the river last week boating and swimming together."

"Is that all?"

"Is that all? Isn't that enough? Calloway looks bad because the four of you were in violation of the Sunshine Law."

"Luddy, during the time of citizen input the commissioners don't respond to questions, and when the audience becomes verbally abusive, we can have them removed from the chambers. Now do you have a point?"

"Junior, don't you start with me. My point is this: you four jokers have ruined our reputation in the county. You broke the law, and I want some answers about what is going to be done."

Applause came from the audience as Luddy finished her point.

Junior banged the gavel. "No noise from the audience. Now, Luddy, we didn't break any laws, and that should answer your question. We aren't going to do anything about it."

"Then you all need to go to jail."

"Luddy, you've gone too far this time. I'm going to have the Chief escort you out if you continue."

"You're going to have the Chief escort me out? What have I done?"

"You're making slanderous statements and personal attacks against elected commissioners," the mayor told her as he signaled for the chief of police with his head.

"I don't need Chief Thomas Jefferson here to escort me out of my city commission chambers. I changed his diapers so he doesn't know anything I didn't help teach him. This place belongs to all of us not just you and your cronies."

"Chief, she's been warned, escort her out."

"Mr. Mayor, you cannot just throw out citizens every time they disagree with you," Chelsea Godfrey said. "I protest your actions."

"Commissioner Godfrey, you are out of order, please contain yourself." Tim banged the gavel although no one could hear the banging of the hammer upon its wooden base because of the loud outburst from members of the audience.

"I don't have to stay here and take this," Chelsea said. "This is not a democracy, and you all will vote the way you want, whether I'm here or not."

With that, Chelsea packed her tall pile of materials she brought to every meeting and packed away her highlighters and pens and stomped off of the dais and out the door.

All sense of order left the room with the departure of both Luddy and Chelsea. The members of the audience stood, yelled, and shook their fists at the commissioners. Molly was there with her trusty camera shooting as fast as the action unfolded before them. Kelly followed the others outside with her tape recorder running. When they got to the front steps of city hall, the Chief went back inside after telling Luddy to go home. The crowd booed and hissed as he hurried past the residents and headed back to chambers for the next citizen to challenge the mayor.

"Luddy, can I ask you a few questions?" Kelly asked when she came within hearing distance of the ousted citizen.

"Sure, go ahead."

"What would you like to see happen next?"

"I want charges brought against those bastards, and you can quote me on that. I want the whole commission exposed. Have you ever heard of a citizen being thrown out for simply trying to get some answers to the questions?"

"It probably happens more in this town than any other. Calloway is notorious for not allowing certain citizens to even speak." Kelly turned off her tape recorder. "Do you really want to see something happen, Luddy? Now I'm speaking to you as a friend, not a reporter."

"Kelly, you and me go way back, and I've always trusted you. Those jokers in there aren't going to do anything. It's just like it's always been."

"A citizen can file a sworn complaint of a suspected violation of the Code of Ethics. The Commission on Ethics in Tallahassee cannot start an investigation until someone files the sworn complaint, even though it's been reported in the papers. Then they do an investigation. If they find a violation, they can fine the official or even remove them from office in extreme cases."

"Do you think they'd do anything here?"

"They might. We can help each other, you know. If I have something I think should be reported, I'll give it to you, and if you think you have something I could use in my articles, you can give it to me. You can be my Deep Throat."

"Deep Throat?"

"During the Watergate scandal the secret source of Bob Woodward was called Deep Throat."

"I remember. Good, I like that," Luddy said. "Luddy Gregors is not going to stand for these good old boys continuing to control us. My daddy lost his land to the Stewarts fifty years ago, and ever since then I've wanted to put them all out of business. It killed my daddy when he lost his property. Maybe this will be the start of getting back what he lost."

"Luddy, they might decide there has been no violation because it's not illegal for two commissioners to talk," Kelly cautioned. "It becomes illegal when two or more commissioners on the same board talk about issues that might later come up for a vote."

"Then it seems to me that commissioners should never be alone together," Luddy remarked. "Anything could become an issue for a later vote."

"I agree, but the Ethics folks will want some proof before they go further. What I'm trying to find out is where had these gentlemen just come from. Why were two Hope Springs commissioners together? Why four from Calloway? I don't believe it was just for a joy ride. Why risk being seen on the busy river?"

"Do I just ask those guys in Tallahassee to start an investigation?"

"You have to fill out a form. If I find out any specific illegal things, we can then consider taking it to the State's Attorney for criminal prosecution, but so far I don't have anything there."

Kelly went back into the meeting where the public portion still continued. Most of the people were getting up to protest Luddy's removal. She noticed Mike for the first time sitting in the back row. She gave him a slight wave and went to the front seats where she had a table for her laptop.

The mayor banged the gavel after the last person spoke because cheering had broken out all around the room.

"This discussion is over for tonight," the Mayor said. "Let me remind you that unless we were talking about official city business, there was no violation of the Sunshine Laws, and I can assure you that we did not talk about city business."

"And this is a democracy, not a dictatorship," Cowan Garcia yelled from the audience.

"Chief, kindly remove Mr. Garcia from the chambers," the mayor directed.

"You can remove me, Mayor, but you can't take away the fact that we hire and fire you folks sitting up there passing judgment and throwing us out of public meetings," Cowan Garcia yelled as the police chief escorted him out of the meeting.

"Life is never dull at these meetings, is it?" Kelly whispered to Molly.

"Hell, no. It sure makes our job easier," Molly said.

"Why?"

"My leads write themselves at these things. I don't even need to think about how to start my stories. Like tonight, 'Cowan Garcia accused the Mayor of running a dictatorship.' Now don't you dare steal that, Miss Kelly."

"No, I thought I'd be clever with Sunshine Laws at a night meeting. You're right. I've never sat staring at the computer screen trying to figure out how to start. It just comes to me, mostly from what some of these officials say themselves."

"Do you and Mike have a date later?"

"No. Why?"

"I just wondered why he was here. He's supposed to be out at the polling places when they open at seven o'clock tomorrow morning so he asked me to cover this meeting for him. I thought maybe you were meeting later."

"Since he's here, he might ask me to meet him, but we don't have anything planned. I think he just likes attending these things."

"He does? That's odd."

"Why odd?"

"We try to get him to cover more stories for *The Chronicle.* We're having a heck of a time getting Millstone covered right now because Mike always says he doesn't have time. Last week he said that Calloway was beginning to be a bit much and asked if I'd do some of the meetings."

Kelly wondered about that. She gained some insight into Mike's character on Saturday night, but something still troubled her about him. He did seem to appear wherever she was and until tonight, she thought it was his love of politics.

"Maybe he's thinking of running for office?" Kelly now suggested to Molly.

"Mike? I don't think so. He's got too much baggage."

The mayor looked down at the two reporters and gave them a stern stare.

"We'd better shut up for now," Molly said. "Let's meet later at Mickey's."

Kelly forced herself to keep her mind on the meeting at hand. What did Molly mean that Mike wouldn't run for a political office because he had too much baggage?

So did she, but it wouldn't prevent her from running for office. She never shared with another living soul what happened to her at the age of seventeen. Not even Bart, the one person she had become the closest to since then. She'd never been as close to her husband Jerry, but then she should never have married him.

Another seventeen years had passed since she had been seventeen herself and when she thought of the months during the summer that changed her life, she still felt the fresh stab of pain in her gut, just as if it happened the week before. Luckily, she didn't think about it often. Kelly was expert at shoving the painful things away from her conscious mind.

When she and Molly settled into a booth at Mickey's Diner, she looked at her friend with questioning eyes. Molly stirred her coffee.

"What did you mean, Molly?"

"What?"

"Mike has too much baggage to run for office."

"He's never told you?"

"I wouldn't be asking if I knew. What is it? Has Mike told you something?"

"Look, Kelly, I wouldn't have brought it up if I thought you didn't know. I figured you were a smart reporter and all that and even though you didn't live around here at the time, you would probably investigate."

"Would you please tell me what you are talking about?"

"I will tell you this. Go back in the paper's archives for the year 1983, I'm not sure of the month, but I'm sure you can figure out how to do a search from there."

"Did Mike do something?"

"Kelly, I don't want to be the one to tell you. Now look who's here. The devil himself."

Kelly broke her intent stare on Molly to look up. Mike stood at their booth smiling.

"Mind if I join you two ladies?" Mike asked. "I wouldn't want anyone to think you two were sharing professional secrets."

"Sure, Mike," Molly said as she moved over on the seat to make room for him. Kelly didn't move.

CHAPTER TWENTY

KELLY BEGAN WITH JANUARY 1983 in the microfilm room of the public library. The paper turned over everything prior to 1990 to the library for safekeeping. The library had more storage space in their new downtown facilities than *The Tribune*.

She stopped on February 20, 1983. "Son accused of setting fire to house," screamed the headline. There on the front page was a picture of a young Mike Green, a yearbook picture.

Kelly quickly put her dime in the machine to have the page printed. She continued her search. For several weeks, every day contained a story on the fire, and then nothing.

She went to 1984, and finally in September there appeared a short brief on the decision of the judge not to try the sixteen year old for murder. The judge ordered him to juvenile hall until he turned eighteen.

"Did you know about this?" Kelly asked as she walked into Bart's office. She placed the articles on his desk.

"About Mike Green and his father? I thought everyone knew."

"I didn't, and I've been dating him for the past few months. Did you know that?"

"Yes, but I thought you knew. It's common knowledge he was an abused kid who's now a hard working adult — a real success story. I really thought you knew."

"I'm not from around here. Mike doesn't go around advertising this information. I can't believe you never talked to me about it. That you didn't care enough to bring it up and ask me questions about him."

"Kelly, what's this all about? Why would I talk to you about your dates? I never thought you were in any danger. It's like I said, he's made something of himself despite his early troubles."

"I should have known there was something."

"I'm sorry," Bart said. "But did I really do anything that was that horrible?"

Kelly relaxed into the chair in front of Bart's desk. She knew she was probably overreacting, but it bothered her that she hadn't been more cautious. Why hadn't she asked more questions? Had she learned nothing in the last seventeen years?

"No, not really," she finally admitted. "I just got a call from Cowan Garcia. Dead tortoise number two appeared in his yard this morning, and he's put up another grave."

"Did something happen at the meeting last night?"

"An uproar occurred over Luddy Gregors getting thrown out, and then Garcia stood up and gave his opinion, which is always forbidden by the mayor. The chief of police works hard at these meetings. Can we run a picture of the graves this time and not have it buried on the back pages?" Kelly asked.

"I'll make sure Rick understands that this is a pattern, and we'd better be reporting on it. You want to do the story?"

"Already started, Boss," Kelly said.

"I knew it. Why do you need me around here anyway? I don't get any respect. Have you had any luck with investigating who's really behind that land annexation in Calloway?" Bart asked.

"Not really. It's been pretty crazy lately. You got anything?"

"I did a cross check of some names and many of them come up on much smaller companies as board of directors. I've just done some Internet surfing when I have time." He handed her a sheaf of papers listing names and corporations of possible owners of the land recently annexed.

"One interesting thing," Bart continued. "One of the guys listed on Calloway Properties? He's just been indicted for fraud in a county in the Panhandle. You might want to check that out. You got anything else you're working on at the moment?"

"I'm still trying to figure out where our boaters had been. One of these days when I have a free afternoon, I'm just going to drive around those roads in Banks County that all lead to the river. I've got a hunch about something."

"Let me know if you ever want company. I'm familiar with the area. It's very easy to get lost out there. Those roads all begin to look alike after awhile."

Rick poked his head in the door right then and asked to speak to Bart. Kelly made her way back to her desk, forgetting to take her papers with her. When she turned back to get them, Rick was asking if they could shut the door. She retrieved the articles on Mike and the packet from Bart before the meeting became private.

That's odd, Kelly thought as she went back to her desk. Bart's door was the one that almost never shut. Reporters, photographers, editors – they all had easy access to the executive editor. Bart insisted on that. He wanted everyone to feel comfortable to just drop in and discuss things with him. That way he kept on top of things, and he told Kelly, it still made him feel a part of the paper rather than a figurehead editor, which his job had danger of becoming.

Kelly put the articles of Mike aside, and she began looking through the stack Bart gave her. Then she started searching on the Internet herself. She finally came to a stop when she realized what she really needed were land titles and deeds. That only meant one thing. She would have to go to the county administrative building and just start digging. She made a list of possible names of people to check and then went through the list of corporations before her and began copying the names of those that were repeated the most.

Interesting how many of the corporations had listings using the name Calloway, but the names of the directors were not familiar to Kelly. Very odd that she wouldn't know anyone among that group. She'd been covering government and politics in the county for almost ten years; someone's name should look familiar.

Before she could start digging away at the courthouse, she decided to finish the story on Cowan and his front yard graves.

"Cowan, is it all right if a photographer comes out this afternoon?" Kelly asked him once she reached him on the phone.

"Not a problem; I'll even put on a suit," he said. "I've also got a digital photo of the shell before I buried it, if you want that."

"Give it to Lonny when he shows up. If there's a next time, call us before you bury it, all right? I promise we won't be burying any more of these stories."

Things began falling into place for Kelly at the courthouse once she pulled deeds. The names from the corporations and the names of individual landowners in Zion County showed the board of directors of many of the companies buying the properties. She made copies of all sales for property more than several hundred acres.

She would come back the next day with the names of mothers, daughters, sisters, and even wives of some of these folks. Sometimes land ownership was hidden that way for tax purposes. Asking the other relatives would do no good because many times they didn't even know they owned the property. The signature could be forged the first time, and so signing it again for the sale proved little trouble. Kelly learned about this method several years ago from a daughter of one of the landowners. She and Bart both talked to the woman, and she was ready to go on the record about her signature being forged. But then her father found out she was talking to the press, and he offered her a new house. No source and no story.

She went back to her car loaded down with copies and Bart's list. When she arrived at the office she made a decision not to take them inside, instead she locked everything in the trunk of her car. No one else besides Bart needed to know she was working on this case. With all the strange happenings lately, Kelly had begun to suspect everyone, except her boss.

CHAPTER TWENTY-ONE

"KELLY, COME ON IN," Bart said when she returned from checking records.

"Your door is open. Must be Rick left."

"Wait until you hear why. He gave two weeks notice and wanted to inform me that a friend of his is starting a new paper in Calloway. He'll be executive editor. Some guy from south Florida, an editor from *The Miami Herald* fallen on good times, always wanted his own weekly in a small town. Seems Rick spoke to him at a conference recently and showed some enthusiasm for helping him."

"That's interesting. Rick running the show at a small town weekly. Not too surprising though. He's always wanted to be the big fish. Now he can be one in a small pond. But can this area support three weeklies?"

"Hard to say. Makes life interesting. Rick said they were calling it *The Zion County News,* and it would cover a broader area than the other two rural papers. You wouldn't be interested in his job, would you? It'd mean quite an increase in salary."

"No, Bart. We've been over this before. I love what I do, and I wouldn't be able to do that as editor. I can't get away from writing."

"We could work something out. Really, we could. Maybe you wouldn't cover as much territory as you do now, but we could still keep you on the political end of it."

"I'm not sure. Let's just both think about it. Advertise the position, and you might get someone a whole lot better than me."

"I doubt that," Bart told her. "But onto the other stuff. Find anything interesting today?"

"Maybe, I found lots of names I didn't know on the corporations' lists. Did you notice that?"

"I didn't look that closely, but now that I think of it, I didn't recognize any names either."

"But when you go to the land deeds, names begin to look familiar. At least the names of the sellers do. And then I started noticing the names from the corporations were often listed as buyers."

"Now this still doesn't mean that anyone has done anything wrong, remember," Bart said.

"I know, but quite a few situations where conflict of interest might have played a role came into my mind when I saw names like Jackson Stewart and others such as Calloway's city attorney, Tony Mayberry. I don't remember Stewart recusing himself on the annexation vote. Tomorrow, I want to compile a list of family members of people like Stewart and Waine and see what happens."

"Sounds good. Now I don't want to insult your intelligence, but you know this is strictly background for now. You don't have a story yet."

"I know. If it's all right with you, Boss, I'd like to keep all the files at home. I can work on pulling together the pieces in my spare time. We're pretty casual out in the newsroom about our stuff. It's not unusual for Carl to come over to my desk and shuffle stuff around looking for a campaign finance report, for instance. I do the same thing."

"Then keep it at home. I don't see a problem."

"Did you vote today?" Kelly asked him.

"Yes, I did. How about you?"

"I was at the polls when they opened. Bart, we've got a few hours of daylight left, want to take a ride?"

"Where? Banks County?"

"You're a mind reader. I've got a hunch that keeps nagging at me. Since it's late in the day, I thought I'd better bring an expert."

"Happy to oblige. I even drove the Jeep today."

"What have you got for us, Rick?" Jackson Stewart asked. They sat around the large oak table on Lucy Burch's screened porch at the river on Tuesday, Election Day 2000, and the day after the disruption at the Calloway meeting. Only a few of the principles had come this time because this was an organizational meeting to prepare for the presentation on the newspaper idea to the entire group. This time they all drove in separate cars.

"To do it right, it looks like a half million to set us up with state of the art equipment and competent employees. I looked into some property in downtown Calloway and found a couple of prime spots. One needs renovation, but we can buy it for a reasonable price especially with Lucy here negotiating for us. The other is a rental, ready to move in." Rick passed around the proposal complete with a budget and pictures of the properties in question.

"If we went with the rental, what's the soonest you could have a paper published?" Billy Winterrowd asked.

"Maybe two months, if we started today."

"Today is November 7," Jackson said. "That means by the beginning of the year?"

"I think we could manage a small edition sometime near the beginning of January. We might be able to put out our first issue as a holiday retrospective between Christmas and New Year's with just photographs," Rick said.

"That means we could be up and running for two months or so before the March elections," Lucy said. "Maybe we couldn't influence the election much, but it might be worth a try."

"I still feel we need to move cautiously with this paper," Rick said. "If we move too fast into the political arena, we'll get labeled right away, and no one will pay attention."

"There are ways to be subtle," Jackson said. "We interview all the candidates and give each equal space. Not like we did in Millstone last year. Gary should never have refused the ad from that tree-hugger, and he should have tried harder to do an interview with her. Gary gets a bug up his ass sometimes."

"I hear talk in the office about Gary and *The Monitor*," Rick said. "Everyone talks about that blatant endorsement, and the reporters at *The Tribune* are constantly whining about the paper being owned by developers."

"So who do we get to be our figurehead publisher?" Lucy asked. "I think they should live in Calloway, join the country club, Rotary, Chamber all that stuff so they look involved in the community."

"I've been thinking about that. That's tricky because it has to be someone never associated with either side. You'd be a good choice, Lucy, but I'm afraid your agenda is too predictable," Rick said. "I have an editor friend from Miami who has been thinking about relocating here; he and his wife are tired of south Florida. No one here knows him. We met at a conference several years ago, and we run into one another occasionally. I think he might be persuaded with the right incentives."

"Can he come up for an interview?" Tony Mayberry asked. "Anthony and B.J. will want to meet him."

Anthony Marcetti and B.J. Winters would probably be contributing the largest slice of money toward the paper since their investment was most at risk. Neither man wanted to lose the movie studio or the development on the Hope Springs River.

"I'll call my friend and see what he thinks," Rick said.

"We need him as of yesterday as far as I'm concerned," Jackson said. "So you become the executive editor, who's going to be our head writer? I want someone aggressive, but not as volatile as Dregs."

"I'd like to ask Mike Green," Rick said.

"Mike Green?" Lucy asked. "That little pipsqueak from *The Calloway Chronicle*?"

"Mike has something we need," Rick said. "He's ambitious. He'll do what we say because he likes money, and he's got some things he'd like kept quiet."

"You mean that thing with his dad?" Jackson asked.

"Exactly. It's been fifteen years or more since it happened and most people have forgotten. Mike would like to keep it that way, especially so he can continue his relationship with Kelly Sands."

"Is that wise – to have a reporter working for us who's tight with that bitch?" Lucy asked.

"It's perfect. He won't want her to know anything. She might even be proud that he's been asked to head up the writing staff of a new paper. Kelly is basically a good person and doesn't get suspicious until things look suspicious. Plus, I know Kelly. I think she might have some things she'd like kept quiet, too."

"Have we ever had her checked out?" asked Billy.

"Just a case down in Palm Beach," said Tony. "But she was the victim. My dad and I have a friend who knew her from those days. Let me ask him if he knows anything."

"Whoever we hire as writer needs to be a son of a bitch reporter. Aggressive, yet able to maintain objectivity. That's where Dregs falls down on the job. He can't keep his mouth shut. Do you think Green can handle that?" Jackson asked.

"I'm sure of it. Kelly and Mike have collaborated on several projects where confidentiality was essential. He never disappointed. He can be aggressive. Look how far he's come. Who would have ever thought that he would be a respected journalist?"

CHAPTER TWENTY-TWO

KELLY AND BART DROVE through Calloway and then Hope Springs. Once they crossed the Hope Springs River, they began a westerly drive toward Banks County. They crossed the river again and began following its course down limerock and sandy roads built in loops.

"If we keep veering to the right here, we'll come by quite a few houses that are on the river. There's a boat ramp, too. Have you considered the place might not be directly on the river?" Bart asked

"I think they'd drive then. That's too much hassle to have a car waiting at both ends," Kelly told Bart as the Jeep kicked up the dust on the road.

"I think we're getting close to Lucy's place. It still nags me that Rick and she were out on the river that day."

"Look, Bart. There's Rick's car. And Stewart's Caddy. That must be Lucy's house."

"Sure enough. What do you want to do?"

"Can we find a place to park to just watch and not be seen? At least so they can't see us sitting in the car."

Bart backed the Jeep onto the side of the road under the low-lying branches of a mimosa tree. Once he'd maneuvered it the way he wanted, it looked as if someone drove off the road and then abandoned the vehicle. While Kelly and Bart could still see out the windshield, the shade of the tree created dark shadows, and no one would be able to tell two people sat inside.

"I feel like a teenager," Bart said. "Want to make out?"

Kelly looked at him to see if he was serious. They had made out in this very Jeep several times in the past. Now they had time to kill alone in the gathering dusk of a November afternoon while they waited for who knew what.

"That would be very smart, Bart. We'd be all over each other and not hear the cars drive away or more importantly miss seeing the driver."

"Worse things have happened. So I guess that's a no?"

"You're worse than a teenager," Kelly said as she playfully tapped his chest. He grabbed her hand.

"I would do anything you want at any time, and you know it." His eyes sparkled as he brought her hand to his mouth for a quick kiss.

"Don't do that."

Bart stared out the front of the vehicle, and wondered if he should tell Kelly what his wife told him the night before. He hadn't been upset by the news, but it did surprise him. He was always skeptical about new medications finally working, but for months, she'd remained on an even keel and had been getting out more on her own. Joyce and Bart didn't enjoy the same activities, and never had. She hated the outdoors; he lived for it. She loved the theater; he was dragged there as her escort. Most of all, she had no understanding of his love of the news and quite often ridiculed his pursuit of the story. She didn't understand how he longed to get back to the actual writing at the paper. She would think this vigilant watching of Lucy Burch's river house a farce and waste of time. But most of all, she would be afraid that someone would see them and not invite them to the annual Christmas party for the Chamber Orchestra at the University Hotel. Despite her depression, she still kept up her outward appearances. In fact, besides her immediate family, Kelly was the only other person to know that Joyce Stanley suffered from debilitating bouts of depression that kept her housebound for weeks at a time.

"I didn't mean to sound so harsh," Kelly said after a few minutes. "I don't want to fight with you. In some ways you're my best friend because you understand doing things like this, as crazy as it seems. We won't get a story out of what we see today, but I'll have a little more background information. You understand that, but not even Mike, a reporter himself, would think this sane."

"Hey, I live for moments like this one. I do understand and encourage it."

The awkwardness of a few minutes before had passed. They sat in a comfortable silence watching, and soon they were rewarded. Tony Mayberry, city attorney for Millstone and Calloway, Jackson Stewart, and Jerry Mueller, Zion County Chamber president came walking out the back door of the house at the same time. They chatted for a few moments before getting in their vehicles. Rick must have remained inside with Lucy.

"Let's see, what do Tony, Jackson, and Jerry have in common with Rick and Lucy?" Kelly asked.

"Remember, just because they were all together doesn't mean there's a story."

"No, I know that, but you have to admit that it is a strange combination."

"Maybe not, Jerry and Lucy have been big in the Chamber for years. Rick went to school with Jerry. Jackson is a powerhouse and probably spends a lot of time with other big shots of Braidwood and Zion County. Now Tony is a little more puzzling, but not too much."

"okay, if you follow your line of thinking it's not so surprising. Millstone has been annexing like crazy and bringing in any kind of business that will settle out in the sticks. I don't know Tony very well, but he impresses me as the kind of guy who would look for the best deal for himself, even if he doesn't know a whole lot about the law. Not only is he the city attorney for Millstone, but also for Calloway and we know what's happening to the growth rate there."

"I would bet it wasn't a social event," Bart said, "even though at this point we can't prove anything."

"Why not a social thing?"

"It's a Tuesday late afternoon. There are no wives present, or mistresses for that matter. Just one female, and I wonder about her because I've always suspected she has balls. Rick doesn't hang out with Jackson's social circle or even Jerry's that much. Joyce drags me to these affairs, and so I see who's with whom. Tony shows up occasionally, but never Rick."

"What now, Boss?"

"Ellie May's for a beer?"

They listened to the election results on the radio as they drove to Ellie May's, a bar on the Hope Springs River. It was just after seven o'clock when they pulled into the full parking lot, and the radio announcer said most of the polls indicated the presidential race would be a close one. Florida's much sought after electoral votes might even be the deciding factor.

"Haven't seen one this close in my career," Bart noted as he found a parking spot.

"I usually pay more attention, but this year all I did was vote," Kelly said. "I'm pulling for the vice-president because one Bush in control of my life is enough."

"Jeb was the one groomed for today's election," Bart said. "George surprised everyone by getting a governorship first in Texas."

The bar offered anonymity to Bart and Kelly. Even though the place was crowded, they wouldn't know anyone and most eyes were glued to the six televisions posted around the bar. Usually sports blared from the speakers, but tonight a sport of another kind kept the beer drinkers enthralled.

Bart and Kelly chose to sit out on the deck overlooking the river after ordering drafts. The lights on the bank shone on the water rippling by.

"Any suggestions for my next step?" Kelly asked as she took the first sip of ice-cold beer. "Nothing beats a cold draft, does it?"

"No, sometimes it's the only thing that will do the trick. As for your next step, I'm not sure. Do you think anyone we saw today would talk to you off the record?"

"They all pretend to like me, but I don't think I could trick any of them into telling me what they're planning. I still say finding out the name of the developer for the landing strip would help. I think something is fishy about how all this is coming down. If it's such a great deal for Calloway, why all the secrecy?"

"The no-growthers have them scared."

"Maybe. Getting time to work on it is impossible some weeks."

"What if you cut back on other things and concentrated on that? If I know you, you're probably working on it during your own time anyway."

"How do I cut back on other things?"

"We'll find a way," Bart said before taking a long drink from his beer. "Want another one?"

When Kelly nodded, Bart went inside to order.

"Looks like your wish came true," he announced when he returned. "NBC just declared Gore as the winner of Florida, which means he has enough electoral votes to take the presidency."

"All right! Now we have a reason to celebrate. Give me that beer."

"Kelly, I've wanted to tell you something all day. Best way is to just say it. My wife asked me for a divorce last night. She moved out of the house today. Seems she's met someone, and she's moving from me to him."

Kelly took another sip of her beer and didn't answer. Lately memories of Bart and her together haunted her. Now he was here in front of her, saying his marriage was over and soon he'd be free. She kept thinking about leaning over and kissing one of his oversized ears.

"How do you feel about that?" she asked.

"Not sad, just surprised. I've stood by her for so long, and then she just breezes in and tells me she's met someone else. Sure hope he's ready for what may be in store."

"Hasn't she been better lately?"

"That's happened before; I just wait for the other shoe to drop."

Bart reached over and covered her hand with his large one. He looked at her with eyes that reminded her of another time when they lay naked on top of the bedcovers trying to recover from a rather athletic session of love making.

"What is it, Kelly? Where did you go?"

She shook her head to clear away the images of a moment ago. "Nothing."

"I don't believe you." He brought his other hand to the table.

She loved his hands, so much bigger than her own. They swallowed hers as he caressed them slowly.

"Do you still love my hands like you used to? Remember what you told me about them?"

"Yes."

"You do remember."

She remembered more than she would ever let him know. Now sitting at Ellie May's she leaned toward him and began kissing his ear as she had longed to do moments before. He turned slightly so that their lips met in a kiss.

"We could get one of the cabins?" he asked keeping his lips close to hers.

She nodded her head. She did not want to speak. If she spoke now it might be to change her mind and that she did not want to do.

And so on an afternoon that began with a surveillance and ended in a cabin on the Hope Springs River, Bart and Kelly once again discovered that they had much more to give one another than a good story.

CHAPTER TWENTY-THREE

KELLY AND BART LEFT the cabin at Ellie May's around 5 a.m. They both wanted to go home and change into clean clothes before heading to the paper.

They didn't talk much on the hour drive back to Braidwood. They held hands while Bart drove. The surreal quality of driving at that hour became enhanced by the news being broadcast on the radio, leaving both of them stunned.

While they made love on the banks of the Hope Springs River, the election outcome took as many twists and turns as the couple had in the double bed of their cabin. Just before they left their beers, the networks decided the election's results were too close to call in Florida. After they had retreated to the cabin, Florida's victory to Gore was rescinded and given to Bush, who was then declared the winner of the presidency. Now in the dawn of November 8, it seemed no one knew who would be the next president of the United States.

"Unbelievable," Bart finally said. "I guess I better get right into the office and see what's happening with the vote in Zion County."

"Just drop me off at my car so I can go home and shower. I don't think anyone will need me right away."

"So what do we do now?" Bart asked as they drove through Calloway. "Do we start dating like a real couple?"

"Seems we're a little beyond that." Kelly squeezed his hand. "But it's a place to start, I suppose. I need to talk to Mike though."

When Kelly finally made it home, she decided to get a few hours sleep before getting ready for work. She slept soundly and pounded the snooze alarm several times. One time it didn't stop, and she realized that it was the ringing of her phone, not her alarm clock.

"Hello?"

"Kelly, aren't you coming to work today?" Carl asked. "You've been getting quite a few calls, and I wasn't sure what to tell them.

Besides that, it's chaos down here. The election has brought out all the wackos calling to tell us about voter fraud."

"What time is it?"

"Almost eleven."

"I am so sorry I overslept; I'll be right there. Is there anyone I should call right now?"

"Maybe Mike Green. He seemed a little agitated the three times he's called this morning. He said you weren't picking up at home either so you might have a few messages from him there. Have a late night?"

"In a way. I didn't sleep very well, I guess, and then when I did finally get to sleep that was it. I'll be in soon."

She sat up in bed and remembered how she had spent most of the night. Bart and Kelly moved slowly as if dancing to a love song. He undressed her first and admired her body before moving to the next step. Bart always made her feel attractive, not like the damaged goods that still haunted her on her worst nights. In fact, Bart was the only man who could block out that awful night almost eighteen years ago. With others it always came back to haunt her even in the context of lovemaking. Bart wiped everything else from her mind.

Kelly put on the coffee and then jumped into the shower. She thought about Mike calling her three times this morning already. She didn't want to see him anymore and had been putting off telling him. She wanted to make sure that her feelings about his past with his father weren't clouding her current feelings about him. No matter what kind of life he had before, he threatened to choke her with his calls and his constant presence in her life. She was lucky he hadn't tracked her down to Ellie May's last night. Now with Bart back in her life, she knew she had to break it off permanently in a kind and gentle way.

The shower worked its magic and revived her. She could face the day, even Mike Green and Bart Stanley. In the past, the worst part of Bart's and her relationship had been the next day at the office. He would look at her with his soft eyes, squinted and smiling just for her, and she would have to turn away; that look always lost her. She would usually blush and mumble some type of greeting and stay at her desk for the rest of the day or find some reason to leave for a story. He usually respected that and didn't come out into the newsroom unless he had to. It would take them a day or so before their easy friendship returned and the guilt abated.

When she came out of the bathroom, she noticed her answering machine blinking five times. She hoped that not all five were from Mike. That would be way over the top, and she had not even turned her cell phone on yet. They had no plans the night before and calling once and leaving a message should be sufficient for anyone.

"Mike, I'm leaving *The Tribune* to start a weekly out here in Calloway," Rick Bellows said on Wednesday morning, after he and Mike had settled into a table at the Wanderer, a breakfast joint in Calloway.

"In fact, see that empty store front across the street?" Rick gestured with his fork toward the front window.

"Where the travel agency used to be?"

"Right, but within a few short weeks, it will be *The Zion County News*."

"You think the area can handle three weeklies?" Mike asked.

"Yes, with the proper slant. We want to be a community-based paper that covers the whole county. Some serious reporting, but lots on the people who live here. You know, the Hope Springs Hidden Hero, the school's citizen of the week, that sort of thing. I don't think either of the other papers hits that market successfully."

"Does Greg Panzer know yet?"

"No, I haven't talked to the editors of the other papers. I gave my notice at *The Tribune* this week, and now I'm recruiting." He paused and looked at Mike who didn't have a clue why Rick Bellows had requested this early morning breakfast.

"Mike, I'd like to hire you as our head news writer. I've been watching you for the past few months and think you'd do a fine job covering hard-hitting news items. To begin, it would consist of following the commission meetings, the sort of thing you do now at *The Chronicle,* except with me, you could design your position. I know Greg has very specific ideas about how a newspaper should be run and that's fine, but I happen to believe in letting my writers set their pace and find the story instead of directing them to the stories."

"What about pay?" Mike asked.

"We'd give you substantially more than what you receive now, plus your health insurance."

"How could I refuse that offer? When do we start?"

"As soon as you can because I'd like you to interview the writers we hire, and I want to have a stable of them. The publisher from Miami has pretty much given us free rein on spending right at the beginning to get the best staff possible."

"okay, I can handle that."

"The writers you hire must have a solid background in journalism and be willing to take direction on the focus of articles. You, too, if needed. Most of the time, I will direct the paper's position through the editorial. It shouldn't affect you writers, but I need absolute loyalty to the company from everyone who comes on board. And in return, everyone receives fantastic benefits and the freedom to be as creative as possible."

"Sounds like I might not always be in charge of the writers and their stories, right?"

"You won't be the editor, just the head writer. Sometimes I might ask you to take a leadership role in assigning stories, but I'm going to have my hands in the mix quite a bit, but I think you'll see that it will be worth it. This is a great opportunity for you, Mike. Greg would never be able to do for you what I can do. Besides us boys from Dansville need to stick together."

"Who's the publisher?"

"Jason Landis from Miami. He wants to move up here, and he will eventually. Right now, he's entrusting all the major decisions with me. We've known each other for a few years. He and I decided it was time to do something together we could believe in."

Jason had not quite said yes to the proposal when Rick reached him the night before. He said he would have to discuss it with his wife. Rick wasn't worried because he could hear the lilt to his voice, and the questions he asked made it clear Rick had his attention. Jason promised to call him within a few days with an answer.

"You've been unhappy at *The Tribune*?"

"Let's just say it's been a battle. I haven't always agreed with the decisions of Bart Stanley or the publisher Doug Collings. I always lost the battles especially when your girlfriend was at the head of the line."

"Kelly? What do you mean?"

"Bart lets Kelly have her way pretty much on everything. I don't agree with what Kelly writes most of the time. Sorry, Mike, I know you like her, and she is a good reporter, but sometimes I think she goes overboard. She never would have gotten that bomb if she'd followed my advice."

"I've been telling Kelly for weeks she and Bart are too close. She tells me that whatever happened there was over years ago."

"I wouldn't be too sure of that, Mike. Not to hurt your feelings or anything, but it might be good for you to know that I've seen them together a few times outside of work lately. One of those times was last night. I was at a friend's house on the river, and I saw Bart and Kelly pull up in Bart's Jeep. They were parked under a tree for a long time, and then they drove off."

"Last night? No wonder I couldn't get that bitch on the phone. She's going to be sorry some day that she messed around with me."

"Then you don't think Kelly can talk you out of this?"

"Kelly has nothing to say about what I do or where I do it. She's just been dating me to cover up her affair with Stanley, but she's going to have to find someone else to do her bidding. When do I start?"

"That's the spirit, Mike," Rick said. "I'd like you with us today."

Mike stared off into the distance clenching his hands into fists. Rick was fairly certain Mike stopped listening to him.

CHAPTER TWENTY-FOUR

MIKE LEFT TWO MESSAGES on Kelly's cell phone after his breakfast meeting with Rick before Carl called from the office to wake her up. Mike wanted to tell Kelly about his job offer. But the more he thought about Bart and her out on a story together, he became incensed and obsessed with talking to her.

She finally called Mike after she arrived at *The Tribune* around noon. He managed to be civil as they made arrangements to meet for dinner that night. She said she needed to talk to him about something. He agreed.

When Bart walked by Kelly and Carl talking at their desks, he asked Kelly to come into his office. Bart went home around eight o'clock after spending a few hours checking on the election results in the county, and now he was back shaven and showered.

"Kelly, let's go over our notes from yesterday," Bart said as he walked by the two reporters.

"Sure thing, Boss." Kelly turned to Carl to finish their discussion of Rick's departure. The morning water cooler talk had been of nothing else.

"Good morning," Bart said when she came into the office notepad in hand. "How are you?"

"Since we were just together a few hours ago, you should know better than anyone how I am," Kelly whispered.

"I'm on top of the world I survey. Thanks for asking."

"What did you want to talk about, Bart?"

"I just wanted to see you alone. That's all. Any problem with that?"

"No. Anything else?"

"Yes, when can I see you again?"

"I've got a date with Mike for dinner tonight to tell him I can't see him anymore. I really can't think beyond that."

"Think there'll be a problem?"

"I don't know. He's been acting a little weird lately, obsessed. He left seven messages on my phones since last night, three of them this morning. Plus, Carl said he called here several times before I got in. We've never been serious enough to keep such close tabs on one another. Even if it hadn't happened with you last night, I would still be breaking it off. I've been independent for too long to let someone tell me what to do now. You just remember that, Mr. Stanley."

"Yes, m'am."

"What about what we saw last night at Lucy's? Any angle I should be pursuing?"

"I was thinking about that, too, believe it or not. Have you done any research on Tony?"

"No, he never seemed like a big player until last night. Now it's all starting to make some sense. He's been behind some pretty big stuff out in Millstone and Calloway. I think that maybe I've been underestimating his influence."

"I agree. Look him up – you know criminal records, land holdings, the sort of thing that you can search easily. Send one of the interns down to the courthouse this afternoon if you don't have time."

"I think they're all pretty busy helping Carl with the election coverage," Kelly said. "I guess everyone in Zion County who ever had a bad experience at the polls is now calling us with stories."

"Funny how all the weirdoes come leaping out of the closet with the weirdest of events. Remember what happened when Elian Gonzalez was being held? You would have thought that every Floridian had a connection to Cuba."

"I'll check to see if Carl needs me for anything, and if not, I'll probably go check out Tony Mayberry myself."

Carl assured her that he and the interns had it all under control. As she prepared to head over to the county building to search records, she tried to think of everything she knew about Tony Mayberry.

He had been in his own private practice until he created a part time job with Calloway when they hired him as a consultant. Prior to that, Calloway never needed an attorney. Then a few years ago when things started happening in Calloway with land zoning changes and new industrial-based businesses moving into the city, Tony managed to convince the city commissioners they needed a full time attorney. He came on with Millstone around the same time.

Now he spent his time justifying both cities' expense, as far as Kelly was concerned. He could take a simple question and turn the answer into a one-hour dissertation on land usage and government rights.

It became a joke around the office, but those jokes never hinted at improprieties. Not like the lawyer in Hope Springs, Bubba Sanders. Now there was someone to investigate.

She drank the last of her coffee as she finished jotting down some ideas for her search. Then she picked up her briefcase filled with notebooks, files, a tape recorder, and lots of pens. Kelly never went anywhere without the means to cover a story. She thought she should even start carrying a small camera, same as Molly. Of course, Molly had to take her own pictures, and Kelly didn't need to worry about that. But she sure could have used a little camera a few times in the past week. The pictures might be just for herself and not the paper, but at least she would be prepared.

Briefly, she thought about having dinner with Mike. What was she going to say to him? She knew after listening to his messages from last night and this morning that she couldn't see him anymore, but she didn't want to make him angry when she told him. Kelly had no problem putting words down on paper, but when it came to real live people and communicating with them, she sometimes lost her gift with words. Often times, she came across as gruff and insensitive when faced with confrontation. Others thought it meant she was just a mean bitch, but Kelly knew it was just her way of dealing with difficult situations. It had been her protective shell in the past.

As she gathered her purse and briefcase and found her car keys where she had tossed them on the desk, she heard Bart yelling in his office.

"Kelly, get in here."

"What?"

"Something on the police radio," he told her as she came into the office. "Shush."

After listening for a minute, Kelly told Bart she was on her way.

"Keep in touch," he told her.

Someone, a female suspect, was holding a man hostage at a residence in Calloway. Kelly jotted down the address she heard over the police scanner before grabbing her purse.

This time she remembered to find a photographer, her favorite freelancer who usually lounged around the city desks waiting for a call. Today turned out to be no exception. Lonny stood eating a donut with some writers, waiting for anything to happen.

"Something going on in Calloway," Kelly told him. "Want to come along?"

"Anytime with you, Kelly," Lonny said as he gathered up his camera bag.

As they drove down US 441, Kelly asked Lonny to call the police department in Calloway. She gave him the number, and he got the dispatcher on the line.

"Hey, Shawna, it's Kelly with *The Tribune*," Kelly said when Lonny handed her the phone. "Who can tell me what's going on out there?"

"They're all out, Kelly."

"Out? On the same call? Then what can you tell me?"

"Not much, you know that," Shawna said. "But I will tell you it's big. I hope you're on your way."

"You bet."

They found the house easily but could not get past the driveway. Police tape draped across the front prevented Kelly from even seeing the house, set back from the road with a large rolling lawn filled with live oak trees.

Kelly spotted a familiar face in the crowd and went over to gain access or at least information.

"Lieutenant, we've got to stop meeting like this," Kelly said as she walked up to John Carson, on duty once again.

"Kelly, can't seem to stay away from trouble can you?"

"It loves me, and I love it," Kelly said. "So, John, what's up here? I can't seem to get any information."

"You know Lester Simmons?"

"The Calloway Commissioner?"

"That's the one. His wife is holding him hostage at gun point inside the house.

CHAPTER TWENTY-FIVE

"HOSTAGE? WHAT'S SHE ASKING for, a longer driveway?" Kelly asked.

"We haven't heard from her yet," John said. "Lester managed to call on his cell phone before she flung that into the pool."

"How do you know she flung it into the pool?"

"We got guys on the back side who said they saw a woman throw a small object into the pool at the same time we lost the connection to Lester. We're waiting from word from the SWAT team right now before we proceed."

"They going to storm the house?"

"That's a strong possibility. The Calloway Police are arguing with our team. Chief Jefferson doesn't seem to think a woman with a handgun is much of a challenge, but some cooler heads are trying to prevail right now. It's a bad sign when the big boys start feeling cocky in this type of situation. Never underestimate anyone crazy enough to hold someone at gun point, woman or not."

"Has anyone talked to the wife?" Kelly asked. "By the way, what's her name?"

"Anne, and no, we haven't been able to talk to her, so we don't even have a motive. That's always a good thing to know in this type of situation."

At that moment, Molly Hale appeared next to Kelly. She had a camera case flung over one arm and her briefcase over another. Kelly laughed at her overloaded friend.

"What you laughing at?" Molly asked. "You think I don't know how stupid I look? But I don't work for a big fancy newspaper like you, Miss 'can I borrow a picture' Sands. I got to do it all myself."

Sometimes Kelly envied Molly. Working with a weekly could be frustrating and low budget, but Molly worked on such a variety of stories. She received a break quite often from the usual politics and murder when she covered stories at the schools, such as kindergartners dressed as mice.

"Like a photographer would help either of us today," Kelly told her as the two women hugged.

"I heard Commissioner Simmons is in there with his wife," Molly said. "Any truth to that rumor?"

"That's what this guy says." Kelly pointed to John Carson still standing at her side.

John was talking into his phone and didn't hear either of the women. When he hung up, he turned to them.

"It's over," he said. "She just shot him, and then turned the gun on herself just as the SWAT team approached the back of the house."

"Who's going to talk to us and give us the gory details?" Kelly asked.

"Chief Jefferson should be out any second," John said.

Gary Dregs joined them. He wasn't popular with Molly or Kelly or most people because of his aggressiveness in getting his story and his arrogant way of pushing himself into the middle of a crowd.

Kelly looked around and saw five people already there from Dreg's paper. One was his mother, always trailing behind him carrying a camera taking pictures of anyone and everything. They ran a whole lot of full-page color photos, too, with no stories. *The Monitor* had an editorial staff of ten, an unusual number for a rural weekly paper with such a low advertising to editorial ratio.

"What's happening here, John?" Gary asked.

"Did you happen to notice that we were in the middle of talking to the Lieutenant here?" Molly said.

"It is a free country, and I can talk to whomever I want."

"Yes, that's true, but you don't have the manners to go along with that freedom, do you?"

"Miss Hale, I run a good business in Millstone, and I treat everyone with respect. It's you that's out of line as usual."

"If you ran a real newspaper, and you don't, then perhaps I'd have more respect."

"Stop it, both of you. Two people just died up there, and we need to get the story," Kelly said.

Mike Green walked up to the group.

"Mike, good to see you," Gary said.

"Same here. What happened?"

Kelly filled him briefly on the little that she knew. He whistled softly and rocked back and forth on his feet.

"Quite a story. What time are we meeting for dinner?" Mike asked.

"I was going to call you because I don't think I can make it now. I'll have to go back to the office and write up the piece for tomorrow's paper. It could be another three or four hours before I get all the information and writing done. I'll need to do background research on the couple, too."

"And I guess Bart will be in the office when you go back there?" Mike asked.

"What does that have to do with anything? He doesn't determine what I write or look over my shoulder."

"No, but it makes it a little more convenient to have your lover right there by your side, doesn't it?"

She heard Gary snort at that comment.

"Mike, I was going to talk about this at dinner, but you're forcing the issue right here," she said as she pulled him away a little from the rest of the crowd that began to form around Lt. Carson.

"I think it's over between us," she said. "We're sort of paddling our feet in the sand instead of water and not going anywhere. That's what I wanted to tell you tonight at dinner."

"You want to stop seeing me?"

"You left seven messages on my phones last night and called work several times, Carl said, and now you're deliberately embarrassing me in public. That's a little over the top, don't you think, when we didn't even have a date last night?"

"I knew you were out with Bart, and I got a little crazy."

"You won't have to worry about that anymore. You never did really. I can't date someone who doesn't trust me or who wants to know my every move."

"Can't we just meet for coffee later? I have some good news to share."

"Tell me now."

"Rick Bellows offered me a job as head writer on the new paper he's starting up in Calloway," Mike said.

"You've got to be kidding!"

"Why? What's so surprising that someone would offer me a job?"

"Are you going to take it?" Kelly decided to ignore his question.

"I'd be crazy not to. He's doubling my salary and giving me an office and letting me run the show. I'll be in charge of all the writers."

"Sounds a little too good to be true. I'd look into ownership and publisher of this paper if it was me before I accepted."

"I'm sure you would, but I don't need to. I trust Rick."

"okay, it's your business, not mine. This is really for the best, Mike," Kelly said.

She walked away before he could respond as Chief Jefferson came from the front of the house to give a statement to the press.

Mike stood watching Kelly for a long time before he turned and walked back to his car.

CHAPTER TWENTY-SIX

KELLY DROVE BACK TO the office and began to research Lester Simmons and his wife Anne. She called other commissioners and met with a brick wall. She finally reached a clerk at city hall, who gave her some names of friends and a little background, although her responses were short and sketchy.

Lester, not surprisingly, was born and raised in Calloway. It was tough getting elected to that Commission otherwise. He served for twenty years and faced reelection in March. Luddy Gregors had begun making noises about running against him, but one of his friends told Kelly that Lester had not been worried.

Getting information on Anne proved to be more difficult. As usual when a tragedy of this magnitude occurred, everyone said they were surprised. There had been no indication of trouble.

Lester and Anne had two grown children who were not at home at the time of the shooting. Anne didn't work, and Kelly couldn't find out about any activities in which she might have been involved. She belonged to the First Methodist Church, but Kelly couldn't find out if she served on any committees or belonged to any group within in the church community. She went to church regularly without Lester.

Kelly finally reached the wife of one of the friends of Lester who seemed eager to talk. She gave Kelly a few leads.

"Anne was different from the rest of us wives," she told Kelly over the phone. "She didn't come with Lester when we had parties, and they never threw any themselves even though they lived in that great big house."

"How did Lester get his money?" Kelly asked her willing interviewee.

"Inherited most of it from Anne's daddy. Lester ran Anderson Dairy after the father's death. The house was given to them on their wedding day. Biggest wedding present any of us had ever seen. They had the reception there. Last time most of us had ever been in that house."

"How else was Anne different?"

"I never talked to the woman. When I would see her in the grocery store, she would smile sometimes, but mostly she ignored us. Everyone knows that; we all thought she was a snob."

"Did Lester cheat on her?"

"Are you kidding? From the day they were married. I don't want to say too much, but he had a steady lover. That's common knowledge around here. Most of the other men did what Lester did. I guess it makes it easier that way."

"What do you mean 'did what Lester did'?"

"Some of the other men have long-term mistresses."

"Isn't that a little weird in this day and age? How do you feel about the other women?"

"As long as I know my husband doesn't have one, I don't care. I keep him happy, and he always invites me to those parties. For one thing, he knows I'll keep my mouth shut, and another, I never refuse any of his requests. A lot of these wives think once they've reeled in the big fish, they're off the hook for the sex. I never saw it that way."

"What about the children?"

Her informant went on to tell her that Lester and Anne's children, Sara and Les, had been model students and athletes. Lester participated in all their activities, but Anne was an absent mother.

"Who else might be able to give me some information? There must be someone who was close to Anne."

"Not really, except maybe Rev. Baxter at the Methodist Church. I think she might have talked to him sometimes. I know I would see her car at the church during the middle of the day when nothing else was going on."

Kelly called the Reverend with little hope he would talk to her. She was wrong, but he wouldn't do a telephone interview.

"You can come out here," he said.

Kelly took a quick look at the clock and saw that it was already past eight. She could be back by ten o'clock and fill in the pieces of the article, if he gave her any information. Bart was still in the office filtering information on the shooting. Everyone else had gone home for the day burned out after a one of the strangest news days in Florida's history. So far, no clear winner had been declared for the presidency.

"Bart, I'm having some difficulty getting info on Anne Simmons, but her minister just told me I could come out there for an interview. Think we should try for tomorrow's paper?"

"How's the rest of the piece?"

"It could go like it is, but it doesn't give much information. Mainly because I can't get much but the basics."

"Go do the interview. I'll tell them to hold the piece. Call as soon as you know something."

Bart looked tired, Kelly thought, as she ran for her purse. Rick had been focused on the election stories when he arrived at work mid-morning, so Bart took care of the other business when the Simmons' incident occurred. With a hot story like the Simmons' shooting, the editor's job became a nightmare. First people called the paper constantly with "news" on the incident. All the calls had to be screened to determine legitimacy and that usually fell to the editor's discretion. The majority of the calls were just from lonely folks who wanted to be interviewed but had little information to provide, and added to the already inundated switchboard on voting problems, the newsroom became the filter for gossip central. Kelly wondered what would happen when Rick left in less than two weeks if things didn't start settling down.

"Miss Sands, come in," Rev. Baxter said when she entered his office at the side of the sanctuary.

"Thank you for seeing me, sir, on such short notice," Kelly said. He motioned her to a comfortable chair while he took a seat on the sofa.

"I know the press will have the tendency to blame Anne for what happened," Rev. Baxter began.

"Witnesses say she held the gun, pulled the trigger, and killed Lester, then she killed herself. It'll be hard to do much of anything else."

"But there's so much more, so much more." He shook his head as he spoke.

"Can you tell me? Maybe I can help others understand this tragedy. No one else seems to know much of anything about Anne Simmons."

"Anne was a quiet woman, but it didn't mean that she didn't feel things. And she knew more than anyone ever gave her credit for."

"What do you mean? She knew more about what?"

"She knew the skeletons." He dropped his voice. "Starting with her daddy."

"Of Anderson Dairy?"

"Carson Anderson, it began with him. He was a mean bastard, if you'll pardon the expression."

He began an old familiar tale of a rich man who wielded power over everyone, particularly at home. It was well known in the community that Carson Anderson beat his wife and abused his children. Anne took the brunt of the abuse by the time she was sixteen when she discovered she was pregnant.

"She came to me then, a frightened child, nearly five months pregnant with nowhere to turn," he said. "She didn't want to tell her mother because Anne was certain Mrs. Anderson would not believe her. From the time she was a young child, Anne was involved in the church. One day, she came to me and confided everything."

CHAPTER TWENTY-SEVEN

REV. BAXTER AND HIS wife helped Anne find a special place where she remained confined until the baby was born. Then she gave the baby up for adoption.

Anne came home to find out her father had arranged for her marriage to Simmons.

"Did her parents know about the child?" Kelly asked.

"I went to them one night soon after Anne confessed to me. At first, Carson tried to argue and deny, and I told him in no uncertain terms that it wouldn't work. He became quiet and listened to the plans we made for his daughter. I never threatened a man before that night, and I pray to my God I never again have to resort to the kind of talk I did that night."

Anne and Lester married soon after her return to Calloway, but there was little love there as far as Rev. Baxter could tell. Lester didn't want to marry Anne Anderson, who never smiled and barely spoke to him. He thought she was a snob even though his family was nearly as prominent in town, having owned a chain of grocery stores throughout the north Florida region. However, his father insisted that a marriage of two dynasties would be dynamite, and Lester had no choice but to comply.

He refused to do one thing. He would not stop seeing the one love of his life. How he got Anne to agree to the arrangement the good reverend did not know, but he knew the relationship continued even to the day of Lester's death. Anne knew, too. She continued to confide in her minister.

Even if Anne had wanted to love her husband just a little bit, he never gave her the chance. Although he didn't beat her, he did something almost as bad. He ignored her and flaunted his relationship with the very married woman who remained his lover for more than twenty years. Lester would even bring her into the house in front of Anne who endured because she didn't know what else to do.

"Who was the woman?"

"Betty Duncan."

"Betty Duncan? Married to Alex Duncan of Duncan and Duncan law firm? Betty Duncan, the city manager for the city of Calloway?"

"That's her. She and Lester had been an item since they were both fifteen, and they never stopped. Everyone speculated that's how she got her job with the city. You've never heard this before?" Rev. Baxter asked.

"Not until tonight. One of the Simmons' friends told me Lester had a long-term mistress."

"It's the truth. I'm surprised you got that much information. They usually cover up everything. They do that for one another, you know."

"What about Alex Duncan? He stood for it?"

"Now we're getting into some territory that leaves me a little troubled. I'm not comfortable discussing Alex with you, but let's say that he had his reasons for allowing his wife to do whatever she wanted."

"Is he gay?"

The reverend refused to answer anymore of Kelly's questions, telling her that he had done what he wanted. He wanted Anne's situation made clear. Not that Kelly could print any of what she had just heard. It was hearsay at this point.

"Was Anne ever hospitalized for those beatings by her father?"

"Not that I know of," Rev. Baxter said. "Why?"

"What you've given me is a start, but I need more proof before I can print anything about this side of Anne. I believe you, but my editor will need more before he will allow us to run the story."

"Let me think. I'll ask my wife; maybe she'll remember something. Can I call you tomorrow?"

"That would be fine," Kelly said before thanking him and heading back to Braidwood.

She called the city desk from the car and asked for Bart.

"Run the story as is," she said when he came on the line.

"Dead end?"

"Not really, but nothing I can corroborate at this late date. But to paraphrase a great heroine, tomorrow is another day."

"okay, Scarlet. Go home and get some sleep. I'll talk to you tomorrow. And I really do give a damn."

With Commissioner Simmons dead, either Calloway would have to hold an election, since it was still over four months until the next regular election, or Governor Jeb Bush would have to appoint an interim commissioner. Despite the mess in which Bush now found himself with the Florida election, the other four commissioners decided at an emergency meeting early Thursday morning to have the governor make the decision. After all, a Republican conservative governor would be sure to appoint someone of a similar ilk, which the majority of the current commission approved. Chelsea Godfrey and Richard Nichols voted against the motion asking the governor for an appointment, forcing the Mayor to break the tie. He voted with Stewart and Waine to ask for an appointment from Tallahassee.

Rumblings in the community indicated that one of the leaders of a new group, the Smart Growth for Calloway or SGC as most referred to them, planned on running in the March election according to the reports Kelly had heard.

After attending the special meeting in Callaway, Kelly returned to work where a message from Molly Hale awaited her.

"Wait till you hear the latest," Molly blasted in Kelly's ear as soon as she got her on the phone.

"I don't think I can take much more excitement, Molly."

"Luddy Gregors is going to run for the Calloway City Commission."

"For sure?"

"For sure. She's put her papers in at city hall even though the qualifying period doesn't begin until February. Once she heard the Commission voted to send the issue to Jeb, she filed the papers. It's calculated to persuade the governor in his appointment."

"Never happen," Kelly said. "He would never appoint a black woman with a big mouth."

"Maybe not, but she's going to try for it. I hear some county commissioners are even going to call old Jeb himself this week to suggest it," Molly said. "What are you hearing about the Simmons murder/suicide?"

"Not much." Kelly hesitated. "What do you know about Carson Anderson?"

"Anne Simmons' father? Owner of the biggest dumper of fertilizer in north Florida. Rich. Bastard. Dead."

"Ever know much about his personal life? Ever hear anything?"

"No. Why? You got something?"

"Maybe. I heard he might have knocked his wife around some, maybe Anne, too. Ever hear anything like that?"

"I've mostly heard about his business dealings. Always on the shady side, you know the type. Must be something in the water out here. Then Lester Simmons inherited everything, as if he needed it. Lester sold off some of the land to developers. You know that monstrous warehouse out on County Road 380? That was a part of the Simmons/Anderson dynasty at one time."

"What are you hearing about Anne herself? Did you know her?"

"Rumor has it she kept to herself," Molly said. "And you know I don't run in those circles. You got something, don't' you?"

"Maybe. Let me work on it some. Nothing I can print yet until I find some corroboration."

"I know you've got more people than me to research this stuff so let me give you a direction. Talk to Betty Duncan. She knows more than anyone about Lester Simmons and what kind of man he is."

"Betty Duncan? At city hall?"

Kelly decided it might be better to play dumb, although she felt guilty keeping things from her friend. She also knew Molly would understand. Kelly would tell her eventually.

"That's the one. The rumors have floated around about the Simmons and the Duncans for years. Never heard it?"

"Tell me."

"Betty and Alex Duncan, a well-connected marriage. Betty's daddy, B. J. Winters, is a real estate magnate and president of Industrial Pines, and Alex's father was his lawyer. A marriage made in heaven except that Betty and Lester fell in love in high school. The fathers all around felt that it would be better to get Alex married as soon as possible."

"Why?"

"Let's just say that when the guys patted each other's behinds in football, Alex liked to keep his hands on the rear ends a little too long."

"And daddy didn't like the fact that his son liked boys?"

"That's grounds for eating your young around here. Haven't you learned anything yet? If they shoot bulls that like each other just a little too much, what do you think they do to the sons of the elite? They sure don't throw them a parade."

"Alex and Betty married for appearances. And she loved Lester Simmons?" Kelly asked.

"That's the way the story goes. All sorts of rumors float around about those two getting caught with their panties down and skirts up more than once around city hall. Why do you think Betty makes $65,000 a year with just a high school diploma and no prior work experience? It's not for her shorthand, I assure you."

CHAPTER TWENTY-EIGHT

LUDDY GREGORS DID NOT get the appointment from Governor Bush to sit on the commission until the regular election in March – just as Kelly suspected. The day after the commission made their decision – just two days after Lester died – the governor made his decision despite the controversy swirling around Tallahassee and his Secretary of State, Katherine Harris. Perhaps a call from B.J. Winters and Anthony Marcetti, gave Jeb Bush an easy out. Most likely, he took their suggestion because after all they knew the area best, and B.J. especially knew the nominee very well, and it was not Luddy.

Someone even more surprising received the nod to serve out Lester Simmons' term. Maybe considering who made the recommendation, not so surprising after all. Lester's lover for twenty years and B.J. Winters' daughter, Betty Duncan, became the newest commissioner for Calloway in one swift announcement from the big white house in the Panhandle.

Betty was sworn in the following Tuesday, the day before the funerals. It was also the same day Bush supporter and Florida Secretary of State, Katherine Harris, certified the election, declaring Bush the winner in Florida, which began the whole long process of court rulings, which continued to block the outright declaration of George W. Bush as forty-third President of the United States.

In Calloway, all of that seemed quite remote, and in one of the only places in Florida and perhaps even the nation, the talk over haircuts and coffee did not concern itself with dimpled ballots and hanging chads in Palm Beach County.

Betty Duncan's appointment to the city commission took precedence over all the overvote and undervote talk everywhere else. Even though Betty wore black at her swearing-in ceremony on

November 14, the cut of her suit did not give the impression of mourning.

Her skirt, a good six inches above the knee, with a slit in the back at least three inches, allowed her no room for crossing her legs, but once she was up on the dais with its desk-like front, prying eyes could only imagine the view when she crossed her legs. But they could see the cleavage. The blouse, of course black, cut low and wide across the top of her breasts, allowed no doubt that this commissioner was all woman.

The meeting in which she was appointed took only a short time to conduct. The trouble came when the public wanted their chance to voice an opinion.

"There's no need for public input," said Mayor Tim Murray. "The Governor of Florida has made his decision and that is it." He pounded the gavel to bring the room back to order.

"This is not a dictatorship," yelled Cowan Garcia from the audience. "The Republicans are already stealing one election in this state; we can't allow it to happen here."

"Have him thrown out," the mayor yelled to Chief Jefferson sitting at the back of the room.

"Mayor, you are out of order here," Chelsea said. "The public has a right to be heard."

Her words met with deaf ears on the dais as the chief once again came to the front of the meeting room to escort Cowan out of the chambers.

Molly followed them out the door, shooting pictures with her little camera. Kelly stayed put. Mike sat two rows directly behind her, but they hadn't spoken since he came into the Commission chambers. She wanted to avoid him, but most of all she wanted a chance to interview Betty Duncan.

When the meeting ended at the drop of the gavel, Kelly headed straight for Betty, who stood gathering her papers on the dais.

"Commissioner Duncan. Kelly Sands, *The Braidwood Tribune*."

Even though Kelly had met her many times in the past, Betty always acted as if she did not recognize the reporter from Braidwood. The two women shook hands.

"I was hoping I could talk to you for a few minutes about the appointment to the commission," Kelly said.

"Well." Betty looked around the room as if trying to find an escape route.

"It would just take a minute or two of your time, I promise."

"It's just that I promised that nice young man from the Millstone paper I would meet with him afterwards, but I don't see him."

Kelly could see Gary Dregs outside the chamber room arguing with members of SGC. She wasn't sure what was happening, but she saw Molly outside listening and knew she would find out soon enough.

"It looks like Gary is tied up at the moment. By the time he's finished, we probably would be, too," Kelly said.

"I guess it wouldn't hurt," Betty said in a soft, halting voice. "But I'm only going to talk about the commission appointment."

"That's fair, but Lester Simmons' name might come up; it's him you're replacing after all."

Betty's eyes filled with tears at the mention of Simmons' name; just the reaction Kelly wanted.

"You were friends with the late commissioner?" Kelly asked.

"Yes, I'd known Lester all his life. And, well, Anne, too, of course."

"Did you and your husband socialize with the Simmons?"

"Not really, Anne was very quiet. She didn't like to go out. But Lester, that's a different story." She sighed and looked away. Kelly followed her gaze and saw that she was looking at the wall of pictures of the commissioners. Lester's photo hung at the end of a long row of photographs of elected officials of Calloway.

"He was very handsome, wasn't he?" Kelly asked.

"Yes. I mean, we'll will miss him very much."

"Did you request this appointment?"

"Absolutely not. It's just that my daddy has known Governor Bush for a number of years," Betty said. "So when he had to appoint someone in Calloway, he naturally called my dad."

"And your father put in a good word?"

"I guess. I know Daddy said that I knew quite a bit about the workings of city government from my years of working here and would be qualified to make informed decisions for the good of the city."

"Will you run for election in March?"

"That depends on a number of factors."

"What are those, Commissioner Duncan?"

The newest Calloway Commissioner looked at Kelly with a frown between her brows and then a smile almost formed in a perfect imitation of the Mona Lisa. Kelly was certain she was the first to call her "Commissioner." The look, smug and content, told Kelly that this appointment wasn't something she shirked.

"The political climate in Calloway, well in the whole county right now, is pretty divisive. Lots of folks don't want us to grow and want us to remain the small two-lane town we've always been."

"You don't want to remain the same?"

"Oh, my no! I grew up here, and it is the most boring place for children to live. We had to make our own fun. Some of it good; some of it not. No wonder we can't keep our young here. Folks keep moving here with children, so we've got to find a way to keep them here. Jobs that pay a decent wage will be the key."

"That's how you and some of your friends managed to stay here, right?"

"My husband, Alex, had a business to go into – his father's law firm. And Les …" Her eyes filled with tears with either memory or just the simple mention of his name.

"You and Commissioner Simmons were very close, weren't you?" Betty looked at Kelly and nodded. "This is off the record, Betty. You look like you could use a friend."

"Thank you. Lester and I grew up together. We would have been married right after high school, if our parents hadn't intervened. Our daddies didn't think it would be the right mix for the two families. So he married Anne, and I married Alex."

"That must have been tough."

"Did you know that Les and I were homecoming king and queen in our senior year? We were voted mostly likely to get married and have ten kids. I guess it was around that time that our parents intervened. They saw we were serious."

"Did you know Anne Simmons very well?"

"I knew her well enough to know that she was the wrong wife for Les." At this point, Betty's voice changed, and the tears disappeared. "She never supported him or treated him like he deserved. I hated that woman."

"You're the first person who seems to have any passion about her one way or another. Everyone seems pretty passive about Anne, saying they didn't know much about her."

"I knew her all right. I really need to go now, Ms. Sands.

"Please, call me Kelly. I'm sorry for your loss. I know it must be a difficult time for you, and now you've just taken on a big responsibility. Maybe we could have lunch one day and just talk."

"Thank you. I must go."

As quickly as she had become engaged in her sorrow, she had disengaged herself from the conversation with Kelly. Good qualities for a politician, Kelly thought as she drove back to the office.

CHAPTER TWENTY-NINE

ON THE DRIVE BACK to Braidwood, Kelly sifted through what she learned about this very strange triangle in Calloway politics. Were the people in this town still living in the eighteenth century, when women had so little say in their lives that they could be carted from home to husband as chattel? It seemed that both Anne and Betty had been victims. So had the men. If Lester really loved Betty, he spent more than twenty years in a loveless marriage sneaking around to be with the woman who stole his heart as a youth.

And Alex Duncan — what about him? He must be a real case. Kelly wondered if he had ever been able to be with a man or had his father castigated him like a steer? What she remembered about Alex made her think he was probably just used as a figurehead with no purpose except to look good and marry well.

When she returned to *The Tribune*, she found Bart at his computer writing, an unusual sight. Bart loved reporting, and Kelly knew that in his darkest moments, he wished that he could get back to those purer days when he just wrote about the scum on the street.

"Bart, can I interrupt?" Kelly knocked lightly on the door.

"Sure. I'm just writing tomorrow's editorial. And I think I'll do a column, maybe even make it a weekly thing."

"Think you'll have time with Rick's departure?"

"Don't know, but I do know I feel better when I'm doing this." He waved his hand toward the computer screen. He turned to give her his full attention. "So how's life in the pristine Calloway. Murder? Mayhem?"

"I think a better name might be Peyton Place. I've learned some interesting things in the last day. I think it might be something pretty big."

"By the way, how did it go with the good Rev. Baxter? We never did get a chance to talk about it."

"He seems to believe that Carson Anderson did more than just love his daughter Anne in a traditional way. He said he helped Anne with a difficult pregnancy when she was a teenager. He and his wife found a place for her to go away from Calloway. She put the baby up for adoption. He threatened Papa Anderson, who Baxter claims was the father, and then Anne suddenly married Lester Simmons when she returned to Calloway six months later. I think the marriage had probably been in the works for some time because it just happened to join two major dynasties together in one neat little package."

"No matter that the package was a little damaged. Anne probably never recovered or saw a counselor except Baxter. And Lester loved another woman," Kelly concluded.

"You trust this Baxter fellow?" Bart asked.

"My sense is he is a good man, but he wouldn't understand how ruined Anne had been by carrying her father's child. But he talked to her probably more than anyone else."

"Why did he confess all of this to you?"

"He wants to be sure people understand Anne was a decent woman and not a lunatic and murderer. I told him I couldn't print any of this without further proof. He said he could appreciate that."

"Who's the other woman?"

"Betty Duncan, or should I say Commissioner Duncan."

"No kidding," Bart whistled. "Betty Duncan: married to Alex Duncan whose father owns the largest law firm in that area."

Bart rattled off the information as if he was going through a Rolodex in his mind. All good newspapermen did that. They kept it stored up there for recall at any time. All they needed to get started was just a few facts, enough to find more information.

"Seems Alex Duncan likes the boys, so Daddy wanted to squelch that and had him marry the most logical choice, his biggest client's pretty daughter."

"So, how does this fit in with your story? So far you've got some pretty good stuff for the *National Enquirer*, but what can we use?"

"Nothing yet, that's why I need permission to keep digging," Kelly said. "I've got a hunch about a few things."

"Want to share the hunches?" Bart asked.

"Only with you. According to the good reverend, it is quite possible that Anne was physically as well as sexually abused; I'd like to search hospital records, insurance claims for the period of her life say from twelve to when Rev. Baxter said she became pregnant. That's one."

"Good, we could probably do a profile on the poor little rich girl theme if we had proof. What about finding the home where she gave birth? Search out those records. That child would be over twenty now, right?"

"Closer to twenty-five. But that's only one angle. My gut's telling me something is not right with Betty Duncan. And I don't mean just because her lover died. I think she knows more about what happened that night, maybe was even there."

"What did she say?"

"Nothing really; it's more a lack of answers, stopping the questioning at certain times – a look on her face or sometimes the lack any particular emotion at appropriate times. Then she became when angry when she talked about Lester and Anne's marriage. She blamed Anne for not making Lester happy."

"The good old Sands People Meter Reader. You ought to market it."

"But you've got to admit, it's accurate most of the time, Boss. Even you have come to respect it."

"But I wouldn't run a story on it."

"Maybe some day when I start batting a hundred you will. Police departments and newspapers from around the world will come with partial stories and photographs and ask me to give an opinion. You'll need to give me my own office then."

"You'll get your own office all right. See that door marked 'Ladies?' That's a start."

Kelly slapped Bart with her reporter's notebook before she left to begin her research. First, she asked Carl if she could borrow an intern. There was not much to report on the election front as ballots were recounted or not in south Florida. Zion County had a clean record from Election Day as far as anyone could tell. Most of the stories now came from the Associated Press. Carl gave her the names of a couple of interns who could help her. She put each of them on some part of the Sunshine Law violation and the annexation of the airport and movie studio property. They could do some of that work while she concentrated on the Simmons' case.

Bart called her back into the office before she could head off to the hospital.

"Kelly, you know Thanksgiving is next week?"

"I vaguely remember. This new story put it out of my mind. Why?"

"Are you scheduled to work?"

"No. Carl and I switch the holidays; he works Thanksgiving so he can be home with his kids at Christmas. Now with the Simmons' case, I'm not sure I'll be going to Palm Beach. What are you doing?"

"I'm going to be alone. The kids have other plans and of course, Joyce will be with her new man."

"How does that make you feel?

"Just a little weird, but not bad. I guess it's what I wanted all these years."

"So we'll both be alone," Kelly said.

"We don't have to be," Bart said. "I was wondering if you would consider going to my little cabin with me for the weekend. You could bring work, and there's a phone line for your laptop. Maybe we could still find time to canoe or hike or sit in front of a fire and talk."

Bart smiled that partial smile from behind half-closed eyes, and then he tilted his head to one side, like a little boy who knew he would eventually get his own way. No woman ever calculated her flirtatious movements more carefully than this man, and Kelly could not refuse him.

"Come on," he continued when Kelly hesitated, "I'd just like to spend time with a friend."

"You mean to tell me you expect that we won't fall into bed together once we're alone in those woods? You haven't been paying attention, friend."

"I meant it's not the only reason. That should tell you something right there. Why can't we stay away from one another?"

"When did you want to leave?"

"Wednesday night? I'll bring the turkey."

Kelly knew they should probably move a little slower, but sometimes heart and head get in the way of one another, and then Bart's smile did not help keep her head clear.

CHAPTER THIRTY

BEFORE SHE HEADED TO the hospital to search medical records, she decided to visit Rev. Baxter again.

This time he insisted Kelly call him Alan, so she obliged.

"Alan, I'm trying to investigate some things, but it's pretty tough with what you gave me," Kelly said. "Can I ask you some specific questions? You can always refuse to answer."

"I guess that would be all right," Alan said. "What kinds of things do you need?"

"I need some specific dates and maybe names of places so I can investigate public records. I need to establish a pattern of abuse by Mr. Anderson. Do you happen to remember if anyone in his family was hospitalized as a result of his behavior?"

"Let me think. It seems that his wife ended up in the hospital one time, maybe twice. I remember her with a broken arm once. Another time she wore a collar brace for a while. They always gave excuses, but you know how people talk."

"I'm glad you remember these things. It will help, but do you remember approximately when these things occurred? Even a year would help."

"I would say in the early seventies people started talking about it," he said. "I came here in 1971 and remember hearing rumors almost immediately. That's one of the reasons I took a special interest in Anne because she was around thirteen, fourteen, vulnerable and shy."

"What hospital do you think Mrs. Anderson would have gone to?"

"At that time there was only University Hospital."

"That's a big help. Now what about Anne? Do you remember the year she became pregnant?

"1975, because she came to me right after we found out we were expecting our first child."

"Where did she go to have the baby?"

"A place in Port St. Lucie, a very nice, secluded home for girls. They only took a few at a time and made them comfortable. We visited her often during those final months."

"Do you have the name?" Kelly asked although she already knew the answer.

"Oak Haven. I'm not sure if they're still in existence, but that's the place."

Kelly managed to thank Rev. Baxter and get into her car without falling apart. She drove to a nearby parking lot and covered her hands with her face. Her past sat right there in the present as Kelly attempted composure.

Kelly thought about the coincidence of both of Anne and her, young girls bewildered by how they had become pregnant in the first place, placed in the same home eight years apart. Now they were in the same place again, except Anne was dead and Kelly was trying to write a story to save her reputation posthumously.

Both of them had been nurtured by the women who ran Oak Haven and trusted their babies to their guidance and safe placement. Two women, Linda Marsh and Tonja Larson – who knew when abortion became legal that not everyone would be able to go that route – opened a rest home of sorts for pregnant women of any age who couldn't raise a child themselves. Catholic Charities helped support them and helped with placement of the babies. They only took in six women at a time because it was just a three-bedroom home. While Kelly stayed there in her final months, the assortment of six women ran the gamut, but they all had one thing in common. They had become pregnant under trying circumstances and most of them would not be able to raise a child alone. A few did leave with their babies, prepared by Tonja and Linda to face the challenges of single parenthood and assured by the women they would always have a safe haven for help if ever needed.

The owners of Oak Haven worked hard to find good families. A local attorney set up legal adoptions after a screening process. Kelly even met the couple who adopted Joely once, just a week before she gave birth. They already had an eight year old and a four year old, a girl and a boy. They wanted a third child to complete their family. The other two children also were adopted.

Kelly met the children and the couple, although she never knew their names. But she knew Joely would be welcomed into the family circle they had created. She knew they would make room for her child as well and take care of all of them. Joely would have a brother and a sister, and because she would be the youngest, she would hold a special place in the family dynamics. And she might even get spoiled a little in the process.

Kelly never felt guilty about her decision. However, nothing ever took away the deep gap – the hole left in her heart when Joely left her arms. They did let her hold her baby for a few minutes before Joely was taken away and given to her new family. Sometimes Kelly wondered if it helped in her healing process or not. One thing she knew for certain – her arms ached whenever she saw a newborn, but she always refused to hold it. She did not want to feel that loss ever again.

"Bart, I need to go to Port St. Lucie for two days," Kelly said as soon as she came into work on Thursday, one week before Thanksgiving.

"What's up?"

"I found the place where Anne Simmons had the child. I'd like to go and talk personally to the women who run the home."

"A phone call won't do it?"

"Not this time. I thought I'd leave as soon as I finish the follow up to the murder/suicide."

"Do I have a choice?"

"No, I guess not. Even without the expense account, I'd go," she said. "I've also got some rough estimates on dates that Anne's mother might have been hospitalized back in the early seventies. okay to put an intern on it?"

"Go ahead. They might want to consider different names to check. Get a maiden name for Mrs. Anderson. You know the routine."

"Sure thing, Boss," Kelly said as she gave him a mock salute. "We still on for next weekend?"

Bart looked at her with raised eyebrows. "That all depends on you."

"I think it might be a good idea. After my trip to Port St. Lucie, I might have some things I need to tell you."

Kelly hadn't thought through what she just told Bart. It came to her quickly, but she realized that perhaps a weekend alone with him would be just what she needed so she could finally tell someone about Joely.

She was not being quite honest with Bart right now either. She wanted to go in person to Oak Haven to see once again the two women who had saved her life. A quick phone call to the receptionist confirmed they still ran the place and provided the same service as they did seventeen years ago and twenty-five years ago when Anne Simmons had come to them as a frightened child pregnant with her father's child.

Kelly planned on finding out what she could about her own child, too. She doubted that the owners, Linda and Tonja, would give her much information on either account, but she hoped that maybe they could give her some peace of mind.

Kelly decided to stop fighting Bart. She might be a fool, but she knew that man, and he never lied to her. She knew he loved her. His fault lay in his inability to hurt anyone, including a wife he ceased loving many years ago, but to whom he felt an extreme sense of responsibility.

Next weekend, they would talk. Kelly smiled to think about where they might do the talking because she knew where they would spend most of the weekend.

When Kelly returned to her desk, she saw a message from Cowan Garcia. Before she started working on her article, she gave him a call.

"I wanted to let you know I got another present – actually, two this time," Cowan said after Kelly reached him by phone.

"They left two gopher shells?"

"Not only did they, but they got artistic this time," he said. "They have names spray painted on the back of the shells. Want to guess whose?"

"Let's see: Lucy and Ricky?"

"Close – Karen and Cowan."

"They're getting clever. You doing the grave thing again?"

"I'm thinking that perhaps these should be displayed next to the graves."

"Let me know when you're ready, and I'll send out Lonny. I'm working on some other stuff right now and have to go out of town for a few days, so I'm going to assign an intern to do more of an in-depth story on you and the graves."

CHAPTER THIRTY-ONE

KELLY PACKED AN OVERNIGHT bag and brought it to work with her, even before asking Bart about going to Port St. Lucie. She knew Bart could not refuse her, and she wanted to be there early in the morning, so she decided to leave as soon as she wrote her assignments.

The four-hour drive to Port St. Lucie down the Florida Turnpike allowed Kelly plenty of time to formulate the questions she needed to ask. She knew certain areas would be off limits, but Kelly had mastered the art of asking around questions to get to the center of her answer. She parlayed with her interviewees like a cat circling a mouse. She saw it as a form of foreplay before the main event.

The next morning she found the place with little difficulty. She remembered the location of Oak Haven as if it had been yesterday. In the year after Joely was born, she visited several times, taking the other girls treats. Linda finally said that she thought Kelly's healing would happen faster if she stopped the visits. She told her in a kind way, but Kelly got the message and had not been back since.

Now she drove down the long curved drive to the home set back into the grove of oak trees hanging low with Spanish moss. The November day in Florida was balmy and sunny, a travel brochure kind of day to lure northerners down for the holidays.

She parked in one of the few slots in front of the house. A girl, maybe seven months pregnant, sat on the front porch swing. She stared off into space not seeing Kelly come up the walk to the porch.

"Hi, there," Kelly announced as she came up the steps.

The girl looked at her with dull eyes and gave a small smile that did nothing to brighten the deadness Kelly saw and understood in the visage of the mother-to-be. It could have been Kelly when she first arrived. If the place still held the same warmth and love that Kelly knew, this young girl would begin to heal and to trust the world just a little bit once again.

"Do you know where I could find either Linda or Tonja?" Kelly asked.

The girl lifted a skinny arm and pointed toward the house. Then she went back to her vigil with space.

Kelly walked into the dimly lit entryway of the house. A long hallway led to the other rooms of the downstairs. Kelly peeked around the corner of the front room, which she remembered had been the office.

Linda sat at the desk, and Kelly was swept back seventeen years. Nothing had changed – the furniture, comfortable but old, looked exactly as she remembered it. She had been in the room in tears and in smiles. Sitting in one of the lumpy old couches brought her closer to healing her wounds.

Linda also looked unchanged. Her big glasses and short-cropped reddish-brown hair gave her the impression of efficiency. And as a nurse she was efficient. She could be gruff at times, but that rough exterior was easily fractured and the soft side of Linda was revealed. She barked and growled, especially at her partner Tonja, but when one of the girls needed her, the demeanor changed, and she became everyone's mother.

She looked up from her work and stared at Kelly.

"Linda, do you remember me?" Kelly asked.

"Kelly? Kelly Sands?"

"You remember."

"I always remember the smart ones, and the ones who have trouble letting go," Linda said as she left her chair and came to embrace Kelly. "I remember you were both."

"It is so good to see you. I wasn't sure how I'd feel coming back, but it's like walking back into a safe haven."

"What are you doing here? Where are you now?"

Kelly gave a short laugh. Linda always shot questions fast and furiously making answers impossible. She didn't do it out of spite, but out of a natural curiosity to want to know things as fast as possible.

"I'm a reporter for *The Braidwood Tribune*, you know the University of Braidwood?"

"Sure, the Rattlers, right? Married?"

"Divorced."

"What brings you back here? Want to do a story on us?"

"Not exactly, but I'm here on a story." Kelly hesitated jumping right into the explanation of Anne's death. "Where's Tonja?"

"Probably in the kitchen supervising breakfast clean up. You remember how she is about that kitchen."

"You are exactly the same, you know."

"Tell that to my back after my fifth trip up those stairs in the afternoon. And tell that to my feet after walking the floor with a slow labor. And tell that to my heart."

Linda smiled, but Kelly could now see the pain of each of the young girls she had helped through a difficult pregnancy etched in the lines of her forehead and around her mouth. Despite the joy Linda brought to those in sorrow, the pain of her girls hurt her almost as much as them.

"Could I see Tonja before I begin?" Kelly asked.

The two women went toward the back of the house where the sounds of slamming cupboard doors and clinking glasses could be heard.

"Tonja, we've got a visitor," Linda said as they entered the kitchen.

A tall blonde woman with curly hair turned around from the sink. She wore a peach-colored blouse and white pants. Without knowing why or who had entered her kitchen, she turned with a smile creating a wake of sunshine in her path.

"Hi, Tonja. You probably don't remember ..."

Before Kelly could finish her sentence, she was swept up into the arms of this angelic-looking being.

"Kelly, my goodness, where have you been?" Tonja asked.

"She's been a good girl, a journalist up in Braidwood," Linda said.

"A journalist? That's right, that's just right," Tonja said now holding Kelly at arm's length so she could get a good look at her.

"She's doing a story and needs to talk to us."

Kelly drove back to Braidwood that night, instead of waiting until Saturday. She was puzzled by the reaction of Tonja and Linda who seemed visibly shocked and upset she was asking about Anne Anderson, even before they learned of her death.

They couldn't give her much or wouldn't. Kelly could tell by their reactions that they knew who the father of that baby was.

Not enough to go on for a story, but at least she knew she had a story. While she would not mention the child, she knew exactly how to proceed with the story on Anne.

She thought about what they told her about Joely. They knew her parents, and knew Joely led a very active teenage life. When she turned eighteen she could look for Kelly, if she so chose. For now, Kelly would accept the fact that her daughter was happy and leading a normal life.

CHAPTER THIRTY-TWO

THE STORY ON ANNE appeared the day before Thanksgiving. With the help of an intern, they corroborated Rev. Baxter's story of abuse with hospital visits by both Anne and her mother for bruises and broken bones over a five-year period. Rev. and Mrs. Baxter both went on the record with information on Anne, although Kelly decided that the birth of a child to Anne could not be substantiated without cooperation of Tonja and Linda, and Kelly knew they would never give it. Kelly created sidebars on abused children and what can happen to them when they go untreated. She interviewed a child psychologist at UB, specializing in child abuse for her expert witness.

Kelly did not have to point out the obvious to her readers because the story spoke for itself. Anne's abuse at the hands of her father resulted in her inability to cope with the realities of her adult life, causing her to become a recluse. The piece did not exonerate her guilt in the crime, but it did offer some explanation on how it could have happened.

Kelly and Bart drove to the river cabin early on Thanksgiving morning. He sent someone out earlier in the week to air it out. Even the Jacuzzi on the screened porch was heated and ready for use. The day was rainy and slightly chilly, rather perfect for an isolated cabin stocked with food, wine, wood for the fireplace, and a view of the river. Neither minded if it rained the entire weekend. They brought work, books, and each other. Occasionally during the weekend, they turned on the small television to see how the recount was proceeding in south Florida, but soon turned if off – nothing would be decided that weekend it seemed.

Bart decided to deep-fry the turkey, so they didn't need to really begin preparations for their meal until an hour or two before they wanted to eat. Heating the oil in the deep fryer would take the longest amount of time. Kelly picked up sweet potato casserole, dressing, and pecan pie at Publix. The mashed potatoes and salad could be prepared while the turkey cooked.

After unpacking, they settled in the living room.

"How was the trip to Port St. Lucie?" Bart asked. "I noticed your research didn't make its way into your story on Anne."

Kelly told him earlier in the week she didn't want to talk about it until they were at the river because she wanted to concentrate on doing justice to Anne's life. Then she promised full disclosure.

"I didn't get much, but enough to know that Carson Anderson was probably the father of that baby. The women who run Oak Haven — Tonja and Linda — were noticeably upset when I asked about her."

"Maybe they're sensitive about all the girls," Bart said.

"No, I know these women. It was something else." Kelly waited for Bart to hear what she had just said. She didn't know how else to begin her story.

"You know the women who run Oak Haven? You didn't tell me that or didn't you know before you went?"

"I knew. In fact, I'd been there before. As a young girl, seventeen."

"For the obvious reason?"

"Yes, pregnant and suicidal. They took me in and helped me get through it."

"And the child?"

"Went out the door soon after I held her for the first time. Nice family adopted her."

"And the father?"

Kelly didn't know how to respond. She promised herself she would finally tell someone, and now she wanted that someone to be Bart.

"I don't know who the father is."

Bart came over to the couch and sat next to her. He wrapped his arms around her and listened to her tale of what happened on the night of her junior prom.

Her date, Randy Robinson, had been her steady boyfriend throughout her junior year of high school. He was captain of the football team, and she was a cheerleader – typical stuff. Randy to party and sometimes lost control when he drank. Kelly usually didn't drink because she had to make sure they got home all right.

On the night of the junior prom, the gang decided to go to the beach afterwards. Randy brought rum punch to the dance and everyone, including Kelly, had a few drinks. On the way to the beach, Randy drank his booze straight from the bottle. They had the top down on Randy's Mustang, and the radio played love songs. Kelly sipped from her plastic glass and thought about how perfect her world was. It was a clear night, a full moon night, a night of promises and dreams.

When they reached their secret place at the beach, only one vehicle sat in the parking area off A1A. They walked over the dunes and saw three of Randy's buddies, but not their girlfriends.

"Hey, what are you assholes doing?" Randy yelled to his friends. He carried the bottle in one hand and the thermos of punch in the other. He staggered over to them, and Kelly reluctantly followed.

"Where are Cheryl and the others?" Kelly asked.

She soon realized the other girls wouldn't be there, and she was alone with four drunk guys. Randy began by kissing her, but she asked him to stop because of the others standing there.

"You aren't going to get away with it tonight," Randy slurred into her ear.

"Get away with what?"

"The tease, the come on and then 'Oh Randy, please, you know I don't do that.' It ain't going to be that way tonight."

He pushed her down onto the sand and fell immediately on top of her. He managed to rip off her panties. She saw the straps from her beautiful prom dress float away in the waves.

Then she told Bart her mind just shut down. She remembered the faces of all of them who jumped on top of her that night. She remembered the slaps across the face to keep her quiet, but she forgot the pain and feelings during the long moments when four boys raped her. To Kelly it seemed as if hours had passed.

As soon as they finished, all of them jumped into the ocean. Kelly realized no one was holding her ankles or wrists. She could move freely, but it came at a great cost. The numbness began to fade as she attempted to stand. She could see A1A from her place on the sand so she went to the road and waited for a vehicle to drive by.

A young married couple pulled over, and after their exclamations and realization that she needed medical care, they drove her to the nearest hospital.

She waited in a cubicle until a police officer came. After assessing the situation, he sent for a female social worker to take her statement. Her mom arrived by then and sat with her while she attempted to tell her story in halting words. Kelly could only manage to get past the part about her date with Randy. From that point on, everyone assumed Randy was the sole perpetrator.

Randy stood trial alone and was found guilty of rape and battery. He never ratted on his friends, but she heard he came out of prison five years later a bitter and nasty man. She always visited her folks with trepidation because she worried she would see him. His folks, more prominent than Kelly's parents, still lived in Palm Beach, and they ostracized Kelly's parents at every opportunity, even though their son committed the crime. Life had not been easy for the Sands since then.

"So when I began to show my pregnancy, my parents and I decided it would be best to go to Oak Haven," Kelly said. "I liked the place immediately, and it was better than being a prisoner in my home with my parents hovering and looking at me so sadly. We knew from the beginning I would put the baby up for adoption."

"Did your folks ever find out what really happened?"

"No. You're the first."

"I don't know what to say, except I think I love you even more."

"Why?"

"You could have succumbed and not done anything with your life. Instead look at you. You managed to become one of the best reporters I've ever worked with because of your humanity. You could have lost that."

It started raining while they talked. Clouds hung low in the sky, making three o'clock seem like nine. They walked slowly to the bedroom.

"I want to hold you close to me for awhile," Bart said as they climbed into bed.

For the first time in their relationship, that's all they did once they lay down on the bed together. Kelly, worn out from the telling of her story, slept while Bart held her.

They eventually managed to cook a decent dinner despite the rain. They pulled in the deep fryer as close as possible to the house without causing a problem. At least it was out of the rain and able to heat nicely to sear the turkey.

Kelly felt so cleansed with the telling of her story, she ate as if she hadn't been fed for days. She even had two slices of pie. Then Bart asked about the part she hadn't revealed yet.

"What about the child?"

"I named her Joely, after my parents, Joe and Lee. That's what I call her in my mind when I think of her. She'll be seventeen in February, and according to Tonja and Linda, she's living a typical teenager's life."

"I just worry about one thing," Kelly said. "Is she wiser than me? Has someone taught her to be smarter? To not trust everyone. I worry about that, Bart."

"That night you went to the beach? Didn't you think your girlfriends would be there, too?"

"Yes, but I also knew Randy got crazy when he drank. He had done things before, nothing like that, but he became violent with me before."

"But you had no idea that what happened would happen, no one would."

"Someone less naïve would have realized and not gone."

"I don't believe that. I also believe once he had you in the car that night, you had no choice. He wouldn't have taken you home. Whether he planned for the other guys to be involved or not, he had plans for you. How could any young girl possibly know that her prom date would be capable of rape?"

"I still think I should have known. No, worse, I know I shouldn't have gone to the prom with him after the way he acted just the week before. I had my warning then, and I refused to take it."

"So now you take every warning, imagined or real, and run before you have a chance to find out anything."

"What do you mean?"

"You've never really given me a fair chance, have you? You make assumptions, and then just run away. I know I'm not blameless; I've taken too long to make a decision about my marriage, but you never waited around long enough to hear what I wanted to do. You just assumed you'd get hurt and got out before that happened."

"Don't think I haven't been hurt already by this, Bart, because I have. I left each time because I wanted to be the one who did it. I couldn't bear it if you walked away from me first."

"That won't happen. Now how about some more pie?"

Kelly groaned and fell back on the couch. Bart joined her and both abandoned thoughts of pie for the moment.

CHAPTER THIRTY-THREE

ON FRIDAY, BART AND Kelly took the canoe out on the river. They decided to paddle up river since the current was never very strong on this part of the Hope Springs if the canoe stayed near the banks. Going up or down, the canoe paddles had to be used, always lazily.

As they neared the boat ramp, they could see activity at the next house on the river. The rain had stopped, and the sun shone down on the folks sitting on the lawn and dock of the river house.

"You know Dallas Redman? The painter?" Bart asked as they slowed to a drift.

"Sure, I love his stuff. I've always wanted one of his river pieces."

"That's his house, where all the people are hanging out. I think I see some other familiar faces, too. Dallas and I have known each other for twenty years. We used to do kayak racing."

"I see Karen Thorne and her husband, what's his name," Kelly announced. "And there's Cowan Garcia."

"The tortoise shell guy?"

"One and the same and the president of the Smart Growth for Calloway."

"Let's pull over and say hello. I see Dallas over there under the tree." Bart began maneuvering the canoe toward the dock. "Hey, Redman, having a party and forgot to invite the press," Bart yelled.

"Your invitation's in the mail, Carl Bernstein," Dallas said. "Come on up. I got a joke or two to share and only a man with your distinguished taste and culture could appreciate them."

They hitched the canoe to one of the pillars on the dock near the stairs and proceeded to join the party. Kelly knew a few people by their faces, not names, but the place seemed to be a virtual who's who of the radical element of the county.

"Did you hear about Thanksgiving dinner at the Bushes?" Dallas began as soon as Bart joined him. "Seems Jeb had to sit at the kiddie table for not winning Florida."

Kelly saw Chelsea Godfrey and decided to leave these two to their political and election jokes. Kelly admired Chelsea because she had the balls to stand up to Jackson Stewart, which was not always an easy task since he had been ensconced in his job for over thirty years.

"Chelsea, good to see you," Kelly said as she came onto the dock.

"Kelly Sands, how are you?" Chelsea reached to embrace her.

"Just fine. This is quite a party. The renegades of Zion County, huh?"

"You know what they say about like minds attracting. Who's your partner?" She nodded her head in the direction of Bart who stood next to Dallas. Both men had their heads thrown back in laughter.

"That's Bart Stanley," Kelly said.

"The editor of *The Tribune*? I'd like to talk to him. Do you think he'd mind?"

"Bart never minds when it comes to talking about politics or newspapers," Kelly said. "He's very approachable."

As Kelly took Chelsea over to meet Bart, she saw Molly and her husband sitting on the swing. Kelly waved, and then introduced Bart and Chelsea. As soon as the two of them began talking in earnest about the Sunshine Law and public records, Kelly made her way over to her friend.

"I didn't expect to see you here," Molly said as she stood from the swing to give Kelly a hug.

"I didn't expect to be here. Did you have a nice Thanksgiving?"

"Yes – you know slaving all day over a hot stove while the men watch football always makes me happy. What did you do?"

Kelly blushed at the question and realized she and Bart had left them wide open to speculation by everyone at this party just by showing up together on the river today. But Molly was her friend, and she needed to confide in someone.

"Can we take a walk?" Kelly asked. She didn't mind talking to Molly, but she didn't want to share the news with Molly's husband, David.

They began to walk back toward the house until they came to the driveway. The two women walked down the limerock drive to a gate.

"This is a state preserve with trails," Molly told her as she opened the gate. "We can walk here without anyone else to bother us. What's up?"

"Did you happen to see who I came with?"

"No, unless it was Chelsea Godfrey, which I doubt. I'm really surprised to see you, since you always talk about not mingling with those you write about."

"I'm here with Bart," Kelly said.

"Your editor? No kidding."

"You don't sound all that surprised."

"Kelly, there's been rumors about you two for years now. I never asked because I really thought they were just that — rumors. Was I wrong?"

What had she and Bart been thinking by showing up at this party, Kelly wondered as she faced her friend. The gossip tongues would surely be wagging after today. She and Bart hadn't talked about when and how they would go public. Now it looked as if the decision was made for them through their lack of thought.

"I'm in love with him, not that it makes a difference to someone looking in from the outside," Kelly said. "And it hasn't been as if we had this long-time standing affair."

"Then what?"

"It's been off and on. Mostly off — it's complicated."

"Most affairs are," Molly said.

"Don't be like that, Molly. I couldn't stand it if you turned away from me."

"Sorry, but I'm having a hard time understanding. Maybe it's just the wife in me feeling more empathy for his wife. So explain."

"I can't talk about much of it, but it has been a troubled marriage. He wife left last week, and we've decided to see where our relationship goes. I came to the river with him this weekend. Today was totally happenstance, and I'm not even sure why we stopped. Maybe it's Bart's way of making a public statement, I don't know. But I do love him, and he loves me."

"What about Mike?"

"Mike? Mike is over."

"Does he know?"

"That we're over? Yes, but it didn't have anything to do with Bart. It was Mike. And me. There wasn't anything there on my part."

"Mike doesn't feel the same way, you know."

"What do you mean?"

"He thinks you'll come to your senses," Molly said. "He's the one that's been feeding the Bart rumor for the past few months. He says as soon as Bart learns you two are together, he'll start leaving you alone."

"Did he really say that? That's so far from the reality."

"Did you know he left us? Going to be a big shot?"

"He told me. Something's up with that, but when I suggested it, he just accused me of belittling him."

"We all said the same thing to him at *The Chronicle*. He left in a rather agitated state, saying he would show us all."

The women came back to the gate and walked back to the party. Kelly could see Bart on the fringes looking around. She knew he was looking for her.

"Where have you been?" he asked as she walked up to him with Molly.

"Talking with Molly. Have you ever met my friend and fellow reporter Molly Hale?"

"No, I don't think so," Bart reached out his hand. "I've heard a lot about you though."

"Same here," Molly said. "Kelly, good to see you, but I need to go find my husband so we can make our way home. Nice to meet you, Bart."

"Let's get out of here," Bart said as soon as they stood alone. "This might have been a mistake."

"Agreed. Follow me, just saunter over to the dock, as if we're not going anywhere in particular. No one will notice, and we'll get out of those pesky good-byes."

Once on the river, they both sat quietly paddling for sometime. The ripples of the water against the oars broke the silence. As dusk settled, they could hear the short whelp of the barred owl from nearby trees.

"Why did we stop?" Kelly asked.

"Not sure. Didn't think it was a big deal, until the questions started."

"Molly told me she's been hearing rumors about us for years." She didn't tell him that Mike had been pushing most of them recently.

"No kidding? I guess there's no turning back now."

"You okay with that?"

"More than okay – I say it's about damn time."

Kelly turned slightly so she could get a glimpse of Bart behind her. He smiled his crinkly-eyed grin, and her apprehension of a few short minutes ago disappeared.

CHAPTER THIRTY-FOUR

COWAN GARCIA MET WITH the members of SGC in the living room of the Redmans. Most of the guests had dispersed from the party, leaving the hard-core members to discuss business.

The group represented a cross section of Calloway who wanted to see change in the leadership direction of the city. Some were extremists bent on destroying property and reputations, others just wanted to go through the legal steps necessary to help take out corruption in the city, and still others simply wanted to have access to public documents in order to be aware of the changes.

"Betty Duncan's appointment to the Commission hurt us," Cowan began. "Those blood-sucking morons down at city hall actually called the governor's office and said, 'Dear Guvnor, We just have the sweetest little sec'tary down here who's been bonking the murdered commissioner for years now, and we think that just by injection, she'd make a lovely addition to our city commission.' And our dear governor, embroiled in seeing that his brother becomes the next president, just rolled over and gave them what they wanted. We need to get her out of there in March."

"What about the other seat?" the giant in the corner asked. Ken Greensides sat smoking a joint by himself on the periphery of the group, but his presence was always felt by the sheer magnitude of his 6'5", 250-pound body. Sometimes he slept through these meetings, other times he rambled, and then there were the times he hit the issue right where it needed slamming most.

"Good question, Ken, but put out the joint. It bothers some of the people here."

"What the hell?" Ken's anger was quickly drawn but just as quickly put away. "Oh, right, you're right. I'm sorry, real sorry, folks."

"We've got Luddy to run against Dungheap, I mean Duncan. That's a doable win with the grassroots support we've got. It's going to be a door-to-door campaign," Cowan continued. "But who will run against Waine?"

"Whoever it is, it must be Waine's opposite. Well spoken, educated, a civic-minded person who's been involved in civic organizations and hasn't been involved in real estate or developing in this town," said Sue Beasley, an elementary school teacher concerned about the possibility of another exchange of I-75 being put right next to her home, if her home survived the construction.

"How about you, Sue?" someone in the group asked.

"I don't think I could. I'd have to quit teaching and this job doesn't pay well enough to do that. Now that's a sad commentary on both politics and teaching."

"How about Donna Downs?" Karen Thorne asked.

"Donna Downs? The Historical Society lady?" Cowan asked.

"Yes, she's involved and lived here all her life with the exception of the year when she was Miss Florida. And she has something that would win thirty to forty percent of the vote with little work," Karen said.

"She's African-American," Cowan said.

"Will she run?" someone else asked.

"I have a feeling she might," Karen said. "I talked to her last week about Luddy's candidacy, and she asked me lots of questions. She knows how it's been in this town, probably more than most of us in this room. You think radicals have a hard time down at city hall, try being black, and then try being a black woman."

"Will you talk to her, Karen?" Cowan asked.

"First thing Monday, I'll give her a call at work and see what she thinks. I think Luddy and Donna would be a great team, running on the same platform."

"Has anyone heard about the new paper coming to Calloway?" Ken asked from his corner.

"Molly Hale mentioned something about it today," Karen said. "*The Zion County News.*"

"Does anyone know if it will be run by the *Millstone Monitor* people?"

"Not sure. Molly said Rick Bellows from *The Tribune* is starting it and has bought or brought Mike Green from *The Chronicle* to be head writer. Rick will be the editor. Mike told Molly it is going to be strictly a community paper, no politics."

"Anyone here want to volunteer services to write some pieces for them?" Cowan asked the group of ten. "You know, get in there, and see if there are what they seem. *The Monitor* was blatant from the start, and the Dregs of society makes his stand known every time he walks into a room. Let's get one of our own in there and find out who's pulling the purse strings. Is it the obvious?"

"I keep hearing rumors about the western limits of town, all that farmland out there close to Hope Springs?" Sue said. "I heard a consortium of developers and real estate agents own more than 1,000 acres. I have a suspicion that Betty's appointment and the new newspaper might have a connection with both the landing strip and the Hope Springs development."

"That's makes it even more imperative to get someone into this paper and be our inside connection," Cowan said.

"I've got some journalism background and have some time for the next couple of months," Lana Mercer said.

"Lana might be a good choice," Cowan said. "She's new in town and hasn't been labeled SGC. But if you go work there, you need to stay away from us."

"Agreed," Lana said. "I see they've already rented an office in Calloway so maybe first thing Monday morning I'll go apply."

SGC began when new residents to Calloway realized that the government of their local city was not responsive to their voice. They realized it when they could not find agendas for meetings. And they realized it when they attended commission meetings that lasted less than an hour because no real discussion of the issues had taken place.

So far they had just found the means to engage in dialogue at the meetings by insisting public comment time be put on the agenda. Prior to that, they were lucky if the chair, the mayor of the city, recognized them after motions had been made by the commission.

There were some contentious meetings when a few of the SGC members were removed for speaking their minds. Cowan Garcia held the record for being thrown out at least once a month for the past year.

One night the meeting ended when the mayor refused to let anyone speak on an ordinance changing zoning from agricultural to industrial on just a few acres on the edge of town.

The residents stood in protest and many of them were removed, particularly after Cowan called the mayor a Nazi. Their methods were not always polite, but before long, the local press took notice and made it a habit of having at least one reporter in attendance at every meeting.

Other communities began taking notice, too. Hope Springs' residents began protesting actions of their Commission. Some of them even attended SGC's meetings to get pointers and advice.

CHAPTER THIRTY-FIVE

JUST DOWN THE RIVER between the Redmans and Bart Stanley's house another group met for the day for some of the same reasons but with different goals.

As Kelly and Bart slowly paddled back to the house, they came upon Lucy Burch's house once again. This time the deck was filled with people, not just Rick and Lucy.

Kelly saw Mike Green first, before he saw her. She noticed the suit right away. It was so out of place on the river that it stood out like a heron would have stood out in downtown Braidwood, but there he was deep in conversation with Lucy. Rick stood talking to someone Kelly didn't know, but she recognized Bubba Sanders and Tim Murray sitting at the table under the umbrella, sipping their drinks. The two lawyers from Hope Springs and Calloway seemed an unlikely couple but probably had much in common.

Jerry Mueller, Braidwood Chamber president, stood off to one side with a woman who was most likely his wife.

"Let's make this quick, Bart. Please don't slow down. If they notice us, we'll just say hello as we cruise by," Kelly said.

"Look at that crew, " Bart said in a whisper. "There's Sen. Jones and the Millstone city manager. What's his name?"

"Fletcher Williams," Kelly told him. "That surprises me."

"Why?"

"He's black for one thing. I see Billy Winterrowd, and everyone knows he's the biggest racist and bigot around. And I guess I thought Fletcher stayed away from one side or another to not be accused of showing favoritism," Kelly said.

"Look there's Bart and his reporter," Lucy said loud enough for everyone on the deck and the river to hear. "Hi, Bart. Nice day for a cruise, isn't? Are you and Lois Lane looking for any commissioners today or maybe stories to turn murderers like Anne Simmons into saints?"

"Hello, Lucy. Kelly and I are just out on a pleasure-cruise today. Why? You got anything you want to share?"

"Bart, you're so funny. Do you know Mike Green?" Lucy asked. "Of course, I forgot. Mike, you used to date her, didn't you?" Venom dripped from the lips of the real estate mogul on the deck. She was in rare form.

"Hi, Mike," Kelly said.

"Kelly," he said.

"Hope you all enjoy the rest of your Thanksgiving weekend," Bart said as they floated swiftly by the deck. He gave a little wave, but quickly put his hands back on the paddle to ensure a swift passage past the den of vipers.

"I never did ask you. What happened between you and Mike?" Bart asked.

"Not much. I told him I didn't want to see him anymore. He agreed, but not happily. I felt sorry for him after I read about his father, but that's about it."

"Is that why you see me? You pity an old man who's in love with you?"

"Yes, that's it exactly. How did you ever guess?" Kelly turned in the canoe to give Bart a big smile and wink. "Who could ever feel sorry for a big old meanie like you?"

"Hey, be careful. I'm still your boss, and you better show me the proper respect."

"Mr. Stanley, if you will kindly get your oar in the water and get us back to the house, I will show you all kinds of proper respect."

The luxury of spending so much time with Bart only equaled the bliss of being able to touch him whenever she wanted, Kelly thought, as she came up behind him on the dock as he secured the canoe. She rubbed his back and began kissing his neck browned and wrinkled from years of fishing on the rivers and lakes of the area. She inhaled deeply and smelled his sweat, which did nothing but entice her further.

Bart turned around to face her. "I'm sorry about the Redmans. I didn't even think about it," he said. "It seems so natural being with you; I didn't think anyone else would even notice. To me it's never seemed liked we were doing anything wrong."

"I realized we hadn't even discussed what it might be like to suddenly appear in public together. Have you ever told Joyce about us? I'm just wondering if maybe you should tell her, even though she's the one who technically left you."

"You're probably right. I never mentioned you before because I never wanted to trigger an episode." Bart pulled her close and kissed her. "On Sunday night I'll call her and tell her everything, and then we'll go from there."

When they came into the house, Bart noticed t his pager was blinking. His wife had called. Kelly wondered if she had heard about their appearance at the Redmans already. News travels fast on a river, maybe faster than on the street. The river carried the messages of time and remained the source of so much life. Why not be the source of all things that multiply?

Kelly sat out on the dock while Bart called Joyce. Dusk was settling on the river and the sweet light of sunset had all but evaporated from the ripples in the water. The owls hooted and the frogs croaked and the crickets thought they could compete with all of that as evening swept in and made itself at home for the next few hours.

Kelly thought about what Bart and his spouse of more than twenty years might have to say to one another. Both spent the weekend with other people for the first time in over two decades. Kelly wondered how that might feel and sensed Bart was not being truthful to either her or himself when he said he didn't have feelings about the end of the marriage. Kelly was only been married a short while, but when it came time for the relationship to end, even though she had stopped loving her husband, a memory lingered of love past and that sense of a failure and even desperation to salvage something from the wreckage. She definitely felt something, and it wasn't all relief. Bart would need to admit that, too. Maybe he did when he was away from her; his sadness may be something he hid away, not wanting her to feel guilty.

Darkness enveloped Kelly on the dock until the little solar lights around the edge came on automatically. The house remained dark, and she wondered if she should go to Bart. She didn't know if he was still on the phone, and she knew she couldn't eavesdrop on words of tenderness between him and his wife. She didn't feel jealousy because she hoped two people who had raised two children together would have some words of love; it was more that she did not want to intrude on a private moment. On the other hand, she did not want to hear yelling and anger either. So she sat and waited and listened to the sounds of the river.

Finally, she heard the screen door of the porch slam. She remained facing the river, but soon his footsteps fell upon the dock, and then he was there. He sat down in the chair across from Kelly.

Bart put his head in his hands, and Kelly suspected he'd been crying. She sat quietly waiting for him to speak.

"She heard about today," he finally said almost so low Kelly thought about having him repeat it. "She wasn't surprised really. Said she was actually relieved it was out in the open. She thinks it's part of the reason she went to Sam so easily, almost a defensive move. She'll be all right."

"It's still sad, isn't it?"

"I never thought I'd feel this much, but when Joyce was so understanding and kind, I remembered why I married her in the first place." Again, he put his head between his hands as his elbows rested on his knees.

"You were married a long time; you shared so much; it's normal to feel this way."

"I was surprised when she said she already knew about you," he said.

"How did she find out?"

"She's been getting letters for a couple of months, telling her about our trips, the time we spend in my office, the lunches, pretty factual stuff, except for most of it we weren't doing anything. I didn't deny it. I told her I loved you, and I had for some time."

"And what did she say?"

"She said she was glad it was in the open. I forgot how reasonable she always was. Makes it nice now, but never made for many fireworks during the marriage."

"What happens next?" Kelly asked.

"First, we need to tell the kids before one of their old buddies decides to drop the news. I told Joyce she could move back into the house, and I'd get an apartment."

"I think Mike sent those letters."

"Maybe or maybe the same person that set that fake bomb on your desk did it."

They sat quietly holding hands in the darkness of the night. Occasionally, they could hear the sound of life beyond the deck when a bird would sweep down upon the river and find its prey. Or a mullet would jump out of the water and slam back down onto the surface.

"Let's go to bed," Bart said as night took over the river.

She didn't hesitate. She stood and pulled him out of his chair, and they walked with their arms entwined around one another so it was impossible to tell where one began and the other ended. They spent the rest of the evening that way, wrapped together forming a strong bond. Kelly would not run away again from this man's strong embrace and their overpowering need for each other.

CHAPTER THIRTY-SIX

ON THE MONDAY MORNING after Thanksgiving, Bart and Kelly dressed for the office reluctantly.

"What you got on the agenda today?" Bart asked as Kelly put on her eyeliner. He looked over her shoulder watching her reflection.

"Some research, check on the interns. Still pulling stuff on the Simmons' case. Tonight it's Calloway; you know the usual boring work until I get to the commission meeting and then fireworks."

"Anything of interest on the agenda?"

"Not on the surface. Maybe the discussion of a loan made two years ago now coming due with a huge payment. Lots of people protested that when it first happened. But you know Calloway; I can never predict what the SGC people will do or say nor can I predict what rabbit Stewart or Murray might pull out of their hat. This is the first regular meeting with Betty on the dais as a commissioner, not to mention the first without Lester. Anything could happen."

"True. Maybe I'll come out later; I always enjoy a good political debate and football game and these meetings are like both rolled into one."

"Lately the mayor has been pulling speakers away from the podium. If they are talking about anti-growth, he tells them to shut up and sit down after exactly three minutes."

"He doesn't do that for the others?"

"Never seen it happen. Even Gary Dregs from the *Millstone Monitor*? He gets up and rants and raves about the SGC people, but Tim doesn't do a thing even when he goes over three minutes. I've timed them."

"Sounds like editorial material to me on several different levels. First and foremost, news reporters write the news, they don't make it. Dregs has no business getting up and expressing his dismay with anyone. He then becomes the center of the news story and how can he report on that?"

"He does though. Have you read that paper?"

"Think I should?"

"I think it would give you fodder for editorials for the next year."

"How about a late dinner afterwards?"

"It will be really late; these meetings are notorious for running past midnight. Maybe you could come over to the house for a drink afterwards."

"Date." He leaned over and kissed the top of her head. "Now I've got to run. Meeting with the boss this morning," Bart said. He meant the publisher Doug Collings.

Kelly turned around and pulled Bart's face close to her own. "Thank you for this weekend." She kissed him on his lips, intending to make it a short peck. He would have none of that.

Bart picked her up and placed her on the bathroom counter and began unbuttoning her blouse.

"I thought you had a meeting," Kelly said as she began doing the same thing to his shirt, after she had loosened his tie.

"This is more important," he mumbled as he reached under her skirt and swiftly removed her panties. "Besides if I can't keep my writers satisfied, how can I tell the publisher I have everything under control?"

Kelly arrived a few minutes early for the Calloway City Commission meeting on the Monday after Thanksgiving. All the commissioners came by the press table to say hello, even the ones who didn't particularly like what she wrote.

Gary Dregs came in with his suitcase on wheels, his mother following closely behind. Mostly they traveled together along with a couple of younger brothers. They reminded Kelly of a pack of dogs. Gary and Kelly spoke briefly, which was unusual. Gary usually spent his time when the meeting was not in session harassing members of SGC. Lately that group took the offensive and began harassing him first. Gary fussed with his laptop and camera with a six-inch lens.

When Molly came hustling down the aisle, Kelly felt relief, not just from the force field of Gary Dregs, but also from the fact that Mike would not be there. Mike usually covered this meeting, but Molly must have been reassigned already.

"Kelly, hello," Molly said as she flung her briefcase and camera bag down on the table between Gary and Kelly. "Gary, move your stuff over. You don't own this press table."

"This is a free country, and I can put my stuff wherever I want it, Miss Hale," Gary said.

"It may be a free country, but this table is for the press, all the press, and I'm sitting next to Kelly." Molly shoved his pads of paper and packet of materials to the edge of the table. "Besides there'll be a new paper joining us soon, so you better get used to sharing this space."

"If you don't stop harassing my son, I'm going to get Chief Jefferson over here," Mrs. Dregs said.

"Go right ahead," Molly said. "And I'll tell him to kick your son out of here for being rude without a license."

"Come on, Molly, they're not worth it," Kelly said as she pulled on Molly's jacket, hoping her friend would just sit down.

After Molly settled in her chair, she said, "I don't know what it is about those people, but they bring out the worst in me."

"I know what you mean, but it's better to ignore them."

"So how are you?" Molly asked with raised eyebrows.

"Just fine, thanks for asking."

Before Molly could ask any questions about Kelly's weekend with Bart a small woman approached the table hesitantly.

"Is this table for the press?" Lana Mercer asked.

"Sure thing. You with the new paper?" Molly asked as she moved her chair closer to Kelly's, making more room at the already crowded table.

"Yes, I'm Lana Mercer with *The Zion County News*. This is my first meeting."

"I'm Molly, with *The Chronicle* and this is Kelly with *The Tribune*. Welcome to the Calloway Circus."

"Would you please shut up, Miss Hale?" Gary hissed from his end of the press table. "The mayor is trying to start this meeting."

CHAPTER THIRTY-SEVEN

THE MAYOR CALLED THE November 27 meeting of the Calloway City Commission to order before Molly could hurl another insult at Gary.

The first thing on the agenda concerned the millage rate in Calloway. Andrew Knowles, the finance director, was asking the Commission to approve the old rate from last year. Kelly watched the finance director make his pitch, and she felt an uncomfortable lurch in her stomach. Knowles gave her the creeps. It was neither the BMW convertible he drove on his $50,000 a year salary nor was it his bleached hair or leather shoes he wore with no socks. It had more to do with his lack of knowledge of monetary affairs over a city with a $20 million budget.

Last year as city manager, Betty Duncan appointed this guy for the position even though his CPA license had been revoked five years earlier. The city was paying for him to have it reinstated. When Chelsea questioned Betty about his lack of certification, Betty said it was as a clerical error.

Chelsea now asked the finance director what the difference would be for the average homeowner if they lowered the millage by 0.02 percent.

"That would mean on a home valued at $50,000 a reduction of $50 per year," Andrew told the Commission.

During the public input portion of the discussion, Cowan Garcia came to the podium.

"I'm not a CPA," he began. "But I can do simple math and your finance director just told you the difference would be $50 per year when in actuality, just using my pencil and paper back there in the audience, I figured that it would mean $5 per year."

"That will be enough, Mr. Garcia." The mayor banged the gavel. "I will not have you up here insulting our staff."

"But he made an error in a public meeting that could make a difference on the way you vote."

"I said you need to stop," the mayor repeated.

"Just because you hired – or rather your newest commissioner decided to hire – a moron to do the city's financial business to cover up Stewart's dealings over the years, does not mean I have to sit back quietly and let it continue."

The mayor banged the gavel as Garcia proceeded.

"You continue to make stupid decisions like the Monster Mart Distribution Center whose trucks are packing our roads, which cannot even handle the normal traffic of its residents. Now tonight you're going to discuss the payback of the loan to bring infrastructure to the poor, poor Monster Mart corporation – money this city does not have.

"In fact, most of your staff is incompetent," Garcia noted as a Chief Jefferson walked toward the podium. "You've got unsafe buildings, and we're in debt $16 million, and this millage rate decision is in violation of state law because it was supposed to have been submitted before the budget in September, but still all the employees working in this building drive brand new Crown Victorias."

The screeching of brakes could be heard outside even over the shouting of Cowan and banging of the gavel from the dais. Suddenly the building began to shake, as pictures fell off the wall behind the commissioners. Lester Simmons' photograph fell right in front of the dais from the row of pictures of elected officials.

Lights hanging from the ceiling fell on the crowd, who began a panic run for the doors at the back of the chambers. Chief Jefferson dropped the hold he had on Cowan's arm. He tried to push his way out through all the people. He found it impossible to move since only double doors provided exit for more than one hundred people crammed into the meeting.

Kelly and Molly tried to go with the rest.

The smell of burning rubber first assaulted Kelly's nostrils when she eventually made it out the door. Molly and she were swept along with the crowd toward whatever caused the problem.

"Keep back, everyone," the chief yelled.

The crowd headed for the road in front of city hall where most of the pandemonium was taking place.

Kelly saw the truck with its cab turned at a ninety-degree angle and its nose seemingly attached to city hall. She saw blood spattered on the wall above the grill of the truck. The trailer remained on the road where several cars had run into the back of it when it took its unexpected turn.

Thomas Jefferson barked orders and the rescue trucks, parked in the building next door, were already on duty. Kelly could see the driver leaning over the steering wheel, but she could not figure out at first what caused the blood on the wall.

"Get over here quick; there's someone between the truck and the wall," yelled the chief when he got close enough to see.

Half of the rescue squad had gone to help the vehicles behind the Monster Mart semi while a few were trying to look into the cab of the truck.

Cowan Garcia pushed his way to the front when he saw no paramedics near the chief.

"I'm a medic," he said.

Garcia saw the small hand of a child reaching out toward him, but when he looked at the truck and the rest of the body, he knew whoever was trapped against the wall could not have survived the impact. Even a full-grown adult would not survive that kind of hit.

"Where's Shelley?" Betty Duncan said as she emerged from the crowd and went toward Cowan.

When Cowan noticed her approach, he attempted to turn her away from what he had seen. She kept resisting Cowan.

"Betty, you don't want to come any closer," he told her as he tried to turn her around by her shoulders.

"You communist pig, I need to find my daughter." Betty tried to push past Cowan.

"Betty, he's right, you don't want to see," the chief said. "Where's Alex?"

"I will not let this imbecile tell me what to do," Betty said. With a burst of energy she pushed past the two men.

Kelly saw her fall to her knees as she came close to the truck's front. Betty leaned her head back and opened her mouth, but with all the noise around them, it seemed her scream was silent. Kelly kept edging closer and saw Betty held a small shoe in her hands.

Just then, the ambulance pulled up as close to the building as it could get. The driver, conscious but with injuries, had been pulled from the cab. A paramedic jumped in the driver's seat and attempted to pull the semi back just a few inches.

It looked like a sack of red just crumbled to the ground when the cab moved just a fraction of an inch. Cowan tried to pull Betty back from the site, but Betty seemed to have gone into another place. Finally, Cowan and another man grabbed her under the arms and pulled her back. She crumbled to the ground still holding the shoe.

Kelly walked over to Betty. She kneeled down and put her arms around her.

"This is Shelley's shoe," Betty whispered. "Alex had come outside to smoke a cigarette, and she followed him. He was supposed to be watching her."

She talked in a monotone, as if it was a simple mistake by a thoughtless father.

"Someone needs to call Lester," Betty said.

"Betty, Lester is dead," Kelly said.

"Lester is dead?" She looked calmly at Kelly. "How can I tell him his daughter died?"

Kelly sat holding her until some of Betty's friends made their way through the crowd. Kelly asked them if they knew where Alex might be. No one seemed to know, so Kelly left Betty with her friends, keeping an eye out for Betty's husband.

"A Monster Mart truck hit that young girl, and you idiots still think it's okay to just put in anything in this town without considering the consequences," Cowan said to no one in particular.

Johnny Waine heard and walked over and walloped him a right hook before Cowan could duck.

"Just shut your frigging mouth, you pig," Johnny said just before Cowan reacted and gave the same right punch to Johnny's chin. Cowan's hit achieved its purpose and Johnny fell back on the sidewalk hitting his head on the concrete planter sitting on the edge of sidewalk. The pansies over Johnny's head swayed slightly in the breeze.

The crowd took a moment to recover from the second shock of the day and began holding Cowan back from doing anything more.

"Do you want to press charges, Johnny?" Chief Jefferson asked as Waine attempted to sit upright without showing his pain.

"Why do you ask him if he wants to press charges, Jefferson?" Cowan asked. "He hit me first. Are you all a part of this system that only protects the GOBs?"

"Chief Jefferson, he's right," Karen Thorne said. "You can't just ask Commissioner Waine if he wants to press charges. We all saw what happened. You can't hide this in your paperwork. I think Cowan should press charges."

"But Garcia here attacked a public official," the chief said.

"And that gives him more rights under the law than the average citizen?" Karen asked. "I think you'd better go bone up on that one in the textbooks, sir. There is no more protection. Sometimes even less because they are an elected official, hired by the public to do the public's business. And you just had one of those public servants attack a resident."

"Miss Thorne, why don't you go back to your veggie burgers and sprouts and leave us alone?" Gary Dregs had come to stand beside her and stood with his hands on his hips daring her to challenge his remark.

"Shut up, Gary," said Molly, who stood next to Kelly. "A young child is dead. You'll probably find a way to blame Cowan for that poor child's accident instead of who should really be blamed."

"And who's that?" Gary asked.

"The greedy bastards at city hall, that's who," Molly said.

Gary looked as if he could hit her, but his mother came and pulled him away. Cowan and Johnny stared at one another with dried blood on their faces.

"Why don't we just let this whole thing drop, Chief," Johnny said.

"Drop?" Cowan began to stir once again. "I want charges pressed against this asshole," he said.

"Cowan, come on, let's not make this worse than it is," the chief said. "It's been a tough night, and let's just say you two got carried away."

"No, I want to press charges," Cowan insisted. "I'm tired of guys like Waine always having it their way. He hit me; there is no dispute there. Look at all the witnesses I have. And you don't think the press here will keep this quiet, do you?"

"Then let's go over to the station and fill out the paper work. Commissioner Waine, I'll get your statement in the morning, if that's all right."

"Sure, Chief."

"Why not tonight?" Cowan asked.

"Because I not only have to do your paperwork, I have to file an accident report on what happened here. It will be a very long night."

CHAPTER THIRTY-EIGHT

THOMAS JEFFERSON HAD BEEN born in the other Calloway — the one literally on the other side of the tracks. The railroad tracks were the center of Calloway life in the 1920s and '30s. Businesses centered around it on the south side, along with the large Victorian and Antebellum houses of the landed gentry. The north side of the tracks housed those who worked for the railroad, the businesses, and the white folks. While most of the whites had moved out to the subdivisions on the edge of town, mostly near the country club, the poorer blacks stayed on the north side of the railroad tracks.

Miami had nothing except sheer size on the drug trafficking that took place in Calloway on the dirt streets, dirt yards, and dilapidated homes in Thomas' world. The drugs, music, and alcohol all flowed freely in the juke joints, which became the local gathering place for young and old alike. Heroin ruled for nearly three decades until the mind-altering drugs of the sixties began making their way into the community. And always-prodigious quantities of marijuana were available.

It was Calloway's best-kept secret. No white person crossed the railroad tracks unless they were in search of drugs. The police turned the other cheek. The town's ruling class liked it that way. The masses are more easily controlled when stoned.

Thomas managed to avoid illegal drugs with the sound principles of his single mother. Some of these women abandoned by their men still had hope; the others who had lost hope by the birth of the fifth or sixth child, were thankful the juke joints existed because then they didn't have to worry about the older children. Thomas' mother still had hope, and she hoped her only child would rise above the hopelessness of the slum and pull them both out. She told Thomas he was better than all of those around him. She told him stories of his father, who she said had died in Vietnam. Thomas would be a grown man before he discovered that his mother had lied just a little bit about the man she turned into a hero for a young boy desperately in need of heroes.

His father, Thomas, Sr., ran away when his number came up for the draft, and he left behind his wife, Merilee, who had just given birth to Thomas. She always hoped he would return, but in fact, no one had ever heard from him again. Thomas had no idea if his father was still alive or not. He had only learned about his desertion from his aunt at a drunken family reunion when he was in his early twenties.

With his mother's guidance and his natural intelligence, Thomas began to excel in school, which by the time he made it to high school was integrated. Blacks who were smart were ridiculed by other blacks for selling out. Thomas played football and wrestled, because he had to become tough in order to survive the taunts and pushes of his peers once they were safely behind the railroad tracks of Calloway. One of his coaches in high school showed him how he could become even stronger and better looking with a simple little pill dispensed by a sports' doctor in Braidwood.

He worked after school at the grocery store in town, bagging and carrying groceries. He was friendly with the customers and soon established a reputation among the wealthy white women who always checked out in the line where Thomas was bagging groceries. It began with a tip here and there, for bringing the groceries out to the car. Then as Thomas began working out with the weights he purchased at the pawnshop with his tips and continued with his little steroid pill-popping practice, these women began requesting home deliveries.

The store manager was pleased and gave Thomas the sole job of delivering their groceries out to the subdivisions west of town. His tips and muscles became larger as did his ego as these women seduced him and easily persuaded him to take a moment to satisfy their basic fantasies. In the two years Thomas delivered groceries, he learned to have sex in every room of the house, on every conceivable surface, and in every available corner and open space. He became the local stud of the country club set. He also saved his money.

Thomas hoped these liaisons would lead to something more for him. But then he noticed something. Whenever he encountered any of these women in other situations, they never looked at him. For them, he did not exist except when he came to their homes in the late afternoons, while their husbands drank at the club, their children played tennis, and their casseroles baked in the oven.

With the help of several teachers, Jefferson managed to go to Zion County Community College on scholarship. He continued to work at the grocery store, but his afternoon deliveries stopped and with that, none of those women ever acknowledged him again until he became a police officer, and he pulled them over for driving under the influence. Then they would try to influence him with seduction and promises. He acted as if he didn't hear them, but he would issue tickets for something less than the actual crime.

As he moved up the ranks at the police department, he began injecting the steroids on a safe schedule. He knew just how much he could take over a short period to give his muscles enough heft to strain his uniforms and not give him pimples or breasts. If he became agitated easily or lost his temper without reason, he always blamed the stresses of the job.

Now he looked to forward to the day when he would not have to deal with the day-to-day grind of police work. He had his eye on the vacant city manager's seat, and the power he could achieve by having control of city hall. He just needed some support to get there. Despite the inconvenience and low priority, he knew he could not refuse to take Garcia's statement, and he knew he could use Garcia's support. Even more than that, he knew he could be a bridge in the community as the loss of first the commissioner and now a little girl sent reverberations out across Calloway.

Kelly tried to record everything that was being said, despite the chaos all around her. Molly told Kelly she had to get back to the office and start writing. This would change the entire front section of the weekly paper. Kelly felt suddenly very alone in this huge crowd of people and tried to look at her watch to see how long she had until deadline.

"Hello, Kelly."

The voice startled her, but she recognized it as Mike's right away. She turned around, and there he stood feet away from her.

"Mike. How long you been here?"

"Since the beginning. I just sat in the back. Thought I should stay on top of things to keep track of Lana."

"When you starting up?"

"They hope by Christmas so we can do a real flashy front page and one whole section on the parades and school Christmas pageants. You know, one of those 'chestnuts roasting on an open fire' issues."

"Sounds right up your alley," Kelly said.

"Why, Kelly, it's not like you to be snide. What's wrong?"

"You talking about me behind my back about my relationship with Bart is what is wrong." Kelly began to walk away. Suddenly she wanted to be back in the safety of *The Tribune* newsroom among her friends.

Mike followed as she walked to her car. When she pulled out her key and tried to open the door, he came up behind her and pressed against her. Keeping the pressure on her back, he turned her around.

"Mike, let go of me now."

"You think you're so smart. You're not, you know. Getting rid of me won't solve your problems." Mike began to kiss her neck, then her face as Kelly squirmed, and turned away each time his lips came close.

The nightmare returned. She felt her panic rise and tried to remember the things she learned from the rape counselor. Fight, fight hard. But he had her pinned, and she could not bring her leg up to use her knee in a strategic place. She kept trying to tell herself to fight, but she felt herself drowning.

"Mike, I'd let her go if I were you." Kelly heard Bart's voice from deep inside her terror. For a moment, she thought she imagined it. "Let her go, boy, or I'll have to do something unpleasant."

Mike slowly released his body's pressure on Kelly. When he pulled away, he stood facing Bart. Mike spit at his feet.

"I think you'd better get out of here before I do something I might regret," Bart said. "And if I ever catch you near this woman again, I will kill you."

Bart then went to Kelly and pulled her close to his chest. Mike walked away and left in his car. Kelly's trembling slowly subsided.

"It brought it back, didn't it?" Bart asked as he continued to hold her tightly.

"It's all right; I did better this time. I thought about fighting, but he had me pinned; that was when I felt panicked. They don't give instructions for that in self defense."

"Let me take you home," Bart said.

"Home? Got a story to write, Bart. Take me to the paper; we can pick up my car later."

Bart looked at her skeptically, but he led her to his car parked just feet away.

Kelly saw a couple holding each other up as they walked to a car in the parking lot. Several people surrounded them.

"Isn't that the Duncans?" Bart asked.

"Yes."

"Let's get a statement."

"I can't do that. Look at them."

"All the more reason to see if they'll talk with us. Here give me your notebook."

Bart caught up with Duncans as they waited for their friends to decide who would drive them and who would drive their car.

Kelly watched as Bart identified himself and offered condolences. She could tell by the wrinkle formed on his brow that he was offering sympathy. The Duncans looked at him blankly while he continued to talk. Then she saw Alex begin to speak as he pulled something out of his wallet; Betty stood crying at his side.

When Bart returned to his car, Kelly asked him what happened.

"The dad said he blamed the city of Calloway because they allowed so many semis to run through the middle of town," Bart said, reading from his pad. "And they didn't know how they would carry on because their daughter had been the light of their life. Just before the meeting tonight, she had asked if she could start volunteering at the nursing home. Said she was like that; always wanting to help people out. Gave me permission to use the words of a poem she wrote that he carried in his wallet."

"How do you do that?"

"Do what?"

"Get people to talk to you so openly."

"I let my heart work for me. I truly am heartbroken for those people. I think about what if it had been my child? It could have been anyone's kid. And I tell them that, and I tell them I want the truth about their child in our report. I don't want it to be a cold reporting of the facts. Every parent wants that, Kelly. They want the life of their child to have meant something."

CHAPTER THIRTY-NINE

KELLY WENT HOME ALONE that night after she wrote her story. Bart helped her until he left to check on Joyce, after she called sounding depressed. Kelly wondered through her fog of the evening's events if life with Bart would always include him "checking on Joyce."

She took what she had about the accident and tried to write a decent piece with feeling. She tried to block out the gore at the scene, keeping it out of her writing. *Let Gary Dregs deal with that end of it,* she thought. It tore Kelly apart to think the life of a child could be snuffed out in just a minute.

As she wrote the piece, something nagged at her, but nothing she could put down in concrete words. Then suddenly as she finished the piece, it came to her. Most of the truck drivers tried to time the light at the top of the hill outside of city hall. They would watch it turn green and then speed up the hill to make the light. Kelly predicted, though she didn't write it in her article, the police would find the driver had been going too fast to brake. There was so much confusion after the accident with the other cars involved that it would have been impossible to detect brake marks until the semi-trailer was removed. She remembered the strong smell of rubber as they came out of city hall; that could mean he slammed on the brakes hard when he realized what was happening.

Before Kelly sent the piece through the computer to editing, she called the hospitals where all the accident victims had been taken. No one else had died. The driver of the truck had been released, although he had several broken ribs. Most everyone else had minor injuries and had been sent home.

A quick call to Chief Jefferson at Calloway Police Department yielded nothing definite. She asked him if Garcia filed charges, and she was told he had, but the report could not be released until an investigation had been conducted. However, the accident's investigation would take priority.

The chief chatted with Kelly for a few minutes. It gave him the opportunity to plant another seed.

"They really need someone in city hall who can manage this whole situation," he told Kelly. "Even though Betty's still on the commission, she's in no position to help anyone but herself."

"Who do you think could do the job?" Kelly asked.

"It would have to be someone who knows the community and understands the way this city runs," Thomas Jefferson told her. "And it would have to be someone who could be fair, yet tough when needed."

"Sounds like you, Chief."

"What do you know?"

After they hung up, Kelly wrote a quick sidebar on the fight between Garcia and Waine as she had witnessed it. She finished with "CPD will conduct a full investigation on the altercation. However, Chief Jefferson said the accident's investigation would take precedence."

The small police departments run by the municipalities usually only had one or two detectives to conduct investigations, and the accident would require full attention because of the high profile case with the death of a child at the centerpiece. Making the police investigation even more difficult were the major players involved. The Duncan name and Monster Mart involvement brought even more notoriety to the tragedy.

Kelly thought about what Betty said about Lester when she saw her daughter was dead, but decided there was no need to poke around that. Based on what she discovered in the past few weeks, would anyone really be surprised if it was determined that Shelley was Lester's child and not Alex's?

When she finally finished and began to gather her things to head home, she realized her hands were shaking. She sat at the desk immobilized while tears poured down her face. No sobs, just tears.

Lonny came into the newsroom just then to show her some proofs he had taken at the scene and found Kelly just staring straight ahead, as the tears continued to fall.

"Kelly, what's up?" he asked.

Kelly jumped at the sound of his voice and turned to see Lonny standing next to her desk despite the layer of tears blurring her vision.

"Lonny, you startled me."

He continued staring at her, waiting for an explanation.

"It was a tough story to write, wasn't it?" he finally said when Kelly remained quiet.

She nodded her head and covered her face with her hands. "If only I hadn't seen that little hand sticking out from between the truck and the wall. That makes it so real."

"I took a picture of the scene, but they decided in layout to go with a long shot of the crowd with Betty on the ground blocking most of the gory stuff."

"Thank goodness. I know this is going to sound silly, but would you mind walking me out to my car?" Kelly asked.

"Come on, I was just leaving."

Kelly did not admit to Lonny the real reason she wanted him to accompany her. She had been crying back then out of fear and remembrance of the feeling when Mike pinned her against the car. She felt so helpless and out of control, both of which were things she did not allow to happen anymore. With just a little pushing, she was right back there on the beach. Thank goodness, Bart showed up when he did, or it would have been worse.

"With all this crazy stuff happening around here, I think I'll just follow you home," Lonny said as she unlocked her car.

"I guess I am a little spooked tonight," Kelly said. "It's been one thing after another, hasn't it?"

Kelly let herself into her well-lit house, and then turned to wave to Lonny who sat parked at the curb. When she attended late night meetings she turned the inside lights on by a timer. She hated the dark.

As she placed her keys and purse on the side table in the hallway, her phone began ringing. She desperately hoped it wasn't Mike.

"Kelly, this is Cowan."

"Yes, Cowan. How are *you*?" Kelly asked.

"Fine. I'm not calling about me. I wondered if you could meet with a couple of us in the morning for breakfast."

"Why?"

"Let's just say, we've got a story for you, if you want it. It's more than me getting more dead tortoises dropped on my lawn. I guarantee you won't be disappointed."

"Who will be there?"

"A couple of us from SGC and Alex Duncan," Cowan said.

"Alex Duncan?"

"You'll have to come to breakfast at Morning Side Up to find out why. Nine o'clock?"

"You certainly have my interest now, but you were counting on that, weren't you, Cowan?"

Cowan let out a sharp laugh. "See you tomorrow."

After Kelly hung up, she poured herself a vodka with cranberry juice and sat in the dark living room with her thoughts, which raced over the evening's events, including the news Alex Duncan would be breakfasting with members of SGC the next morning.

Although Alex didn't often speak up at meetings, he did attend them. One night after Cowan had questioned the city's fiscal responsibilities by keeping one million dollars in a non-interest bearing bank account, Alex stood to speak on behalf of the bank.

Alex represented the Calloway State Bank as its counsel. The Bank held the city's money for as long as anyone could remember.

"You know nothing about financial matters, Mr. Garcia," Alex said.

"Mr. Duncan, you must direct your comments to the Commission, please," the mayor said.

"Mayor, the account Mr. Garcia is referring to is what those in business call a 'liquid" account. The city can access that money at anytime without penalty."

"That's bullshit, and you know it, Duncan," Cowan yelled from the back row of the audience.

"Chief, please remove Mr. Garcia from the Chambers," the mayor said.

It was another typical meeting in Calloway. Now these two were coming together to break bread.

Kelly remembered what Alex said to Bart earlier.

"I blame the city of Calloway."

That would be the connection to Cowan, who had been itching for the perfect vehicle to challenge the city's granting Monster Mart the permits to build a one million square foot distribution center on the edge of town.

Kelly still didn't feel sleepy so she poured herself another drink and continued to sit on her couch. Her thoughts jumped from one thing to another, and she felt if she did try to sleep she would dream of a child's hand sticking out from the grill of a semi, helpless and crushed, the breath taken away.

When she tried to block that picture, the scene with Mike at the car began rewinding and playing itself repeatedly in her mind.

She poured yet another drink.

CHAPTER FORTY

WHEN KELLY WOKE IN the morning after three hours of sleep, she had a headache and a dry mouth. She had an hour to make it to the breakfast. First she called the office to let them know she would be late because of an interview. Bart hadn't arrived yet, so she talked to Carl for a minute about the events of the night before. She didn't mention her breakfast meeting.

When Kelly walked into Morning Side Up, she told the hostess she was meeting a group of people, and she was led to the back of the side room where Kelly found Cowan, Alex, Chelsea Godfrey, and Karen Thorne.

"Good morning, everyone," Kelly said as she approached the table.

"Everyone here know Kelly Sands with *The Tribune*?" Cowan asked.

They all nodded and greeted her. Kelly had probably quoted or interviewed everyone sitting at the table.

Alex looked like he hadn't slept a wink. His normally combed hair looked as if rakes brushed it. Kelly could never remember seeing him out of a suit. Today, he wore an old white T-shirt that advertised Corona beer.

Kelly sat down in the only empty chair situated between Alex and Karen.

"How are you and your wife holding up?" she asked Alex.

He looked at her with dull eyes. "My wife? I haven't seen her since last night. I spent the night at Garcia's house."

That explained the T-shirt but not much else.

"I know you are just chomping at the bit to know why we are all here," Cowan said. "I won't stall any longer. SGC has decided to file a lawsuit against the City of Calloway for entering into an illegal contract with Monster Mart, which has brought 900 trips per day of semis through our downtown's two-lane streets. Alex and I will also be listed as plaintiffs."

"Monster Mart will probably be asked to be added with the city since they are named in the suit," Alex said.

"Who is your attorney?" Kelly asked.

"Jimmy Slaughtery," said Cowan, "out of Tallahassee. He specializes in this sort of thing."

"When will it be filed?"

"As soon as Jimmy can draft it. Actually we've been working on something for quite awhile, but now we have proof that it is dangerous in Calloway with children and semis," Cowan said.

"Your wife is on the commission. How does she feel about all this?" Kelly asked Alex.

"Who cares?" said Cowan. "Alex here certainly doesn't. Last night he left her. Right, Alex?"

"But it's so soon. Shelley just died last night," Kelly said.

"It doesn't matter anymore," Alex said. "I loved Shelley, but she wasn't my child, and Betty made that abundantly clear to me last night. She kept asking me to call Lester until I just couldn't take it anymore. I've been humiliated too many times."

"Have you always known that Lester was the father of Shelley?" Kelly asked.

"Of course, but it was all so civilized until Lester died. When we're alone, Betty talks as if Lester is still alive. In public, she held up just fine. Last night was the worst. She said she was finally going to divorce me because Anne had agreed to divorce Lester. She said Lester was going to adopt Shelley, and if I didn't agree, she was going to expose me. She's lost her mind."

"There's more, Kelly." Cowan said.

"We were having a political strategy meeting before you arrived," Karen said. "You know Luddy's running for the commission in March."

Kelly nodded. "Against Betty?"

"No, we've looked into the election laws, and she can run against Waine if she wants and she does," Karen announced. "Someone else is going to run against Betty."

"Who ..." Kelly stopped talking when she realized that everyone, including Alex, sat looking at her with sly grins on their faces.

"Not Alex," Kelly said.

"Yes, Alex," Cowan said. "It makes perfect sense. He's going to run against his then ex-wife for the seat. He won't pull any punches. Alex knows where all the skeletons lie, and he plans to go public."

"Why the sudden change of heart, Alex?" Kelly asked.

"Nothing matters anymore. Up to this point, I've lived my life the way others determined. I married Betty, even though she loved someone else, but I stayed with her while she carried on a very public affair. Now my father is dead, so I don't have to bother with that; Lester is gone, so he's off my back, too. I don't have to protect Shelley anymore either, and I really don't give a crap about Betty at all."

"And now the million dollar question," Kelly said. "Why am I here?"

"We trust you to do a fair and impartial job; you're a respected journalist all over Zion County," Chelsea said.

"And *The Tribune* has the largest audience," Cowan said. "As soon as the local papers see that you've picked up the story, they'll be all over it. We want you to write the first piece."

"When are you ready for the news to hit the paper?"

"We should have the lawsuit in hand the day after the funeral which is next week," Cowan said. "We need to honor Shelley first before the news takes precedence."

"That's very thoughtful of you," Kelly said. She managed to keep the sarcasm out of her voice, just barely. No one noticed.

"I think we should keep the lawsuit story, and Alex running as two different pieces," Chelsea said.

"I agree," Kelly said. "But I want to make something perfectly clear to all of you. You don't have a say in what I write, and I will write these stories in my own way. No one will be looking over my shoulder and dictating to me, and no one will read the stories before they go to press. Separating the two stories makes sense if you want both pieces to have an impact.

"And remember, I'm the one who made the decision to do it that way just because it makes good sense news wise, not because you told me to do it that way."

"We understand, Kelly," said Karen. "We trust you to be fair. And since we're in the right, there will be no problem."

CHAPTER FORTY-ONE

KELLY LEFT THE MEETING feeling squeamish. She barely touched her pancakes and gulped down the coffee. Her antenna remained posed in the up position because such a drastic change in a person did not seem possible. It had been barely twelve hours since the child's death, and Alex Duncan had made all these major decisions about his life, which would turn not only his existence up on end, but also the entire structure of politics as usual in Calloway. Who knew what else he might reveal in the coming days and weeks? She wondered if he might be setting up the SGC people. Her instinct told her he was not because of the personal events that had caused his turn around.

When she got in her car, she made a call to the Calloway Police Department. Chief Jefferson took her call right away, not a usual occurrence, particularly after such a busy night.

"We don't have the report ready yet, Kelly," he said.

"That's not why I'm calling. I didn't expect it. I wanted to ask a couple of questions, off the record," she said.

"Shoot."

"Were there any witnesses who saw the whole thing before the semi hit her? I wondered about her stepping off the curb."

"The cars behind the semi noticed Shelley, but that's about all. I think one of them said they remembered she didn't look either way. They began honking their horn to alert her."

"Where was Shelley's father, Alex Duncan? He was supposed to be watching her, according to his wife."

"Don't know. I remember he was at the scene afterwards, but before that I have no idea."

"Seems to me if he was watching her, he should have seen something, even if he was just sitting at the picnic table smoking a cigarette."

"I guess I'll be asking him that question," he said. "And I'll fax the police report as soon as it's done, but I've still got a lot of people to interview."

When Kelly finally made it to the office, she only wanted to go into Bart's office and collapse and share the morning's news. To her disappointment, when she headed for his office, the door was closed and the lights off.

"Where's Bart this morning?" Kelly asked his secretary, Mary.

"He'll be in this afternoon. He said he had some kind of an appointment."

The piles on her desk looked higher than usual this morning. When she began looking through the stacks, she realized one of the interns had been able to pull some information on the companies buying up property in the area.

Julie, the intern, highlighted some repeated names in different colors to match similar or related names. One of those names kept drawing her attention, as she glanced at the page.

Anthony Marcetti held many board positions on the various companies. In the same color highlights were other Marcettis. And then some similar names like Alan Martin, Adam Marconi. She owed Julie a lunch for this work; noticing these similarities took some scrutiny and most interns just made the copies.

It looked as if board members from one of the companies, Marcetti and Sons, had recently been buying parcels of land until they owned the 2,000 acres now annexed into Calloway. Then something else came up. Those same board members were doing the same thing with river properties, just outside of Hope Springs, from Lucy Burch's house east to the Zion County-owned boat ramp, further south. Further, Julie had uncovered just what Kelly needed. Marcetti and Sons was a subsidiary of Industrial Pines, owned by both B.J. Winters and Anthony Marcetti.

She went to the GSI map on the computer and began looking for owners of property nearby to see if there was a pattern.

What wasn't owned by I.P. connections on the adjoining lots were owned by some very interesting people. Billy Winterrowd, a commissioner in Hope Springs owned one large tract of land just south of the boat ramp, on the Zion County side of the river. Lucy Burch owned some other pieces. A Mazie Kane was listed as owner of property that would join all the properties together in a two-mile riverfront unit.

Mazie Kane was a name she'd heard before but she couldn't figure out where. Anthony Marcetti also sounded familiar. She did a search on both and only found information on Marcetti.

That's when it hit her who Anthony Marcetti was. The Internet gave her some information, but it also jogged her memory. Marcetti came from Miami, and he owned large tracts of land around Lake Okeechobee and up to almost Ocala. Kelly always suspected the developer of the movie studio and landing strip had connections to I.P. Now it looked as if those other rumors about a large development on the Hope Springs River might be true also. I.P. developed most of central Florida and sections of the south with little concern for dwindling mangroves and wetlands in the state. Now it seemed they were ready to make their move into north Florida.

Kelly remembered stories from a few years ago. Marcetti needed somewhere to put some cash, so he convinced the city of Eustis, located between Orlando and Ocala, to let him build a beautiful ranch for rich folks, complete with a landing strip and African animals. He claimed the animals came from a Rescue African Animals program in Kenya during a year of drought. He brought back elephants, zebras, rhinoceros, and even a tiger or two. The rich and famous came for pampering while looking out over a vista that resembled an African veldt.

Two years ago, a famous movie star wanted to give her husband the thrill of his life by petting a white tiger. She brought him to the ranch, and the caretakers let the husband into a fenced area with the white tiger. Just as the caretaker said the animal was very tame, the tiger attacked the movie star's husband, immediately severing an artery in his neck. Then the tiger picked the lifeless form up by the back of his shirt and trotted around the field with the man in his mouth and blood dripping onto the white fur of the rare animal.

The ranch closed almost immediately, and as far as Kelly knew, Marcetti vanished just as quickly, only to turn up now in Zion County.

"Good morning, Kelly," Bart said as he walked toward his own office.

TORTOISE STEW

"Hey, Boss, got a minute?" Kelly asked as she began to gather all of the papers together.

She didn't wait for his reply. Bart always welcomed his reporters, especially her, into his sanctuary.

"What's up?" he asked once he had settled at his desk.

"Julie turned up some pretty interesting stuff yesterday," Kelly began. "Even more impressive, she looked at the stuff and started making parallels."

"Let's hear it."

"Have you ever heard of Anthony Marcetti?"

"Marcetti, owned the ranch in Ocala where the tiger mauled somebody's husband, mob connections, land owner, developer, started Industrial Pines with B.J. Winters from Calloway."

"You're amazing," Kelly told him. "How do you do that?"

"I don't question a gift."

"Board members of Marcetti and Sons, a subsidiary of I.P., now own the 2,000 acres in Calloway, plus tracts of land on the Hope Springs River. And even more amazing, what he doesn't own on the river is owned by Mazie Kane, Lucy Burch, and one of the Hope Springs commissioners."

"Interesting, but where's the story? Have you contacted I.P. yet on their intent to develop either parcel?"

"Not yet, but I will. I thought I could begin with a profile on Anthony Marcetti. I contact him for an interview. We really haven't done anything in depth on the plans for the airstrip/movie studio so maybe I could get tech drawings, representations, that sort of thing."

"That could work, but what is your ultimate goal in doing all this work? To shut down the project? To get Marcetti?"

"I want the public to know exactly who is building this complex, where the money is coming from. It's going to change the whole character of those communities. Do you remember if Marcetti has ever had trouble with the law?"

"As far as I know, he's managed to keep himself fairly clean. I'm not so sure about his sons. As I recall he has three sons all involved in the business. Before you start anything, why don't you start investigating them and see what shows up."

"Good idea. How are you this morning?" Kelly asked.

"Beautiful."

"Bart, that's what you say to everyone; don't say that to me."

"I'm fine. How are you? Is that better or did you have something else in mind? Any other way you'd like me to respond?"

"I can tell you're in a fine mood this morning, so I'm going to get back to work."

"Sorry. I had a rough night with Joyce. She's having doubts about everything. It's turning out that the new boyfriend isn't very sympathetic. I took her to the doctor this morning."

"And?"

"The doctor talked about hospitalizing her until she stabilizes."

"How do you feel about that?"

"I'm working on it. It might be the best thing," Bart said. "I told the doctor and Joyce that no matter what happened, the marriage is still over. Joyce seems to understand, but it doesn't help her depression."

"Let me know what I can do to help."

"I'm sorry, Kelly. I know you needed me last night, too. I'm sorry it's always you I let down. That's what I want changed."

"Just the fact you told me means a whole lot, Boss." She smiled at him, and he forced a fake smile back, but at least it was a start.

She placed a call to the public relations office at I.P., but the spokesperson said they had no comment at this time regarding any developments in Zion County.

Kelly then began an Internet search on the Marcetti brothers. She couldn't check criminal records on her computer, but she could do a name search with the company *The Tribune* used online. She had no trouble finding two of the sons, Paul and Mario. They'd both had arrests for fraud and embezzlement, but charges were dropped both times against them. Anthony Marcetti, Jr. proved to be a little more difficult to find.

Kelly sent in an advanced search that would show a driver's license with photo of the oldest son. While she waited for a response, she again looked through the papers. Suddenly she noticed something interesting on all the documents of incorporation. Tony Mayberry had been the agent of record for all of it. On the Calloway property, there was another attorney listed, but that was it. Kelly turned back to her computer.

"I don't believe it." Kelly said when a picture appeared on her screen.

"Hold it down over there," Carl said.

"No, Carl, come here. You've got to see this."

She picked up her phone and called Bart. "You better come out here and see this," she said.

Kelly sat at her desk with a small smile on her face. The pieces of the long-quested puzzle just began falling together. Carl and Bart arrived at her desk at the same time and looked at the computer screen.

"Why is Tony Mayberry's picture on the driver's license for Anthony Marcetti, Jr.?" Carl asked.

CHAPTER FORTY-TWO

TONY MAYBERRY, JACKSON STEWART, and Sen. Sam Jones rode in silence to the ranch of Anthony Marcetti in Eustis. He summoned all three of them, which could not be a good sign. Marcetti liked to remain anonymous and used others to give his orders. Only lately, he'd been forced to attend commission meetings where he always sat in the back, arrived late, and left early.

When Tony pulled up to the tall cast iron gates blocking the entrance to the road that led back to the house, he pushed a button under the steering wheel, and the gates opened slowly. They drove past the "Closed" signs and the tall grasses on the front part of the Marcetti acreage visible from the road. Except for the gate, it looked like abandoned property found more often in the Panhandle of Florida. However, as soon as they rounded the curve in the drive and became invisible to outsiders, the scenery changed. Bison roamed with a lone elephant on the left of the car and a ten-foot waterfall dominated the other side. Made from the limestone found all over the cleared property, the waterfall ended up in a large pond where geese swam and deer drank. One zebra stood alone to the side of the stone structure casually eating grass.

"So Anthony didn't get rid of all the animals after the accident?" Jackson asked.

"No, just the tigers and one lion," Tony said. "He likes to feel he's living on a big game preserve."

"I'm impressed," Jackson said. "I've always wanted to see this place."

"I better warn you," Tony said. "He wears safari clothes all the time when he's here on the ranch – you know the khaki jacket with the hat. Not to alarm you, but just so you're prepared, he usually carries his

186

Winchester, slung over his shoulder. Sometimes he'll just shoot into the air when he's out walking around. It's one of those high-powered rifles so it'll make quite a noise."

"He's more of a character than I thought." Jackson said as he chuckled to himself in the backseat.

"Just don't let him know you think that," Tony said. "I better warn you about something else; sometimes he does more than just shoot into the air. Sometimes he pretends he's on safari, and he'll shoot one of the animals."

Jackson whistled under his breath. Anthony Marcetti was more than a character. Jackson was used to being the cock in the small barnyard, but here he was just a chick visiting the head rooster, who sounded like a lunatic. When Anthony recently started attending their meetings, he sat in the back and said nothing. Jackson envied his power and wanted to be as close to it as possible, lunatic or not.

The ranch house spread out in front of them. Just one story made from cedar shank, oak beams and cypress trim, it looked like one of those western ranch spas except for the limestone facade around the foundation.

Walking down the steps on the long porch running the length of the house, just as his son described him, came Anthony Marcetti himself. He wore hunting boots and shorts along with the belted safari jacket. His hat folded up on one side, and with his white beard and outfit, he could easily win in the Hemingway look-alike contest held in Key West every summer.

"Hello, Father," Tony said as he walked around the front of the car toward the hunter.

"Son," Marcetti said. He shook Tony's hand, wrapped the hand holding the rifle behind his back, and pounded his son with it.

"Sam, good to see," Marcetti said to the Senator. "And Jackson Stewart, the King of Zion County."

"I wouldn't go that far, Anthony," Jackson said as he extended a hand.

Anthony led them into the ranch house. No surprises here with its natural wood floors and exposed beams with high ceilings. The study held the heads of several exotic animals placed strategically around the room so no matter where anyone sat, the glass eyes of the stuffed heads seemed to follow.

A black bear rug joined the comfortable leather chairs with the large mahogany desk gleaming from the fire roaring in the large stone fireplace next to the chairs. It was a man's room in all ways.

Anthony went to a cabinet and pulled out four glasses and a carafe with brown liquid. Then he brought out a silver case decorated with turquoise. He opened it and offered each one a real Cuban cigar.

Jackson Stewart knew he had a comrade as he lit the big fat stogy and accepted the glass of whiskey.

"You know how to live, Anthony, I'll say that for sure," Jackson said after taking a long puff on the tasty cigar.

"That's what it's all about, my man. Why would I do if I couldn't enjoy it?" Anthony then pushed a buzzer on his desk and a side door opened.

Into the room, walked two of the most beautiful women Jackson had ever seen. They were dressed identically in cropped tight white T-shirts showing off their tanned midriffs and tight blue boxer shorts. They both had long frosted hair. They walked over to Anthony, standing behind him with all the confidence of lionesses protecting their den.

"Meet my assistants, gentlemen," Anthony said. "Unity and Pusella."

The men offered greetings and the two beauties simply smiled in return. They did not need to offer anymore than that.

They sat in an easy companionable silence for a few moments while each man savored the gifts of the good life. Unity began passing around a silver tray with white lines and a straw. The Senator turned it down, but Tony and Jackson took their turns snorting the pure cocaine to the very back of their sinuses. The assistants did not offer the tray to Anthony.

"Good stuff, Dad," Tony said. "New shipment?"

"Only the best. okay, boys, let's get down to business," Anthony said. He sat up straight in his chair and took off the hat. "Zion County seems to be giving me some headaches. What's going on up there?"

"Sir?" Tony asked.

"We got a commissioner dead, six commissioners in the water, bomb threats, protestors every time we turn around and now a lawsuit," Marcetti informed them.

"A lawsuit?" Tony asked.

"Don't they tell you anything? Some group is getting ready to file a lawsuit against the city of Calloway over that Monster Mart warehouse because B.J.'s grandkid was killed by one of their trucks."

"SGC," said Jackson. "Those son-a-bitches."

"Zion County is within our grasp, but not if we let these dirt lickers make more publicity plays like this lawsuit," Anthony said. "Something needs to be done."

"We have done a few things, Anthony," Jackson said. "We're starting that new paper in Calloway with our own people and your help."

"What will make this new rag any different from the others?" Anthony asked.

"For one thing, we're starting slow. We hired a squeaky clean publisher coming up from Miami and Rick Bellows from *The Tribune* is doing his editor bit. It's a flawless plan. We get the community to like it with kids and parades and sports – lots of it," Jackson said. "Then by March when those two crucial seats come up for reelection in Calloway, we will have been up and running for at least two months, and we'll make an endorsement."

"Dad, we had nothing to do with the bomb," Tony said. "There have been some other things, not worth mentioning, but we were not involved."

A tall, broad-shouldered man walked in the room. His reddish hair was parted on the side and carefully combed back to create another inch of height. His tanned face and arms stood out from his white golf shirt.

"Gentleman, let me introduce you to my new assistant, Randy Robinson," Anthony said. "Randy has been brought in to deal with some of the problems up in Zion County. He'll be working for Industrial Pines. With B.J. dealing with family problems right now, I need someone I can trust in Calloway."

Randy went around the room, shaking hands, while the other men introduced themselves.

"I need you to find me a place, preferably in Calloway." Randy addressed no one in particular. "I'd like a housekeeper, too. One who will cook meals."

"I'll make some calls as soon as we get back," Tony said.

"Randy has an old friend in the area. High school sweetheart, right, Randy?" Anthony said.

"I sure do. Ever heard of Kelly Sands?"

The men looked from one to the other uncomfortably. "Yes, we've heard of her," the Senator finally said.

"There a problem, gentlemen?" Randy asked.

"She's a reporter for *The Braidwood Tribune*," Jackson said. "She sometimes gives us trouble. The bomb was left on her desk at *The Tribune.*"

"Sounds like Kelly," Randy said. "She always liked stirring up trouble. She got me into a few messes, that's for sure. That's why I broke it off with her. She probably won't be too thrilled to see me, so let's keep it quiet between us until I speak to her."

"Sure, I can understand that," Jackson said. "Women pain us something horrible, but then we keep coming back for more."

"Something like that," Randy said.

CHAPTER FORTY-THREE

JASON LANDIS DROVE UP from Miami alone on his first trip to Calloway to visit Rick and the offices of *The Zion County News*. He wanted to look around and be sure his wife and family would be comfortable. He was fairly certain his oldest daughter, Elizabeth, was moving with them even though she was twenty-five. She wanted to work as a reporter, and he thought it might be a good idea. She hadn't finished college; in fact, she hadn't finished much of anything in a very long time, but she wrote volumes in those notebooks of hers. Maybe the move would do her some good, especially if she had a job she enjoyed.

His middle child, the only son, Jaycee, was twenty-three. He would probably stay in Miami. Recently graduated from the University of Miami, Jaycee planned to attend graduate school after working as an architectural intern for a year. Someday, he'd be pulling down much more money than his old man, especially if he started his own firm like he wanted.

Maggie would be more of a problem. She turned seventeen soon and was in her junior year of high school. He and Jean, his wife, discussed the option of Jean and Maggie staying in Miami until the school year was finished. In the meantime, Jason would find a house and become acquainted with the area. Maggie didn't want to leave the school in her last year and had made her feelings known over and over again.

Maggie gave them the most trouble. Elizabeth worried them with her quietness and dark moods, but at least they didn't have the rages that sometimes overcame Maggie when she wanted something very badly. Jaycee did everything according to the plan. He played football in high school, received good grades, finished college in the usual four years, and now was dedicated to his career goals.

Maggie was the most striking of all the children, with auburn hair and blue eyes that mesmerized most people, particularly the boys. Boys started sniffing around the house ever since Maggie turned fourteen. At least they didn't have to worry about that yet. Maggie was aloof with the opposite sex and never dated anyone seriously. She liked her girlfriends much better and preferred spending time with them. When Maggie did date, it was because all her girlfriends had dates.

Now Jason had accepted the job of publisher for a newspaper in Calloway where he and the editor would run the whole show. He was attracted by the idea when Rick first called. The challenge of starting up a new paper and doing things he would have liked to do while working for larger papers had always been a dream of his. He was moving to a rural area where the cost of living would be less, and his salary increase would allow an easier lifestyle than he and Jean could have imagined living in Miami working as an editor. While he would have liked to actually own the paper, this was the next best thing and could be the stepping-stone he had always wanted.

"Now what do we know for sure and what do we have?" Bart asked after they had all calmed down after seeing the driver's license.

Carl and Kelly sat in Bart's office as they tried to regroup and decide what to do with the information they had.

"And, Carl, I'd like to put you on this, too," Bart said. "I know we have interns, but we're getting into an area where it might be risky to use anyone, except for the one who led you here. Any problems with that, Kelly?"

"Nope, Boss. I could use the help. I'm feeling like I need a chart or something to keep it all straight."

"How about you, Carl?"

"That's fine. There's still the mess with the election, but it's not really a local issue."

"I'll put someone else on it. The interns will jump at the chance – it's history in the making and won't be forgotten in a long time," Bart said. "But what we're working on here will affect us even more locally. What do we have?"

They went back over the information. Individuals somehow connected with Industrial Pines and Anthony Marcetti had been buying the property that everyone thought I.P. would be developing for the movie studio and landing strip in Calloway. It looked like the same group might be getting ready to do something with large tracts of land on the Hope Springs River. For the past year, rumors kept surfacing about a development and resort there, which would make perfect sense if movie stars, directors, producers, and studio heads would be flocking to the area. They would need a place for rural pampering.

None of what they had on record was illegal, except for two things. Billy Winterrowd owned some of the property on the river, which was on the drawing table for annexation into Hope Springs. He would have to be watched carefully when it came before the commission for a vote to see if he recused himself, which the law required since he would stand to benefit from the annexation. Tony Mayberry served as city attorney in negotiations for the annexation of the 2,000 acres in Calloway, which was a major conflict of interest since he was the son of the potential buyer.

"What else?" Bart asked.

"We know that Jackson Stewart and other elected officials meet regularly at Lucy's house on the river, and Tony Mayberry goes to some of those meetings," Kelly said.

"How do you know that for sure?" Carl asked. "We've all speculated those meetings occur, but could never prove it."

"Bart and I have been doing some surveillance since the river baptism," Kelly said. "I haven't had a chance to tell you with everything else. We've seen them."

"But do we have a story?" Bart asked.

Carl and Kelly looked at one another and then back at Bart. "Don't think so yet, Boss," Kelly finally said.

"How about trying to do that profile on Marcetti you mentioned earlier?" Bart asked.

"Not a bad idea," Kelly said. "Should we do the good cop, bad cop routine?"

"You'll have to let Carl be the good cop. You are on the shit list of certain people."

"You are so eloquent. We also know a new paper is starting in Calloway," Kelly said. "Who did the market research to see if the area could handle one more paper?"

"They took Rick, who has always aligned with the business side," said Bart. "And Mike Green, who seems to be quite a chameleon."

"But we still don't have a story," Carl said.

"Then we keep digging because as sure as I'm the executive editor of this paper, there is a story here somewhere," Bart said. "We might just uncover the giver of the bomb, too, if we keep digging."

"What about a feature on the area's weeklies?" Kelly asked. "We look at whether the market can support them, and we profile the publishers and editors, that sort of thing."

"Good idea," Bart said. "That one is yours."

"I think I'll start with an interview with that new publisher who is coming from Miami to start the *Zion County News*."

CHAPTER FORTY-FOUR

TONJA LARSON AND LINDA Marsh decided to open Oak Haven after both of them experienced incarceration in a Catholic home for girls in Miami. Tonja had been fifteen; Linda a year older.

Tonja was brutally raped by the older brother of her best friend. In 1968, no one treated her like a victim. When she dragged herself home from her friend's house, her face was bleeding and her clothing torn. Her parents asked what had happened and when she told them, they were horrified.

However, they didn't take Tonja to the police station or the hospital. They didn't call anyone. Her mother told her to go to bed. When she came to breakfast the next morning, with a black eye and torn lip, her father could not look at her. He kept the paper in front of his face. Her mother, Daisy Larson, said plenty.

"First, Tonja, you are not to tell anyone about what happened," she said. "Teddy is such a nice young man that you must have done something to provoke him. I've told you not to wear those halter-tops and shorts. Young men just can't help themselves. We're going to forget it ever happened. Do you understand, sugar?"

Tonja stared blankly at the scrambled eggs and bacon set before her on her mother's stoneware with daisy imprints. The whole room reeked of daisies from the wallpaper to the tablecloth to the vase with the real thing in the middle of the table. Her mother capitalized on her name in a big way. She thought of herself as a middle class Daisy Buchanan from *The Great Gatsby*. Born in Charleston, South Carolina, to a family deep in tradition and roots, Daisy Southwell grew up in the privileged life of a southern belle. When she met Tonja's father at a dance in 1948, they fell in love and married. Her father hailed from

Savannah, just a short drive away across the Georgia border, but both cities reveled in their deep southern tradition.

They moved to the Miami area when Tonja and her younger brother were preschoolers. Her mother continued to play the southern belle to the hilt among the pastels and palms of suburbia in Miami.

Daisy did not count on her daughter coming to her five months after the rape to tell her she hadn't had a period since before that night. Tonja's mother pursed her lips together and immediately went to the phone to call the priest. Within a week, Tonja was packed and whisked away to the sheltered home for unwed mothers. Tonja wasn't even sure where she was or what was happening to her. She knew the nuns were cruel, especially when they made her change her first name and would not allow the use of her last name. She became Sally for the next four months; even her identity was stolen.

She might have lost all her spirit and hope if not for her roommate, Linda, or as the nuns called her, Patti. The two of them promised always to use their real names when they were alone. Linda refused to follow the rules at first until she realized being put in the small closet, they called the thinking room, kept her away from her new friend. So only when they were alone at night did they do the things the nuns forbade, such as touching one another's bellies when the babies kicked and sleeping in the same bed. The nuns acted as if they weren't pregnant at all, and they received no instruction about what was happening to their bodies or what would happen when labor began.

Tonja and Linda whispered at night about how they would raise their children. No one told them they wouldn't be allowed to keep them. Linda had a boyfriend who was willing to marry her, but her parents refused to consider it. They intended Linda to go to college and become either a lawyer or a doctor. Her mother found a new religion called feminism, so the things denied to Mrs. Marsh, were suddenly heaped upon the shoulders of Linda, who simply wanted to be a teenager and go to dances and watch American Bandstand. She didn't want to stand in line at the cafeteria in Burdines and protest the separate dining rooms for men, who were served at the tables by waitresses, while the women with children had to go through a cafeteria-style line to get their food.

If Linda's mother had not been raised Catholic, she might have sought out an illegal abortion for her daughter, but instead she called upon her first religion to offer a solution. However, she forgot to tell her daughter the baby wouldn't be coming home with her. Neither of the mothers never suspected two pregnant teens might fall in love with each other.

They had their babies within two weeks of each other, with Linda going first. She held her son for a few moments before Sister Mary Margaret stepped in and whisked the baby from her arms.

"Wait, I want to keep him here with me," Linda cried.

"That's not possible, dear," the nun said. "The baby's parents are waiting downstairs to meet their new son before we take him to the nursery."

"The baby's parents?"

"Yes, of course, the people who are adopting him."

"No, you don't understand, I'm his mother," Linda said.

"No, I'm afraid not, Patti. You will put all this in your past and go on back to your normal life. These people are prepared to take care of an infant."

With that pronouncement,Sister Mary Margaret swept out of the room.

"My name is Linda," she yelled to the walls.

Linda stayed in the home for ten days after the birth. In that time she tried to prepare Tonja for what would probably happen to her once the baby came. They vowed to find their children and steal them away the first chance they got. Four days before Tonja gave birth, Linda was discharged. The girls exchanged addresses and phone numbers and knew they would stay in touch.

Oak Haven was the antithesis of what they endured. By the time they went to college and opened the doors of Oak Haven, times had changed some. Neither Tonja nor Linda had been able to find their own children in the ensuing years, but they could provide help and choices for the young women who came to them. Their girls were given options. During their pregnancies, they received education about their bodies and the birth process. They counseled the girls, both mentally and physically. Most of the girls left reluctantly as if they were leaving home, but Tonja and Linda encouraged them to go out into the world, with or without their baby, and make a difference.

One young girl who always worried them had been Anne. She came to them, the victim of incest, which she finally confessed. However,

Linda and Tonja already knew the truth from the guarded statements made by the Baxters when they brought her to Oak Haven. Anne had no hope left in her. She clung to them and didn't want to leave, but her father finally came and got her, and they did not have any recourse except to release her into his custody. The nice minister assured them the father would not touch a hair on her head again. When Kelly brought the news of Anne's suicide, they were saddened, but not surprised.

In cases where adoption was the best option, Tonja and Linda also became close to the adoptive parents as they made their placements through an adoption lawyer. They felt it was important for both parties to meet, and they screened very carefully the girls to be certain they would not change their minds in six months – the legal waiting period for the adoption to become final – and ask for the child back. Both women agreed they would have handled the removal of their own babies better if they were assured they went to good homes.

When they received the note from Jason and Jean Landis, they eagerly ripped open the envelope, happy to get a progress report on Anne's child. They knew they would have to write them back and tell them that Anne was dead. However, their joy in hearing about the adopted daughter dissipated once they read the Landis' news.

"Jason has decided to take a new job as the publisher of a small paper up in Zion County," Jean wrote. "Elizabeth will be coming with us to work as a reporter on *The Zion County News*, and Maggie will finish her last year of high school in Calloway. As you know, Maggie is very independent minded and doesn't like the idea of this move one bit."

Neither did Tonja and Linda. Calloway was the place where Elizabeth's mother had lived and just died. Jason and Elizabeth would be working on a newspaper in the same area where Kelly was a reporter. The two women, who usually had an answer for everything, turned and looked at one another and wondered what could be done to avoid a major collision. Kelly was already investigating the death of Anne, and they knew Kelly would do a thorough job.

CHAPTER FORTY-FIVE

BETTY DUNCAN WAITED AT the restaurant for her father, B.J. Winters, and Tony Mayberry. The waitress came by twice to ask if she wanted to order a drink. Her daddy frowned on her drinking, but she had been patient for long enough.

"Vodka on the rocks," Betty finally told her. After all, if these two men couldn't be on time she deserved a drink.

"Daddy," she said as she rose to place a kiss on her father's weathered cheek. "Tony, hello." She accepted a brief hug from Tony before all three sat back at the table.

"Kinda early to be drinking, isn't it, baby?" her father asked. "But I guess if I'd been through what you've been through this month, I'd be drinking, too. Sugar, bring us all a round of drinks."

He didn't need to tell the waitress what to bring. B.J. Winters practically owned this restaurant within the country club and golf course on the edge of Calloway. He was the original owner of the property where they now sat, and no one ever forgot his contribution to this exclusive and private club that gave Calloway its cache – something the other small towns in Zion County could not claim.

"I'm so sorry about your daughter," Tony said. "I didn't get a chance to see you the other night with all the crowds and everything."

"Thanks, Tony, I know Betty appreciates that," B.J. said. Betty just stared into her drink.

"Betty, now we've got to talk," her father said once the other drinks were set down on the table. "I've met with the funeral home, and the body will be released to them late Friday after the autopsy is completed. I've set the funeral for Monday afternoon at the church."

Betty managed to nod her head. She had not been able to help with any of the arrangements.

"Lester will do the eulogy," she said.

"Betty, honey, you know Lester died three weeks ago," her father said.

"No, he didn't, Daddy. That was Anne that died, but not Lester," she said.

"Betty, for God's sake, knock it off. I can't have you saying things like this in public. Pull yourself together, daughter."

"This has been a shock for you, hasn't it?" Tony said, as he covered her hand with his.

Betty looked at him with grateful eyes that filled with tears the instant she made the human contact.

"More than I think I can handle. He's really dead, isn't he?"

"Yes, Betty, Lester died. Anne shot him and then she killed herself. And Shelley, your daughter, was killed two days ago. It's a lot to absorb, isn't it?" Tony talked in a soothing monotone, which seemed to relax Betty.

"I've lost everything. At least when Lester died, I still had his child; I had a part of him – now it's all gone, and I want to die." She began sobbing, loud racking sobs that caused everyone sitting in the club to turn around and stare.

Most everyone there knew what had happened and who Betty was, so the looks came from more than the mere curiosity seeker. The open stares directed at their table held open pity and something else – something not pretty, something that showed the human nature that permeates the worst of the species. There was glee. The look that said, "It's about time that family was brought down; they have always had too much of everything," appeared everywhere in that room that day, despite best efforts to hide it behind the pity. The worst of them felt sheer joy in the fact that someone who had always been on top had been suddenly brought down to the bottom of the heap.

"Betty, pull yourself together," her father said. "There's plenty of time for all that. Show what you are made of, girl."

Somehow, the words permeated through the wrenching pain of her sobs, and she began to take deep breaths as she took the handkerchief offered from Tony. She delicately blew her nose into the white cloth; she wiped under her eyes checking for traces of mascara, then she took a final gulp of her drink and signaled the waitress for another. She needed help to pull herself together.

"Anthony has been in touch," B.J. said. "He's very concerned."

"That's right, Betty," Tony said. "Dad would like to visit with you as soon as you are able to travel to the ranch."

"What does he want? I did everything he asked me to do."

"Now, sugar, he just wants to offer his condolences in person, but he can't come up here for the funeral. The press will be all over, you know that."

"But, Daddy, I did what he wanted."

"I know, baby, I know. Sometimes that just isn't enough, is it?"

"Actually, Dad is most concerned about your husband right now. Do you know what Alex has been up to the last two days?"

Betty shook her head and realized she hadn't seen her husband since the night of the accident. That really wasn't a concern to her. They always lived separate lives. There was no reason to think a tragedy would bring them closer together.

"I haven't seen him since Monday night," Betty said.

"It seems he's been pretty busy. The rumor mill has been working overtime, saying he's bringing a lawsuit against the city," Tony said.

"A lawsuit?"

"With that SGC organization, you know the Garcia fellow," B.J. said.

"Alex and SGC? No, that doesn't make any sense."

"That's what we think, Betty, and we need you to talk to Alex; persuade him to stop this nonsense," Tony said. "And something else. You really need to keep quiet about Lester and Shelley. Have you told anyone outside the family?"

CHAPTER FORTY-SIX

ALEX DUNCAN THREATENED TO topple the carefully built house of Winters and Marcetti. Years ago, B.J. hoped for a short time his only daughter, Betty, would marry one of Anthony's sons, preferably Tony because he was favored as the oldest. But he let Sonny Duncan talk him into the marriage between Alex and Betty. At the time, it made sense. The Duncan's holdings in the area combined with the Winters gave them great power in both Zion and Banks counties. Even though Industrial Pines spread itself over the southern part of the peninsula, B.J. wanted to strengthen his hold in the north where he knew growth would inevitably spread.

Now B.J. sat looking at his daughter and wondered if maybe he had asked too much of her. She'd always been so complacent, even though he knew she loved Lester. He cautioned her before the wedding to be careful. He told her he would understand if she had to go elsewhere than her marriage for love. He knew as well as anyone that Alex would not be able to give her that.

Betty agreed and told him she would never stop loving Lester nor would she stop seeing him. When she became pregnant several years after the marriage of economic makings, B.J. knew deep in his heart Alex was not the father. Betty had never hinted at it until now.

Now she was falling apart, having lost Lester and her only child within weeks of one another. He thought briefly of sending her away after the funeral to recover. But they needed her on the commission, and they needed her to make a successful run for Lester's seat in March. He would have to help her get through this right here in Calloway.

"Now, sugar, is there anything special you want done at the funeral?" B.J. asked his daughter. "Any special song for the organist to play?"

"I want to see that reporter from *The Braidwood Tribune*. That nice young woman who was so kind to me that night," Betty said.

"Betty, it's wonderful to see you, but not under such sad circumstances." Anthony Marcetti wrapped Betty in his large arms after laying his rifle down on a chair in the entryway.

"Thank you, Anthony," Betty said as she pulled away.

"Let's go in the study and have a little brandy, okay?" Anthony did not wait for an answer but turned to his right and headed into the animal-decorated den with overstuffed leather chairs and rugs that looked as if they'd recently been skinned off the backs of a large game animal.

Betty only agreed to come if she could meet with Kelly in the next few days. Her father and Tony assured her they would arrange it.

Anthony made her nervous from the first time she met him when she was twelve. He hugged her then in the same way, with a cigar burning in the hand that wrapped itself around her small body. He always smelled of cigars and whiskey, and something more primal. The smell of the animal hung about him, she thought, that musky rank smell as she imagined Pan smelling as he trampled through the fields violating everything in sight.

Anthony had that energy about him, and it made her nervous. It hadn't prevented her from calling him the night Anne and Lester died. Anthony might be unpleasant to an innocent girl, but he knew how to undo and outdo problems. There was no one else to call.

"My father said you wanted to speak to me," Betty said once she settled in the chair across from his desk. She allowed the warmth of the brandy to slide down her throat. The glow from the alcohol might help with what she knew could only be a messy conversation.

"Your husband, Alex? Where is he?"

"I don't know, don't care," she said. "He left the night Shelley died."

"Your father tells me you've been talking about Shelley's father," Anthony said. "You know you must keep quiet about that and so must Alex."

"Who cares now?" She took another sip of the medicine that would anesthetize her mind.

"You better care, my dear, because I saved your pretty little behind that night with Lester and his wife. You better care because if anyone finds out that Lester is the father of your child there will be nosy reporters and lots of accounting to be done.

"I've already got my hands full with the Calloway Police Department and keeping officers from talking about seeing you in that house that night, so you had better well start caring right this damn minute."

Anthony's voice rose with each word, spoken slowly and methodically. The slowness allowed his anger to simmer and the loudness helped it explode.

Betty took a big gulp. "Don't you understand, Anthony?"

"I understand that we've got a mess here. I've heard your hubby is getting into bed with those stupid dirt lovers and might even be doing something crazy like suing the city over the warehouse. That cannot happen."

"I just don't care. I've lost everything that ever mattered," Betty said.

"Do you want to go to the chair? Do you?"

Betty didn't answer him, but she stared at him as if he had just asked her if she wanted to go for a walk.

"The chair is fine; I don't care."

"If they even think you killed your lover and his wife; they'll fry you in this state. Already the media is portraying Anne as the long silent wife. Pretty soon, someone might start asking questions about you and Lester. Then what happens? The whole thing falls apart, and it will be all your fault, so you had better start caring or your father and I will have to do something drastic."

"Drastic?" Betty began to laugh, beginning at first as a quiet little laugh as if Anthony had just told a cute little dirty joke. Then it began rising in intensity until she was holding her sides and rocking back and forth in the chair. Tears fell down her cheeks and Anthony pressed the button at his side.

Between tears and gasps for air she managed, "What could you do to me that would be more drastic than what has already happened?"

B.J. appeared in the doorway and looked first at his daughter who was hysterical and then to Anthony, who stood poised at his desk the telephone to his ear.

"Yes, send an ambulance. She's suicidal; yes, that's right, Baker Act."

"No, we can't do that," B.J. said, but Anthony ignored him and continued giving directions to the ranch.

When he hung up the phone, he looked hard at B.J.

"We don't have any choice, B.J. I know she's your daughter, but right now in her state, she is very dangerous to us. Putting her away for the next seventy-two hours will give us some time. They'll put her on some medication, and no one will ever know, okay?

Betty had to be restrained with handcuffs when they finally arrived for her. By that time, she had stopped laughing. Anthony gave her another snifter full. She became more belligerent. When they came in the study to take her away, she began fighting the policeman and the paramedic like a trapped animal.

The men handling her towered over her small body, but she fought as hard as she could. Finally she gave up, her strength depleted for the moment. They walked her out handcuffed, passing under the head of a wild boar hunted down one summer morning during one of Anthony's safaris.

The glass eyes stared down in sympathy at the beaten woman.

CHAPTER FORTY-SEVEN

BART CALLED KELLY FROM his house late on a Friday night in early December.

"She's not doing too well," Bart said. "I'm not sure what to do, but I'm a little afraid to leave her alone."

"Then you'd better stay there tonight. Are you going to call her doctor?"

"In the morning. She's upstairs now getting ready for bed, but sometimes she wakes up and can't get back to sleep. That's when I worry about her the most."

After they hung up the phone, Kelly decided to soothe her aching heart and body in her one indulgence: a hot bubble bath. She poured a glass of wine and lit the candles sitting on the white tile surrounding her tub. She usually read a novel while soaking, but on this night, she wanted solitude.

What did her life amount to at this very moment, she wondered. She had no children, although she had given birth almost seventeen years ago. She wondered how she and Bart could ever have a relationship if he had to rescue Joyce continually. She felt betrayed in one sense for even allowing hope to creep into the equation. How did she let Bart make her this vulnerable? Over Thanksgiving, she had even confided in him her one dark secret.

She felt no better when she emerged from the bath. She toweled herself off and thought about the things she could do to shake the feeling of hopelessness taking up residence in her brain. She sat down at the computer and began to write. Soon the screen before her took precedence over everything, and she forgot about Bart and Joyce. Most of all she forgot the pain of loving someone. When she finally went to bed, she slept soundly until she heard the phone ringing. The bedside clock showed she'd slept until ten o'clock.

"Kelly," Bart said when she answered. "Joyce is in the hospital. She took an overdose of tranquilizers last night. They pumped her stomach. She's going to survive, but I just put her in the private hospital next door."

"How are you?"

"I'm numb. This is the first time she actually tried to go through with it. I went in to check on her in the middle of the night and found the bottles tipped over and empty."

"It's a good thing you spent the night there then. What can I do?"

"Nothing right now. I'll see how things are on Monday. Then I might need you to pitch hit for me at the office."

"You got it, Boss."

For the rest of the weekend, Kelly continued to write without any particular goal. She wasn't much a journal writer, but as she wrote about her feelings and about Bart, she realized the cathartic benefits in exorcising those demons that had settled for so long around her heart and brain. The more she wrote, the more she realized she sympathized with Joyce. She knew what it was like to want to die, although Kelly's depression was situational rather than a chronic state. For Joyce, hope never appeared. For Kelly, hope resurfaced when she got through the worst moments. She remembered back to her suicide attempt all those years ago, just two years after Joely's birth. She never knew what triggered it, but she knew she would never forget the experience of being locked up in the indigent ward at the hospital until her parents could come to Braidwood and have her moved into a private place. Kelly wrote about that experience over the weekend as she thought about Joyce.

Kelly stayed in the hospital for almost a week. When she was released, she threw herself into school and work at the newspaper. Now fifteen years later, she realized she was blessed with the ability to pull herself out of that depression despite the lingering pain associated with the rape and the birth of her daughter.

Bart called Sunday night as she settled down with a silly novel to take her mind away from the darkness that settled around her over the weekend. In between reliving her own experience, she tried to imagine what might be happening with Joyce.

"She's better, but probably won't be released for a few days yet," Bart said. "Can I come over?"

"Why aren't you here now?"

"On my way."

He fell into her arms when she opened the door. He looked as if he hadn't slept for the entire weekend.

After Bart finished giving Kelly all the details, he paused.

"Something very strange happened," he said.

"Stranger than your wife attempting suicide? That seems to top the list of strangeness."

"I can top it. I'm just not sure about the ethics here. I think maybe I'm too tired to be a good judge."

"Can you tell me? Or is that the ethical part?"

"It's probably all right because the other patient is the one who asked me to do this favor for her."

"Now you've got me; you're going to have to tell me now."

Bart heard a commotion out in the hallway soon after his wife was admitted and settled in her room, which was positioned across from the nurse's station. If Joyce wanted, she could see most everything that went on. She wasn't allowed to shut her door and shut out the chaos because they'd placed her on suicide watch. Bart hoped that whoever was being admitted would not be put in Joyce's room.

He decided to go out and see what was happening. Most of the patients from the floor were shuffling over to the glassed walls of the nurse's station. The main entertainment of the day came with the admittance of a new patient. He saw the police officer first and knew that the new patient had been brought in against his or her will.

Bart walked closer to the glass. Sitting on a chair with her head bowed and handcuffs still in place sat Betty Duncan. Her hair was a mess and her mascara runny, but it was still Betty, no doubt about it. Bart recognized her from the night her daughter was killed.

Betty looked up when she sensed Bart staring at her. For the moment recognition flashed across her face, but then it was gone.

Joyce lay on her bed, and Bart sat in one of the uncomfortable recliners in the corner when an unhandcuffed Betty appeared in the doorway with the head nurse at her side.

"Do you mind if I share a room with you?" Betty asked.

"She's supposed to have a private room, but we don't have any," the nurse said. "She said she knew you and wondered if she could be put in here."

"Actually, I know him," Betty said.

"Joyce, this is Betty," Bart said. "I interviewed her for a story the other night. Do you mind if she stays in here?"

"I'd like that, Betty," Joyce said. "I recognize your picture from the paper."

"I want to remind the both of you that whatever happens in this place and whatever comes out in group discussions, stays here in this place," the nurse said. "I'm a little uneasy with the two of you knowing each other, but I'm going to trust that you are both smart enough to know how to handle it. Maybe it will help."

" Thanks, we'll be fine," Joyce said.

"I'll bring your clothes and things once we've gone through them," the nurse told Betty. "Then we'll do an inventory sheet. I'll also have to ask you some questions at that time, so, Joyce, if you would make yourself scarce when I come back, I'd appreciate it."

"It's been tough, hasn't it?" Joyce asked Betty when the nurse left.

"You have no idea," Betty said. "Your husband was so kind to me the other night."

"Did you try to kill yourself, Betty?" Joyce asked. "I'm sorry to be so blunt, but we're going to know all that stuff eventually. It's the reason I'm here."

"No, it's not why I'm here although I can't say I haven't thought about it since my baby was killed. No, I did something much worse. I told my father and a couple of the other men trying to run my life right now that I wanted to talk to that nice reporter, Kelly."

"Kelly Sands?" Joyce asked. "Why?"

"I think she might be able to help me."

"They put you in here because you wanted to talk to one of my reporters?" Bart asked.

"Not exactly, but it's something I told Daddy before I met with the others, and it upset him. I'm in here because they think I'm going to spill my guts to the press and lose a whole bunch of money for all of them, so they told the police I was threatening suicide."

Just then the nurse came back to do inventory with Betty, and Joyce and Bart walked out into the main room.

"That's strange, isn't it?" Joyce asked when she and Bart settled on a couch.

"How do you feel hearing Kelly's name?"

"It's okay, Bart. I'd actually like to meet her."

Betty soon joined them and told them a little more. First, they put her in a hospital near Eustis for the seventy-two observation required by law. When it looked as if she would need more time, her father made the decision to move her to Braidwood.

"I made sure to tell them I wanted no visitors or no calls," Betty said. "I wouldn't even let my father bring me here, so I got the royal police treatment."

"Then she asked me if she could see you," Bart said as he finished telling Kelly the absurd story. "I told her I didn't know about that based on what the nurse had said earlier. I suggested she write you a letter, and I would give it to you."

Bart pulled an envelope out of his pocket and handed it to Kelly.

"I don't know what it says," he said, "but if it has anything to do with what she told Joyce, it's big."

CHAPTER FORTY-EIGHT

B.J. WINTERS, BETTY'S FATHER, once dynamited fish on the Hope Springs River. He learned from his wife's uncles how to cut a quarter stick of dynamite, light it and throw it in the water just before the fuse burned down to the explosive. The fish would float up to the surface, and the ones that didn't die were temporarily slowed down enough to find themselves trapped in a net. The lazy fishermen then pulled up the net containing dozens of dead and stunned fish. They would spend the next few hours cleaning those mullet. The fish that had received the most impact from the blast had exploded spleens.

One of the uncles only had four fingers on his right hand. He failed to let go of the powerful stub in time. B.J. heard stories of some of the best dynamiters in the area who only had one arm. Nub, the most famous of the fish blasters, had no arms after attempting to use more than a quarter of a stick. *If just a stub could bring that many fish to the surface, imagine what the whole stick would do,* the slothful fisherman thought. He even used both hands to hoist the stick high above his head before tossing it into the water. Only trouble was the fuse was shorter than usual and Nub decided to show off for his buddies as he made a production of winding up and rotating the stick a few times over his head. If he had just done one less round up, his arms might have survived.

But Nub was a persistent fellow. For the rest of his life he used his toes to toss in the smaller sticks of dynamite. He died with his feet intact.

B.J. thought of Nub now as he drove back to Calloway after following the police car with Betty in the back seat and seeing she was safely admitted to the Braidwood private clinic. His daughter was playing with dynamite herself right now, and he was powerless to do anything about it. There was nothing he could hold over her head anymore. With the death of both Lester and Shelley, Betty's ability to be moved by anything was removed. She might even face criminal charges if she did not come out of this state where she felt she had nothing to lose. She had finally stopped asking to speak to that pesky reporter, and B.J. hoped that was a sign that his complacent and agreeable daughter had returned.

Betty could be as stubborn and persistent as old Nub, but B.J. would be damned if she took the rest of them down with her. He needed to instill in her the values instilled in him so long ago on the banks of the Hope Springs River. No matter what, they stood together, even when it went against the established law. B.J. felt he and his partners knew best and should either ignore or work to change those laws that made no sense.

When the state decided to put officers in charge of the rivers and woods of Florida, the state started to go downhill as far as B.J. was concerned. They tried to pit neighbor against neighbor, and then they tried to tell them what they could or couldn't do with their own private property. The further downfall in Florida came with the advent of the Environmental Protection Agency in the early 1970s. The EPA stuck their nose into things that just did not or should not concern them.

If people could feed themselves a little more easily by dynamiting those fish, then so be it. No government should be allowed to come in and regulate a man's way to feed his family.

B.J. believed the same thing applied to the closing of his father-in-law's turpentine camps. Everyone was happy with the way the system worked. The owners of the property enjoyed the rents paid by the turpentine companies, and the turpentine companies made huge profits on that thick pine juice imported mostly to Germany. And the workers made a living and were given a place to live. When the camps closed, where were these men supposed to find work to support their families already destitute from the conditions inherent in the depression?

B.J. saw one view and one view only. He thought that survival of the fittest applied mostly to the human race rather than the animal kingdom. And those with the strongest and most successful survival skills should be afforded some of the luxuries associated with being on top of the pile.

He loved Betty, his only child. He loved Shelley, his only grandchild. He could not let everything be destroyed now. Alex proved to be the most immediate and challenging obstacle. Betty was away for now, and he had to believe that she would come to her senses. She would see that he had always looked out for her best interest, and she would discover that it was in everyone's best interest to continue with the family tradition.

Even after her marriage to Alex, B.J. tolerated the open affair with Lester. She should be grateful for the years they did have together without interference from either of their spouses, parents, or children.

"Did you do it for love?" Betty asked after they turned out the lights.

"Do what? Try to kill myself? No, I just didn't want to live anymore; it's more a state of mind," Joyce said.

When Bart visited Joyce on Sunday, she took him to the outside patio where the sun warmed them as they sat in the privacy of the walled garden. Joyce and Betty grew close over the past two days, and Betty shared the details of the past few weeks of her life. Joyce shared some of that with Bart at Betty's request. The story Joyce related shocked even the hardened journalist, Bart Stanley.

"I loved Lester, but I hadn't counted on one thing," Betty told Joyce the night before.

"What was that?"

"Lester fell in love with Anne sometime during their marriage. I heard them talking right before they died. And Anne loved him."

"You heard them talking right before they died?" Joyce asked. She read all the newspaper accounts because something about Anne's picture touched her deeply. She saw in Anne a little bit of herself.

"I walked in on them in bed."

After Betty told Joyce the whole story of the events of that afternoon when Anne and Lester died, Joyce had one question.

"The newspapers reported they were alone when it happened. How did you manage to escape unnoticed?" Joyce asked.

"I made a phone call to the only person who could have possibly helped me."

"Who?" Joyce asked.

"Anthony Marcetti."

Kelly finished the letter from Betty and handed it to Bart.

"It's big all right, Boss. Now we've got to figure out how to get me into that hospital."

CHAPTER FORTY-NINE

ANTHONY CUT THE END of his cigar and lit it before calling his son Tony.

"Is she still locked up?" Anthony asked.

"She's in Braidwood now in that private clinic. She hasn't been cooperating, so she stays."

"You tell them at that clinic who they're dealing with – mention new equipment – you know the routine."

"I know the routine. By the way, I'm having difficulty tracking down Alex Duncan."

"Why?"

"He isn't answering his phone. I don't think he's living at the house. We tried Garcia, but he has that place with all the weird underground shelters; he's a real paranoid jerk, that one. Now he's put up barbed wire around the yard where he's got a tortoise cemetery going."

"We need Alex Duncan. What you got on the annexation in Hope Springs?"

"All the annexation requests are in place, and Lucy just transferred the deeds in Waine's name to hers yesterday. The first public hearing on the annexations will be next month, after the first of the year. If that passes, which it should, then they go to the state for approval. The zoning changes for the airstrip will come before the Calloway Commission at the last meeting in December."

"You bought that large tract of land west of downtown Calloway?"

"Randy Robinson is set to make a bid on it, but it won't be any problem. The owners have been waiting for this to happen; they wanted the right owners, that's all."

"Zion County has been much easier than I anticipated, my dear boy. Now I advise you to go out and get laid tonight and drink lots of scotch

215

because once all this starts, you won't have much time on your hands. No, not much time at all."

Tony Mayberry had all the traits of a coddled yet well-trained first-born son. His younger brothers, while pampered, did not enjoy the easy satisfaction Tony experienced. Tony knew that whatever he touched would turn to gold, and if it didn't happen on his schedule, he had the means to make it happen. He got whatever he wanted.

That included women, too. After he hung up the phone with his father, he reached for the naked body lying next to him and began caressing it. He kissed her shoulders and when she began to stir and turn toward him, he wasted no time in entering her roughly and without any preparation. His lover was not surprised. This was Tony Mayberry, and she knew how to please him. and he knew how to please her. She smiled as he pumped harder and harder over her and thought about the couple of hundred dollar bills Tony would leave on the bed stand before he left the room.

Alex Duncan stood facing Cowan Garcia in the underground studio built by Garcia years earlier as his refuge from the world. Alex had been staying in the shelter since the day after Shelley was killed.

"They're looking for you everywhere," Cowan said. "I've got Mayberry calling here two and three times a day. They must be pretty afraid of what you know."

"They like to keep everyone in order. Mayberry has received his orders from his father, and so he's performing like a good soldier."

"Your wife seems to have disappeared, too."

"Betty? The good little soldier? If she's disappeared, it's because they wanted her to disappear. B.J. probably wants to keep her out of sight until they've spoken to me."

"Maybe. Something's a little fishy about it though. Shelley's funeral was today. Rumor has it, Betty didn't show up."

"Too distraught, or she finally lost her mind completely. She was talking crazy that night like Lester was still alive and needed to be told. Maybe she finally cracked. And if she did, she probably went into fine little pieces because she was really tightly strung."

Cowan sat down on the couch covered with an old army blanket. He patted the seat next to him, and Alex obediently came and sat at his side. Cowan placed his hand on Alex's knee and with his other hand he turned Alex's face toward him.

"How come I never noticed you before," Cowan said before he leaned down to kiss Alex on the lips.

Lt. John Carson pulled the car up to the building, leaving it idling in the circular drive of the wing of the mental hospital.

"You sure you want to go through with this?" he asked his passenger.

"We've gone over this, John." Kelly said. "It's fool proof."

"Except I'm driving you here in a police car without invoking the Baker Act."

"You're my good friend, and you know I'm depressed. You're just helping me because you know the ropes, that's all."

"Good thing I trust you."

Bart called Kelly an hour ago to let her know Joyce had been released, and Betty now had an empty bed in her room. Betty knew to be looking for Kelly, ready to ask to become her roommate.

Molly made it through the security check and then her name check at the nurse's station. They told her Kelly was in her room.

When Molly walked through the door, she saw a small blonde woman sitting on the bed with her back to her.

Kelly sat on her bed facing the woman as they talked. Molly was most of the way in the room before she realized that an intense conversation was taking place between the two women. By that time, it was too late to back out because Kelly looked up and saw her standing there.

"Good morning, doll," Molly said as she approached Kelly's bed. "Looks like you've got company."

The other woman turned toward Molly and full recognition hit her. She sat down hard on Kelly's bed.

"What's this about?" she asked.

"You know Betty?" Kelly asked.

"You don't cover politics in Calloway for very long before you know Betty Duncan. I'm so sorry about your little girl. It must be very difficult for you." Molly wanted to stop talking, but when she became this nervous her mouth and tongue worked without the help of the brain.

"Molly, did they make you sign that confidentiality agreement today?" Kelly asked.

"Yes, but what does that have to do with Betty?"

"She's a patient. No one else knows we're in here together, except Bart and now you. Betty isn't allowing any visitors or calls, but she told her father and a couple of other people right before she was admitted that she wanted to talk to me."

"Why?"

"I had some things I wanted to share with Kelly. That's one of the reasons my father started worrying about me," Betty said.

"Excuse me, ladies, but I'm having difficulty taking all of this in," Molly stood and began pacing back and forth between the ends of the beds. The two other women watched her. "I thought you came here because of your depression over Bart."

"I lied about that to get you here," Kelly said. "I couldn't admit anything over the phone. Molly, we need your word on this, or we could all be in trouble. Betty has told me some things that are explosive."

Molly looked at Betty. "You wanted to tell Kelly something that could be published?"

"Yes, I want to go public with what I know. When I suggested that to my father and his friends, they locked me up in here until I come to my senses."

"Betty, would you mind if I talked to Kelly alone for a minute? We can go out into the lobby, but I just need to talk to her about some touchy matters," Molly said.

"I trust Betty explicitly, if that's what this is all about," Kelly said. "You can talk in front of her; you can trust me on this one, Molly."

"All right then." Molly paused and continued to look from one woman to the other. "Betty, I'm sorry, but it's just that you've been the enemy for so long, not granting interviews, blocking public records requests whenever you could legally do it, generally making things extremely difficult for *The Chronicle*. It's hard to switch my thinking."

"I understand, but maybe if I share something with you that would help?"

"I'm listening," Molly said.

"I know who really killed Lester and Anne Simmons," Betty said.

"Who killed them? It was a murder suicide."

"No suicide. Everything got cleaned up and rearranged."

CHAPTER FIFTY

"WHAT HAPPENED?" MOLLY ASKED.

Betty proceeded to tell her story to Molly while Kelly filled in the gaps where needed.

"I don't really care what happens to me, I would just like to come clean with everything. I want to tell everything I know about everything."

"okay, let's slow down here and think about this whole thing," Molly said. She began pacing. "We have to be careful because once they find out you've spilled the beans they will come after you and whoever knows."

"I'm not taking my meds," Betty said. "That's what they want me to do so they can control me, so I just fake swallowing."

"No one knows you two are rooming together?"

"Just Bart. You're the only visitor so far for either of us." Kelly said.

"Do you and Bart have a plan?" Molly asked.

"That's why you're here, my dear friend," Kelly said. "Bart wants to bring *The Chronicle* in to help. He's calling Greg this morning to figure out how we can best put our resources to work. He thinks we're going to need a month to pull everything together."

"And Betty? You want to cooperate with us?" Molly asked.

"I don't see any other way. Either way I'm going to spend some time behind bars, which doesn't bother me. If I come clean, perhaps I can atone for some of my past. I was always such a good little soldier, but when I saw Shelley's helpless and lifeless hand sticking out from the front of the truck, I suddenly lost all hope and connection to that past life. It's over. My daddy and Anthony Marcetti can rot in hell, but I don't need to go with them."

219

"We may be able to get Alex to help as well," Kelly said. "I had breakfast with him and Cowan Garcia and other SGC members last week. He's bringing a lawsuit against the city, but maybe we can get him to help with dates and names, too. Also, can you access that research Mike should have done on ethics complaints in the past?"

"I found his files," Molly said. "Everywhere he turned ended up at a dead end. No files or complaints can be found implicating Jackson Stewart in any wrongdoing in his thirty years on the Commission."

"What about Luddy? Have you talked to her lately?" Kelly asked.

"Thanks for reminding me," Molly said. "I ran into her yesterday. She received a letter from the Commission on Ethics regarding her complaint. They told her there was not enough evidence of wrongdoing for them to conduct an investigation."

"Looks like we're going alone on this one," Kelly said.

"Betty, I need to tell you something else before I leave," Molly said. "Your father held the funeral this morning for Shelley. He told people you couldn't attend because of your grief."

Betty's eyes filled with tears, but she did not allow them to turn into sobs. "That's all right. That was Daddy's show anyway. He wouldn't let me do it the way I wanted, but I would like something." She looked around the room.

"I know a minister in Calloway who would probably help. He helped Anne Simmons years ago." Kelly said. "Did you know she had a child fathered by none other than her own father? She gave it up for adoption and when she came back, she married Lester."

"Anne did?" Betty's surprise gave way to understanding. "That sure explains a lot. We all make too many assumptions about others, don't we?"

"Molly, will you call Rev. Baxter for me?" Kelly asked. "Tell him I asked you to call. See if he can come here today or tomorrow and conduct a private service for Shelley."

"I'll see what I can do. If he can't do it, I'll ask my minister," Molly said. "Just remember, ladies, this is big, bigger than a fake bomb, bigger than a dead armadillo, bigger than a tortoise grave. And we have everything to lose if word gets out that we are working on the story of the century in Zion County."

"Right, Boss," Kelly said as she gave her friend a little salute.

Jackson Stewart paced the office of Tony Mayberry. Tony's announcement that that Alex Duncan officially filed the lawsuit against the City of Calloway for the construction of the Monster Mart warehouse on a road that could not handle the traffic came as no surprise, but it angered him just the same.

"We think Alex has moved in with Garcia," Tony said.

"Now that's a real sweet love story there," Jackson said. "We need to do something now. I mean it. If we have investigations going on, who knows what might get out? We need to get someone strong in position at city hall to stop the nonsense."

"I know we need to replace Betty as city manager," Tony said. "We could put someone in who is unexpected, who wouldn't care what others think, who could handle Luddy Gregors if she should get elected."

"How about Thomas Jefferson?"

"The chief of police?"

"Why not? He's black so that's a plus; makes him easy to control if we give him a little power. He's got a good reputation in the community, and even those tree huggers like him."

"Not bad, not bad," Tony said. "He might even be accepted by SGC as one of them or at least we can make it seem that way. I know he's friends with some of them, including Garcia. Godawful even likes him, and she hates everyone."

CHAPTER FIFTY-ONE

THOMAS JEFFERSON DID ONE thing exceedingly well. He took credit for things he did not do. His assistant, Susie, had been in love with him since they started school. She didn't fit his bill as a woman with whom he could be seen in public. He saw her outside the department, but not where anyone knew about it. He kept her hidden from others, but he used her as often as he could. He preferred to date high-profile women, white and black. His bulging muscles, good looks, and position as Calloway Chief of Police attracted some of the most beautiful women in Braidwood.

Thomas saw to it that a youth center opened in an old abandoned schoolhouse on the other side of the tracks in Calloway. The building volunteers renovated the building using donated products. He received recognition from the Chamber of Commerce, Rotary, and Lions Club for his efforts. There was a big media-laden ribbon cutting ceremony where Thomas stood pumped up and proud in his uniform as he accepted accolades from the mayor.

These days the youth center sits vacant, and no one remembers the promises made by Chief Jefferson to help make the streets safe with a community center in the middle of the neighborhood. Thomas received what he craved and then forgot about funding and staffing the center. It never really opened its doors except on that day when the VIPs and press trooped through the building oohing and aahing over the brightly painted walls.

Susie lovingly wrote all of his correspondence and reports. Thomas did little at the department except attend official functions and board meetings of several large charitable organizations in Braidwood. He never missed an opportunity to talk to the press.

He liked most of them, even Kelly Sands. She was fair and responsive. She even wrote a profile of him. The photograph showed him standing in front of an American flag in his uniform. He looked intimidating and strong. He framed and matted the article along with the picture and hung it in his office with his other awards.

Thomas hoped Kelly Sands would be around to do another piece on "Calloway's First Black City Manager." Maybe that would even make the front page instead of the local section in the *Tribune*.

"Thomas, it's good to see you," Tony Mayberry said, as they settled in the comfortable leather chairs in the darkly decorated office of the Calloway city attorney.

"It's always a pleasure," Thomas said.

"As you know we need to get a new city manager in place," began the mayor. "And I'd like to make a recommendation at tonight's meeting for my choice. Jackson is poised to make the motion."

"Anyone I know?" Thomas asked.

He courted the mayor for this position, and he knew the answer as well as he knew how many steroids he could shoot into his veins before he developed a moon face.

"You might know this fellow," Tony said. "It's Chief Jefferson."

"That's an honor, Sirs, a real honor," Thomas said. "I just have one request. You know I've been with CPD for a long time, and the community views me as someone who can protect them.

"I'd like to have the title of Police Commissioner along with City Manager," he said. "That way I can still serve as a police officer and carry a weapon. I would hate for someone to come to me because that's how they've always viewed me and request police protection, and I can't give it to them."

"I don't see why we can't arrange that," the mayor said.

"You could have Commissioner Stewart make it a part of his motion," Thomas said, although he'd already asked Chelsea Godfrey the same thing. No sense in taking any chances.

"Let me check on the legality of it," Tony said. "We probably can get around any hurdles, but I want to be sure."

Thomas wanted to feel that sense of security knowing he had his .38 Colt Snubby Revolver securely attached to his ankle holster. The Snubby with its two-inch barrel had been a present from Jackson when he became chief of police.

"This sweet little thing belonged to my daddy," Jackson said. "They don't make them anymore, thanks to those anti-Constitution peace lovers. But there's nothing like this little Colt for keeping a weapon always at hand. I feel safer just knowing you'll be wearing it."

Thomas took great comfort in feeling that holster on his right ankle, ready to pull whenever necessary. It gave him even more peace of mind than the regular issue police handgun inside his holster. Lately, he suspected he needed to protect himself at all times.

The other day one of the officers questioned his policy on sick leave at the police department, and Thomas was certain it was a personal attack on his leadership ability as chief.

"I can paper trail you out of this job, just watch," Thomas told the officer. "You go straight to the union, and I'll see that some things in your past you'd probably not want made public will come to the forefront. Just try me."

The officer, although angry, worried more about his reputation and his marriage. Surveillance cameras at the station captured him massaging one of the dispatchers not with his hands and not with his pants on. Thomas was sympathetic at the time when he called the officer into his office to show him what the cameras captured. Thomas liked to keep tabs on those around him, and he kept separate files on each officer and staff hidden in a locked cabinet in his office.

"Greg, have you talked to Bart Stanley today?" Molly asked her editor when she returned to *The Chronicle* after her visit with Betty and Kelly.

"I've got a message from him, but I haven't had a chance to call him back," Greg said as he continued to work at the computer. "Why?"

"Not here."

Greg looked up from the screen. He waited for Molly to explain.

"Let's walk around the block," Molly said. "I don't feel comfortable here."

As they began walking around downtown Calloway, Molly began the unbelievable story that unfolded in the room at the mental hospital. Greg said little but he kept his head down, frowning as they walked, and Molly's words spilled out, one on top of the other.

"And now Betty is ready to spill her guts, and Kelly is ready to write about it," Molly said as she finished the saga. "She said Bart wanted to bring *The Chronicle* in to help."

"I guess I better call Bart," Greg said. "If Betty is telling the truth, this is big and serious, more serious and dangerous than anything I've ever worked on; we're talking murder and cover-up here and corruption in government and probably just about everything else."

"I know, but isn't this what you wait for as a journalist?" Molly stopped on the street waiting for Greg to reply.

He turned slowly when he realized she no longer walked along side him. When he lifted his eyes from his reverie with the sidewalk, Molly saw the twinkle, the glint, even though his countenance remained stern.

"First, I need to talk to Bart," he said. "And you do not do anything without my knowing about each step of the way. I won't enter into it until Bart promises me that the four of us are in this equally, and I need reassurances that no one else knows anything."

"What about Betty?" Greg asked. "She's really a wild card here, and everything depends on her cooperation. Without that, there is nothing. What do you know about her release?"

"I've been thinking about that. If she's released, she might be pressured to stop; but if she is uncooperative, they will keep her indefinitely. They only release those who follow the program. She might risk a shock treatment or two, but it might be worth it to keep her inside while we compile our facts."

"Is she willing to do that?"

"I think she'd be willing to do just about anything to strike back. As she told me several times today, she's got nothing to lose now."

"Molly, you are the best thing that ever happened to *The Chronicle*," Greg said. "And you have proven me right once again. I thought I'd lost my touch with Mike Green, but you've convinced me I just had a momentary lapse."

CHAPTER FIFTY-TWO

"MOLLY OR I WILL visit you every day until you are released," Kelly told Betty.

Kelly's small bag of clothes sat on her bed. She waited for the doctor to sign her release forms, and Molly to arrive to take her from this place. Despite the memories it brought back, Kelly managed to put the past in its proper place as she concentrated on helping Betty through her losses and quest for revenge.

"Did you put our names on your visitor's list?" Kelly asked.

"Last night; it's all set. The doctor seems to be getting tired of my lack of ambition."

"They might put you in the wacko ward down the hall. Can you handle it?"

"Let them. They said yesterday I need shock treatment. Don't they realize that's what the last month has been? Major shock treatment."

"I know right now you're motivated by getting revenge, and sometimes we need that anger to fuel us, but at some point, you might start thinking about what is best for Betty."

"If I do that, I won't be able to go forward."

"That's what you say right now, so keep that anger for now," Kelly said, "but believe me, at some point, you have to let it go and move on."

"To what? That's the problem; I can't see anything for my future."

"Maybe I can help there. I've felt that way before, too. I want you to know you can always talk to me, no matter what it is. I learned a long time ago not to judge anyone until I've walked in their shoes."

Molly walked into the room as the two women hugged.

"You ready to blow this joint, Kelly? Betty, I thought you might want some cheerier company than your old roommate here," Molly said as she placed a vase filled with evergreen branches, white mums, and red ribbons on the night table next to the bed.

"Thank you, very Christmassy," Betty said. "Shelley loved Christmas and flowers. You and Kelly are all set to be my only visitors, Miss Hale. Quite a turnaround, isn't it?"

"You bet. You know what they say about politics and bedfellows."

Molly pulled the door shut and brought out a small pad and pen from under her sweater.

"Here you go. Don't let them see you with this – they told me no pens – but it's a way for you to start writing down dates and names and events so we can start the paper trail on our end."

"I can't wait. When do you think something will go in the paper?"

"It could be up to a month so we've got to be diligent and careful. Hopefully we'll get you out of here well before that."

"I don't mind staying in here as long as it takes. Here are my choices when I'm released: I could be in the clutches of Anthony and my father who would be insisting I begin campaigning and passing zoning changes and annexations to make this Marcetti County, or I could be in prison, or I could be dead. This place doesn't look so bad."

"That's true," Molly said. "I worry that Marcetti or your father might start putting pressure on this place for you to be released so you can get back to the commission business."

"Not as long as they think I'm unpredictable and unstable. They do not want me to do anything to jeopardize the next steps in the process. Christmas is what, ten days away? That means the commission only has one more meeting in December. That gives you some time."

"That should give us plenty of time, don't you think, Molly?" Kelly asked.

"As long as we continue getting information to research from Betty and Alex."

Molly and Kelly finally made their way outside the building. Kelly breathed in the fresh air and gloried in the sun beating down on her face. The morning radiated the best in a north Florida almost-winter day – warm and clear. She felt something shift inside of her, and she realized it was gratitude. She felt gratitude for being alive and for the ability to make something good come out of the darkness. She lifted her face to the sun and vowed to herself that she would get those bastards who had hurt and destroyed Betty Duncan and Anne

Simmons. It was the same thing Randy and those boys had done to her, although her rape was as literal and fast as it was damaging. Betty's rape took years, but she'd been used, and so had Anne. It was time for someone to take a stand against those bastards. Kelly knew in her heart she had the ability in her to do the right thing and make them pay. It was one way Kelly could finally fight back.

Joely never strayed far from her thoughts and on this morning, she felt gratitude for having a daughter. She wondered if Joely would try to find her once she reached eighteen. That in itself was incentive for her to continue to fight.

She thought briefly of Bart and the way he looked at her between his crinkled brown eyes, and just as quickly she remembered Mike Green pushing her against the car after the commission meeting.

"What are you doing?" Molly asked when Kelly flicked her middle finger against her thumb.

"I'm flicking away some memories. Let's go get them, Mol."

"I haven't had a dead tortoise left in a few weeks," Cowan said as he and Alex settled on the couch in the fallout shelter with a couple of beers. "I guess they got tired of killing those poor defenseless creatures."

"Cowan, there's something I should tell you about those tortoises," Alex said. "I know who put them there."

"Really? Now who would that be, I wonder?"

"Not who you are probably thinking. It was Gary Dregs."

"Dregs of Humanity? I can't stand the bastard, but I didn't think he had it in him. How do you know?"

"He told me," Alex said. "He goes out to where they're plowing up the land for the airstrip and flushes them out of their holes before the dozers get there. He's got plenty more to deposit, so I'm not sure why you haven't gotten more."

"I didn't realize you and Dregs were so close."

"We were as close as you and me are now."

"What happened?"

"I disappeared after Shelley's death, and I haven't talked to him since."

"Maybe it's time you made a tear-jerking love call to him. Make something up about how I'm holding you hostage and encourage him to dump some more of those tortoises, maybe something even more dastardly. Only this time, I'll be waiting and so will one of my favorite photographers," Cowan said as he reached over and hugged his roommate. "You are full of surprises, Mr. Duncan."

CHAPTER FIFTY-THREE

"WE WANT TO PUBLISH the first issue the Thursday after Christmas, before New Years," Rick Bellows told the group before him.

Jason Landis arrived in town a week ago, and Lucy was looking for a place for him to buy. Nothing seemed right yet. He was staying in a bed and breakfast in Hope Springs.

"Do you think you have everything in place?" Jason asked as he looked around the room. It seemed amazing that all of the equipment needed was assembled in such a short time.

"It's all here and *The Tribune* is all set to add us to their schedule for printing," Rick said. "We've got lots of pictures and will continue to take them during all the holiday events. Mike, you got anything?"

"I'm working on a piece on the benefits of a movie studio to the area. Thought I'd bring in some of the growth that could take place. Do you want me to mention a river development as a possibility?"

"Not yet," Jackson said. "We want to hold off on that. Calloway isn't ready for the vote on annexation yet."

"I thought we might do some 'Man in the Street' interviews," Mike said. "Take a picture of residents and ask them what they think of the results of the presidential election."

"That's good; everyone loves to see their picture in the paper," Rick said. "Make sure what we publish is well balanced with those agreeing with the Supreme Court decision to stop the vote counting and those who disagree that Bush should become the next president."

Only two days before the U.S. Supreme Court voted in a 5-4 decision to suspend the ballot counting in Palm Beach, which left Katherine Harris' decision as Florida Secretary of State certifying Bush won Florida to stand. After six weeks, the presidential election had finally been decided in one of the most historic and bizarre pages in U.S. history.

"When does it look like Betty will be back on the commission?" Rick asked.

"I've got to check with B.J., but I think she'll be fully recovered by January," Jackson said.

"okay, we have photos, and we have a feature, and we have something that ties our local area with national news. What about commission meetings? What about a story on a business? What about the schools?" Jason asked.

"Lana Mercer has been attending the commission meetings and pulling together some fluff pieces from the schools. Mike has a new business he's going to profile," Rick said.

"Ads?" Jason asked. "I keep hearing that the first clue that the Millstone paper might be controlled by financial interests was the lack of ads in the first issues. We've got to have ads."

"We've taken care of that," Jackson said. "We'll have ads, don't worry about that."

"I do worry, gentlemen," Jason said. "I'm uprooting my family, and I quit a good job to come here and do this paper because I thought it could be something that would benefit the community and would be good for my family. But I've got an uneasy feeling about this whole thing."

"There is nothing to worry about, Jason," Rick said.

"I'm very uncomfortable with an elected official sitting in on a staff meeting. No offense, Mr. Stewart, but it's just not the way things are done ethically."

"I don't see a problem with me being here," Jackson said. "Why would anyone want to turn away good, sound advice?"

"It's not that I don't value your advice about the community. In fact, I would like to have lunch with you one day, but to have you here while we discuss editorial decisions is not wise. What if we have to report on something you've done one day? We would be compromised because of your closeness to the paper."

"Rick? Didn't you talk to this man?" Jackson asked.

"I will. Let's call it a day. We all know what we have to do, and Jason and I need to meet."

When Jackson left he immediately called Anthony to tell him that they might have some problems with the publisher. He also wanted to find out about Betty.

"The doctors say she needs to stay there for maybe two more weeks," Anthony said. "B.J. wants her home for the holidays, but they are saying that will only make things worse. They believe she should be in a controlled setting because the holidays might trigger an episode."

"I suppose it's better that way. But we need her back by the first of the year. The first public hearing on the zoning district for the annexation was scheduled to come before the commission at our next meeting, but I can get our new city manager to postpone them until January."

"She'll be back by then, don't worry. Nothing will stop us, nothing."

Anthony lit his cigar and leaned back in his chair. He had accomplished many things in his life, but the thought of owning an entire county brought a smile to his tanned and heavily lined face. He hoped one of the projects would bear his name. He always remained in the background on everything he did, but now he was ready for recognition. Since the Zion County project would be his last, he wanted it done right.

Randy would take care of any headaches. Tony, his son, could handle things in the legitimate way. In some ways, Randy was more like his son than Tony. Randy did what needed to be done, despite the consequences. The consequences only became another hurdle to overcome. Both he and Randy thrived on jumping hurdles and sidestepping piles.

Randy Robinson rented one of the old Victorian homes on Main Street in Calloway. He liked the proximity to the downtown restaurants and *The Zion County News*. He walked the streets often, getting to know the community. After just two weeks, the storeowners knew him and greeted him warmly. After picking up a bagel at the coffee shop, he wandered down the street to the paper.

"Rumor has it you used to be pretty close to Kelly Sands at *The Tribune*," Randy said as he settled in the chair in Mike Green's office.

"We dated, but I let her go when I found out who she really was."

"And who is that?"

"She's a whore to be perfectly honest, and I'm ready to give her some serious competition with this new paper."

"Did you know that I once dated Kelly?"

"You? I told you; she gets around.

"Mike, how about we show her who's really boss?"

"I can't imagine why anyone would want to press the issue on voting of this very important project for the City of Calloway at this time," said Jackson Stewart at the last December meeting of the Calloway Commission. "I move to continue the public hearing on the new zoning district until next year."

"Second," Johnny Waine said.

"Discussion," Chelsea Godfrey said. "We have all the information we need to vote tonight. I want to ask Commissioner Stewart why he wants to stall on this project. What's in it for him?"

"In it for me? I just think we should be more respectful of Commissioner Duncan's tragedy. That little girl was buried just over a week ago. We got some people up here on this dais with no compassion at all."

"I completely sympathize with Commissioner Duncan's loss. It was horrible to see what those big trucks you voted on coming through our city could do. And I'm not about to see an airstrip get put here for more industrial hauling."

"Industrial hauling? What are you talking about?" Jackson asked. "That air strip is going to bring people to this town to spend lots of that green stuff. You do like green, don't you, Ms. Godfrey?"

"You can't fool me into thinking the only thing landing at that airport will be small passenger planes. Cargo planes will be coming here too and the semis will line up for miles around to fill up and then drive through our city. I cannot support any project that would put more cargo on the road."

"Question," Waine said.

The motion to continue passed 3-1.

"Next on the agenda is the appointment of our new city manager," the mayor said. "Are there any nominations? If so, make them in the form of a motion."

"I move that we appoint the police chief, Thomas Jefferson, as the city manager," Chelsea said.

"The Chief of Police?" Jackson said. "Now why would you make a fool motion like that? I think Thomas has done an outstanding job with the police department but that does not mean that he can handle the city's business."

"I think it's precisely because he's handled the police department so well that we should give him a try, Mr. Stewart," Chelsea said.

Molly watched in awe and contempt as Jackson Stewart manipulated the proceedings on the dais. She heard that Commissioner Stewart was meeting secretly with the chief for this very purpose. She also knew the chief courted the SGC folks. Now Jackson put on a show for all to see, making Chelsea even more determined to go through with her suggestion.

Molly turned in her seat and saw Thomas Jefferson sitting in the back in full uniform, his arms across his chest, staring straight ahead. She underestimated him. She saw him as nothing more than a figurehead at the police department, a figurehead who liked the things that went along with a job like his. She believed his bodybuilding occupied most of his spare time. Now she knew Jefferson knew how to work both sides to get what he wanted. She would have to watch him more carefully.

She saw Rick Bellows in the audience with someone she didn't recognize. Mike Green sat in front of them taking notes, also sitting with a newcomer.

After the meeting, she asked Mike how he liked his new job.

"Much better than *The Calloway Chronicle* and old Panzer, that's for sure," Mike said. "Where's Kelly tonight?"

"I think she's sick. Who's your friend?" Molly asked as the stranger stood listening to their conversation.

"This is Randy Robinson. He just moved here after taking a job with Industrial Pines. Strange coincidence – he's from Palm Beach and knows Kelly. Randy, this is Molly Hale, a former colleague of mine."

"You knew Kelly in high school?" Molly asked as the two shook hands.

"You might say that. She was my girlfriend; we even went to the prom together, but I haven't seen her in quite awhile. I was hoping I'd see her tonight."

CHAPTER FIFTY-FOUR

"I'M HOME," MOLLY ANNOUNCED as she threw her car keys down on the credenza in the hallway of her home.

Kelly came out of the kitchen to greet her. She had come over to the house earlier to find out what happened at the meeting. Carl was filling in for Kelly sometimes so she could devote more energy to the Calloway story.

"That was a very long meeting," Kelly said. "I've been here bothering David for about an hour."

"It was long enough to stall the zoning issue and appoint Thomas Jefferson city manager."

"No kidding? Chief Jefferson?"

"No kidding, and it was quite a show. Chelsea nominated him, and Jackson balked, although the word is he really wanted him in that position. Jefferson's been courting Chelsea, too. So eventually Jackson acted like someone had tortured him to vote, and then you know how the rest of the vote went."

"Interesting tactic. What else?"

"Rick and Mike were there and the new publisher, although I can't remember his name. Some guy from south Florida wanting to take advantage of our bucolic setting here in the north with his kids."

"Young guy?"

"My age. He said he had a teenager and one daughter grown, who wanted to work for the paper. I almost forgot. Mike Green introduced me to someone who said he dated you back in Palm Beach."

"Dated me?"

"A Randy Robinson? You never mentioned him, but he said you went to the prom together."

"Randy Robinson was at the Calloway Commission meeting tonight with Mike Green?"

"Yes. What's wrong? Here sit down, you look like you're going to faint."

"What's he doing here?"

"Mike said he's working for Industrial Pines. He came to the meeting tonight hoping to see you."

Kelly let loose the longest sigh of her life. Her past had finally caught up to her completely. She imagined Randy and Mike standing together talking to Molly, and she felt the breath kicked out of her. Molly stood over her.

"What is it, Kelly?"

"Randy and I did not part on very good terms. I really don't want to see him."

"Do you want to talk about it?

"Not tonight. Let's get back to work on the story."

Kelly pulled out files from her briefcase and began filling Molly in on her research so far.

"I worked on some of the stuff Betty told us this week. Right now, it's a fairly arduous task, but I think it will get easier as everything falls into place. We have to begin requesting some public records. I want to trace some revenue streams."

"What do we want Betty to do?"

"How about specific places to check on money? She mentioned the police department as a source at one time."

"Yes, that's a good start. Are you going to meet with Alex tomorrow?"

"I have an appointment with him first thing. I need him to corroborate some of Betty's details. Did you find out how Betty is doing with the doctors?"

Once Kelly had been released from the hospital, Betty began obeying all the demands. She went to art therapy; and she played Trivial Pursuit with the other patients. She painted Christmas ornaments during craft time. She turned out her lights when told. She even ate all of her meals. But they had not quite figured out how they would manage her release. Neither Molly nor Kelly was certain Betty was ready to make a convincing play at pretending to follow her father's and Marcetti's orders once released. So they waited.

"Betty thinks they might consider releasing her right after Christmas. I asked her to tell them she felt safer there, just to give us more time to be sure of her."

"Molly, do you mind if I sleep on your couch tonight? I don't really feel like driving all the way back to Braidwood."

Thomas wasted no time moving into his new office in city hall. His deputy of police stepped into his former position, but with the knowledge that Thomas was really still in charge of the police department as commissioner of police in Calloway.

"I want you to keep me up to date on everything that goes through this department," he told Craig Holloway as he packed his trophies and certificates and awards. "I'll be watching you pretty closely, remember? I don't want any mess ups."

"You got it, Chief. You still want the books handled through you?"

"Always. And remember you don't talk to the press unless I give you permission, got it?"

Thomas ordered officers to haul the boxes out to his new Crown Victoria that came with the job of city manager. He no longer wore the uniform of his office, but instead wore a suit and pressed white shirt. He personally carried his special box to city hall, something he never entrusted to anyone else.

When he arrived at city hall, three blocks away, he carried the small box into his new office and ordered his new staff out to his car to carry in the other boxes. His appointments started at noon with the local media, and he wanted to be ready to greet them. He called maintenance and asked them to get over there on the double to hang the certificates and pictures of him with the governor and senators and even Janet Reno when she was the Attorney General of the United States. It was an impressive host of pictures, and Jefferson had dreamed of how they would hang in the office and how the chairs would be positioned so anyone talking with him would face those pictures and know he held power. He had been headed here all his life.

"Get in here, Susie," he yelled. "I need your help."

"Yes, Thomas?"

"Get these drawers cleaned out," he commanded. "I want to put some special files in here."

Susie went immediately to the drawer in question and began pulling out files left by Betty Duncan. Betty hadn't had a moment to clean out her desk between everything that recently happened.

"I want all traces of that Duncan woman out of this office in an hour," Thomas said. "We are starting fresh."

"But what if some of the files have information you need?"

"What could I possible need from her? Are you questioning my ability to know how to do this job? If you are you know where the door is. I can get you out of this job faster than you've ever seen me do anything before."

"No, Thomas, no. You know how I feel about your abilities. I just wondered if some of the papers might come in handy. I tell you what. I'll put them in my drawers, just in case. That way you don't have to be bothered."

"Fine. Now write a memo to the staff. You know what to say. And where is maintenance?"

By the time Thomas met with Mike Green at noon, the office looked as if he'd been there for months instead of a few hours. He even had time for a shot from his special box before Mike arrived. He also put his special files away in a locked drawer.

"Mike, let me tell you, as I'm sure you know because of your own personal history, my early life was not that easy. I grew up in the projects down the street from here and believe me no one from there would have ever thought one of us would be sitting in this chair now."

"What do you attribute your success to?" Mike asked.

"I worked hard. I will tell you that Thomas Jefferson always takes care of the City of Calloway."

"But was there one person who helped along the way? Your mother? Father?"

"Yes, yes, my mother. I'd say my mother."

"What are your plans? I've heard some of the staff mention they are a little afraid of losing their jobs because of your previous handling of employees at the police department."

"I will say to you, Mike, that anyone who wants to work hard for Calloway and has the interest of the city and the wishes of the commission as their first priority will have no trouble working under this new city manager. Thomas Jefferson is fair and only here to serve at the whim of the people and the Commission."

CHAPTER FIFTY-FIVE

RANDY ROBINSON VISITED THOMAS Jefferson later in the afternoon. The two hadn't met, but each had knowledge of the other.

"Anthony wants you to know he expects the rest of the process on the 2,000 acres to go smoothly," Randy said as he settled in Thomas' chair in the new office. Randy's back faced the pictures on the wall.

Thomas seethed at the affront and resented the orders from Anthony Marcetti.

"Whatever the commission wishes," Thomas said.

"No, that is not good enough, Jefferson. We've got a lot at stake here, and we expect cooperation."

"I think you'd better stop right here. I am no man's puppet, Mr. Robinson. Thomas Jefferson is his own man."

"We'll see about that, Jefferson, we'll see about that."

The next week *The Millstone Chronicle* ran an editorial calling Thomas Jefferson a moron with a gun. They predicted a short term of office because of his connections with SGC, and his lack of preparation and education for the job. The following day Commissioner Stewart paid Thomas a visit.

"I'm going to sue," Thomas told Jackson when the subject of the editorial came up. "They can't do that to me. I only want to do what is best for Calloway and its citizens."

"Shut up, Thomas, and listen to me," the commissioner said. "I got you into this position, and you stay here on my whim. And my whim happens to coincide with that of Marcetti's. We expect the zoning changes on the 2,000 acres to go smoothly, and we expect other things, also. Do I make myself clear?"

"I'm nobody's lackey, Mr. Stewart."

"Now, boy, nobody said you were. I'm just telling you what is expected of someone in your position. Besides there is a great pay out at the end, you know."

"What does that mean?"

"We've got plans for you outside of this office. Calloway is just the beginning if we get what we want. You know Sam Jones, don't you?"

"The senator? Of course, we went to school together after integration. We both played football for Calloway High."

"He's running for governor in 2004 and needs a running mate. We've been thinking with the right PR, you could be the man."

"My press is not that great right now, remember."

"No, Thomas, that's right. But you know how you can turn around, don't you?"

"I think I'm starting to get the picture. Help pass along the zoning and then other things as they suit you and Mr. Marcetti."

"I knew I hadn't made a mistake in suggesting you for this job. Now the zoning situation – we got it postponed until the first of the year, but after that, let's do it fast. Betty will be out of the hospital and ready for a meeting. I want it in a big meeting, at the auditorium. We'll have lots of supporters there."

"okay, I can handle that. Is that it?"

"You don't allow anyone from staff to speak. I hear that new city planner has some reservations about the roads out there and maybe even the wildlife. We don't need Garcia harping on the gopher tortoise issue. We can get the water district and environmental protection agency to pass us through with Sen. Jones' help, but we can't risk that planner woman to get up and start talking about the negatives. That will give SGC more fuel. We limit public comments at the last minute to two minutes instead of three. All my people will know, of course, and plan their statements accordingly. There might even be a movie star or two out in the audience."

"Brilliant. What about the votes?"

"That shouldn't be a problem. Tim, me, and Betty. Chelsea and Richard can hang out to dry."

"Then why do you need all of the other?"

"Public perceptions and media play, my young man; it's all paper mache and mirrors, and we give the public what they want, and they'll support us all the way. No roadblocks will be placed in our way."

Thomas gave himself a little shot after Jackson left his office. The lesson in public relations took their toll and left him a little shaken. Even though he hated to be manipulated, the thought of being lieutenant governor brought a smile to his face as he imagined standing on the dais on Election Day with his arms raised and thanking the cheering crowd. He forgot for a moment he wasn't the governor himself in this daydream – at least not yet.

Susie knocked on the door and came inside. He nearly knocked his box off the table.

"Knock next time, damn it," he screamed as he scrambled to pick up the contents. He didn't know Susie already knew about his not-so-well-hidden secret.

"Sorry, but here's that letter to the editor you wanted me to write to *The Monitor.*"

"Just put it on my desk. I won't be sending it now, but I'll keep it in my private papers. I want to see Andrew Knowles now."

"He's in a staff meeting with the finance department," Susie said.

"I don't care. Aren't I the city manager around here? When I say I want one of my workers that means I want them now, immediately. Now get out of here and get that asshole in here."

Thomas eased back into this chair and wondered why he was surrounded by such incompetence. Maybe he should just start firing them all, starting with that ridiculous finance director with his leather shoes and BMW convertible. He needed a way to feel back in control.

"I don't like you, Andrew," Thomas said when the finance director was finally seated in front of him, facing the wall of pictures of famous people.

"The feeling is quite mutual, I'm sure," Andrew Knowles said. "You didn't deserve this position, and most people know it."

Thomas felt the blood rise to his face. He stared at this small man with the smart mouth sitting in front of him. He wondered at his gall in speaking to him in this manner.

"I could fire you right now," Thomas said.

"But you won't. Jackson Stewart put me in this job, and I'm quite happy here. You can't do a damn thing about it."

"I wouldn't bet on that," Thomas said. He reached for his ankle and pulled out his Stubby.

Andrew drew his hands over his head as Thomas pointed the gun at him.

"Now who is responsible for your job here in Calloway?" Thomas asked.

"You are, of course, Mr. Jefferson."

"And Mr. Jefferson doesn't like to be told that someone else is in charge, so I'm going to ask you to leave real quiet-like now. Pack the things in your desk and get out of here in fifteen minutes, understand?"

"Loud and clear, yes, sir." Andrew Knowles scrambled as soon as the gun was lowered from its pointing position at his head.

He ran to his office and began pulling open drawers and piling everything on his desk. He yelled for his assistant to get a box. When it was all packed, he left with the other employees throwing questions at him, which he ignored. He kept stealing glances at the closed door of the city manager. When he was outside, he got on his cell phone and made two calls – one to *The Millstone Monitor* and the other to Jackson Stewart.

CHAPTER FIFTY-SIX

JASON LANDIS DROVE BACK home the week before Christmas with doubt on his mind. Rick made it abundantly clear his position as publisher was simply a figurehead one. Not much would be required of him except to see that everything was run according to the real publishers' wishes. Jason went to the ranch of Anthony Marcetti several days ago. What Rick had left unsaid, Anthony managed to fill in the gaps. Randy Robinson took care of any of the other little details.

He had a decision to make, but he wasn't sure how much he should tell his wife. He had a feeling if he backed out of the Calloway deal now, trouble would follow from that Marcetti fellow, who was used to getting his way. He was well aware of Anthony Marcetti's reputation from his reporter days of covering vice in Miami before becoming an editor.

On the other hand, he could try and make the paper work, no matter what. He could ignore the editorial decisions and concentrate on content other than the political mess. But he knew that all issues on *The Zion County News* would be turned into political issues, from whose child was featured in the basketball game to which civic group received the most coverage for their annual banquet. As his visit progressed, it became clear this new paper sought to change public opinion and sway politicians for one reason only – to create Marcetti County.

"Jason, I'm so glad you are home," Jean said when he finally walked in the kitchen. "Maggie has been driving me crazy with her incessant nagging about staying here for the rest of her junior year."

"I'll talk to her. Jean, we need to talk, too, but let's wait until after dinner."

Once they settled in the den with glasses of wine, Jason began telling his wife about his visit to Calloway and Zion County.

"It's quite a little town; not quite what I expected," Jason told her. "The town itself is run by one commissioner, but he is really just a puppet for this Marcetti guy who lives on an African veldt in central Florida, for God's sake."

"Can you really take this job?"

"I'm trying to figure that out. I have thought of nothing else ever since that Randy Robinson fellow first threatened me. I am almost afraid not to take it. They have so much at stake right now, and the first issue is due off the presses in less than two weeks."

"Could you hope to change things if you took the job?"

"I'd like to think I could, but I doubt it. I could try by concentrating on the wholesome sort of coverage that small towns love. Of course, at first they are not going to be blatant about their agenda. It will be subtle. I could take it and gradually ease myself out. I haven't closed any doors down here."

"I'll support whatever you decide, but I have a feeling we're going to Calloway. Look at it this way. This will be good for Elizabeth. She doesn't need to know about any of this."

"The commissioner I told you about? Jackson Stewart? He's having a Christmas party on Saturday night, and I'd like all of us to attend. In fact, they made it clear it's a mandatory appearance. That way I can show you the house."

"Did you find a house?"

"They are giving us a house, if you'll agree."

"Why wouldn't I agree?"

"Because the house comes with a sordid history. It seems last month a commissioner and his wife died there."

"What happened?"

"She killed him and then turned the gun on herself. The house has been cleaned and gutted. I couldn't even tell where it happened."

Gary Dregs and Jackson Stewart sat facing Thomas Jefferson's wall of pictures. The new city manager sat stiffly in his chair.

"You will hire Andrew Knowles back as finance director," Jackson said.

"Or if you don't, we run the interview with Andrew on how he was run out of this office by a gun-wielding, steroid-laden city manager wholly unequipped for his new position," Gary said.

"You don't really have any choice, now do you?" Jackson said.

The next morning, Kelly went into Bart's office and shut the door.

"How's Joyce?" Kelly asked after she settled in the chair in front of Bart's desk.

"She wants to meet you."

"Me? Why?"

"Something about any woman I love must be pretty spectacular. She's actually doing quite well. I think I'll be able to move into an apartment soon and let her have the house. We both think that might be best, and I don't mind, unless I get a better offer." Bart crinkled his eyes and smiled in the way Kelly always found irresistible.

"Normally, I would have said no way to that suggestion. It's just so soon. But I may have to reconsider."

"What's up?"

"Randy Robinson moved to Calloway recently. Seems he's taken a job with Industrial Pines. And he's hanging out with Mike Green."

"Randy Robinson – how do I know that name?" The old Bart Rolodex could not recall the facts on this person.

"Randy, my prom date."

The tension Kelly had been holding in since the night before when Molly broke the news, spilled over into the tears running down her cheeks. She fought the fear, but now with Bart it threatened to overcome her.

Bart moved from behind his desk and knelt in front of her, taking her hands into his big ones. With one arm, he pulled her close and let her cry.

"I'll pack a bag this afternoon and stay at your house until we figure out what's going on, okay?" he finally said.

Despite Kelly's commitment to remain strong, she only nodded her head and continued to hold onto Bart as if he was a buoy in the water.

CHAPTER FIFTY-SEVEN

"IT BECOMES INCREASINGLY EVIDENT that we need some proof about the charges for utilities and the money that actually goes into the city coffers," Kelly said one morning as she and Molly drank coffee at Molly's house.

"How do we do that?"

The two women sat in silence as both contemplated the next steps. The lights from the Christmas tree twinkled from the corner of the living room, but neither Molly nor Kelly thought much about the coming holiday. They both were consumed with the information coming from Betty and the job of sorting it all out.

Molly still had to make her deadlines at the paper, and she hadn't done the first bit of Christmas shopping. The kids would be home in two days. David would just have to pick up some of the slack. Luckily, her two children did not concentrate on the material aspects of Christmas. Many years ago, they'd foregone gifts for one another to help another family less fortunate. As far as Molly could tell, the whole family viewed those years as the ones with the best holiday memories. This year would have to be the same.

"Have you decided what you are going to do for Christmas?" Molly asked. "You are very welcome to come here."

"Bart and I are going to spend it together. Joyce will be with their kids. My parents have lots of friends in Palm Beach so they won't miss me, not really."

"Then that's settled. You and Bart are having Christmas dinner here, and Christmas Eve, if you want." Molly said as she took their empty cups into the kitchen. "We need a paper trail for the money. I'm going to start by requesting numbers of tickets issued by CPD and then compare on a month by month basis on what goes into the budget."

"What about drug busts?" Kelly asked. "Alex is convinced those high-profile busts engineered by Thomas Jefferson ended up with no follow up. He remembers B.J. Winters and Anthony Marcetti talking about it one time when they didn't know he was in the other room."

"There should be public records on drug burns and amounts, so I guess we would compare the amounts confiscated through busts and then the amount burned," Molly said. "Lots of work, but maybe Betty can help when she's released this week?"

Since Betty was cooperating with both the hospital and the two reporters, she revived in spirit. She told Kelly the thought of making her father and Anthony pay for all they had done kept her alive. Molly and Kelly felt certain she was ready to come home and play her role until all the pieces fell into place for them.

Jackson Stewart and his wife always threw the most elaborate Christmas party the Saturday before Christmas. Most of Calloway and the surrounding area were invited. The booze poured freely, and the food slid down throats greedily. He called it his gift to the community that had given him so much.

Jason and Jean Landis decided to spend the holidays in Calloway with all three children. The bed and breakfast where Jason had been staying in Hope Springs also had a house available for corporate retreats, and the owners graciously offered it to the Landis family. Jaycee and Elizabeth thought it was a great idea to begin their parents' new life with the first holiday in Hope Springs. However, Maggie complained on the entire ride north about being pulled from all her friends while school was out.

The couple spent many hours discussing what to do about Maggie. The girl – who wasn't really a girl any longer – had long wavy auburn hair, tending more toward the red side. It poured down to her lower back where her very small yet noticeable buttocks sprang out from the hollow curve in the small of her back. Her breasts, though not large, demanded attention on her small frame. She stood only five feet four inches, but her hair and blue eyes commanded an authority that belied her sixteen years. Maggie was a force of nature and anyone in her orbit knew it. Mostly her parents observed young men noticed it as they followed Maggie around waiting for her attention, which Maggie doled out as it suited her.

In the end, Jason and Jean decided there was no other choice but to all move together to Calloway. Jean worried that without the male influence of her husband, Maggie would be difficult to keep under control. Besides whisking her away from her lusty followers would be a good thing. They both hoped the boys in Calloway would be different. Hope always springs into the hearts and minds of parents who feel much safer ignoring the obvious.

The first public event for the Landis' would be Jackson's party. Jason not only displayed denial about his daughter's charms, but he also naively thought he could manage the obvious bias at the paper. He still believed if they wrote the truth, the rest would follow. He did understand his bosses controlled the paper, not him. However, he believed with time, he would prove to them they had nothing to worry about, and the paper would flourish. However, Jackson Stewart worried him the most. A commissioner insistent upon controlling the local press gave him nightmares. Jason decided to take it one story at a time. He was determined to keep Jackson under control.

On the night of the big party, Maggie dressed very carefully. She planned on letting everyone in Calloway know they were horribly backwoods hicks who had no idea what Maggie Landis represented. She knew she had to be careful because if she dressed in too provocative of a way, her parents would simply make her change before she left.

She settled on black, her best color. The dress was nothing special except it fit her body perfectly and showed every one of her curves. The neck was a round scoop and the hem came down to within two inches of her knee. Demure indeed until combined with her long shiny hair and burgundy ribbons tying the hair back from her face and revealing clear white skin, sparkling eyes, and a small button nose detracting nothing from the rest of delicate facial features. She was simply stunning and sensual without revealing a thing. Her parents could only sigh when they saw her and realized Maggie could wear rags and still manage to come away looking like a vixen.

Elizabeth, on the other hand, could have used some of Maggie's style, her parents thought. While a good-looking young woman, Elizabeth did nothing to enhance her features. She had short black hair, wore no make up, and preferred gauze skirts with boots and tank tops. Tonight she succumbed to her mother's wishes and at least wore a dress; one with embroidery on the bust and cinched waist. She even wore some silver sandals her mother pulled out of the closet. If not standing next to Maggie, she would have been a pretty sight in her own right. But next to her younger sister, Elizabeth disappeared, and Maggie stood alone.

CHAPTER FIFTY-EIGHT

MIKE GREEN AND RICK Bellows stood talking to Randy Robinson in a corner as the party swirled around them. All three held drinks, but each seemed more concerned with the conversation than the amber liquid in the cut crystal glasses.

"I think we need to go slower," Rick said. "If we come out with an editorial in the first issue praising the efforts of Industrial Pines, we'll let everyone know."

"We don't have much time," Randy said. "I'll take your word on it for this first issue because you know the community better than me, but I tell you we won't be patient much longer. After the first of the year, we go for it."

"We have to establish a readership that trusts us first or none of the rest of it matters," Rick said.

"Who's that?" Mike asked as he watched the Landis family enter the front door.

"Who? You know Jason; you mean his family?" Rick asked.

"I mean the only one who matters, the one in black," Mike said.

"That's Maggie, Jason's youngest." Rick looked at his head writer and saw that Maggie had spun her web. "Stay away, Mike. She's only sixteen."

"That's old enough in my book," Mike said.

"She's a dangerous one, all right," Randy said. "She reminds me of someone. Who's the other one?"

"That's Elizabeth. She's going to be writing for us. She's twenty-five and a hard worker. But it looks like they'll have their work cut out with Maggie."

Mike put down his drink and headed straight for the magnet despite Rick's warning. *It wouldn't hurt to welcome the young girl to Calloway*, he thought, as he left the two men. Rick was soon standing alone because Randy decided to welcome the other daughter. Ever since Kelly, beautiful women held no attraction for him. He liked the earthiness, sensibleness of Elizabeth. He wanted a woman who would be willing to stay a foot behind him, and Elizabeth impressed him as just that sort of woman. He was lonely since moving to Calloway even though he had managed a regular sex life. That was not the same as having a relationship, and except for those years in high school with Kelly, he'd never been a part of a couple.

"Jason, I see you and your family found the place," Mike said as he approached his new boss.

"Mike, good to see you. I wondered if we would know anyone here," Jason said as he shook Mike's hand. "Let me introduce you to my family. Everyone, this is Mike Green, our head writer. Mike, this is my wife Jean, my son Jaycee. This is Elizabeth; you two will be getting to know one another very soon, since Elizabeth will also be writing for us. And this is our youngest, Maggie."

Mike ignored everyone else and turned to the real reason he had come over to his boss in the first place. No one paid much attention because Randy came up behind him, and Jason went through the introductions once again.

"What do you think of Calloway?" Mike asked Maggie.

"So far it's not far from what I expected, but that could change." She looked at Mike, and he thought he had never seen such beautiful eyes, except on one other person. The comparison startled him.

"Is that good or bad?" he asked.

"It depends. What do you have to offer?"

"Mike, Maggie, I hate to interrupt, but I wanted to introduce Maggie to Randy Robinson. Randy just moved here to take a job with Industrial Pines. Randy, this is my youngest daughter, Maggie."

"Maggie, it's a pleasure. Your daughters are both beautiful. They take after their mother," Randy said.

"We're adopted, Mr. Robinson. We don't look anything alike," Maggie said.

"We adopted all three of our children," Jean said. "Maggie likes to shock people, but she doesn't mean to make you feel uncomfortable."

"No, not at all," Randy said. "Maggie reminds me of someone."

"Me, too," said Mike. "But the person she reminds me of is much older."

"Mr. Green, I'm offended," Maggie said. "I always thought I was unique."

"You are, you are certainly. It's just for a minute that you looked like Kelly Sands. I can't even see it now."

Randy heard Mike mention Kelly and knew in an instant Maggie reminded him of Kelly as well. He hadn't seen Kelly since she was just about Maggie's age, and the resemblance was uncanny. Except that Kelly's hair was always raven, not auburn like Maggie's. He ran his hand through his reddish hair and guzzled what remained of his drink. Standing near Maggie gave him an uncomfortable feeling although he could not place it. He decided to turn his attention to Elizabeth. She didn't leave him feeling unsettled.

"When do you start working at the paper?" Randy asked Elizabeth.

"The day after Christmas, which is Monday," she said. "They want the first issue to come out the following Thursday. There probably won't be much for me to do, but I can nose around the area, get to know something about it before I plunge in."

"You won't write anything for that first issue?"

"Maybe, I'm not really sure. I just met Rick today, and he didn't really say. He told me to report for work on Monday morning."

"I'm new in town, too," Randy told her. "Maybe we could get to know the town together. I've been here a few weeks, so I know a little bit. That's a start."

"I'd be grateful," Elizabeth said. "I love to write and research and interview, but putting myself out there and poking around in an unfamiliar town makes me a little uncomfortable. Do you have a family here?"

"No, I'm all by myself. I've never married, never had kids. Been too busy building my career."

"What are you doing for Christmas? I mean, I just thought maybe …"

"I thought I'd find a restaurant serving Christmas dinner and have a quiet day."

"You could come to the house we've rented for the holidays in Hope Springs," Elizabeth said. She kept her head down so she couldn't see the expression on his face.

"That would be great, if you're sure your family wouldn't mind?"

"We always had lots of people over for Christmas Day down in Miami. This year we don't know anyone, so I know it would be fine with everyone. We're just going to cook too much food, and it would be great to share it with someone."

"Then it would be fine with me, too, Miss Elizabeth."

CHAPTER FIFTY-NINE

"MOLLY INVITED US TO spend Christmas Eve and Christmas at her house," Kelly told Bart after he had brought a few bags over and unpacked in Kelly's bedroom.

"Do you want to go?"

"I think it might be nice. The last few years when I haven't gone back to Palm Beach because I always work, so I've gone to the Calloway parade on Christmas Eve and then gone over to the Hales for dinner, sometimes I go to church with them at midnight. It's very cozy and warm."

"How about we try some of that here?" Bart asked as he pulled Kelly toward him. Ever since her confession about Randy and Mike in his office that morning, he'd wanted to make love to her in an attempt to drive that haunted look from her eyes.

She led him into the bedroom, and they undressed one another very slowly. Bart removed her blouse and began kissing her shoulders before moving lower while Kelly attempted to loosen his tie and unbutton his shirt. They did not bother to roll back the bedspread or remove any of the pillows Kelly had tossed casually upon its top. Kelly lay propped up on the pillows and watched as Bart removed his trousers. They were ready for one another and all thoughts of the last twenty-four hours left Kelly's mind as Bart came to her. They made love slowly, looking into one another's eyes. Kelly felt lost in another world whenever they looked at one another in that way. Neither had known love in this way, and it's what kept them coming back to one another despite everything else in their lives. Kelly felt sometimes she had always known Bart, and he could see things in her that she could not.

She slept soundly after they finished making love. The night before, her sleep was interrupted by the usual fearful panics of someone holding her head underwater or taking something away from her that was very valuable. When wrapped in the safety of Bart's love, she slept with no nightmares or monsters under the bed.

"What do we do now?" Bart asked when she woke. He lay sideways next to her propped up on his elbow.

"About what?"

"You're going to have to wait a little while, if you expect a repeat performance from me," he said crinkling his eyes and leaning down to kiss her.

She began molding herself into his body and soon his body responded.

"I didn't have to wait that long," she said.

"Remind me to fire you someday. You're awfully disrespectful to an old man."

When they did manage to talk, Bart asked once again how she wanted to proceed with Randy's presence in Calloway.

"I don't feel strong enough to see him," she said. "But I'm going to work on that; I can't let him hold that kind of power over me, not after all these years."

"Do you think he took this job because of you?" Bart asked.

That question had plagued Kelly since Molly had told her. It seemed too much of a coincidence to have him show up here after all these years. The hang up calls increased in intensity since the bomb threat. She decided to tell Bart about that part of it, too.

"We need to call John Carson," Bart said when he heard about all the other strange happenings in Kelly's life for the past two months. "He would want to know. Who knows? Randy could be connected with the bomb."

Mike and Randy met the morning after the party for breakfast in Calloway.

"Kelly doesn't scare easily," Randy said once they ordered. "I've been trying."

"You've been trying to scare Kelly?" Mike asked. "Are you the bomb guy?"

"Didn't touch that bomb, but it didn't do its job either. Neither have the calls."

Mike sat back and reassessed the man sitting across the table from him. Randy obviously worked for Marcetti, but he seemed to have a more personal vendetta against Kelly than he did.

"She must have really done a number on you, man," Mike said. "What did she do? Stand you up, dump you for someone else?"

"She sent me to prison for five years."

"Prison? What for?"

"She claimed I raped her, and a jury believed her when she turned those baby blues on them. I didn't stand a chance."

"You must really hate her."

"Let's just figure out how to even the score. What does Kelly love above all else? What are her Achilles' heels?"

"Her career and Bart Stanley. And with Bart as her boss, the two are connected."

"Mike, old buddy, you just earned yourself a gold star. Can you get me access to *The Tribune* offices? I've got a plan already."

"We're going to have to go there," Tonja told Linda the week before Christmas.

"And say what? 'Oh, by the way, Kelly, the daughter you gave up for adoption seventeen years ago? She lives down the road with Anne Simmons' daughter?'" Linda said.

"I don't know what we're going to do once we get there, but we need to go and at least let Jason and Jean know the truth about both of their daughters."

Never in the thirty years of operating their home had so many lives come together so intimately, as far as they knew. Since they kept in fairly close contact with former patients and adoptive families, they felt secure knowing accidents like the one about to occur in Calloway did not happen easily. The two women made plans to spend Christmas in Hope Springs at a lovely little bed and breakfast. They would decide how to proceed from there. Luckily none of the girls presently housed at Oak Haven had imminent delivery dates, and their assistants could handle the running of the house for them. They didn't know how long they would have to be away, but they planned on at least through New Years. They felt responsible for whatever might transpire up in north Florida.

"Gary, I'm sorry I haven't been in touch," Alex said when he called Gary Dregs several days before Christmas. "I'm just playing along with Cowan to see how far he'll go to stop the landing strip."

"You've got a funny way of doing that," Gary said. "What about the lawsuit?"

"Cowan forced me to do that, to prove my loyalty. I'm not even supposed to be telling you this. You know how those guys are, so please don't say anything to Jackson."

"I find it unbelievable, and it's Christmas, Alex. I miss you."

"I miss you too, but this is the way it is for now. I have to follow his orders. By the way, Cowan was gloating the other day about how he's really scared the opposition because they haven't been leaving any tortoise carcasses lately. He thinks he's won."

"We'll see about that. Santa's going to leave him a little present, my dear."

CHAPTER SIXTY

ON CHRISTMAS EVE, BETTY walked into her house in Calloway and greeted her husband. The doctors were so impressed with her recovery and her husband's willingness to help, they decided she could be released for the holidays. Her father left the two of them alone with instructions to be at the family house at seven o'clock.

"You know how your mother fusses for this dinner with all of our friends, so don't disappoint her, either of you," B.J. Winters commanded before he departed.

"No, Daddy, we won't. I know I've been a terrible bother lately, but that's all over. You don't need to worry about me," Betty said.

"Me either, sir. I lost my head when Shelley died, but that's all over now," Alex assured him.

Kelly and Molly managed to convince Alex and Cowan that playing along with Marcetti for the next month would yield far better results than fighting him. Alex withdrew his name from the lawsuit the day before, leaving only Smart Growth for Calloway as the plaintiff. Alex and Betty would play the bereaved couple through the holidays and as long as it took for something to be published.

Mike Green received a call from Anthony Marcetti that same day. While he knew Marcetti had something to do with the new paper, he never expected to hear directly from him.

"Mike, I want you to do a profile on me," Anthony said. "I got a call from a Handler fellow at *The Tribune* wanting to do the piece, but I thought why let that mullet wrapper get my first interview in Zion County? Why not let this new paper get the extra attention?"

"That would be fine, sir. When do you want to meet?"

"No need for that. The angle will be that I am one of the major investors in the landing strip/movie studio project. I'll send you some publishable details, and then you manufacture the rest. Do some phony interviews, that sort of thing. Make it all lollipops and balloons. Understand?"

"I can handle that. How about a picture?"

"I got that, too. I'll email that later today. No need bringing up that nasty business with the white tiger a couple of years ago at my ranch, okay?"

John Carson came over to Kelly's house after Bart called him. They told him the whole story, and in turn, Kelly admitted to Bart how she first met John fifteen years earlier.

"Why do you think Randy Robinson has come to Calloway?" John asked after hearing about the rape.

"It could all be a coincidence, but I tend to think not," Kelly said. "I really don't know, but I know the Randy from seventeen years ago would want to settle an old score. To him I represent the ruin of his life. I'm sure he blames me completely for all the time he spent in prison, unless he had a major transformation of personality while behind bars. From what my parents tell me, I seriously doubt that."

"Unlikely, I agree," John said, "at least from my experience. And also from my experience, there is usually no such thing as a coincidence."

"The good news is there are no more Calloway Commission meetings for the next ten days," Bart said, "so she won't run the risk of running into him there."

"And if I do run into him, what do I do? He might be at the Christmas parade tonight."

"I really don't want you to have much contact with him, until I find out more," John said. "But if you do run into him, act surprised and then move on."

"Can you handle that?" Bart asked Kelly.

"I've been thinking a lot about since I found out he was in Calloway with Mike. And I discovered something pretty amazing about myself," Kelly told the two men sitting in her living room. "I'm not afraid anymore. The worst has already happened. I was raped and my daughter was taken from me, and I haven't seen her in almost seventeen years. That's the hell of it. Randy can't touch me anymore and neither can Mike."

"That's my sweet lady," Bart said as he came over to her to give her a hug. "I always knew you had it in you."

"That's the best thing you could have told me," John said. "Fear is the worst thing to present to a criminal mind. They'll go after it every time, just like a dog."

It was not a difficult task for Randy to find his way into the offices of *The Tribune* as staff began to vacate the premises on Christmas Eve afternoon. His press identification had been even easier to duplicate. Mike gave him a rudimentary lesson on the layout of the paper and its offices so finding Kelly's desk had not been too difficult. A call to the office told him Kelly had left for the day and would not be back until the afternoon of Christmas Day. Hacking into her computer proved to be easy also. The December 25 issue was almost done. Kelly had one front-page story about a homeless family finding shelter for the holidays. Randy made the switch, turned off the computer, and made his way out of the office in time to drive to Hope Springs to escort Elizabeth to the annual Christmas Eve parade in Calloway.

As Tonja and Linda checked into the bed and breakfast late Christmas Eve afternoon, the proprietors told them about the Christmas parade, just seven miles down the road.

"It's really spectacular with all the white lights decorating the floats," one of the owners said. "It's a real family tradition around here to go to the parade and then go to church or home for Christmas Eve dinner."

They unpacked and decided to enjoy themselves for the evening. Perhaps they'd figure out what to do next. They soon discovered things might fall into place on their own. As they approached their car to drive to Calloway, they saw Jean and Jason Landis leaving from the house next door with three men and two young women. They knew immediately who the women were. Jason saw them before his wife.

"What are you two doing here?" Jason asked.

He and Jean made their way over to the car while the others tried to figure out which cars to take the seven of them to the parade.

"We decided to get away for a few days," Tonja said. "We've always heard how pretty it was up here during Christmas. Actually your letter put the idea into our heads."

"We're going to the Christmas parade," Jean said. "Would you like to join us?"

"That's where we're going," Linda said. "Wouldn't we be a little difficult to explain?"

"No, the girls know all about you," Jean said. "We've always been completely honest. The only thing that might be difficult is Maggie's questions. She doesn't ever mince her words."

"Why don't we just go on for now, and we can meet them later," Linda said. "We came here to see you, and we need to talk, but it can probably wait until after Christmas. Maggie's questions might make things more difficult."

"You came all the way here to see us?" Jason asked. "That sounds fairly ominous. Maybe we should ride with you and let the kids go on by themselves. What do you think, Jean?"

"I think we need to know why you two are here," Jean said. Then she turned to her children standing at the curb in front of their cars. "Kids, we're going to ride with our friends. You all go on, and we'll meet up at the parade or back here for dinner afterwards."

Linda and Tonja found they had no choice but to give the couple the details of the situation on the ten-minute ride to Calloway and its nighttime Christmas parade.

"So both mothers came from Calloway?" Jason asked after Linda explained the basics.

"Kelly originally came from Palm Beach. We just found out she moved to this area when she came to Oak Haven to investigate Anne's death," Tonja said.

"She has no idea that you have either of the girls," Linda said. "And while Kelly's investigation left us slightly concerned, we didn't see a major problem until we received your note saying you were moving to Calloway."

"Oh my God, Jason!" Jean looked panic stricken when Linda saw her face in the rear view mirror. "The house they gave us — it's the house where Elizabeth's mother killed herself."

CHAPTER SIXTY-ONE

THE STREETS OF DOWNTOWN Calloway teemed with people on Christmas Eve as families with strollers and teenagers with dates and shoppers with bags settled down on the sidewalks to await the parade, which ended with Santa Claus riding on the back of the town's ladder fire truck. Children knew this was Santa's last stop before beginning his journey to fill all the stockings and dreams of those who still believed in the magic and miracle that is Christmas.

Molly promised Greg she would help distribute the Christmas edition of *The Calloway Chronicle,* so she and David pushed a shopping cart loaded with papers up and down Main Street before the start of the parade. She looked for Kelly in the crowd and finally spotted her in front of the hardware store, sitting with Bart in lawn chairs, drinking hot chocolate. Even though it was Florida, the December night had turned chilly requiring sweaters and hot liquids to keep the chill of the humid night from permeating through to the bone.

"Want a paper?" Molly called as she passed the couple.

"Who reads that rag?" Bart called back.

"Anyone who wants to know the truth," Molly said. "Why aren't you passing out *The Tribune*?"

"Gotta pay a quarter for that rag," Bart said.

"Hate to tell you, Boss, but it's two quarters these days," Kelly said.

"Save us a place," Molly told them. "I've got to take this back to the office, then I'll be right back."

Kelly assured both Molly and David they would save a spot for them, as she and Bart spread their chairs apart to make more room for their friends. After they settled, she looked across the street and noticed Mike Green. Right beside him stood Randy, who looked almost the same as he did in high school, except for the receding hairline. She would have known who it was anywhere. She watched the two of them for a few minutes before she alerted Bart. The two men seemed more focused on the two young women sitting in chairs in front of them than they were in each other. She reached across the space made for Molly and David and touched Bart's arm.

"Look across the street," she said. "See Mike? Look at the tall man next to him, and you'll see my worst nightmare."

"So that's the son of a bitch," Bart said. "What I wouldn't give to be able to go over there and knock both of their heads together. Do you know the females?"

"No, never seen them before."

"Look at the beauty, the one with auburn hair. She looks familiar."

Kelly stared at the young woman sitting in front of Mike. She turned slightly as Mike leaned down. He laughed at whatever she said, and for a moment, Kelly felt relief that Mike had a new love interest.

"Never seen her before," Kelly finally said after scrutinizing the girl with Mike. "Maybe it's Mike's new girlfriend."

The beautiful Maggie captivated Mike. She turned her full attention on him and for once, he knew what it was like to have someone adore him. He didn't think about her age because Maggie acted as if she was years older. For Maggie's part, Mike represented the first male who ever intrigued her enough to keep her attention.

Randy and Elizabeth seemed to be enjoying themselves as well. As Kelly watched Randy buy a hot chocolate from a Girl Scout walking up and down the street, she wondered if perhaps he had changed. The woman he handed the cup to appeared shy and totally unlike anyone that she could imagine Randy dating. Perhaps she was his wife.

"okay, you two, move it over, we've got to put our chairs down here, too," Molly commanded when she and David returned. "Look over there; looks like Mike Green's got a new girl. Feeling jealous, Miss Kelly?"

"I'm relieved. Bart thinks the girl looks familiar. Do you know her?"

"Can't say I do. How about you, David?"

"She looks like Kelly," David said.

As he said this, Maggie turned and looked directly across the street at Kelly at the precise moment that Mike also saw Kelly. He nudged Randy.

"There she is," he said.

"Who?" Maggie asked.

"Kelly Sands," Randy said. "What do you know? She hasn't changed much since high school."

"Isn't that the name of the woman you said I reminded you of?" Maggie asked.

"She does look an awful lot like you," Elizabeth said. "It's hard to tell from here, but you two could pass as sisters."

Kelly stared into the face of her daughter without knowing it. Most people do not recognize resemblances in others, so Kelly didn't notice the similarity of expression. The gathering dusk didn't show the particular shade of blue in Maggie's eyes that so set Kelly apart from other blue-eyed creatures. The set of the eyes and the small nose and the dramatic cheekbones drew the attention of others looking across the street at the two women.

"She could be your sister," Molly said. "Don't you see it?"

"My sister? She looks about fifteen years younger than me."

Just then, a man and a woman walked up to Randy and Mike and began talking. Two women appeared from behind them, and the girls turned around as the small group greeted one another. The four people on the other side of the street continued to stare at them for various reasons. Bart had forgotten temporarily about Randy as he realized Molly was absolutely correct. The reason the girl looked so familiar was because of her resemblance to Kelly.

The sirens began, signaling the start of the Christmas parade. Kelly rose from her chair and crossed the street without a word. The honor guard leading the parade remained a good block away.

"Kelly," Bart called, but she did not turn around.

Kelly walked toward Tonja and Linda as if in a trance. It all came together for her in an instant, especially after she recognized Jean and Jason Landis as the couple who had taken Joely from her at Oak Haven. She would never forget them. Maggie continued to stare at Kelly as she crossed the street.

"Here comes trouble," Mike announced when he saw Kelly rise from her chair. "She's got more guts than I would have thought. Are you ready for this, Randy?"

However, Kelly didn't approach either Mike or Randy. She went directly to the two women who had come up with Jason and Jean.

"Tonja and Linda, this is certainly a surprise," Kelly said. "What brings you to Calloway? Or perhaps I already know?"

"Kelly, we didn't expect to see you here tonight," Linda said. "We just got into town. We were going to call you."

"Maybe we should talk now," Kelly said.

"We can go to my new office," Jason said. "I'm Jason Landis, Kelly, the publisher of *The Zion County News*."

By this time, Bart had followed Kelly across the street and introduced himself. The parade getting nearer, and the sound of the sirens increased, making talk impossible. Randy and Mike watched in fascination as Kelly completely ignored them and concentrated on the two women introduced simply as Tonja and Linda. Then the two women turned and followed Jason and Jean back to the newspaper's office as Bart and Kelly trailed behind. Kelly had just enough time to explain to Bart who all these people were before they reached the front door of *The Zion County News*.

CHAPTER SIXTY-TWO

"THIS IS NOT HOW we envisioned this all happening," Tonja began. "In fact, when we came here, we had no idea what we were going to do, but things seem to be out of our hands here."

"Let's just start at the beginning," Linda said after Jason brought enough chairs for everyone into his office. "Kelly, we thought we'd better come up here when Jason and Jean wrote to us about their move to Calloway. We knew you worked in this area and were working on a story about Anne and her death."

"What does Anne have to do with all of this? Is my daughter here?" Kelly asked.

Bart had already figured out what Kelly seemed to be blocking. That beautiful young woman talking with Mike was actually Kelly's Joely. Once Linda and Tonja began their story, it didn't take Kelly long to make the same realization.

"Her name is Maggie?" Kelly finally asked after she had absorbed the first part of the story. "That's her out there – that beautiful girl – that's my daughter?"

"Yes, that's Maggie, the girl you gave birth to almost seventeen years ago," Jean said.

Kelly began crying then, surprising everyone, including herself. Bart knelt in front of her, and Jean reached over and grabbed her hand.

"I don't know why I'm crying," Kelly said. "All I ever wanted was to know she was happy. I know you gave her a good life, and I am grateful. It's just a shock to see her. She's beautiful."

"She looks just like you," Jean said quietly. "And she is going to want to meet you. Maggie has always been curious about her birth mother, more so than our other children."

"Your other children?" Kelly asked.

"Yes, we adopted three children," Jason said. "Another girl and a boy. Maggie's the youngest."

"Kelly, there's more," Tonja said. "The odds of all of this happening are probably a million to one, yet it happened. Jason and Jean also adopted Anne's child, Elizabeth. We just found out that the people financially responsible for *The Zion County News* have given them the Simmons' former home as their new residence."

Just then, Elizabeth poked her head in the office.

"We're going back to Hope Springs," she said. "Is everything all right?"

"Just fine, Lizzie," Jean said. "You all go along, and we'll be home soon."

"I can't quite absorb all this," Kelly said.

"Maybe everyone should go on to their Christmas activities, and we'll figure something for the next day or two," Bart said. "How long will you two be in town?" he asked Tonja and Linda.

"We planned to be gone a week," Linda said. "We want to stay and help all of you through this; after all, we feel responsible. I'm not sure how we could have predicted everyone coming together in this part of Florida, but it happened, and now we want to help."

"Can I meet her?" Kelly asked.

"I think it might be best if Jason and Jean tell both the girls what they know," Linda said. "They've always been honest with them about everything and this is not the time to stop that, I would think."

"Jean and I have not had time to even think about this," said Jason. "We just found out before the parade, too. We'll talk tonight, and we'll be in touch. You two are staying right next door, and you know how to reach Kelly, right?"

"Yes, that' right. That's a good idea," Tonja said. "If you want us there when you tell them, just ask."

"I want you to know that I don't expect anything," Kelly said. "Seeing her tonight was enough for now. And if she does want to meet me, I would never try to come between you and Joely, I mean Maggie."

Thomas Jefferson played Santa Claus in this year's Christmas parade. He rode on the back of the fire truck still packing his handguns on both his ankle and underneath the pads. Just before he dressed, he gave himself a little shot to pump himself up. Since his appointment as city manager, he gave himself does without consulting the calendar. He'd yet to notice the pimples on his back.

Jackson Stewart suggested the Santa thing to show the community how fair minded they were. A black Santa Claus certainly pleased the minorities and liberals in attendance. For Thomas, it was a humiliation, but he had no choice but to follow Jackson's orders.

When he passed Randy Robinson, he heard him shout, "We got Aunt Jemima for Santa Claus this year, folks."

He didn't notice the woman with Randy hit him nor did he hear the admonishments from others around him. He only heard that Robinson fellow's smart remarks. He hopped down from the fire truck and strode over to where Randy stood. He reached into his boot and pulled out the Stubby.

"What did you say to me?" Thomas asked as he pointed the gun. He was so far gone he didn't hear the screams from the crowd on the street.

"I said 'we got ourselves Aunt Jemima this year for Santa Claus' or should I say 'we got Uncle Tom.'"

"Randy, please," Elizabeth said.

"I thought that's what you said," Thomas said. "And you're going to be sorry you ever set foot in this town let alone make comments like that in front of the children here."

The new chief of police made his way over to the ruckus. He spoke quietly into Thomas' ear and managed to pull him away before anything happened.

"I want this man arrested," Randy shouted after the chief.

"It's all right, nothing happened. Everyone can go home now," said the officer who remained behind after Chief Holloway and Thomas walked away.

CHAPTER SIXTY-THREE

BART ASKED KELLY IF she wanted to go home or go back to Molly's house as they left the office. When they came outside, Molly and David waited expectantly on the sidewalk.

"What happened?" Molly asked.

"It's quite a story," Kelly said. "Are your kids going to be at the house when we get back?"

"They just called me on the cell phone, and said they wanted to go to some friend's house for eggnog," David said. "We're going to meet them at the midnight service at church."

"I'd like to go back to Molly and David's," Kelly told Bart. "I want to tell them the news, too."

"Whatever you say. Tonight you're the boss," he said as he gave her a quick hug.

Mike and Maggie rode with Jaycee to the parade. Randy wanted to show Elizabeth his house in Calloway afterwards so Elizabeth rode with Randy.

At the house in Hope Springs, Mike asked Maggie if she'd like to drive around the town and see the Christmas lights. Hope Springs may not have a parade, but the town lit up at Christmas time. The town Christmas tree, from a local tree farm, sat in the middle of the Hope Springs River on a floating deck. Maggie had not yet seen it. Jaycee said he would stay at the house and start cooking their late dinner before everyone else made it back.

Mike drove along the deserted dirt roads following the river until he came to a deserted spot overlooking the water and the Christmas tree. The stars shone brightly above providing even more illumination over the water.

"It's beautiful," Maggie said after Mike had parked the car. "And so quiet. We don't have anything like this in Miami."

"You're the beautiful one," Mike said as he pulled Maggie close to him.

He began kissing her neck as he lifted her long hair away from her skin.

"That feels good," she said. "You can keep doing that."

He did, and then he began doing more. Maggie had never been with a man before, never even wanted to be with a man, but something about the way Mike touched her and the peaceful setting made her relax and enjoy his hands exploring her body. She began to respond and soon Christmas became a whole lot merrier for both of them.

"You're a virgin?" Mike asked at one point. It never occurred to him that she might be because she came across as so sophisticated and experienced.

"Is that all right?"

"It's better than all right," he said as he continued.

When they finished rather clumsily in the back seat of the car, Mike looked at the clock and saw that they had been gone for more than an hour.

"I'd better get you back or your folks will have the police out for us," he said. "You know you can't tell anyone about this, don't you?"

"Do you really think I'm that naïve? I may have been a virgin before tonight, but that doesn't mean I don't have a brain," Maggie said as she attempted to comb her abundant hair with her fingers. "Was I better than that Kelly Sands?"

"I will never compare the two of you again," he said as he kissed the tip of her button nose. "You are the best."

"No one could ever write this in a novel," Molly said after Kelly finished telling the story and the remarkable events of the evening, "because no one would believe it."

"What happens next?" David asked.

"I haven't thought very far into the future," Kelly said. "It's in Maggie's court now whenever Jean and Jason decide to tell her. As much as I want to meet her and talk with her, I know she needs time to absorb it all, too. It could take awhile."

"And Elizabeth!" Molly said. "She's going to have much more to absorb. Imagine finding out who your birth mother is and finding out she's dead and then to learn her father is actually her grandfather. Talk about the Oedipus complex."

"I just remembered something," Bart said. "For the time being, Elizabeth will think that her birth mother not only committed suicide, but she also killed someone else."

"You don't think we can tell her the truth?" Kelly asked.

"That's not our story to tell," Bart said. "Betty can't go public yet or much more is at stake. Besides wouldn't it be better for Elizabeth to hear the worst thing first and then find out it isn't quite that bad?"

"I suppose that's one way to look at it," Kelly said. "I'd like to talk to her, too, after they tell her. I might be able to help. I think Rev. Baxter would be good to contact also. I forgot to tell the Landises about him, but maybe Tonja and Linda will."

"Wait a second!" Molly yelled. "We've forgotten something here! Mike and Randy – they left with the Landis' girls tonight."

"How could I have forgotten that," Kelly said. "Bart, we've got to call Jason and Jean and tell them about Randy. We never told them, and Tonja and Linda don't know. I forgot all about him with this news."

"Do you want me to call Jason and tell him?" Bart asked.

"Yes, please, somehow make it clear to them they shouldn't let Elizabeth be alone with him. It was Elizabeth he seemed to be with, right? Not Maggie?"

"When they left, Mike, Maggie, and another young man went in one direction. Then Randy and Elizabeth started walking down Main Street," Molly said. "I remember because there had been an altercation between Thomas Jefferson and Randy at the end of the parade. The chief came and pulled Thomas away, and Elizabeth and Randy walked the other way together."

When Bart returned from making the phone call, they knew right away something was not right.

"Maggie just came home with Mike Green after viewing the Christmas lights in Hope Springs," he said. "But Elizabeth has not been heard from since she and Randy left the parade to go to his house."

"Where does he live?" Kelly asked.

"He bought that Victorian down at the end of Main Street," David said. "I talked to him the other day when I saw him walking downtown. His realtor introduced us."

"We've got to go find her," Kelly said. "She shouldn't be left alone with him."

"Jason agreed after hearing the story," Bart said. "He said he was going to drive over to Randy's house, if he couldn't reach Elizabeth on the cell phone. He also said he began worrying when Maggie and Mike related the Thomas Jefferson story to him. It seems the fight started when Randy started yelling racial epitaphs at Jefferson."

"This is a beautiful house," Elizabeth said as Randy showed her around.

"It was renovated right before I bought it, and it came fully furnished. I didn't have to do a thing to it. How about a drink? A little white wine?"

"That would be lovely," Elizabeth said as she gazed at the Monet print over the fireplace. "Whoever fixed it up had good taste."

Randy felt his agitation rising. It began as he watched Kelly at the parade. And then, she crossed the street and totally ignored him. His hatred of her grew, as did his rage toward all women. That Jefferson fellow really pissed him off, too. Waving his gun and humiliating him in front of Elizabeth was unforgivable. He tried to maintain his cool with Elizabeth, but he knew he was going to have her one way or another tonight, and she was going to give him what he wanted.

"Here you go," he said as he handed her the wine glass. "You know you are quite beautiful, Elizabeth."

"Randy, can I ask you a question?"

"Shoot – anything for you."

"Why did you say that to Santa Claus tonight?"

"What do you mean why did I say that? He's the one who came after me with the gun, and no one did anything."

"But you said some ugly things to him. Why?"

"Because he's an uppity nigger, and I don't appreciate you questioning me in this way. You've got a lot to learn, little girl."

He removed the wine glass from her hand and threw it against the fireplace. Then he grabbed her and began to kiss her. When she protested, he did the only thing he knew to do. He began to hit her with abandon until her face began to resemble the one that haunted him for seventeen years. That's when he shoved her to the floor and began to vent all the anger he'd pent up inside of him since his conviction.

CHAPTER SIXTY-FOUR

"I WANT TO TOAST my daughter and her husband tonight," B.J. Winters said as he held a glass of eggnog up to the gathered guests in his living room. "They faced one of the worst tragedies ever imaginable, but they have come out on the other side stronger and more determined than ever to do the right thing for all of us gathered here."

Anthony Marcetti raised his glass to the couple as did the dozen other guests in the Winters' house on Christmas Eve. He watched carefully as Alex pecked his wife on the cheek. Betty did seem like her old self and Anthony was very grateful. He'd already directed Tony to donate a large sum in the hospital coffers.

"And here's to Anthony, who is going to put Calloway on the map," B.J. further offered. "We all owe him a debt of gratitude."

"Thank you, B.J., but I couldn't have done it without everyone in this room right now," Anthony said. "Sen. Jones, Commissioners Stewart and Duncan, and my son, Tony, my partner, B.J., you've all been a part of this development, and you will all be greatly rewarded as it comes to fruition."

"Don't forget about Lucy here," Tony added. "Without her real estate acumen, we might still be fighting through the quagmire of deeds and brokers getting those lands turned over to us in such a timely manner."

"How could I ever forget the beautiful Lucy Burch," Anthony said as he went over to her side and offered a personal tip of his glass.

Actually, Lucy and Anthony had only met a few times before this night, but it looked to be a union of two kindred souls. Either that or it would prove to be a combustible combination. Lucy gave Rick the heave-ho when Lucy discovered the lure and seductiveness of animal skins and Cuban cigars. Lucy visited Anthony's ranch the week before to bring some papers for him to sign. Once the two were alone in the den with just the stuffed animal heads to keep them company, they found they had much in common. Before long, they were rolling around on the bear skin rug in front of the fireplace. Lucy had the bite marks in her ass from the still intact bear's teeth when she rolled just a little too far south.

"When can we get out of this extremely boring party?" she whispered when all the toasting ended.

"Meet me in the bathroom in ten minutes," Anthony said. "They'll all think I'm giving you a line of coke if they catch us coming or going."

"They might catch us coming, but never going," she said as she moved away from Anthony to mingle for a few minutes.

"Should we call the police first?" Molly asked as the four of them headed to the car.

"We might be overreacting," Bart said. "We'll be at the house in just a minute, and then we can tell if we need to do anything."

When they pulled up in front of Randy's house, Thomas Jefferson, minus his Santa hat and beard, but still in the red suit, stood on the front porch banging on the door. As they got out of the car, Elizabeth lurched out the front door, making it to the front lawn before she fell on her knees.

"I think I killed him," she screamed when Kelly approached her. "I think he's dead."

"Get out here you son of a bitch," Thomas yelled from the porch. "We're going to settle what you started earlier tonight."

"Now you better call the police," Bart told Molly as he approached the gun waving city manager.

"Thomas, what's going on here?" Bart asked as he and David slowly approached.

Thomas swung around still waving the gun in the air. "That pig in there insulted my dignity tonight, and I will not stand for that type of treatment from anyone. Thomas Jefferson does not allow that to happen in his town."

"The girl back there thinks she already killed him," David said. "Maybe we should go inside and take a look around. Aren't you still the police commissioner here in Calloway?"

"You bet I am. I am the law in this town, and no one will forget that. I serve at the wishes of the commission, and they wish me to be the chief person in all matters in this city."

"Then I suggest you stop waving that gun around before you hurt someone in this city and go inside and see if a murder has been committed," Bart said.

"What happened?" Kelly asked as she knelt on the lawn next to Elizabeth cradling the crying girl in her arms.

"I hit him; I hit him with that thing next to the fire place."

"The fire poker?" Molly asked. She too knelt on the grass next to them. "Where did you hit him?"

"I don't know, I just struck out, and then he fell backwards on the rug, and I ran out here."

"Was he hurting you, Elizabeth?" Kelly asked.

"Yes, he was hitting me and then he tried to rip my clothes, and I grabbed that thing and just struck out."

"You fought back," Kelly said. "That's a good thing. He deserved whatever you did to him and probably more."

Jason and Jean arrived at about the same time as the police. Bart and David entered the house, leaving Thomas ranting on the front porch about his responsibilities as harbinger of law and order in the fine city of Calloway. When the officers arrived, Bart and David came back outside.

"He's alive," Bart said. "It seems to be a fairly superficial wound to the head."

"But it was enough to stop him so she could escape," Kelly said. "That was a good thing, Elizabeth. You did the right thing."

"That's right, baby, that's right," Jean said as she took over for Kelly and cradled her daughter in her arms. "You were very brave, Lizzie."

"I knew I shouldn't have come here with him when I heard him yelling at Santa Claus in the parade. He was saying some awful things, and I knew something was wrong with him."

"Don't do this to yourself," Kelly said. "The important thing is you found the strength to get away from him. If you hadn't, it could have been much worse."

"She should probably go to the hospital," Molly said. "They need to check her over and do some tests."

"Do you want me to go with her?" Kelly asked. "I can help her through it."

"Let's both go," said Jean. "I'd be very grateful for your help. Jason, you go back to Hope Springs and try to make something good for the others out of tonight."

Kelly made it back to her house and Bart sometime after midnight. Despite the late hour, he waited up for her.

"It's been quite a night, hasn't it?" he said as she fell into his arms.

"He didn't rape her, thank goodness," Kelly said. "But he made a mess of her face. She'll be all right, but Jean wants to wait before telling the girls anything, and I agree. Elizabeth is such a fragile thing, but she fought back."

For the second time that evening, Kelly fell into Bart's arms and sobbed. When she brought herself under control once again, Bart made her laugh finally with his description of Thomas Jefferson and his zealous proclamations on being the savior of Calloway.

"Is he going to get into trouble for his gun wielding nonsense?"

"I doubt it. Who's going to do anything? I get the impression that Randy was brought here by someone from what Thomas was saying, and so whoever put him here certainly will not be able to defend his actions of tonight."

"That's interesting. I can't even think about it tonight. There has just been so much. Thank goodness for you, Boss. Knowing you would be here when I got home from the hospital made it all better after one of the most event-filled days of my life. And that's after one crazy month of craziness."

"How about we go to bed, and I'll give you your Christmas present?"

"Do I get to unwrap it before morning?

"Sweet lady, you get to unwrap it right now."

CHAPTER SIXTY-FIVE

BART AND KELLY WOKE early, but they did not venture out of bed on Christmas morning until a few hours later. They would wake and make love and then drift off to sleep once again.

When Bart returned from getting *The Tribune* from the box, he went into the kitchen and laid out the front section, unfolded on the table.

"When did you write this story about homelessness in the Big Apple? And why would you write it, when your story about that family was local and very poignant?" Bart asked.

"What are you talking about? I didn't write any story about New York."

Kelly came from the sink where she'd been preparing coffee and stared at the headline. "New York's homeless find little shelter on Christmas Eve by Kelly Sands, *Tribune* reporter."

"I didn't write that, Bart. That's not my story."

Just then, Bart's cell phone rang.

"Who changed that story?" Kelly heard him yell at the phone. "You better find out pronto because we're in big trouble here."

"What?" Kelly asked when he ended the call.

"That story is the front page story in the *New York Times* this morning written by none other than Pulitzer Prize winner Rick Bragg. Somehow it got switched with your story, and no one noticed until *The New York Times* headquarters called this morning for an explanation."

"How could that happen? And why?"

"I don't know, but they've already sent someone down here to investigate. Kelly, is there any chance you could have accessed the AP wire and sent this in by accident?"

"How could I do that? I don't even know how to do that. That's production's job."

"I had to ask because I'm going to be asked a whole lot of questions before the day is over. The story came from your computer. Right now, I've got to call Doug Collings and try to figure this out. We definitely go with an apology and correction for tomorrow's paper, but it's going to be tough convincing everyone."

"Do I need a lawyer?"

"Not right now. I'm going to make sure Collings puts our legal department on it. You might want to call John Carson, though. Doesn't it seem a bit odd this would happen at the same time as everything else? Who will this hurt the most if it's not contained?"

"My credibility is on the line, isn't it?"

"You bet. What time did you file the other story?"

"I left the office around two o'clock so it would have been sometime around one. After I sent it, I cleaned up some paperwork and worked on a few things for today."

"Jim in production says he remembers receiving your story, so that's good. I have to go into work. What time were you supposed to come in?"

"We were scheduled to have Christmas dinner with Molly around two, and then I was going in after that."

"Cancel with Molly and come with me," Bart said. "I think it would be a good idea to have you there. And besides we've got to get tomorrow's issue out."

The call from Randy to Anthony's ranch provided no results since Anthony decided to stay in Braidwood at Lucy's house after the party in Calloway. Neither could he find Tony Mayberry who had holed up for the night with one of his expensive call girls.

He finally settled on B.J. Winters.

"I need some help, B.J.," Randy said when he finally reached him.

"It's Christmas Day; you're going to have to wait," B.J. said.

"I'm in jail, and I need to get bailed out."

"In jail? How the hell did that happen?"

"You got one crazy nigger running the city, B.J. He's trumped up some charges against me. Claimed I tried to rape a girl."

B.J. made one phone call to the chief of police. When he heard about the evening's happenings, he ordered Randy's release and said he would be talking to Jackson Stewart about Thomas Jefferson. All they needed at this point was someone to know Randy was associated with them, and that the city manager was on a steroid rampage. They were too close to the finish line now.

Lonny met Kelly and Bart in the parking lot of *The Tribune* on Christmas Day.

"What are you doing here today?" Kelly asked the photographer.

"You're not going to believe what I captured on film last night," Lonny said.

"I'm afraid we'd believe just about anything at this point," Bart said.

"I got a call from Cowan Garcia, asking me to come over to his house last night. He said something was going to happen, and I should be there."

Lonny then proceeded to tell them another bizarre Calloway story. Shortly after nine o'clock, Lonny and Cowan waited inside the house with the lights off, peering out on the front lawn. They did not have to wait long to be rewarded. Gary Dregs from *The Millstone Monitor* appeared with a pillowcase stuffed with dead gopher tortoises, which he proceeded to empty into Cowan's front yard.

"Cowan said 'Start shooting,' and then he turned on the front yard floodlights," Lonny said. "I came to check on what the lab was able to do. If they turned out, I caught Dregs red-handed trespassing. I did a little research, too. They're not endangered in Florida as Garcia keeps saying – it's only west of the Mississippi although Florida has them 'under review' as a threatened species right now. It's unclear whether he can be charged for outright killing them although developers can plow them under when preparing sites for building."

"Can it get any weirder around this place?" Bart asked the sky. "Let me know how the photos turn out. Sounds like front page, full color, if you get something. AP will probably pick it up, too. Kelly, while I begin dealing with the other thing, you start on this story."

CHAPTER SIXTY-SIXTY

ON NEW YEAR'S EVE day 2000 the first issue of *The Zion County News* hit the stands. The front page introduced the area to one Anthony Marcetti smiling and standing with Sen. Sam Jones. There were stuffed, dead animals anywhere.

The article by Mike Green, Senior Executive Writer, showed Mr. Marcetti to be a kind and benevolent philanthropist, having made his fortune in real estate in Miami during the 1960s. "Now he spends his time trying to put that money back into charitable causes around the state," Mike wrote. None of the charities had a specific name.

A Mrs. Irma Cronkite of Eustis, was interviewed and provided a glowing report of Marcetti's neighborliness when he moved into her town in the article. "He practically fell over himself to help the schools and churches," the article quoted her as saying.

Bart received a call from Irma Cronkite the same day.

"Someone suggested that I call you," she said. "They said you would be fair and could perhaps do something about the article that appeared in this new paper up here."

"Are you referring to *The Zion County News?*" Bart asked. He searched his desktop until he found the copy Kelly had dropped there just an hour earlier. She told him to read the piece on Marcetti and mentioned that Mike had never written such a real profile with great quotes from those he interviewed.

"Yes, the article on an Anthony Marcetti on the front page," she said. "I happen to be in Calloway visiting my niece and her family this week, and they brought this paper home with them today. I read the article because I remembered this man has that awful ranch near my house."

"What can I help you with?" Bart asked as he scanned the article. He saw Irma's quote almost immediately.

"I never spoke to anyone from that paper."

"But you're quoted here about what a great neighbor this Marcetti fellow is. You're sure a Mike Green never called you? Maybe you didn't hear the name of the paper correctly."

"The first time I have ever spoken to anyone at any newspaper is right now," Irma said. "And I would have never said Mr. Marcetti was good at anything. Those animals he keeps over there do not belong in Florida, and he hasn't done one thing for our town except bring it a bad reputation when that famous fellow was attacked at his ranch.

"I'm calling you because my niece said your paper had a good reputation and could perhaps set the record straight," she concluded.

"Let me get your number, and I'll call you back later today after I do some checking. I appreciate your trust, Mrs. Cronkite, and I'll find a way to make it right for you."

"Kelly, get in here, now," Bart yelled when he had hung up the phone.

"Settle down, Boss. I swear I haven't swiped any stories from *The New York Times* today," Kelly said when she entered his office.

"I just got a call from a little old lady down in Eustis who says she was never contacted by anyone for this story." Bart tossed the paper over the desk to Kelly.

It had been easier than Bart thought to clear Kelly. Luckily, the paper maintained a sign in and out sheet for its employees. Kelly had signed out at two o'clock. She produced a couple of charge receipts with the times stamped on them between three and five o'clock, and from then on she had been at the parade in Calloway. Jim in production remembered receiving the story before two because he was relieved that he could get the front page done and ready to go so early. He left around three o'clock. They narrowed the time of the switch down to sometime between four and five.

John Carson agreed with both Kelly and Bart that it was more than a coincidence that this had happened so near to the other events in Kelly's life. He received permission from his superiors to investigate. He began by securing the mug shot taken by CPD of Randy Robinson when he was arrested for attempted rape. He questioned all the employees on duty during that time on Christmas Eve and found two who could positively identify Randy as being in the building during that time. Both wondered who he was, but didn't question him because he wore a pass. Sometimes temps are hired during the holidays. John was working on a warrant for trespassing, but couldn't find evident he hacked into Kelly's computer.

It was enough for Doug Collings, who wrote a piece about the whole fiasco and exonerated Kelly. Kelly's real Christmas Day article ran on December 27.

Linda and Tonja spent the days after Christmas relaxing and enjoying the beauty of Hope Springs and its river. They canoed, fished, and read while they waited for Elizabeth to recover enough to be told the truth about her parents. So far, hadn't talked with either of the girls as they tried to let the Landis family cope with one situation at a time.

On New Year's Eve day, Jean found them sitting on the front porch of the bed and breakfast, swinging.

"I think she's ready," Jean said as she came up the front steps. "The last two days have been good, and she's anxious to begin working on the paper. Maybe today would be a good time to break the news. We also have to make a decision about the house. They called this morning and said it was ready."

"How do you want to handle it?" Linda asked.

After some discussion, the three women decided they would begin by introducing Tonja and Linda and then one of them would explain how placements are made, leading them into the specific instances of both Elizabeth's and Maggie's births.

"I can't get away tonight, Mike," Maggie whispered into the phone as her mother and two women walked passed her in the hallway. "My mom has just called a family meeting so I've got to go."

She listened for a moment. "I love you, too, but things are just a little crazy around here. If you love me like you say, you'll love me tomorrow, too." Then she hung up without waiting for a reply.

CHAPTER SIXTY-SEVEN

KELLY WAITED AT A coffee shop in Hope Springs for a call from Jean. They planned to tell Maggie and Elizabeth, and requested Kelly stay close in case either girl wanted to see her. Bart wanted to come with her, but he now had a mission from Irma, and he wanted to follow it through to the end.

"We can't have him around here," B.J. told Anthony over the phone. "He's a loose cannon. Now they've charged him with trespassing at *The Tribune* offices the day before that bogus article appeared by Kelly Sands."

"Tell him to come to the ranch this afternoon," Anthony said. "I'll take care of it."

Bart met with Doug about the false interview in *The Zion County News*. Both decided to proceed carefully and both determined that Bart should do the investigation. They already damaged the reputation of *The Millstone Monitor* this week, now they had to take on another weekly.

"Good thing they could trust Greg Panzer at *The Chronicle*," Bart said as he and Doug considered how to determine what Mike Green had falsified.

He would first begin taking the article apart to determine if any of it was true. After he left Doug's office, he found John Carson waiting for him.

"John, got some good news for me?"

"Maybe. I just charged Robinson with trespassing, but it won't hold him in jail, even with the attempted rape charge," John said. "But I might have something a little more incriminating. I began to get curious about this guy after we talked. I may have traced him to Kelly's bomb."

"Do you remember us telling you about the kind women at Oak Haven where both of you girls were born?" Jean said as they all gathered in the living room of the rented house. "These are the two women who run that place. I'd like you to meet Tonja and Linda."

All three children shook the women's hands and greeted them warmly. Their parents had always portrayed these two women as saints and none of the children had a reason to think anything else.

"They came to Hope Springs to bring us some news of Maggie's and Elizabeth's parents," Jason said.

Maggie sat up straighter on the couch, and Elizabeth simply tilted her head to the side, waiting to hear the news.

"Who wants to hear first?" Jason asked.

"Let Maggie; she's wanted to know more than me anyway," Elizabeth said.

Tonja began explaining about the young girl who had come to them seventeen years ago, frightened and alone after a brutal rape left her pregnant. The rapist was sent to prison, but that did not mean the girl's nightmares ended.

"There were nights when her screams awakened the whole house," Tonja said. "I'd hold her and rock her to sleep. She made a deliberate choice to give her baby up for adoption as much as it killed her to do so."

"She didn't feel emotionally equipped to handle a baby," Linda said. "And we agreed. She made a very mature decision. We felt your parents would be a good match. They wanted another child; Elizabeth and Jaycee were such happy children. This young woman agreed after meeting your folks."

"Do you know where she is? My birth mom?" Maggie asked.

"Yes, we do. She's the reason we came to this area. She came to us last month investigating a story about Elizabeth's mother, not knowing the connection. Then your folks wrote and said they were moving to this area where your mother lives, and we thought we'd better get up here and help everyone."

"Who is she?" Maggie asked. "Can I meet her? Does she want to meet me?"

"Your birth mother loves you very much," Tonja said. "In fact, she worried us for some time after your birth because she seemed to be having such a hard time letting go. But she has managed to become a very successful journalist. She works for *The Braidwood Tribune.*"

"It's Kelly Sands," Elizabeth said. "That nice woman who helped me that night; I kept thinking she looked so familiar. Remember, Mike said you looked like her that night. She sat across from us at the beginning of the parade and then she went off with...," Elizabeth faltered. "She went with you, Mom and Dad?"

"Yes, Kelly saw us and recognized us," Jean said. "She also saw you, Maggie, and she was so moved. She wants to see you very much, and she's just around the corner waiting for our call. She has abided by our wishes all the way."

"Kelly Sands is my mother?" Maggie asked. "She was raped?"

"That's why she was so understanding," Elizabeth said. "She knew just the right things to say to make me feel as if I'd done the right thing."

"She was raped," Linda said. "But that is her story to tell, if she chooses to tell it."

"I've got to think about this," Maggie said. "I'm not sure I want to see her right now."

Maggie left the others and went upstairs to the bedroom she was sharing with Elizabeth. Her mother started to follow, but realized Maggie needed to absorb this on her own. The reality of learning who her mother was and what her father was, did not bring Maggie the joy she once thought it would. She could not forget that Mike Green, the first man she had ever slept with, had also slept with her mother. She knew she would never be able to see Mike again.

"You said Kelly was doing a story on my birth mother?" Elizabeth asked after Maggie's surprising departure.

"Yes, that's right," Linda said.

Elizabeth listened quietly to the horrific details of her birth and then her mother's subsequent suicide.

"On top of that, the house they have given us is the very same home where your birth mother died," Jean said.

"Did Kelly know her?" Elizabeth asked.

"I don't think so, but she wanted to make your mother more human than the other papers," Tonja said. "That's the kind of writer and person she is. She was in contact with the minister who helped Anne. He and his wife were very fond of your mother. We've spoken to him this week, and he would love to meet you and tell you about Anne."

"That would be nice," Elizabeth said. "But right now I think I'd like to see Kelly. She must be waiting for Maggie. I think she'll be hurt when she finds out Maggie doesn't want to see her. I'd like to be the one to tell her, if that's all right? She was so kind to me."

"I think that would be extremely appropriate," said Jean. "She's at the coffee shop right around the corner waiting for our call."

CHAPTER SIXTY-EIGHT

WHEN KELLY'S CELL PHONE rang, she nearly spilled her coffee on the book she was reading. Her nerves had been jangling ever since she had arrived in Hope Springs. Three cups of coffee and Danish had done nothing to quell her nervousness.

"Bart, hello," she said. "No, I haven't heard anything. I'm just going to wait a little while longer because the longer it's been, the more I know her reaction isn't a positive one."

Bart told her the news from John Carson, which only made her feel slightly better. They were discussing their plans for New Year's Eve when Kelly saw Elizabeth enter the shop.

"I've got to go; I'll call you back in a little bit."

"Hello, Elizabeth," Kelly said. "Do you want to join me?"

"Yes, I was looking for you," Elizabeth said. "I wanted to thank you for the other night."

"I was just glad I was there."

"Mom and Dad just told us everything. Maggie is taking some time to digest it all, I guess."

"That's understandable. Did she send you here?"

"No, this was my choice. I knew you'd be anxious. Maggie's locked herself in the bedroom. Her reaction was kind of surprising."

"In what way?"

"Maggie always wanted to know who her birth parents were. I think she had some kind of glamorized version of who they might be. Learning you were raped might be causing her some trouble right now. There's something else. What about you and Mike Green?"

"I dated Mike for a while, but it's over now," Kelly said. "I'm seeing someone else; actually it's someone I've been in love with for a very long time. Why are you asking about Mike?"

"I think Maggie is seeing him. She probably knows you two dated. I can't say if they're sleeping together, but Maggie has never given any guys the time of day until Mike. I know he calls her regularly, and then she's been going out at night, she says for long walks around town."

"Doesn't he know that Maggie is only sixteen?"

Elizabeth shrugged. One other thing nagged at her, and she finally asked Kelly.

"How did you happen to be the first one at Randy's house the other night?"

"Because Randy Robinson is the person who raped me, and your parents told me you had gone to his house. I got scared for you."

"Randy is Maggie's birth father? Did he come here because of you?"

"It's beginning to look that way," Kelly said. "I'm so sorry you got caught in the middle of it all. There is some good news: I just heard there may be more charges brought against him. He's probably the one who hacked into our computers and placed that story from *The Times* with my byline."

"I guess I was pretty lucky that night," Elizabeth said.

"I was so proud of you, Elizabeth. I never fought back, and I have regretted it ever since. Seeing you do just that, made it feel better for me. Does that make sense?"

"It's like we're connected somehow, isn't it? It sounds silly, but it's like you're my birth mother, too, as well as Maggie's."

"When you're ready, I'd like to tell you about her. I didn't know her, but I've found out quite a bit about her life. She was a victim of circumstances."

"I would like that someday, but for now I'd just like to help you and Maggie, if I can."

"One thing you could do for me. Watch over her with Mike. He's not very stable right now, and he's pretty angry with me for dumping him. Give Maggie my cell phone number and tell her she can call me any time."

Kelly wrote the number on the back of her business card and handed it to Elizabeth. The two women hugged before leaving the shop together – Elizabeth to go back to the house and Kelly to go to Calloway and the offices of *The Zion County News*.

Kelly did not stop at the reception desk but headed past the receptionist to the offices. She found Mike sitting with Rick Bellows in the large corner office in the back.

"You son of a bitch," Kelly said when she saw Mike sitting in front of Rick's desk with his feet perched on the desktop. "You leave her alone, do you hear me? I'll have you arrested if I ever hear of you being alone with her again."

"Kelly, what's the matter with you?" Rick asked.

"She's just jealous because I've got a new girlfriend, that's all," Mike said.

Kelly knocked his legs off the desk and leaned down into Mike's face. "She's only sixteen, for God's sake. What are you thinking?"

"What do you care? You got Bart to keep you warm at night. What do you care who's keeping me warm?"

"I care because she's my daughter, you fucking asshole, and don't think I won't tear you apart if you hurt that girl."

Rick stood at this point and came around the desk. He took Kelly by the arm and began leading her out of the office.

"He got the message, Kelly," Rick said as he saw her to the front door. "I'll talk to him."

He went back to his office where Mike sat grinning and shaking his head.

"You better wipe that grin off your face before I do," Rick said. "If what she says is true, then I agree with her."

"It's Maggie Landis," Mike said. "I don't know how she could be Kelly's daughter."

"Put two and two together. The Landis children are all adopted. Don't you notice the resemblance between Kelly and Maggie? But the real issue here is you going against my express order to leave that girl alone. You better stop it right now or Kelly won't be the only one trying to bust your balls."

When Elizabeth came back to the house, she went to the bedroom where Maggie remained. She knocked on the door, and Maggie invited her inside.

"How are you doing, Maggie?"

"All right. How about you?"

"I just came from Kelly. She gave me this and said you could call her any time." Elizabeth tossed the card on the bed next to Maggie.

"I'm so ashamed, Lizzie." Maggie began to sob. "I slept with him, and so did she."

"Shush, Mags, it's all right. I warned her that might be the case."

"Is she mad?"

"At you? Never. She wanted me to give you a warning that Mike's been acting strange lately. If she's angry with anyone, it's him."

"Should I call her?"

"She's really a good person, Mags. You'd be fortunate to have her in your life. I know I want her as a friend."

CHAPTER SIXTY-NINE

KELLY SHOOK SO MUCH it took her a few minutes to get the key in the ignition of her car. She had never been so angry in her life, but she at least did something about it. As she pulled onto U.S. 441 to head back to Braidwood, she called Bart.

"You did what?" Bart's laughter across the phone made Kelly grin herself for the first time that day.

"I knocked his feet off the desk and got in his face. I even called him a 'fucking asshole.'"

"Good for you. It's about time you started fighting back. Now what about Maggie?"

"I gave Elizabeth my cell phone number and asked her to pass it along to her. So we'll see. Bart, is it okay if we just stay home tonight?"

"I think it's the best thing. I'll pick up some lobster and champagne on my way home. I love you, sweet lady."

As soon as she cut off the call to Bart, her phone rang. She didn't recognize the number showing on the window.

"Kelly Sands," she answered.

"Hello, this is Maggie."

"Maggie! You called."

"Can we meet?"

"When?"

"You could come here."

Kelly didn't need to hear anymore. She got into the left lane and turned around at the first chance and headed back to Hope Springs and her daughter.

"I named you Joely," Kelly said as she and Maggie sat down on the couch in the living room. "It was a combination of my parents' names,

Joe and Lee. They were so good to me when I went through the trial and the pregnancy. They would have helped me raise you, too, if I had chosen that route, but I didn't. Can you understand that?"

"The women from Oak Haven said you didn't feel emotionally capable of raising a baby."

"That's right. I was so confused, and Jason and Jean seemed to be so loving—I knew you'd be safe."

"I've had a good life," Maggie said. "Did you ever have any other children?"

"No. I married once briefly after college. It took me a long time to trust anyone again, but I think I've just found that person."

"It's not Mike Green?"

"No, Maggie, it never was Mike Green." Kelly paused and looked at her daughter who seemed uncomfortable with this discussion. "I did something today that I hope won't make you angry."

"What?"

"When I heard you might be dating Mike, I became so angry with him that I went to his office and threatened to kill him if he ever saw you again."

Maggie looked at her newfound mother in horror. Then she realized the situation with Mike had been solved for her, and even better, Kelly had gone to bat for her just because she was her mother. Maggie began to laugh.

"You're the second person who has laughed when I told them. Maybe I'm not such a convincing bully after all."

"I think it's great," Maggie said as she leaned toward Kelly to give her a hug. "Thank you for sticking up for me."

"Get yourself down to Miami and lie low," Anthony said as soon as Randy had made himself comfortable in the study of the ranch. "I don't want to hear one word about you doing anything except selling Girl Scout cookies. You might have screwed it all up with your damn pecker making you do stupid things."

"I swear I didn't do anything," Randy said. "It's that damn nigger you need to watch."

"I don't care what you did or didn't do, and Thomas Jefferson is the best thing for us up in Calloway."

"He's a moron on steroids."

"He's a respected member of the community, and you are not. Especially now. If *The Tribune* doesn't hang you, we're going to consider ourselves extremely lucky. Right now, we're working to distance any connection with you and our organization. I want you in Miami by tonight."

After Randy left the ranch, Anthony made one other call before beginning his New Year's Eve celebration with the real estate agent waiting for him on the leopard skin bedspread in the room above his head.

"Now's the time for payment," Anthony said. "You want it all, then prove it. He's gone to Miami. You can find him at my house in South Beach. And lay off the steroids for one night, please."

Molly had been meeting with Alex and Betty every day since Christmas. Kelly was indisposed with the plagiarism charges and then with her daughter, so Molly was handling it alone. Alex and Betty came to her house in the woods where privacy was assured.

They planned how Betty would handle the first commission meeting in January when the zoning for the landing strip came before the board. Alex assured the two women that Chelsea and Richard would vote against it. They had to figure out a way for Betty to stall it while not raising suspicions.

"Maybe I should just let it go through," Betty said. "It's only a first reading and then it goes to Tallahassee for its recommendation. That will take at least ninety days before the final reading comes back before the Commission. By that time, I'll be gone and Alex will be on the Commission along with Luddy."

"Are you sure Alex will win?" Molly asked.

"He will, if my daddy and Jackson think he should win," Betty said. "If I go along with the first reading, everything will be fine."

"How are you doing with tracing the money?" Alex asked Molly.

"It's a long process, but it's all coming together thanks to you two," Molly said. "Here's the plan: sometime by the end of January, *The Tribune* will publish the breaking story about revenue streams going elsewhere, and not into the public coffers. We're almost there. Then *The Chronicle* will follow up the very next week with an entire special section devoted to where the money has gone and any other stories we can uncover."

"Is Kelly all right?" Betty asked.

"She's working on it. I think the story from Christmas Day has been resolved. Now she has some personal issues to deal with, but as soon as New Year's is past, she'll be back on track," Molly said.

Kelly drove back to Braidwood with promises to return for dinner on New Year's Day with Bart. She smiled to think about how life had changed in the past week. The new year would begin on a hopeful note with her daughter and the Landis family who embraced her as one of their own. She also smiled when she thought about Maggie's birthday this year. No more hiding under the covers until the day passed.

Bart and Kelly quietly toasted each other at midnight grateful for the peace surrounding them. As they kissed, they heard the sirens and horns honking outside the warm house, and for the moment only thought about themselves.

CHAPTER SEVENTY

THE DAY AFTER NEW Year's, Molly reached Kelly at *The Tribune* just before she left for the day.

"Your nightmare might be over," Molly said. "We just received a story about a murder in South Beach. Seems a Randy Robinson of Calloway, formerly of Palm Beach, took a shot to the head and then took a swim. Sound like your guy?"

"Randy murdered?"

"So it seems. The AP report says there are no suspects and nobody heard anything. He was found floating in the Intercoastal on New Year's Day."

"Thanks for letting me know, Molly," Kelly said. "We probably got the same report so let me go check."

When she found the AP story online, she read with interest the short piece on the death of someone who had brought her much pain. His death suited the trouble he had caused on this earth. The only positive thing he had contributed had been sperm to create her beautiful daughter, Maggie.

The first meeting of the Calloway Commission meeting in January was held in the auditorium of the high school to hold the anticipated crowds. Both sides on the rezoning issue had come out in force. Members of SGC passed out signs and buttons outside that read, "No Jets." The Mayor banned them from the meeting. The other side wore T-shirts with a large movie screen, proclaiming "Callowood" broadly across the front. Mayor Murray did not ask those to be removed.

From the bang of the first gavel, the fireworks began.

"Because of the number of people here and our willingness to hear what the public has to say, I move that we limit each public comment to two minutes instead of the usual three," Jackson Stewart said as soon as the meeting began.

"Second," Johnny Waine said.

"Discussion," Chelsea said. "This project is one of the most important ones we have ever had come before this Commission. If we have to stay here until 7 a.m., then that is our job as elected officials. To cut off public comment time by saying we're actually promoting it, is doublespeak and a violation of the public's trust."

Members of the audience lined up to the microphones set up on both sides of the chairs. Cowan Garcia and Ken Greensides both stood poised to begin the protest.

"We will not entertain public comment on the motion," the mayor said. "I will now ask the commissioners to cast their votes."

The motion passed 3-2, with Chelsea and Richard casting the dissenting votes. And that's how the rest of the evening went. When Chelsea demanded to hear from the city planner what impact a change in zoning would have on already stressed roads, the city manager spoke.

"Ms. Gammon is not prepared tonight to make a presentation about roads," Thomas Jefferson said. "Staff will be happy to make a note of your concern and bring something back to you at a later meeting."

"How can we vote on such an important issue if we don't have all the facts?" Chelsea asked.

"I'm prepared to vote on this right now," Betty Duncan said. "We've been talking about this for hours, and this is just a first reading. We'll have another opportunity to address all these issues in a couple of months."

"If staff cannot come to this meeting prepared," Chelsea said, "how can we expect they will be prepared then?"

Thomas Jefferson began rocking in his chair to a beat only he could hear. He closed his eyes and gripped his cell phone sitting on the table in front of him. Jackson Stewart, sitting to the right of Thomas, reached over and touched his arm and whispered in his ear.

"I'd like to know what Commissioner Stewart and Mr. Jefferson are saying," Richard said. "This is a public meeting and all comments should be in the open."

"Do you want to know what we're saying? I will always let you know what I have to say when I say it," Thomas said as Jackson threw him a look of caution. "Commissioner Stewart told me to stay calm even though Ms. Godfrey is not."

"I can't understand why anyone would argue with changing an agriculturally zoned piece of property within our city limits to a special usage," Stewart said. "It just makes good sense economically for our community. It's the best thing that's ever happened to Calloway. Some people want to stop our growth, that's all, and I'm sick of it. I move that we pass this ordinance for the zoning exception on first reading and send it on to the Department of Community Affairs for approval."

"Second," Waine said.

"I call for the question," Betty Duncan said.

The meeting ended as it began, with a 3-2 vote approving a special zoning exception to be added that would include the development of an airport in Calloway.

After the meeting, Lana Mercer approached Kelly as they left the auditorium.

"Kelly, you're pretty good friends with Molly over at *The Chronicle*, right?" Lana asked.

"We know each other from covering the same things. Why?"

"I know you know Mike Green, and Molly used to work with him," Lana said. "I need some advice on ethics. Karen Thorne said I could trust you. Could I buy you a drink?"

When they were settled in the booth at Shot Bucket, a local establishment, Lana told Kelly that she had gone to work at *The Zion County News* at the suggestion of Cowan and SGC. She'd not been able to determine if the developers had also set this paper up, but she had discovered something about the "executive head writer" that caused her concern.

"He never leaves the office," she said. "But he writes these beautiful interview pieces. On the last one, profiling that new equestrian stadium's grand opening in Millstone? I know for a fact he never spoke to any of the sources quoted in the story, and he never attended the event."

"How do you know that for sure?"

"I walked into his office while he was writing it to ask why he wasn't covering the grand opening. I wondered if I had misunderstood, and I was supposed to be there instead. He didn't have any notes on the desk; he was just happily typing away. He said he had it covered.

"I had been suspicious, so I asked around to some of the people he quoted. They hadn't even known about the article and had no idea they had been quoted in it."

"Lana, do you mind if I tell my boss at *The Tribune*? He'll know what to do."

"No wonder Mike's writing has improved," Kelly said after she told Bart about her meeting with Lana. "He's been writing fiction and doesn't have to deal with people at all."

"I guess I better call Rick and Jason for a meeting."

CHAPTER SEVENTY-ONE

THE ZION COUNTY NEWS was in trouble almost from the beginning. The ad base had not grown and most people seemed reluctant to advertise in a third local weekly paper. They couldn't even give the paper away most weeks. B.J. and Anthony kept it afloat, but they wanted more for their money than Jason or Rick supplied. Jason felt powerless to do anything as he had imagined because he was thwarted every chance by either Rick or Jackson. He didn't know how much longer he could take it. The day Bart walked into the offices of the paper brought him the perfect opportunity to leave.

"Doug and I have decided that we can no longer sit quietly and let you publish falsified stories," Bart told the two men after he explained the investigation he had completed on Mike Green. "Some of his supposed interviewees are eager to go on the record that they never spoke to a Mike Green. And I have other witnesses who also will admit he was not at events he claimed to have covered."

"Go ahead and print it," Rick said. "We stand behind our reporters."

"That's ludicrous, Rick," Jason said. "Bart has the proof; we've got to cut our losses here and admit we have also investigated and let him go."

"No, we don't."

"Who's the publisher here?" Bart asked.

"Certainly not me, not anymore," Jason said as he walked out of Rick's office and out of the building.

"The story runs tomorrow, Rick. I'm sorry."

Bart caught up with Jason in the parking lot.

"What now?" Bart asked.

"I guess I go home and tell Jean and then call my old boss at *The Miami Herald.*"

"How about giving *The Tribune* a try? You're already here, and I've had no luck in finding someone to replace Rick. I need you, Jason."

On Jason's first day in his new position, Kelly and Bart brought him up to date on the article scheduled for publication on the last Sunday in January. With the help of Betty and Alex, Kelly and Molly had pulled together some damning facts and figures. They were all certain there was enough information to begin an ethics investigation. Doug Collings himself promised to file the formal complaint with the Commission on Ethics. He also was asking his reporters and *The Chronicle* to turn over all their notes to the State's Attorney office so they could begin a criminal investigation.

"It's good to be on this side again," said Jason. "Thanks for getting me out of there, Bart."

"A man's got to do what a man's got to do," said Bart.

In the end, Rick had no choice but to fire Mike because the evidence against him had been so damning. Anthony Marcetti seethed down on the ranch when he heard about both Jason's and Mike's departures. To make himself feel slightly better he went out to his veldt and shot one of the wild animals roaming. His agitation was so great he didn't even know what he hit when it went down. Woe to those other animals because the worst had only begun for the big game hunter. He imagined he just shot Bart Stanley who had done everything in his power to thwart Anthony's plans. First *The Millstone Monitor* looked like it was in its final days after Gary Dreg's picture appeared on the front page of *The Tribune* pouring tortoise shells on Cowan Garcia's front lawn, and now Stanley threatened the newest paper with its credibility by exposing Mike Green.

"Calloway's Drug Busts Come Under Scrutiny" screamed the headline in the *Tribune* on a Sunday in late January. A sidebar graphed the busts for the past three years and the amount of drugs seized with another line showing the amounts listed for burning during the annual drug burns. Many more drugs had been seized than had been burned. Chief Craig Holloway provided the records on what was locked up in the storage room and still the figures did not match.

Kelly wrote another article on a shortfall in revenues for traffic violations when compared to the tickets that had been issued by CPD.

"Andrew Knowles, finance director of Calloway, said that it was not unusual for the books to reflect different amounts than the actual tickets," the article stated.

The article quoted Knowles. "We call that undiminished returns in the world of finance."

She followed up with a quote from the finance director of Zion County who said he had never heard of anything even resembling an "undiminished return."

The article ended by stating, "Thomas Jefferson, city manager of Calloway, said he had no comment on the discrepancies, and would only comment at the 'whim of his commissioners.'"

The following Thursday, Molly's pieces in *The Chronicle* further laid open the questionable financial practices in Calloway. She interviewed experts in finance and pointed out other areas in the budget where revenues fell short of the expected income, particularly in the area of utilities. Calloway charged more for electric and water than any other municipality, yet the return into the budget did not match what was being collected and had not for more than twenty years.

By the following Monday, the Ethics Board in Tallahassee announced a full investigation into the finances of Calloway. However, Molly and Kelly were not finished. They still had some research to do, but they were beginning to match annexations to sales of properties by at least three living elected officials within the city. They needed just a little more time before going public.

"This is the stuff Pulitzers are made of," Bart said as he held up a glass of champagne in the home of his new editor. "Here's to Kelly and Molly before they get snatched up by *The New York Times*!"

"I'm not going anywhere, Boss," Kelly said as she stood next to Maggie and Elizabeth.

"We won't let her," Maggie said.

The Landis family never did move into the Simmons' old house. Jean insisted they buy their own home and not take any handouts. It turned out to be a wise decision because they needed their own home when Jason took the job with *The Tribune*. They ended up buying a ranch house just down the road from Molly and David between Hope Springs and Calloway. Bart and Kelly spent much of their spare time at one house or another, and even talked of building a home of their own in the area. Kelly spent no time these days pushing Bart away. He was in her life for good as was her daughter Maggie and Elizabeth.

CHAPTER SEVENTY-TWO

WHEN THE PHOTOS OF Gary Dregs appeared in *The Tribune,* the money behind the *Millstone Monitor* disappeared. Without the support of the Marcetti group, *The Millstone Monitor* could not continue to publish. By the time of the March elections in Zion County, the weekly stopped publication, and Gary Dregs and his mother were out of a job and looking for some other small town to peddle their services.

"I don't think I can handle it, Daddy," Betty told her father as the end of the qualifying period for the Calloway election neared a close at the beginning of February. "But Alex thinks he would like to give it a try."

"Alex?" B.J. said. "That's not a bad idea. Anthony will agree."

Alex Duncan filed his papers to run for Lester Simmons' seat on the Commission. No one opposed him. Johnny Waine, however, had a difficult race against Luddy Gregors, particularly after the reports in the newspapers suggesting he might have voted improperly on annexations that benefited him financially. In fact, most people either blamed or praised the duo of Kelly Sands and Molly Hale for determining the outcome of the Calloway election in March of 2001. Johnny Waine received only a quarter of the votes, and Luddy Gregors was elected to the city commission.

"We've got to do something," Anthony barked into the phone the day after the election. "What good was that paper if it didn't change the results of the election? They've got a majority now, and we've got a crucial vote coming up in two weeks."

"Don't worry; we'll think of something," Jackson said. "I'll put Thomas to work on it right now. First, we'll poll Luddy and Richard and see if they might be the swing vote. Short of that, we'll keep one of them from coming to the meeting that night so Tim will have to cast the deciding vote."

"You better do something, or it's all over," Anthony said. "What do you hear from Tallahassee?"

"Sam's helping there," Jackson said. "It will be just like last time, don't worry."

Richard Nichols, the Calloway commissioner who usually voted with Chelsea Godfrey, pulled out of his driveway onto Main Street the night of the meeting on the rezoning. He turned toward the auditorium where once again the public hearing would be held. Flashing lights appeared on the dash of the unmarked Crown Victoria behind him. He pulled over, slightly annoyed the city manager hadn't recognized his car.

"Thomas, aren't you headed to the meeting, too?" Richard asked when Thomas approached the car.

"Did you know that you were speeding through here?" Thomas said. "Please get out of the car. What have you been drinking?"

Nothing that Richard said could convince the city manager that he had not been drinking prior to getting behind the wheel of his car. He offered to take a breathalyzer, but Thomas said they would have to wait until someone could take him to Braidwood to use their machine.

"I'm going to call one of our officers who will put you in a holding cell until we can run that test. I've got to get over to the auditorium."

"So do I! Come on, Thomas, you can't do this."

"Are you trying to tell me how to do my job, Commissioner Nichols? Because if you are, I'm going to charge you with resisting arrest. You appointed me the chief law enforcer in this city, and I intend to protect Calloway from drunk drivers and angry citizens."

CHAPTER SEVENTY-THREE

WHEN THOMAS JEFFERSON CAME into the meeting, one minute after seven, he announced that Commissioner Richard Nichols had been detained by the Calloway Police Department for undisclosed charges. Mayor Murray pounded the gavel and the meeting began.

"We really don't need to waste anyone's time here," Alex said after the mayor explained the procedure for the hearing. "Everyone on this dais knows exactly how they will vote on this issue and no matter what anyone says, it will not make a difference."

"How can you say that?" Chelsea asked. "Have you so much disregard for democracy that you will not allow the public to speak?"

"I move that we pass Ordinance 01-03 on second reading," Jackson Stewart said.

"Second," Alex said.

"Let's vote," Jackson said.

"We'll do this by roll call," the mayor said. "Please do the honors, Mr. City Manager."

"Commissioner Godfrey?" Thomas Jefferson asked.

"No. And I protest the way this is being handled. You have not given this due process nor followed the intent of a public hearing."

"Commissioner Stewart?"

"Aye. I don't know why anyone would even doubt the benefit this project will bring to the City of Calloway."

"Commissioner Gregors?"

"No. I agree with Commissioner Godfrey. I have too many questions I'd like answered and unlike some of you up here, I certainly did not know how I was going to vote before I came here tonight."

"Commissioner Duncan?"

"No."

With Alex Duncan's vote, pandemonium broke out all over the room. Kelly felt a wad of paper hit the back of her head. She turned and saw Cowan Garcia in the face of B.J. Winters who looked as if he was fighting not to hit someone. Cowan taunted him and B.J. took a swing. Alex ran to Cowan from the podium and put his arms around him.

"What do you think you're doing?" B.J. yelled at his son-in-law.

"I'm sticking it to you, Daddy. And I'd say it's about time."

Kelly threw her laptop in her briefcase and attempted to get outside where she could call Bart. She stood under a live oak tree and fumbled to find her phone in her briefcase. She hurried because at any time, John Carson would be arriving with Betty, fresh from giving her confession on the events that occurred the night Anne and Lester Simmons died.

Thomas Jefferson squared off with Ken Greensides near the dais.

"I thought you were on our side," Ken said. "What happened? Did they offer you a sweeter deal?"

"I serve at the whim of the Commission," Thomas said. "Now you need to back off, Mr. Greensides, or you'll be sorry."

"Are you threatening me, you pimple-faced traitor?"

Despite the drug-induced hulk of the city manager, Ken still towered over him as Thomas stepped down from the behind the dais. Ken began moving in close to him pounding his chest.

"Come on, Mr. City Manager, if that was a threat, let's take it outside."

Thomas reached for his ankle and pulled out his safety net and pointed it directly at Ken Greensides chest.

"I'd step back if I was you," Thomas said. "You are a menace to society, and you can't tell Thomas Jefferson what to do."

"Put the gun down," Luddy said as she pushed her way between Ken and the barrel of the gun. "This will come to no good, Tommy. Put it down."

"No, Miss Gregors, I will not do that," he said. "I have had it with these white boys telling me what to do and threatening me and ordering me to kill this one and that one. I did not want to kill Randy Robinson, but they made me. Said I would lose this job. And I got the job because of Lester and Anne and Betty. I didn't want to do that either."

Thomas was waving the gun now and sweat poured down his face from his hairline. His chest heaved as his breathing became labored. The make-up he had used in an attempt to hide the acne on his face began to streak. Pimples stood out in red and white mounds against his black skin, which began to shine under the lights of the auditorium. His eyes, filmed over with a creamy liquid, darted from side to side as the chaos around him slowly stopped as the words of Thomas Jefferson could be heard even above the shouts of Cowan and Alex and B.J.

"Come on, Thomas, you don't want it to end this way," Ken said quietly. "If you put the gun down now and come outside with Luddy and me, we can help you."

"He's right, Tommy. You've just listened to the wrong people all this time; it doesn't have to be this way," Luddy said.

"You're both wrong; you're trying to trick me just like the rest; you're all jealous of what I've achieved. Look at me! I am Thomas Jefferson, the Governor of Florida."

He stopped with his legs spread as a smile spread across his face and his glazed eyes left the auditorium and looked into the future. He brought his Stubby, a gift from Jackson Stewart, up to his temple, and pulled the trigger.

"It's all your fault you know," Anthony Marcetti said as he approached Kelly who had managed to find her cell phone. They were the only two outside as the main entertainment continued inside. "I bet you think you're pretty damn smart. Maybe going for the Pulitzer?"

He continued to come closer until Kelly was backed against the building. He pinned her wrists to the metal behind her although he did not notice the phone she held in one hand. He also didn't know that she had already pushed the call button to Bart's office.

"Get your hands off me, Mr. Marcetti," she said loudly. "I'm warning you."

"Now aren't you a tough little girl, and so pretty," he said as he lowered his mouth to her neck. "Randy always said you were a hot little number. I often wondered what he meant, but now I know."

"Anthony Marcetti, you are a pig!" she screamed. "Get off of me, right now."

"No, I don't think so, Miss Sands. You've ruined everything for me with all your articles and investigations, and now you are going to have to pay me back for all I've lost. Believe me, you are going to enjoy this; all the women do. Just relax and enjoy."

As Anthony began kissing her, Kelly heard the sirens. When Anthony turned his head to listen, she brought her knee up to his groin in one swift motion. The grip he held on her wrists loosened, and she broke away while he bent over double.

"Bart, did you hear all that? I kicked him in the balls!"

"You bet I heard, and I even managed to call the police as soon as I heard you mention his name the first time. Are they there yet?"

"Just pulling in. I'm afraid Mr. Marcetti will not be able to shake their hands just yet. I wish you had been here for the vote; it was beautiful."

"John should be there any minute, too, with Betty," Bart said. "He called just before you and told me he had a warrant for Anthony's arrest and for Thomas Jefferson. I'm leaving the office right now so I'll see you in a few minutes."

"Hey, Bart? I fought back this time."

"Sweet lady, you've been fighting back for some time now; you just wouldn't believe it."

CHAPTER SEVENTY-FOUR

"ANTHONY MARCETTI, YOU ARE under arrest for conspiracy in the murders of Anne and Lester Simmons," John Carson said as an officer placed handcuffs on Anthony's wrists. "You have the right to remain silent."

"What do you mean? I didn't murder anyone," Anthony protested although he was bent over slightly from Kelly's hit to his groin. "You're going to be very sorry; I'll make you all pay."

"I'm sure you will. Now, you have the right to an attorney," John continued.

Kelly stood off to the side watching as Marcetti was placed in the police car. Maggie and Elizabeth came running out of the auditorium to find her. They told her what had just happened inside. They watched as Betty got out of the police car and came to stand with them.

"You did it, Betty," Kelly said as she hugged her new friend.

"We all did it, Kelly, and I thank you."

Bart and Kelly drove back to the office together, promising to meet with Maggie and Lizzie the next day.

"What do we lead with?" Bart asked. "Thomas Jefferson's suicide? Alex Duncan's switch? Marcetti's arrest? Lester and Anne?"

"It's a tough one, but I think we should lead with Thomas," Kelly said. "I didn't know he had gone so far to the edge, but there's been a lot going on."

"Poor guy; he was a victim of sorts, too. I guess we do teasers on the front page for the rest of the stories. Are you up to writing tonight?"

"You bet, Boss. In fact, I've never felt more ready."

Betty's story appeared in its entirety the next day. Kelly fleshed out most of the story, but Betty kept some details from her until she made her confession. She didn't want Kelly implicated in any crime. Alex arranged immunity for Betty for full disclosure.

The afternoon that Anne and Lester died, Betty went to the house to see Lester. When she came around the back to the pool and patio area, she saw Lester and Anne in bed together through the sliding glass doors.

"Isn't this cozy," Betty said as she walked into the couple's bedroom. "What are you doing, Lester?"

Lester proceeded to tell his lover that his wife was pregnant. For all these years, Lester had told her Anne and he never slept together after their second child was born. Now she learned that Anne carried Lester's child.

"I love her," Lester said. "I guess I always have, but I didn't want to hurt you."

Anne sat on the edge of the bed with her head bowed and her hands on her lap. Betty could see the slight smile on Anne's face, and it infuriated her. Anne didn't even try to cover up her nakedness.

"You love her? How could you? Look at her, Lester."

At this point, Lester stood up and asked Betty to leave. That's when Betty pulled her handgun out of her purse. She always carried it, ever since her father had given it to her when she married Alex. The handle was engraved silver, and the .44 Magnum fit snugly in her hand. Lester grabbed the cell phone sitting on the table in front of Anne and made the call to the police, but Betty turned the gun on Anne, and Lester dropped the phone. Betty ordered Anne to take it over to the pool and throw it in, which Anne did, grabbing her robe on the way.

Betty then picked up her phone and called Anthony Marcetti.

"I need some help here, Anthony, at Lester's place. Send someone who can clean up a mess, please," Betty said.

Anthony sent Randy Robinson and soon in response to Lester's call to the police, Thomas Jefferson showed up. Betty told the Chief to call Anthony to find out how to proceed.

"Thomas, you don't need to call Anthony," Lester said. "You need to escort Mrs. Duncan from my premises. She's trespassing."

"Mrs. Duncan, you need to put the gun down," Thomas said.

"Did you say I was trespassing?" Betty asked Lester. "How about all those times you had me come around here to the back so we could screw while Anne slept in that back bedroom. Was I trespassing then? Was I?"

Lester reached for the gun Betty was now swinging in the air. Before he grabbed it, Betty managed with her thumb to throw the safety. As they struggled with the gun, it went off. The bullet passed the long-time lovers and hit Anne in the temple. She fell over the table and blood spread out all over the glass.

"Look what you did!" Lester screamed as he ran to Anne still holding the gun he had managed to wrest from Betty. "You killed her, you bitch."

He then pointed the gun at Betty but before he could fire, Thomas Jefferson reached for his gun and fired. Lester fell back, hitting his head on the table. He lay in a pool of blood at Anne's feet.

Randy Robinson appeared at this exact moment and took in the scene before calling Anthony.

"Let me talk to the chief," Marcetti said after Randy finished.

"Make it look like a suicide/murder," Marcetti said. "Betty is not there. No autopsies, no questions. Anne was depressed over Lester's affair and shot him before turning the gun on herself. Keep it simple, case closed."

"Now that's a story," Bart said when he finished reading. "I'd say you've gone a long way toward saving Florida from some of its finest animals. Maybe you've even helped to make some of them extinct. And frankly, my dear, I do give a damn."

"I guess I got the last word for once, Boss," Kelly said as she leaned back in her chair. "That'll teach them to leave a bomb on my desk."

THE END

ABOUT THE AUTHOR

P.C. Zick describes herself as a storyteller no matter what she writes. And she writes in a variety of genres, including contemporary fiction and creative nonfiction. She's won various awards for her essays, columns, editorials, articles, and novels.

The three novels in her **Florida Fiction Series** contain stories of Florida and its people and environment, which she credits as giving her a rich base for her storytelling. She says, "Florida's quirky and abundant wildlife—both human and animal—supply my fiction with tales almost too weird to be believable."

Her contemporary fiction novels contain elements of romance with strong female characters, handsome heroes, and descriptive settings. And all her works express her philosophy of living lightly upon this earth with love, laughter, and passion.

Zick offers a variety of nonfiction books, which include a book on vegetable gardening, a compilation of her essays and short stories from her decades-long career as a writer, and a primer for writers on taking an idea and turning it into a published book. She has also published and annotated the journal of her great-grandfather based on his experiences as a Union soldier during the Civil War.

She and her husband live in Tallahassee, Florida, where they enjoy gardening, kayaking, and hiking.

For more information, visit www.pczick.com.